Surprises

M. D. Williams

A GhettoLectual Book

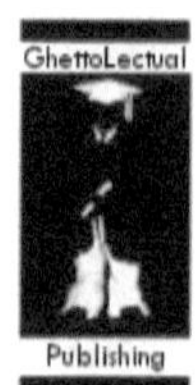

GhettoLectual Publishing
P.O. Box 24693
Fort Worth, Texas 76124-1693 USA

ISBN: 978-0-9912511-0-0
ISBN: 978-0-9912511-1-7 (ebook)

Library of Congress Control Number: 2013956291

Back Cover Thumbnail Photo by Glamour Shots

First Edition

Printed in the United States of America

To my maternal Grandmother Mary Quabner White (RIP), and my paternal grandmother Lorene Jones. The wisdom from you both is etched in my memory for life.

Also to my baby brother Mitchell, and my 1st cousin Melvin Atchison Jr. Y'all left us much too early, but you're never forgotten.

Sometimes what you seek is right in your grasp, but it's up to you to discern it.

—**M.D. Williams (2014)**

1

Mitchell wanted to floor it to feel what he was working with under the hood of the new Cadillac, but something from his past made him rebuke the reckless thought, and he realized the beauty he was rolling wasn't for speed, but for cruising and looking distinguished like somebody who had money. As the wheels purred smoothly, the beaming pearl-beige SUV effortlessly exited highway 75 into North Tulsa. Mitchell bounced and rapped along to an old school cut called "Out North" by Big Bur-na, one of his favorite Tulsa rapper's. He scanned familiar surroundings and frowned at shabby, rundown buildings, disregarded eye-sores of empty lots, and wished his dollars stacked sky high like Bill Gates' so he could do a complete overhaul of the black side of town and make it look brand new. He knew some areas in the predominantly black north side were trying to develop for the better, but compared to the white side of town, the differences stood out like a black eye.

Damn, I wish North Tulsa could prosper like the Greenwood District did when it was dubbed the Black Wall Street before the 1921 race riot.

It was still home, and he felt good being at the crib. "T-Towwwn!" he yelled. "Guess who's back in the hi-zouse?"

Rolling solo, Mitchell was in his hometown to see his family after his longest period without seeing them. The past eight months he'd been consumed with renovating and decorating his town house in Norman, and some important business matters. He could've easily made the trek home anytime, but he'd held out til today, both his mama's and sister's birthday.

Moments later he was near his destination, a pre-school program doing its best to enrich the lives of the young and carefree. He surveyed the playground. It was due for a facelift because the equipment was outdated by decades. He made a right turn and slowly rode down the street parallel with the front of the school. He was as excited as a kid on Christmas morning.

He parked a couple of car lengths behind the vacant school buses waiting in the loading zone, emerged with his eyes shaded in smoke-black sunglasses. He stuffed the keys in his pockets and palmed a cellular phone as he slightly gangsta-limped down the sidewalk leading to the entrance. He was a molecule under six feet tall, had on an extra-large crimson Oklahoma University T-shirt and baggy white denim shorts. True it was after Labor Day, but the heat seemed oblivious to that fact. On his head was a white OU baseball cap turned sideways, and hanging from his neck was a modest platinum chain with the letter M emblem.

Across the street, a sequence of houses began from the corner of the block and extended the length of the street. He imagined the kids who only had to make that brief hop, skip and jump to school loved that short trip.

Though the heat wasn't bothering him, he felt it. It was dang near mid-September, and Tulsa, like most of the state, willfully lay under a stubborn sun spreading a blanket of miserable heat, without interference from an unblemished, far-as-the-eye-can-see blue sky. Carrying over from a smothering August, that big ass, angry ball of fire was up there raising hell like it was pissed off at the world.

He thought of his mama driving around the entire summer in such suffocating temperatures without air-conditioning in her car. He partially grinned, knowing she wouldn't be subjected to that misery again if he had his way.

As he approached the entrance, he noticed the humming of laboring air-conditioners bracketed in every other window and was amazed that in the 21st century a school didn't have central air.

Ain't that a bitch? Only *in the hood could a school be this neglected.* He shook his head, hoping the overworked air conditioners were keeping the school cool. He greeted three bus drivers—black, and white females, and an older black gentleman talking on his cellular—as they stood off to the side of the stairway making use of the minimal shade while waiting for school to let out.

He smiled after entering the building as a jolt of nostalgia grasped him, because the walls of lockers rehashed memories of his childhood, walking similar halls. Presently hollow, soon bunches of four and five-year-olds would pervade with idle chatter and cheerful chaos, scrambling noisily to reach the buses, or waiting to be picked up. The floors shone, appearing to be freshly waxed and buffed, bringing back memories of when he'd cleaned school buildings one summer as a teenager. The water fountains were so low he would need to get his midget on to get a drink.

He entered the office, where a little butterscotch toned girl was sitting in one of four wooden chairs wearing a despondent expression, rubbing over what looked to be a recently applied band-aid on her left knee, while her swinging right foot almost brushed the bluish-gray carpet. A small backpack sat in a chair next to her. Her lips were stuck out so he didn't speak to her.

He advanced to an oval-shaped counter and rested his forearms on top. From one of two desks behind the counter, a stern-faced, thickset, fiftyish black woman hung up the telephone, rose from a computer, and came forward. She wore a pair of horn-rimmed glasses; her short cut hair had streaks of black and gray. Creases in her forehead, probably from years of frowning, caused her to look sort of mean. The wicked witch popped into Mitchell's head.

"Hello. May I help, you, young man?" she asked, giving Mitchell a once over.

A loud rosy scent made contact with Mitchell's nostrils. *Maaan! She sure has that perfume on strong.*

"Yes ma'am. I'm Mitchell Thomas. Mackenzee Morgan's brother. I've come to ask if I can pick her up?"

The woman sent him a condescending smile.

"Do you have a parent or guardian's permission? Policy prevents us from releasing students to anyone unless they are authorized."

That threw Mitchell for a curve, though he agreed with the policy. "Well ... no ma'am." He then proceeded to explain that he'd just come in from Norman, where the University of Oklahoma was located, and wanted to surprise his little sister since she had no idea he was coming to town.

With a glint of stern skepticism, she folded her meaty arms over her ample breast. "Mr. Thomas, you've gotta come with a better tale than that, young man. OU? I don't believe that one bit." She shook her head incredulously, her doubt stemming from the fact that he didn't look a day over sixteen; if that. His face was absent of any facial hairs except for a tease of mustache. If she hadn't been looking into his almost hypnotic brown eyes, she wouldn't have noticed that. *And those baggy clothes ... who in the hell does he think he's trying to fool? Still wet behind the ears and trying to be slick.*

From experience, Mitchell anticipated her reaction and instinctively retrieved his wallet from his right rear pocket, producing his old college ID and driver's license, and handed them to her, unfazed by her assumptions. His young face was always misrepresenting his actual age. It was irksome, but it was the face he'd been given, so he had to work with the hand he was dealt.

She skimmed the cards, and her mouth gaped like a child getting caught digging in the cookie jar. "I-I'm sorry," she uttered in a hushed tone, wearing a self-deprecating expression. "I can't believe you're actually twenty—"

"Twenty-one," he helped her out as she mentally tried to calculate his age. "I'll be twenty-two shortly. There's no need to apologize though, I'm so used to that reaction toward my age." He wanted to say, "That's what you get for judging a book by its cover," instead, he smiled.

"Let me see what I can do," she said hurriedly, returning his ID, attempting to regain her equilibrium.

"Thank you, Ma'am."

Though embarrassed, she smiled at his manners, mentally complimenting his parents. She was so accustomed to crudeness, and being answered with *yeah,* or *mm-hmm.* She disappeared into one of the side offices. She returned and informed Mitchell that he could go and speak to Miss Johnson, Mackenzee's teacher, about his request.

She wasn't as mean as she appeared, Mitchell decided.

"Thank you for your help M-Ma'am," he stammered, searching for a wedding ring on her finger, trying to determine if she was a Mrs. or not.

"Mrs. Green," she said, noticing the direction of his gaze. Before getting it approved for him to go speak with Miss Johnson, she'd wondered about his last name differing from Mackenzee's, but didn't make an issue of it since it wasn't that unusual for siblings to have different last names these days, especially in the black community. Besides, finding out his real age still had her a bit unbalanced, but it explained why he seemed so mature and well spoken.

He thanked her and she gave him the simple directions to Miss Johnson's class. The bell rang as he was leaving. The once lifeless hallway quickly filled with pandemonium.

℘ↄଔ

In her classroom, Jazelle Johnson knelt face-to-face with a student who'd been fighting. Jazelle was slightly annoyed that the *munchkin conflict* had started. She couldn't stand when her students got into it with one another, but she was gently letting the child know fighting wasn't allowed. Unlike last school year, when she had three bad-ass boys causing friction off and on, Nikki Smith, a little gorgeous girl she would've never perceived as being problematic, had began her campaign of disturbances the third week. She tried to bully her classmates, and today she'd targeted Mackenzee Morgan, who wasn't having it. Now in her second year of teaching, she sometimes wondered if she should have majored in business instead of dealing with other people's kids. She'd got the teaching bug after working at a daycare for two summers during her teenage years, wanting to reach kids' impressionable minds before all the negative elements—sex, drugs, money, gangs—of the world distorted them. Public school generally got a bad rap, so she wanted to be a teacher that made a difference instead of throwing in the towel with the public education system. Unfortunately a lack of love at home often caused some to act out at school, just for attention. Ironically, some received plenty of love at home, but were disruptive from being spoiled rotten.

At this point she wasn't sure what Nikki's problem was, but Mackenzee wasn't unruly or troublesome. Like anyone, she hated being teased.

"Do you understand what I'm telling you, Mackenzee?" Jazelle asked tenderly, hating that she had to discipline her for something she didn't start. But all students had to abide by the rules.

Sniffling, mostly from embarrassment for getting in trouble, Mackenzee nodded, and mumbled, "Mm-hmm," while wiping her teary eyes with the back of her hand.

Mitchell appeared in the doorway, squinting because of the bright sun rays beaming through the windows, only able to make out the silhouettes of what appeared to be the last two people in the classroom. He quietly eased into the room, realizing one was a little girl with her back to him; three, fluffy, braided ponytails with wine barrettes affixed at the ends hung a little past her shoulders. The other, a young lady— presumably Miss Johnson—was kneeling down talking to her. Suddenly he recognized the wine colored pants and gray shirt with wine collar and sleeves worn by the little girl. He'd sent the outfit to his sister over the summer. He hadn't spotted her in the cluster of kids in the hallway, now he knew why.

"Miss Maaac," he uttered, wearing a mischievous grin. The reason she wasn't trampling to the buses with the other kids never crossed his mind.

Miffed at hearing the familiar voice calling her name, Mackenzee's eyebrows furrowed, and she quickly spun around.

"Mitcheee!" she screamed, completely surprised and excited to see her brother. She rushed toward him. "Mitcheee!"

Mitchell squatted, spreading his arms.

"Miss Mac!" She jumped into his arms into a bear hug. He pecked her on the lips. "How's my favorite li'l lady?"

"Fine," she replied, wearing a big smile.

Mitchell held her away from him looking her over. A laminated name tag hung from a string around her neck.

"Maaan, Miss Mac ... what has G-Lady been feeding you? You've grown so much since I last seen you." She giggled, fully exposing delightful dimples. "But you're still pretty as a swan." He kissed her on the forehead.

"Ooh, Mitchee, you smell sooo good."

"I better. You wouldn't want some stinky boy kissing you, would you?"

She giggled. "Where'd you come from, Mitchee?"

"Outta nowhere. You know I'm magic," he teased, nuzzling her neck.

Mackenzee squirmed and laughed for a second, then all in one breathless, hurried sentence, poured out how she had pushed Nikki because she kept teasing her.

At that moment she was so cute there was no way he could be disappointed with his little sister. "Ohhh Mac ... you know you're not supposed to be fighting," he said very gently. *Man, it seemed like just yesterday she was a baby crawling around the house destroying anything she could get her little chubby hands on. Now ... here she is in pre-school, and already trying to settle disputes the wrong way.*

"But Mitchee, she-she made me so mad ... teasing me about my picture I was making for you. I didn't try to hurt her though." She had her arms around his neck looking contrite.

"Well—"

"Hi. I'm Miss Johnson, Mackenzee's teacher."

The voice startled the two siblings who'd been so caught up in their reunion that Miss Johnson's presence had become oblivious to them.

His attention on his sister broken, Mitchell's eyes settled on a plain, yet attractive twenty-something sista in blue slacks, blouse of a lighter shade of blue, and complementing shoes. Her hair was pulled tightly into a bun secured by a hair band matching her slacks. She had a make-up free, smooth, caramel toned face. And, something he normally resisted observing on a woman was that she had *body*.

"Hello, Miss Johnson." He was slightly abashed because he'd pictured Mac's teacher as being much older; middle-aged in fact, likely in a flower-print, shapeless dress that hung to her knees. As she smiled, revealing a sexy dime-sized gap, he couldn't help but notice, even though he preferred not to, her kissable-looking plump lips gleaming in lip gloss. She was definitely no old lady. Not by a long shot. "I'm Mitchell. Mitchell Thomas."

"Hello, Mitchell Thomas," she said, moving toward them, wondering why this little boy wasn't at school. It wasn't time for high school to be out, she thought, reflexively scanning the clock above the blackboard. She'd been caught up in the endearing greetings between her student, and this ... Mitchell, whoever he was.

Mitchell lowered Mackenzee to the floor.

"I'm Mac's brother." He extended his right hand and clasped Jazelle's hand. "I came to see if I can pick her up."

"You came to get me?" Mackenzee asked, surprised.

"Yep."

"Ooooo weee," she sang.

Smiling, Mitchell glanced at his sister. Then to Jazelle said, "Mrs. Green said I must get your approval, because I don't have authorization from"—he swept the cellular in his free hand back and forth between Mackenzee and himself—"our mother."

Now knowing he was Mackenzee's brother, Jazelle released her hand, which Mitchell held longer than he'd realized, and smoothed the hand over her blouse. She was slightly flushed by how soft his hand was. She'd never had a massage, but if she ever did, hands similar to his are what she'd want working the kinks, aches, pains, and tension from her body. And the scent emanating from him ... if she'd had a man, and he wore whatever that cologne was, she'd be all over him like a dog in heat. Mackenzee was definitely on point about him smelling good. "Mi ... ahh..." She'd forgotten his name that quickly. Unnerved.

"Mitchell." He refreshed her memory. "But you can call me Mitch. Either is fine with me." There was a time when he probably would've jokingly added, "But Miss Mac is the only person I'll allow to call me Mitcheee." But he'd turned reserved over a certain period, and pointless dialogue was a rarity for him. Definitely with anyone he didn't know well—women mainly. "So will you okay it?"

"Right. Mitchell," Jazelle said, a bit embarrassed by the impromptu amnesia. As for him wanting to take Mackenzee, she was curious about the difference in their last names, but refrained from asking about it. It was plain to see they had a very close bond. She subtly studied his face, seeing the similarities they shared: thick pretty eyebrows above his magnetic brown eyes, a not too flat or too wide nose, attached to a somewhat oval peanut butter face. The big difference was his absence of dimples. But his smile was engaging enough to win you over. There was something about him she couldn't pinpoint, though. "Mitchell it is," she uttered with unintentional sultriness; sultry enough to startle herself.

The utterance also startled Mitchell, and he stiffened. She had said his name like something that tasted delicious. It made him uncomfortable. She'd almost reminded him of...

"So is it okay if I take her?" he asked impatiently while absently fidgeting with the cellular phone, surveying the room. He imagined his classroom must've been similar when he was in pre-school. The letters of the alphabet in capital A, small a, through capital Z, small z, were strategically placed above the chalkboard on the wall behind Miss Johnson's desk. Ten double-sided paint easels stood in the back of the room. Neatly lettered blocks, board games, toy cars, dolls, and a selection of toys were all in what he assumed was the play area. Small plants sat on the window ledges, and about twenty miniature-looking desks were neatly lined in rows of five. On the wall coinciding with the doorway, SEPTEMBER in bold lettering was above a calendar which he imagined Miss Johnson had created. Small animal figures cut from red and yellow construction paper with stenciled numbers served as the date markers. Next to the chalkboard, the American flag was bracketed at an angle, and he wondered if the preschooler's learned the Pledge of Allegiance at such an early age. He couldn't remember when he'd learned it; it had been too long ago. The major difference he noted from his pre-school days was the presence of a computer.

"Miss Johnson?" He said it realizing she still hadn't answered his request, but wishing she would agree to it. Quickly.

His voice snapped her from her reverie. She was still tripping on his strange affect on her. "Oh—yes. Normally I'd check with the parent, but I can see by you all's reception, that it should be fine if you take her."

"Yesss!" Mackenzee blurted.

Jazelle then had a thought as she absently fidgeted with some papers on her desk, trying to extinguish the unsettling disturbances this youngster had somehow stirred in her. "What about her aunt who usually picks her up at the bus stop?" she asked, purposely omitting the aunt's name.

Mitchell peeped out the test. His mama and her baby sister, Carla, had an arrangement where Carla picked Mac up every day except Monday, when his mama was able to pick her up, since it was her day off.

"I already talked to Aunt Carla, and let her know I was getting Mac from school."

Mrs. Green abruptly appeared in the doorway, informing Jazelle that the bus driver was waiting on her, and that Nikki had gotten on her bus, but wanted another band-aid for her knee in case the other came off. "I obliged the little munchkin then walked her to the bus," she said, laughing as she turned and walked off.

Nikki must've been the little girl in the office, Mitchell thought.

"My God, I'd forgotten about it being my scheduled day for bus monitor," Jazelle said skittishly. She took a quick glance at the clock. "We've got to get outta here. The driver is waiting on me."

That's what I wanted to do anyway, Mitchell thought.

"Okay," he said. They gathered Mackenzee's back pack and stuffed her things in there. "It's time to go celebrate y'alls birthday li'l sis." *And get away from this lady.*

"It was nice meeting you, Mitchell," Jazelle said.

"Nice meeting you also," he responded, holding Mackenzee's hand, stopping himself from adding, "After hearing so much about you." Mac raved about her every time he'd talked to her on the phone over the past few weeks. "Oh, and thank you for letting me take her."

Smiling, Jazelle nodded. "You're welcome, but if you have your mother provide authorization, you can pick up Mackenzee anytime."

"Alright."

"Mackenzee, you have a nice birthday, baby," Jazelle told Mackenzee, "and tell your mother the same."

"Okay. 'Bye Miss Johnson," Mackenzee said, cheesing big.

ഇൗ

"Where's your car at, Mitchell?" Mackenzee asked when they got outside. They were standing near the flag pole, looking at the noisy kids on the buses.

"Behind the last bus." Mitchell pointed at the Cadillac, relieved to be out of Miss Johnson's presence.

Mackenzee shook her head. "Unh-unhhh. That ain't yours—your car's red."

Mitchell grinned. His smart and perceptive little sister wasn't about to let him fib to her.

"You're right, Miss Mac, it's not my car. But it is what I'm driving."

"Ohh."

"And it's your car." He loved playing games, and trying to trick his little sister.

Her eyes shot open quickly. "My car? Unh-unhhh!" She was grinning and shaking her head. "I dunno how to drive, Mitchee."

"I'm gonna teach you."

A completely awestruck expression adorned her face. "Fa real, Mitchee?" she sing-songed.

He started cracking up. "Gotcha!"

For some get back Mackenzee started swinging at him. Mitchell juked and side-stepped her flailing arms, dodging her like a game of freeze tag. While they giggled and played around, Jazelle came hurrying from the building, passing them as she climbed onto the bus. Mitchell paused, quickly glimpsed at her, and then gently tugged Mackenzee's hand, motioning her toward the car. "Come on Miss Mac, I'll tell you 'bout the car on the way home."

He pivoted, stealing a last look at the bus Miss Johnson boarded. With all the raving Mac had done about her, she'd never mentioned how pretty she was. *Guess little kids don't pay much attention to looks.* He saw fine women on a daily basis, but for some reason, Miss Johnson disturbed him and it freaked him out.

He'd get authorization to pick up Mac, alright, but for the sake of peace of mind, he'd just wait for his little sister out by the buses next time. If he never laid eyes on Miss Johnson again, it would still be too soon.

₭‘⊊

From the bus, Jazelle cast a passing glance at Mitchell and Mackenzee as they walked by. With it being Friday, the kids were overly hyper, and she was barely able to get them to settle down because her mind was elsewhere. She was aware that it was hot as heck on the bus, though, because her armpits and forehead were already feeling damp. She dug out a paper towel from her pocket, dabbed at the beads of sweat before it ran down her face.

Her thoughts continued to linger on Mitchell. Something about him had her perplexed. Exactly what, she wasn't sure. Doubting him being Mackenzee's brother wasn't it; she had no doubt they were brother and sister. It had more to do with his mannerisms. For a teenager, he seemed too mature. There was an adult-like aura about him. Only, he was certainly the high school brother Mackenzee often mentioned. And the affection he showed for his little sister was abnormal for a boy. *They acted like they hadn't seen each other in months.*

Though ashamed and embarrassed for thinking it, she was almost empathizing with the rash of teachers around the country lately that had gotten in trouble for illicit relationships with students. He was the type who'd have a teacher tempted.

Hearing the driver prodding the accelerator before pulling off, she snapped from her thoughts. After instructing the few kids who were standing to sit down, once they were seated, she sighed.

As the bus began to move, she claimed a seat also.

2

Mitchell pulled into the driveway at his mama's house and got out of the car to raise the garage, since it didn't have an electric garage door opener. He smiled about the manicured yard which was free of any loose trash. The house had been recently painted the same brownish tone with darker brown trimming, making it look decent enough, but other than that improvement, everything looked the same since he'd last visited. A simple three bedroom, Section 8 house, it was located in an area Mitchell felt comfortable with. Their previous house was a hot mess, with peeling paint, missing window screens; no front screen door, faulty plumbing, and only God knew what else. And the landlord had been, in his mother's words, *a piece of shit*, neglecting the house as much as he was able to get away with. Thankfully they were able to keep it respectable looking and livable.

Their present landlord was dependable and made sure everything was up to code and functioned properly. The neighborhood, sprinkled with slightly less whites than blacks, a pinch of Mexicans, was a far cry from their old neighborhood. That area had been like a miniature war zone. Something happened nightly. Break-ins, shootouts and drive-bys had been the norm. It was a wonder none of them was jacked, shot, or killed in their own home. Many nights, sleep was hard to come by from fear of something terrifying happening. Mitchell had been reluctant to leave for college, afraid something would happen to his family while he was away.

Thinking about those days, he could only shake his head. He glanced at his watch and quickly returned to his initial intention. After lifting the garage door, he hopped back in the luxury SUV, parked it inside. That morning he'd jubilantly picked the SRX up from the Cadillac dealership, writing a check for the full amount. He'd been highly thrilled watching the eyes of the salesman almost pop out when Mitchell handed him the check. Mitchell imagined him intensely pondering over whether a black kid actually had that type of money in the bank. It took all of his will power to suppress the laughter trying to break through as he watched the salesman's expression once he verified the validity of the check.

Since childhood he'd only imagined being able to afford a brand new car for his mother. She'd never owned anything of significant value that was brand new. Unused. Today, that ended. His mama would feel like a ghetto queen in her brand new ride.

As Mac and he arranged a big red bow on the roof of the car, he remembered his mama's aggravation when he was only four of five, while the two of them waited at the bus stop in either miserable heat or numbing coldness.

"I'm so tired of waitin' and ridin' the damn bus, I dunno what to do. If I ever get enough money for a new car, believe me it's gonna go on me a Cadillac."

Mitchell smiled at the memory. *Little do you know, Mama, you've finally gotten your wish.*

₞₡

Next to each other on the couch, Mitchell and Mackenzee absently mindedly watched cartoons and drank a mix of grape and lemonade kool-aid. Impatiently, Mitchell peered through the slightly opened drapes behind the TV, anticipating his mama's arrival. Realizing he hadn't told Mackenzee not to mention anything about the car, he warned her now to keep the secret.

Mackenzee was confused. "Why cain't I tell, Mitchell?"

"Because ... it's a surprise." He began tickling her. "You don't wanna spoil the surprise, do you?"

Squirming and laughing, she pleaded, "Nooo ... nooo, Mitch-Mitchee!" She toppled to the carpet, screeching with laughter as he tickled her all over.

Outside, a door slammed. The sound instantly caught their attention. With Mitchell hovered over his sister, who was on her stomach, they looked at one another. Together they rose, eased to the window and gingerly peeked out.

"It's Mama," Mitchell whispered. He gave his sister a warning glare. "Remember ... you can't say anything about the car, Miss Mac."

With what appeared to be a blow-off to his warning, Mackenzee ran to the door, opening it just as their mama was approaching the porch.

"Mac ..." Mitchell warned, but he might as well have been talking to the wall.

"Heyyy, Mama," she said, holding the screen door open, one foot on the porch.

Glaring sideways, Gwendolyn Miller abruptly stopped. Surprised, and slightly alarmed, she cried, "Girl! What in the world you doin' home?" She dropped her keys, bent to pick them up. "Where's—"

"Hello, G-Lady." Mitchell had given her the nickname years ago, deciding she didn't look old enough to be called mama. Wary of Mac blowing the surprise, he shot another warning glance at her as he stepped out onto the porch.

"Mitchell?" Gwen was now shocked, but happiness replaced her alarm, and she almost let the drugstore bag she clutched slip from her hand after seeing her firstborn. "When did you get here, boy? I didn't know you was comin' home."

Mitchell smiled at the woman he loved most in the world. Until now he hadn't realized how much he'd missed her. In an elegant cream pantsuit, she was looking good.

"G-Lady, now you know I wouldn't miss my two main girls' birthday. I'll never be that busy." He stepped down into a hug and kissed her on the cheek.

After separating, he grabbed the bag from her as they headed into the house.

"I gotta use it," Gwen announced, zooming into the bathroom. She shut the door behind her and yelled, "Put that sack on my bed, Mitchell."

He tossed the sack onto his mama's bed, whispered something to Mac, and then hurried out and parked the Cadillac on the front lawn. He took a reproachful glance at G-Lady's raggedy-ass car, which she always parked at the curb to prevent the incurable oil leak from scattering its gook all over the driveway. It was a disgraceful hoopty. The rear was smashed-in, the tailpipe dragged, the muffler growled, the doors were defective, and the interior was jacked up. They called it "The Big Misery." Around the neighborhood, people talked real bad about it when it rode down the street. It was fucked up, unsafe and embarrassing—especially to his teenage brother, Montell. Mitchell hated the pile of junk with a passion. After today, anybody could come haul that load of garbage and burn it to hell if they wanted to.

After going back in the house and closing the door, the toilet was flushing.

"Mitchell, how did you and Mac get here? Where's your car? Mackenzee ... what was you doin' at that school house fighting?"

Mitchell shook his head at how she was rattling off questions before getting out of the bathroom good. He knew she was in her room when he heard "Where did your brother go, Mackenzee?"

"Outside," Mackenzee replied.

He could tell by the softness of her voice, Mackenzee was scared about what happened at school. He walked toward the room, glanced in to see if G-Lady was still dressed. She wasn't. While she dressed, Mitchell checked himself out in a hallway mirror, thinking of his mama. The second of five children—two brothers—Gwen had dropped out of school at fifteen, lied about her age, and obtained a cleaning job at a hotel. It was there that she'd met and began seeing David Thomas. Within months she'd become pregnant, subsequently giving birth to Mitchell at sixteen. Mitchell was three months old when she got her first apartment, cohabiting with David. They never married.

She continued working at the hotel, and was doing okay until she became fed up with David and his inability, and lack of desire to maintain a job. Not one to continuously put up with bullshit, she had packed her and Mitchell's stuff and moved to Missouri with a cousin. She'd warned David she would leave but he had always figured she was only blowing smoke. Gwen always said, "He didn't believe fat meat was greasy." Six months later she received word that he was killed at a gambling shack over a money argument. Six months after that she moved back to Tulsa, mainly because she missed her mama and family.

Together with her mama, G-Lady had practically taught Mitchell everything he knew about life. Life hadn't been easy, so upgrading hers—making it materially better— was one of the main reasons he'd excelled in the classroom, determined to repay the woman who'd given him life and many intangible gifts.

"She kept teasin' me, so I … I pushed her," he heard Mac say, her words snapping him from his thoughts.

"Girrrl, you don't be havin' yo' ass at that school house fighting!" Gwen shot back.

"She-she should've lef' me alone."

Mitchell tactfully entered the room, stepped behind Mac and started toying with her ponytails. Gwen had changed into a sundress and was putting on sandals.

"G-Lady, what time does M-Morg usually get home?" he asked, already knowing the answer. M-Morg was what he called Montell. He was trying to distract his mama's focus off Mac and the incident at school. Gwen had a tongue capable of hurting a person's feelings, and didn't bite it for anyone. Once, she'd cussed out a policeman for racial profiling, and didn't back down when he threatened to arrest her. Mitchell was rescuing his little sister before she became a victim on her birthday.

"Oh, there you are," Gwen said after seeing him behind his sister. She checked her watch. "He oughtta be here in a minute. Where's yo' car?"

"Aunt Carla has it. She's bringing it over when she's finished taking care of something." He knew that white lie would strike a nerve with his mama.

Gwen checked her appearance in the dresser mirror. "When did you see Carla? Why she got yo' car? Something wrong with hers?"

She was a pro at bombarding a person with questions, but Mitchell had dealt with it his entire life, and knew when to completely evade some of her questions, how to talk around others. "I saw her this morning, a little after I made it to town." Mitchell had plotted for today with Aunt Carla weeks ago. She rode with him to the Cadillac dealership to pick up the car and was keeping his car until he notified her to bring it, after he sprang the surprise on his mama.

"She didn't say nothing to me about it when I talked to her on the phone this morning."

"That right?" Glad his aunt had kept the surprise intact, he figured now was the perfect time to lure her outside before someone came and spoiled the surprise. "Maa-ma," he drawled with generic concern, "why is all that smoke coming from your car? Is it overheating?"

"What, boy? Please don't tell me something else is goin' wrong with that damn car!" She frantically hurried toward the front.

Mitchell and Mac were at her heels when she opened the front door and abruptly pulled up short.

"Surpriiiise!" they yelled, almost in unison.

Slowly, Gwen pushed through the screen door, looking like she'd just seen a ghost. Only, it wasn't fear in her eyes. "Who-whose car is that?" She asked blankly, her heart pumping like an overworked engine. Her stomach was fluttering, and disbelief circled like a pesky fly. She didn't want her hopes to rise, and suddenly plummet like a shot down quail.

"Happy birthday, Mama," Mitchell murmured from behind her, rubbing her shoulders.

"Don't be playin' with me, Mitchell Eugene Thomas!" She was sure her son was playing a joke on her; he was good at playing tricks on somebody. Even though he'd been giving her and his siblings some nice things lately, a new car was off the chart. She figured it was a rental. She remained glued to the spot, leaning on the open screen door and gazing at the glowing vehicle which, radiated a calm beauty, posing as if wanting to be photographed right on her front yard.

"For real, Mama," he assured, "See the bow up there? It's a present." To convince her, he handed her the keys: complete with a personalized sterling silver key chain with medallion he'd had engraved with 'GWENDOLYN'S CADDY'. "Here, G-Lady, it really is yours."

Stunned, her free hand finally covered her mouth; tears welled up in her eyes. Her head shaking back and forth, she murmured, "Oh ... my ... God. Oh ... my ... God." Tears now crawling down her face, noticeably shaking, she realized her son wasn't bullshitting her at all.

She stepped onto the porch, placed a hand on one of the columns supporting the roof to steady her jittery legs, slowly stepped down the two steps, eased her way to the car. She delicately rubbed a trembling hand over the contours of the beautiful machinery, still filled with disbelief. But she now knew there was such a thing as *love at first sight*. Tentatively, she glanced back at Mitchell, exhibiting more gratitude than she could put into words. The cat definitely had her tongue.

"Get in, Mama," Mitchell cajoled. "Take her for a ride."

Hesitantly, she opened the door and climbed in inhaling the cherry scent from the air freshener. While she scanned the interior, she slid a nervous hand over the immaculate upholstery; cooed over the modernized instrument panel. Still, she couldn't believe it.

"A Cadillac! Brand ... fucking ... new," she mumbled.

Waving a hand, she called for Mackenzee to come get in. The enthusiastic child quickly hopped in, climbing over Gwen. Gwen pulled the door shut, sighed, and bowed her head. "Thank you, Jesus," she quietly whispered. She never gave a second look or thought to the old piece of shit at the curb, or the smoke supposedly coming from it.

3

Job number two had Jazelle at her cubicle rapidly tapping at the keyboard while simultaneously scanning the monitor for possible errors. She wasn't a big fan of typing, but for the past three months in order to manage bills and other debts, she'd been moonlighting five days a week as a data entry clerk. Jazelle's duties included receiving personal information from phone calls and mailed in credit applications, then inputting the information for processing.

The need for this second job still angered her. Ignoring common sense, she'd jumped into the same pit of foolishness visited by thousands of simple-minded, too-trusting, think-they-got-to-have-a-man women. A lousy situation that any intelligent woman should stay clear of after all the disturbing, lousy-ending stories floating around covering the exact subject.

In the wake of an inadequate month of dating, she'd green-lighted Kevin Ballard, her last so-called boyfriend, to move into her apartment with her. Being the ignorant dummy she was, she allowed him to drive her car and gave him access to her credit and debit cards, trusting him the whole time. Turned out that during that five month period, he'd only been using her for money, thrusting her into a small-scale financial crisis. On top of that, she found out he had another woman the entire time she'd known him. He'd claimed to work for a janitorial service, when in reality, he wasn't employed. During the hours when he pretended to be working, he'd been at his baby's mama's house. Worse, he'd been helping her out with Jazelle's money. Prior to meeting him, she'd been saving for a home, fastidiously maintaining student loan payments and car note. He put a huge dent in the dream for a house, even caused her to struggle to pay bills on time. Before she'd gotten hip to what he was doing, she'd already been burnt. But a fine ass man with some stupefying hazel eyes could screw up the head of any woman, which is what happened to her. Now she knew being fine could equate to being fictitious, because his ass was a fraud.

How could she have been so naïve? Stupid? She asked herself those questions again and again and again.

"How may I help you?" Jazelle said into the head-set after it buzzed in her ear. She asked the relevant questions, and entered the data as quickly as the caller relayed the information. "Thank you. Have a nice evening." The applicant went off the line.

"Ready to take a break?" asked Amanda from the cubicle next to Jazelle.

"Mm-hmm. I could use one," Jazelle replied, removing the headset and hanging it on a hook.

White as could be, thanks to Irish lineage, Amanda was a true redhead, top-heavy, and freckles. Married with two kids—a boy and a girl—she had a hilarious sense of humor which had easily drawn Jazelle. Being stationed next to each other had enhanced their friendship.

In the break room, they sat at a table snacking on chips, drinking soda. Amanda was a homemaker who didn't need to work; her husband was a well paid electrical engineer. She worked part-time to get out of the house for a while during the week, attempting to hold on to the little sanity her kids were constantly seeping from her. One evening during Jazelle's second week on the job, Amanda had come into the office emotionally spent and poured some of her off-spring-inflicted frustrations on her. In turn Jazelle divulged how Kevin had used her, and the resulting ramifications. Since that day their friendship blossomed.

"Jazelle, I told my husband I'm gonna put those rotten kids of ours in a juvenile facility."

Jazelle chuckled. "Maybe that'll scare 'em a little."

"Something should; I refuse to let them drive me cuckoo. The little boogers have already destroyed my figure." Scowling, she swept her eyes over her body. "One day they and my husband are gonna come home to a house with no Amanda. No more, 'Mama, can you do that? Can you do this? Mamaaa, Danny hit me!' Or, 'Mama, Rachel been in my room!' "

Jazelle listened with a knowing grin.

Turning up the can of coke, Amanda took a deep throated swallow, lightly belched and excused herself. "And my husband with his, 'Aw honey, all kids fight and bicker. It's natural.' "

Jazelle cracked up at her friend mocking her husband.

"When I'm gone," Amanda continued petulantly, "then we'll see what's '*natural*!' "

Jazelle was still laughing. "Girl, you are crazy." She rose, stepped over to the snack machine and deposited some coins in the slot. "I had a little altercation in my class today."

"What kind of altercation?"

Jazelle removed the package from the vending machine and tore into it with her teeth as she sat. "Remember that precocious little girl I told you about, Mackenzee?"

Amanda thought, and then nodded.

"She pushed one of her classmates down, causing her to get a tiny scratch on her knee."

"So it wasn't bad?" Amanda looked minutely concerned.

"Unh-unh. Nikki—that's the classmate's name—kept teasing Mackenzee about her painting and she got fed up, so she let Nikki know how she felt about it."

Jazelle gestured, offering Amanda a cupcake.

"Just leave it in the package, I'll eat it later. Your students sound like my kids—fighting and fussing over anything."

Jazelle bit into the cupcake. "Nikki just needed a little band-aid. She's been trying to bully the others since the third week. I knew it wouldn't be long before one of the kids stood up to her."

"Well, that's what the little heathen gets," Amanda said, crunching on chips. "Maybe she'll leave her classmates alone now."

Jazelle was skeptical. "Maybe?"

"What are you doing for the weekend?" Amanda asked, wanting to store the subject of kids.

"I'm thinking about going to shake a leg," Jazelle said. "I haven't been out in over three months, and my girlfriend's been bugging me to go out with her for the longest."

Amanda snorted. "Hell, I couldn't tell you the last time Steven and I went out. What a fun husband he is," she said sarcastically. "But I'm going home tonight; the four of us are having a nice, looong talk." She rose to dispose of her trash. "The shit at that house is about to stop!"

Laughing, Jazelle stood and threw away her trash, thinking how funny Amanda was. Though they only had a job-site friendship, it surprised her how naturally they'd connected since she had never been close with a white person. She'd attended school with whites but they'd only been friendly, no bonding had taken place. Even now her relationships with white colleagues at the pre-school were mostly cordial. Why? She had no idea. Up until recently, she'd never thought about it. Befriending Amanda was a refreshing change from the ordinary; it provided a different spin on life situations culturally and morally, and was informative. Good diversification for a teacher. The friendship also came at a time when she needed a new, objective perspective. Because of Amanda, she often looked forward to her second job. Their time together temporarily rescued them from the stress of their lives outside this building.

Two co-workers entered the break room interrupting them with small talk. A minute or so later, she and Amanda ended their break.

Sensing Amanda was tired of discussing kids, she didn't re-open that subject.

Settling the headsets on their heads, they returned to the stack of applications needing to be inputted. As was the norm each evening, they conversed back and forth while they worked, chitchatting until time to call it a night.

ഓരു

Returning home from Incredible Pizza, where they'd celebrated McKenzee's birthday, Gwen parked her CTS on the lawn and Quincy parked in the driveway behind Mitchell's Optima. The nine bodies languidly got out the two cars into dark surroundings, as most houses on the block seemed to be stingy with the porch lights. No one noticed the seventy-something Delta eighty-eight out at the curb behind the Big Misery. Before anyone reached the porch, a strange utterance came from the direction of the Big Misery. All heads but Mac's sleeping one turned to the voice they couldn't immediately identify.

The person then got out of the unidentified car. They could only see a staggering form. "Where's my baby girl?" demanded a man's slurring voice.

"*Charles*?" Gwen yelled. "Is that you?" Intuition told her it was her ex; something warned her that he would show up tonight. Charles Morgan was Montell and Mackenzee's father. Though she'd put him out when she was six months pregnant with Mackenzee, he'd shown up at the hospital for the birth, and never missed his daughter's birthday.

"Yeah, it's me!" Charles yelled back.

What had been a smooth evening instantly became bumpy. Gwen could tell Charles was drunk as hell. Gwen had spent ten wasted years with him; the only good thing to come from the relationship was her two youngest. No thanks to him, she'd had to deal with the pain of another man gone bad, and go it alone as a single mother. Prior to the fall out he hadn't been the greatest provider, but he was there. Present in her two boys' lives. He worked construction when work was available, had been a decent man, so-so daddy for the most part, but the thing was that Montell and Mitchell had a male figure around. Then his drinking increased, eventually becoming unbearable, and drugs sometimes entered the picture, which caused him to squander paychecks, and derailed his mental stability. He never laid a hand on any of them, but became verbally abusive, displaying drunken rages, and turned more intolerable by the day. One gloomy night during one of those rages he expressed his true feelings toward Mitchell: he simply didn't like him. In his eyes, Mitchell was a spoiled mama's boy. Pussy. Sissy. Later, once he sobered, he tried to deny ever making those remarks. But an intoxicated person spoke a sober mind, and his truth had come out.

Already sick and tired of his shit, Gwen decided enough was enough. It was time for him to step. She didn't play with anyone fucking with her kids. They were her heart and soul, and Mitchell was her first born; the first thing she loved that was hers.

Charles had crossed the wrong line.

She dismissed the pleading, begging, and heartless apologies and put his ass out. And she did it without procrastinating. Put all his belongings out in the front yard.

"Mama, Mac don't need to see him like that," Montell said with a disgusted tone.

"I know," Gwen replied, totally agreeing with her middle child. Drunk as he was, not only would the sight of Charles scare Mac, but it would also present an undesired image that no small child should be exposed to. Not from a parent. "Take her in the house and lay her on my bed, Montell."

Mackenzee had fallen asleep during the ride home. The day's festivities had worn her out. Montell carried her up to the house, her small head still wearing the birthday hat rubber strapped to her chin. He was glad she was sleep. He didn't want her to see the pitiful scene. He cared for his daddy but at the same time, Charles made him sick. He was nothing but a worthless drunk only caring for his liquor. It seemed like his kids weren't that important to him.

Montell and Mac hadn't seen nor heard from him in over four months, so why when he decided to show his face, was it in this condition? Things used to be good with him around, Montell reflected now and then, when he wished his daddy would show up to one of his games. Charles used to be his role model; they'd had a cool bond once upon a time. Back then he only drank socially it seemed, on a Friday or Saturday, keeping it to a minimum. Then all that changed and the drinking slowly went from being social to a way of life. Weekend drinks turned into an everyday thing. The sloppiness started and turned completely out of hand. Not long after, the potentially all-American family became another all-American casualty. Montell didn't know who his daddy was any more.

He unlocked the door and carried his sister into the house. He was heated.

Gwen told the others to go inside. She was going out to have a talk with her ex. Reluctantly, the others went inside.

The porch light came on as she approached her ex. The smell of liquor trounced on her nasal passages before she was within ten feet of him. Jack Daniel's—a smell she remembered all too well. He still wore the same old boots from when they were together, dressed as usual in well-worn jeans and, as hot as it was, he still had on a flannel shirt; the same chain with a pocket-knife case linked to it still dangled from his hip. Once a masculine, handsome brother, his six-four frame had shriveled up like a prune. She realized Montell was growing physically into an almost duplicate of how Charles once was. His scraggly, bearded face looked to have aged about twelve years. He looked old and tired. She ached a little at seeing the father of her kids, a man she once loved, torn down to this shameful version of a human. She wasn't sure if it was disgust or sorrow she felt, because she'd tried on several occasions, before and after putting him out, to get him to seek help.

A familiar voice said, "Hello, Gwen," from the car when she was an arm's length from Charles. Gwen bent over a bit, trying to see who it was in the dark vehicle. It was Charles's long time friend, Ralph Lucky.

"I told Charles we shouldn't come ovah here since we been drinkin', but he kept pesterin' me. Said he'd drive his self if I didn't bring 'im." He sounded scared, Gwen noticed, probably because he'd been cussed out by her before.

"You don't haf ta tell her shit!" Charles asserted.

"No he don't!" Gwen snapped. "But I can surely call the police on both o' y'all, 'cause y'all both drunk." She was being calm as possible. "And you, Charles, with yo' drunk ass—I told you I didn't want you comin' around my kids drunk— Especially Mackenzee!"

"Gwen, please don't call the laws on us," Ralph begged.

"If you would've came over sober—with a sane mind—I would've let you see Mac. But nawww, you ain't seeing my baby while you're drunk, smellin' like a whiskey distillery ... and lookin' like a fuckin' creature feature!"

"She's my baby too. And ... I wanna see her!" Charles tried to demand.

Being rational with an intoxicated person was usually a lost cause. The mind doesn't function properly and Gwen recognized all the symptoms with Charles: incoherence, slurred speech, irrational ... he couldn't even balance himself. If not for him leaning on the car he'd probably be lying on the ground. She was disgusted by his appearance. There was no way in hell she was about to let him see Mac!

Over a half hour passed while the hopeless exchange carried on. Gwen's temper was beginning to boil and she was having malevolent thoughts, wanting to slap the shit out of his drunk ass. She would've if Montell hadn't finally come and pulled her away. He told Charles he needed to leave 'cause he wasn't seeing Mac. Charles fired back with the, "I'm yo daddy" speech, which Montell couldn't care less about. Back in the day, that *daddy* stuff would've worked, but now Montell considered his daddy nothing more than a sperm donor.

"Boy, if you wadn't my son, I'd knock you on yo ass!" Charles said maniacally. "You must be getting like that sissified brotha uh yourn. The way he use'ta hang around the house— always up unda' his *mama*," he said sarcastically, "you coulda swore he was fuckin' her!"

Why had he made his mouth say some shit like that? He would've been better off calling his own mother a bitch to her face. The heat in Gwen's eyes could've melted steel. She lost all understanding, blew a fuse, and verbally tore into Charles, calling him everything except a child of God. The mix of cuss words she fired at him probably had Pope John Paul I turning in his grave. Even Charles was probably convinced his name was now *Drunk Sonofabitch*. If she'd had a gun it wouldn't be the liquor threatening his life, but the bullets she'd be capping in his ass!

Neighbors were peering out their windows, porch lights blinked on, some folks even stepped out onto their porches to see what the commotion was.

"Ralph! You get yo fuckin' friend," she ordered, "and y'all get the hell away from my house!" Montell had to hold her back. If she charged at Charles and he ended up hitting his mama, he'd have to lay his pathetic daddy out. He had the strong desire to do that anyway. "And don't you never ever bring his drunk ass back over to my house, or I'll have you and him both locked up quicker than you can park that raggedy ass car you drivin'!"

"O-okay, Gwen. Okay ..." Ralph was spooked.

With a glare that would've proselytized the devil into being an angel, Gwen pointed at Charles. "It'll be a cold day in hell before you see Mac again, mista! What you need to do is go get yo' self some help, boy, 'cause that shit you keep pouring down yo' throat done turned you crazy as hell. Now y'all get the hell on away from here!"

Charles didn't budge.

Gwen glared. "Boy, you betta do it quick, fast and in a fuckin' hurry!"

"Charles, bring yo' ass on, man!" Ralph yelled. It took him a few minutes of pleading, coaxing and coercion to get Charles to get in the car. He wanted no parts of the jail house. Especially on a Friday night; they'd be there all weekend.

When they were both in the car he pulled from the curb like a bat-out-of-hell, tires screeching, and grazed the fender of the Big Misery as he hightailed away. "To hell with you, Gwen!" Charles yelled in a drunken slur halfway down the block.

Gwen and Montell stood there with pained expressions, watching the car's tail lights as it sped away.

੪ාੜ

From the porch, Mitchell watched the episode unfold. The way he felt toward Charles he would've knocked him out if he'd gotten involved. That's why he kept his distance after flicking on the porch light. He knew his mama could hold her own with Charles since he was too drunk to really be a threat. A part of him wanted to walk out there and put hands on Charles for the hell of it; not because he'd popped up drunk, nor because of what he said or thought about him—Mitchell could care less about Charles Morgan's feelings about him. He resented Charles for deserting his responsibilities as a parent. Reducing your own children to anything less than the most important aspect of your existence deserved an ass kicking.

To hell with Charles. Montell and Mackenzee were the ones he was concerned for. After living his entire life without his father, Mitchell wanted different for his brother and sister. Kids deserved both parents' nurturing. Involvement. And he knew Montell wished his daddy played an active role in his life. Wished he was there supporting, boasting, and being proud of his athletic accomplishments.

It was Charles's loss. Whether he was around or not, his son and daughter wouldn't suffer. As he'd been doing for years, Mitchell would fill that fatherly void as much as possible. Be the male figure in their lives, providing an example whose lead they could follow. A role model they could always look to for encouragement, guidance and support. He'd provide them with the necessities and wants—tangible and intangible—which Gwen couldn't provide, and that their father was incapable of. Son, brother, father figure, friend; he was all of those rolled into one. Dysfunction wouldn't limit his siblings from having a good sense of direction and stability. Not if he could help it. "Mama and M-Morg, come on in the house," he said to them. "Your audience has seen and heard enough for tonight."

4

Early Monday morning, Mitchell traveled the Turner Turnpike back to Norman. The overcast sky confirmed the potential strong winds and heavy rains that had been forecast. Farther southwest, thick, spooky clouds rapidly developed, moving eastward. As usual when he made the hundred-plus mile journey, hip-hop thumped through the speakers, keeping him motivated during the trip.

The past weekend replayed in his mind while he bobbed his head to the sounds. Not even drunk Charles had put a dampener on the outcome. The images of G-Lady's expression when she first saw the 'Lac, and Mac's wide-eyed look when she'd turned and seen the bicycle he bought her for her birthday, were moments that dreams were made of. The party for Mac at Incredible Pizza had been plenty of fun and they'd capped off the night with a good time during G-Lady's little bash at the club…

It seemed everyone in the club had been gathered around the two tables filled with food reserved for Gwen's party. About fifteen or so were friends and family, but a cluster of others swooped on the free eats like vultures on a dead carcass, welcoming themselves to the spread while it lasted.

Mitchell navigated his way through the maze of people, leading his tipsy mama from the dance floor. Most of the night, she'd been sipping from the oversized glass snifter honoring the birthday person. On the way to their seats, Mitchell spoke to and briefly mingled with folks he hadn't seen in ages. When they reached their area, he noticed a seemingly familiar sista conversing and laughing with Aunt Carla. The area was decorated with sparkling party paraphernalia, and whoever this female was embellished it more. People were getting their party on, and wanna-be players were trying to get their mack on, while many of the women dismissed the advances, unimpressed by what they knew where mostly lies. Some women tuned in, seeming interested, but were probably just being nice. But there was something about this sista talking to Aunt Carla...

Once he got closer, he did a double take. *Miss Johnson, Mac's teacher*. Those lips—tantalizingly voluptuous—he would recognize in any setting. Even in the dim club he identified the owner of those lips. *Man*. He couldn't help but admit that she looked delicious dressed in an eye catching strapless jumpsuit with rhinestone trim around the waist, perfectly enhancing *that body*. Her silky hair hung mid-shoulder, making her excellent eye candy. She'd definitely improved since their earlier meeting.

"Ahh, here comes the birthday girl," Carla announced, sipping something intoxicating as he and Gwen edged up to the table. "And my handsome nephew."

Aunt Carla is tipsy as hell too, Mitchell thought, briefly catching the eye of Miss Johnson as he pulled out a chair for Gwen. He winced at the notion of being around a bunch of drunken folks tonight. Aware of how Miss Johnson had roused something in him at the school earlier, he planned on keeping his distance from her. He saw that she had on make-up and eyeliner, unlike at the school, but it enhanced her looks. The plain but pretty woman he'd met earlier had transformed into a straight up *dime piece*.

"Look who's here, Gwen," Carla said, drinking whatever sauce was in her glass, "Mac's teacher."

"Happy birthday, Miss Miller," Jazelle said slightly bowing.

"Heyyy, Miss Johnson, and thank you," Gwen replied with a smile matching the mood she was in. "And call me Gwen. I don't need to be reminded that I'm getting old, girl." They both laughed. "Who told you 'bout my party?"

"Oh. No one. I decided to get out the house tonight, and here is where I ended up. I was lounging around, trying to keep an arm's length from some of these touchy-feely men, and noticed someone was celebrating a birthday. Carla recognized me and motioned me over, so I've been talking with her while you were dancing."

"You by yo'self?" Gwen asked.

"Nooo—with my girlfriend." She looked toward the dance floor. "She's somewhere over there being fast."

"I know that's right," Gwen said, reaching for her drink. "Have you met my son?" She motioned the hand holding her drink toward Mitchell, who was filling a paper plate with food.

Mitchell looked toward Jazelle when he realized his mama was referring to him.

"Yeah, Mama ... we met when I picked Mac up from school today." He said it casually, trying to conceal his lasting surprise at Miss Johnson being there.

"I thought you got that girl from the bus stop," Gwen said.

"Mitchell?" Jazelle said, looking baffled.

Mitchell was perplexed. "Ah ... yeah."

"You're only in high school ... how'd you get in the here? Do you have a fake ID or something?" Jazelle continued, still looking startled, knowing the club was twenty-four and older.

"High School?" Carla chimed.

"Girl, my baby been done graduated high school," Gwen said. "And he don't need no fake ID—his damn cousin on his daddy's side owns this place. But don't tell nobody," she said conspiratorially, and laughed. "We don't wanna get him in trouble just 'cause he let my college baby in to party with his mama."

Mitchell laughed internally at the surprise written all over Jazelle's face, her mouth hanging open longer than necessary. Now he realized what the surprise in her eyes earlier had been about: she hadn't recognized he was the person she'd met at the school earlier, and like many others, she'd thought he was in high school. Whoever said age was only a number probably needed to rethink that notion, because it was often much more with him.

Right then the DJ played Funkadelic's "(Not Just) Knee Deep" and some dude Mitchell didn't recognize came over and ushered Gwen to the dance floor. Mitchell was relieved for the time being, because he knew his mama would've started going off at the mouth; especially with the good mood she was in.

Aunt Carla grabbed Quincy, who'd just returned from the men's room, and followed her sister to go shake a leg.

"So, you're the one who attends OU?" Jazelle asked.

Attended, Mitchell was about to say; instead, he answered, "Yep."

"Well then, what's your brother's name—the one in high school?"

"M-Mor—I mean Montell."

Jazelle pondered that for a second. "*Dang*. Guess I certainly mixed you up with your brother. Plus, without"—she made a gesture with her hand over her head—"the cap. And with those glasses you're wearing … You're really in college?"

"I'm the 'college baby', as G-Lady put it." He was almost smiling, and realized he was actually relaxed around this lady who had rattled him earlier that day. He was even holding a little conversation with her.

That, he thought, was unbelievable.

He then noticed she was avoiding eye contact with him as she nervously picked at the finger foods. *Why the nerves? Hopefully it's not because she's embarrassed for mistaking me for my little brother.*

"Living It Up" by Ja Rule started bumping and, impulsively, he asked, "Would you like to dance, Miss Johnson?" Hearing his cut motivated him to temporarily dump his women boycott. He might as well get into the spirit of his mama's birthday. Hell, he loved to dance, and it might be nice to dance with someone other than family all night.

"Hunh?" She appeared to be taken off guard. "Oh, yeah," she replied hesitantly. "And please, call me by my first name. Miss Johnson sounds too formal in this setting."

"And what is your first name?"

"Jazelle."

"Jazelle," he pronounced almost whispering, liking the name. "That's original." *And pretty.* But he cuffed that thought.

"Thank you." She smiled, slightly blushing...

A frightening cacophony of thunder boomed, startling and abruptly snapping Mitchell from his thoughts, and wicked streaks of lightning lit up the sky as bloated, angry raindrops began pounding his car. He'd already gotten a late start, and the storm would likely add to his tardiness.

He clicked on the windshield wipers, grabbed his cellular, and called the office to notify them that he'd be running late. All lines were busy, so he punched the phone off and dropped it in the passenger seat.

Though near-sighted, he normally made use of his eyeglasses—couldn't adapt to contacts—only when driving at night, or when he wanted to try to look more mature. So with the clouds darkening the daylight, rain splatters blurring his vision, he fumbled with his eyeglass case, then scooped the glasses out and slid them on. He then pumped up the volume of

E-40's "Function" and mimicked the lyrics, paying close attention as he rapidly but cautiously rode the slick highway.

To his chagrin, Jazelle entered his head. He wondered why he was thinking about her, disturbed that he was even thinking about a woman, period.

Oh yeah, I better hurry up and get back to Norman, so I can blot Miss Jazelle Johnson completely out of my mind.

₧₧₧

The morning began in a bad way for Jazelle. She woke up sneezing, which in turn seemed to lead to an intermittent runny nose. She considered calling in sick because she didn't want to infect her students, but missing a day with her kids wasn't an option, particularly if it meant spending the day in her dull ass apartment; she wasn't that sick!

Unless she had something highly contagious, or was physically unable—neither was the case—she was going to work.

Though not too fond of taking medication—she had an emotional-psychological hang up about drugs—she swallowed more than a tablespoon of liquid cold medicine, popped a couple of non-drowsy allergy tablets, assisting the pills down with orange juice. She decided that the weak mixture wouldn't be harmful.

After dressing, she fixed herself some bacon, scrambled eggs, toast and jelly along with another glass of OJ, hoping the vitamin C would help combat the cold symptoms.

Adding to the discouraging morning, she approached her Chevy and found one of the tires flat. *Damn*! She wanted to scream, but held it in, knowing that whining over something uncontrollable was useless. Rumblings of thunder and spooky streaks of lightning damn near made her run back inside. Instead, she reluctantly retrieved the fixing-a-flat tools from the trunk and slid the jack into position under the car, then loosened the lugs with the four-way before jacking the car up. Changing a tire was one of the useful lessons she'd absorbed from an ex. While hunched over, engaged in the inconvenient task, she looked up, scanning the cloudy sky. *Please don't let the rain start dropping while I'm doing this.*

She inertly replaced the flat tire with the donut spare, being very careful not to stain her clothes. Being a single independent woman had its educational moments, and this was definitely one of those times. Afterwards, she inspected her handy work, and decided she would get the flat tire fixed after work, because the donut made her car look like a hoopty.

Hurrying, she returned the tools to the trunk, got in the car and dug out a wipette and some hand sanitizer from her purse. After cleaning her hands, she put the key in the ignition, checked her hair and face in the mirror, then turned the switch.

Nothing happened.

She tried again.

Nothing. No buzz, not even a click. Now that she thought about it, the instrument panel hadn't lit up, the interior lights hadn't come on, nor had she heard the dinging bell once she'd put the key in the ignition.

She pressed the horn.

Nothing.

"Well I'll be *damned*," she uttered. This was just like her luck. After the maintenance warranty expired a month ago, her car wanted to start acting an ass.

Frustrated, she laid her forehead on the steering wheel, wondering why this was happening.

Other than changing a tire and some minor tricks, she knew little about cars. Nonetheless, she aversely pulled the hood lever, to go see and see if the battery terminals were loose. But right when she opened the door to get out, the rain pounced.

ജଔ

School was out, the students were gone, and Jazelle sat cross-legged on one of two couches in the teachers' lounge, finally enjoying the hot link sandwich she'd brought for lunch but had been unable to eat because she didn't have an appetite earlier. Now, she was hungry as a hostage, and she was getting busy on the sandwich.

Fortunately, the day had turned out better than it started after she reluctantly called Speedo, the ex who'd taught her the little she knew about cars. He was a mechanic and wrecker service owner who she'd met at an auto parts store while buying motor oil one evening. He had come and dropped her off at work, then went back and checked out her car. He'd detected that the problem was the alternator, and fixed it on credit since Jazelle was short on funds. Like all her other exe's, he was something of a man-whore, and she preferred not having anything to do with the men from her past. But he was her only option. She realized Speedo had matured some since their days together—was now engaged—but that hadn't prevented him from making subtle hints of *hittin' it* again.

Once a dog always a dog.

On pay day she would promptly pay him. She had no desire to be indebted to any man. They always wanted some *ass* for doing a woman a favor.

Mrs. Green quietly stepped into the lounge carrying a small stack of papers. She'd sat with the class until Jazelle made it to work. "Thank you again for watching the kids," Jazelle said, finishing off the sandwich. It was the first opportunity they'd had to talk since she'd arrived to work.

"Anytime you need me," Mrs. Green dismissed the gratitude with the wave of a hand. "Did everything come out alright with your car?"

"Yes—thank God. The alternator had died, which drained the battery, but all is working now."

"Good for you." She leafed through the papers, handed a sheet to Jazelle. "Not having transportation can be a bugger."

"I know," Jazelle said, glancing at the paper, something about a *Bachelor's Auction.* "Cars always break down at the wrong time."

"That's how it always seems to turn out." Mrs. Green was now removing dated papers from the bulletin board and tacking up replacements. "Least you're back up and running."

Jazelle sighed, absently nodding.

"How were the kids when I left?" Mrs. Green asked. "Everything seemed pretty peaceful."

"All was calm with the kids, thankfully," Jazelle answered. "I think they sensed I wasn't in a real good mood."

Mrs. Green chuckled. "I have a feeling Nikki won't be bothering Mackenzee again. She found out that one has a mean streak, too." She gathered the papers she'd removed from the bulletin board and headed to the door. Before exiting she paused and pivoted. "Did you see that car Mackenzee's mother was driving? Wasn't it nice? Her birthday sure must've been good to her. And I know she's happy to put that other thing-on-wheels to rest. Lord, that old car ..." She walked out shaking her head.

Jazelle wondered how she knew the car was Gwen's. Mrs. Green sometimes reminded her of her grandmother with her nosiness. She could be all up in your business without you even knowing it. And she was quick to cite one of those old sayings: "Problem with kids nowadays is that they don't get their butts whooped." The thought brought on a smile. Then, sighing, she shook her head in wonderment. The term *nosy* definitely fit Mrs. Green perfectly.

Yes, Jazelle had seen the new Cadillac. Gwen had been driving it when she picked up Mackenzee from school earlier. Mackenzee had already told the class about her birthday and the gifts she'd received. She'd privately told Jazelle how Mitchell had surprised her and Gwen.

It occurred to her that Mitchell full of surprises; even unintentionally.

She'd finally decided to go to the club with Dawn, and she had certainly been *surprised* in there. Hell, she was still stupefied. Not only had Mackenzee's too-young-to-be-in-the-club brother been in there, but she'd come to find out he was the brother in college Mackenzee was always talking about. After that revelation, she'd stood there with her mouth agape, dumbfounded. Before that, no one could've paid her to believe that boy was older than sixteen.

It was difficult to accept that he wasn't in high school. The glasses, the low cut fade, and how he was dressed compared to when she'd met him earlier made him look intellectual, a bit more mature, and she didn't recognize him. He still looked sixteen, though she now believed he was eighteen. Despite his age, though, the black mesh T-shirt he'd worn to the club, which clung to his torso like a sweatband, had her drooling like a high school girl. It outlined his buff chest and enhanced his sprinter's physique. She was sure he'd gained the attention of half the females in the club. Maybe even some of the *fairies* too, she considered, frowning.

College boy or not, he was still a teenager, and she couldn't believe the flutters he'd caused her to have. They slow danced, and the fruity but masculine aroma of his cologne had her wanting to taste him. As he lightly wrapped his arms around her she'd felt and uncharacteristic yearning between her legs, and the moistness that came with it.

Although she hated to admit it to herself, and was embarrassed by the thought, she actually wouldn't have minded if he'd come onto her. But unlike the occasional bold, egotistical, disrespectful young brothers running around in his age group, Mitchell conducted himself like a perfect gentleman. And that was a first. Most men weren't capable of that type of restraint. Even many of the older, supposedly mature men were at her like some horny little devils. He hadn't tried to make any advances on her, and they'd been virtually glued together when they danced. He'd been rather taciturn and reserved, hardly saying much of anything. Yet, there was a level of confidence about him even with his quietness. He hadn't seemed shy, just ... not too talkative.

Her grandmother had warned her about the quiet types, though. They were the worst kind, hid many secrets, and had agendas and skeletons in their closet. Plus they were sneaky and clever as hell.

What did all that matter, though? Other types of men had run game on her too. It wasn't like she was thinking in terms of a relationship with him anyhow; with any man for that matter.

Suddenly, the thought of the jacked up things men had done to her snapped her to her senses. She chastised herself, and cursed Mitchell for the romantic BS he'd stimulated in her. He'd been a gentleman alright, probably putting on a front in the presence of his mother. He was probably just as bad as, or worse than, all the no good sons-of-bitches she'd been involved with over the years. He wasn't fooling her by trying to play that innocent role. No way. She was up on the game this time. All men were dogs; even Mitchell Thomas with his *young* clever ass.

Something else that had her mind in a quandary started with Gwen's car. How was he able to buy such an expensive car? Any car for that matter? He was too damn young, and like Jazelle, too broke. Even though Gwen kept Mackenzee well dressed and groomed, she received state assistance, so money wasn't just dripping at will in their household. Like so many young black men in the community flossing around in their fancy cars, name brand clothing, and expensive jewelry, he had to be hustling.

What a waste. He certainly had potential to be something worthwhile. Being in college was a positive, so why was he taking a chance of wasting a bright future? And the example he would set for his little brother and sister...

I must be losing my mind, Jazelle thought, ending the unfounded insinuations about Mitchell. She knew nothing about him, but was accusing him of being a hustler. To be judging his character like that showed her ill feelings toward men were at an all time high.

She sighed. Mitchell seemed like a decent person. But being too credulous was what had been her main adversary with men in the past: too damn trusting!

Still, what concern was it of hers to be sitting around analyzing the livelihood of someone that in all actuality, she knew nothing about?

Damn, I need to get a life, she told herself, feeling as pathetic as one of those old ladies who were always in somebody's business. It was nobody's fault but her own that her life was in social misery and a financial noose; that she was stupidly and, even after numerous disappointments, she constantly got burnt by the doggish men roaming T-Town.

She glimpsed at the clock above the pop machine and sighed. It was nearing the time for her to go to her other j-o-b.

5

Tuesday now, and the storm had ceased wreaking havoc. A day earlier when Mitchell rode up to the modern one-story office building housing Omnity Sports, the sports management firm he and Travis Wingham owned as partners, Travis had been closing up due to the storm. As was the case all over Norman, neighboring towns, and Oklahoma City, their building had been affected by electrical outages, phone lines were down, and some electric poles had tilted, causing hazardous loose cables, blackouts, and plenty of disarray. Utility workers had labored steadfastly during the night, battling torrential downpours, lightning, and heavy winds, trying to restore utility services. But with the dangerous conditions, the workers could only do so much. Many households went without power the entire night.

As he'd done yesterday, Mitchell pulled into the Omnity parking lot. Travis's red BMW was the only car present, and he parked next to it. Travis was normally the first to arrive each morning.

Mitchell emerged from his Optima under a sky still dominated by clouds, only they were light and genial instead of leaden and somber. Remnants of the storms heavy hand—tree limbs, trash, mud patches, and other debris—were scattered all about, and some areas were flooded. Tired-looking city and utility workers were cleaning and repairing, attempting to put the area in order again. He opened the driver's side back door, removed his blazer off a hanger and retrieved his briefcase from the backseat.

He slowly padded across the parking lot, scanning the mess. He was glad not to be a blue collar worker; they had plenty to keep them busy.

Travis was perched on the edge of the receptionist's desk in the lobby area holding a coffee mug when Mitchell walked through the doors. He was wearing a curiously playful smirk, and right away Mitchell new something favorable was up.

The two had met at OU's student recreational facilities during Mitchell's freshman year, and Travis's final semester of law school. They'd each been one of the best players on their team in a campus intramural basketball league, and after a game one evening, players from both teams ended up at the same restaurant, where Mitchell and Travis discussed playing together in an off campus league. From that outing until the time Travis graduated and passed the bar, the two often balled together. They earned the nick-names 'Sugar' and 'Spice'; Travis being the white guy with a sweet jumper and Mitchell, the black kid with a flavorful all around game.

Becoming business partners had happened by sheer coincidence two years after they'd met. By then, Travis was employed at a law firm in OKC, working in Contracts, while Mitchell was an honor roll student, scheduled to graduate that coming summer because he always took a heavy course load for fall, spring and summer semesters. Along with being an outstanding student, Mitchell was also a tutor, and friends with several athletes. During a tutoring session, one of the football players had confided in him thoughts about entering the NFL draft, but didn't want to contact an agent and jeopardize his status to play if he instead decided to come back for his senior year. Knowing how intelligent Mitchell was he wanted his advice.

With the athlete's permission, Mitchell and Travis researched and contacted a few knowledgeable people regarding the draft, requirements, what to expect, and becoming an agent. Mitchell then relayed the information to the athlete, and in an unforeseen occurrence, the athlete asked Mitchell to be his agent if he got an acceptable draft position.

Mitchell was shocked and flattered, but hadn't attained the requirements to be an agent. Also, he was more focused on completing his degree requirements. Instead, he suggested the athlete use Travis. With the okay, he then passed the idea along to Travis, and after a week of weighing the pros and cons, Travis, who'd been flabbergasted when Mitchell had ran the notion by him, said, "What the hell! I've heard he's going to get a decent draft position, but I'll keep my day job just in case." Travis's only request had been for Mitchell to be his accountant if things went accordingly, even though he hadn't graduated. Reluctantly, Mitchell agreed.

He was drafted mid-second round. Omnity Sports was born, and sports management was introduced to its newest associates.

Mitchell clearly recollected the day when Travis and he had sat in Travis's apartment living room watching that draft, and the NFL Commissioner had announced the name that steered their lives in a completely different direction from anything they'd ever anticipated.

That relaxed, confident smirk of adulation Travis wore then was the same as he now wore. And, Mitchell noted, he was dressed in casual polo shirt, slacks, and loafers instead of his usual suit and tie.

"What's poppin', T-Dub?" Mitchell asked, using the nickname he'd given his partner.

"They're ready to meet. Bet they're ready to agree to our terms." The hand not holding the cup motioned back and forth like he was a maestro. "We've got 'em by the *cojones*, Mitchee-my-man."

Mitchell grinned at Travis's last words. It always tickled him when his partner, a white guy from a white suburb, tried to sound hip, attempting to imitate the lingo of black folks. It often reminded him of the time Travis came to a costume party decked out in an afro wig. Mitchell just shook his head. T-Dub didn't quite have the proper swag.

"Have you contacted Main Man yet?"

Known to all by just his nickname, Main Man was the very same football player who'd changed their lives three years earlier. He'd been holding out from his team since the beginning of training camp for a new contract. A year was remaining on his present contract, but he wanted to renegotiate for a lucrative long-term deal. They'd tried to work out a deal prior to the beginning of training camp, but talks broke down and they'd been at an impasse ever since.

"Nope. Not yet." Travis sat the cup on the desk, stood, and dipped his hands in his pockets. "I was waiting for you so we could give 'im the news over the speaker together. As you know, he's expecting to hear from us regarding any developments."

"Ahh, that's right—it slipped my mind." Mitchell stepped up to the desk and posted his briefcase beside it. "We won't see his reaction, but we're surely gonna hear it."

Travis nodded, grinning.

"Got some ear plugs ready?" Mitchell joked. "Because he's gonna be yellin' his ass off. Loud."

"That's for sure."

"Knew they'd come running any time soon," Mitchell said excitedly. "Watched half of their game Sunday, they *sucked* without him!"

"Yep. Been that way since pre-season." Travis had a confident expression. "They don't have a rat's chance in a pack of female cats to win without Main Man."

Mitchell chuckled.

"And they know it!" Travis stated emphatically.

Mitchell motioned at the phone. "Let's give 'im a call." He clicked the phone on speaker then Travis punched in the numbers.

It rang twice.

"What up, Trav?" Main Man answered, sounding relaxed.

"Whadoyousay to a signing bonus with lots of zeroes?" Travis asked jauntily.

"You shittin' man! You serious?"

"Yep," Travis said, winking at Mitchell. "Main Man, right about now, I imagine you can ask for your own jet and you'd be in the air within thirty, forty minutes."

"Hell yeah!" Main Man roared jubilantly.

"Pack your bags, dude," Travis said, grinning, "we're heading to the Lone Star state to sign a contract."

"We? Mitchell there?"

"Fo' sho," Mitchell chimed in, "What up, Main Man?"

"Mitcheee ..."

"It's going down, homeboy."

A loud yelp echoed from Main Man, then the line went dead. Mitchell and Travis stared at each other, then both began laughing.

₧₧₧

Later that night in his plush town house, Mitchell lay comfortably sprawled on the sofa in the living room; remote resting on his chest as he idly scoured the newspaper. His mind was more entranced by the propitious day. Not much felt as good as success. Considering the distance he'd traveled financially, the results of success left a sweet taste in his mouth he wished would never fade. He'd covered miles since the days when he had to wear his cousins' hand-me-downs, or second hand clothes bought from rummage or garage sales; days of coming home from school near the end of the month, hungry, only to find a milk jug filled with water, or maybe some spoiled leftovers in the refrigerator. There was a time when the only thing they had to eat was old bread with no meat or condiments to spread on it. Different instances of poverty carried over to other aspects of their lives as well. Like when he'd played sick and missed school on field trip days because his mama lacked the five or ten dollar fee for the outing. The next day at school he would lie, telling his friends his mama wouldn't let him come because he could've spread his sickness.

He used to feel like being poor was a plague. A curse. But as he'd matured, started realizing he could overcome the status of life he'd been dealt. Thus, he began learning that achieving success took plenty of action and dedication. It took setting goals, planning, hard work, and a stroke of good luck was always a plus. Though he'd always hated being poor, he never allowed it to deter his mental or moral persistence. That social and financial stigma was the primary motivation for his unyielding drive in the classroom, during recreation, work, or whatever he set out to do. To this day he feared being broke, which in turn, steadily motivated him. He'd already had enough of the ghetto life.

Yet, as he got older, and experienced more of his surroundings, he recognized the positives of having been poor. It's what taught him how to cope with adversity. Poor people were survivors, mentally and spiritually strong, and knew how to turn nothing into something. With that edge, Mitchell aimed to climb from poverty. He had nothing to lose. But he would never forget where he came from, and was one of the most gratuitous, altruistic people there was.

As he introspected about the past, the present which was flourishing more rapidly than he ever conceived, and the undetermined future, he smiled for his family. Success was so sweet. And financial success opened avenues that were otherwise dead ends.

At times he felt as though he was living in a dream, and without warning would wake up back into reality; poor, struggling to make ends meet, and unable to get ahead in life. Realistically, though unbelievable, he knew he'd invested himself to reach the successful plateau he now inhabited.

As sweet as all the prosperity was, it still contained a pang of bitter sweetness. He used to think people were merely being cliché whenever he heard *money was nothing without someone to share it with*. But now he understood what they meant. All that he'd gained and achieved dwarfed in comparison to what he'd lost. No amount of money or good fortune could replace that loss …

He thought of that loss as he often did when he was alone; when something good happened; when something or someone roused the images of his greatest tribulation. Many a sleepless night the dreadful memories had dogged him. Plagued his thoughts day in and day out, migrating with him like a hitch-hiker with no clear-cut destination. His present life was packed with good things in several ways, but romantically, it had been a long stretch since he'd enjoyed the companionship of a female; intimate moments with the opposite sex was a pleasure virtually untapped. A simple embrace from a female was like a delicacy he'd never relished. And sex … hell, he couldn't even jack off because his own hand was unable to take him to that blissful world.

For some unknown reason *she* drifted into his thoughts, and suddenly he was revisiting the night of his mama's party. The sweet smell of her perfume as they slow danced staggered him. During those moments he'd wanted to be stuck to her like the flap of a sealed envelope. She was so squeezable, firm and soft. And her butt ... basketball round, and cushiony delightful, he'd inadvertently brushed over it, and then as they'd gotten deeper into the dance, he couldn't help but let his hands roam over its pleasant shapeliness. When she turned and pressed her butt just below his mid-section as they swayed to the music, she had to have felt his erection, because it stood at attention like a soldier, prompting him to craftily dip inside his pants and shift it upright. She maneuvered the motions of her body sensuously, bedazzling him like he hadn't known in a long time. Awakening feelings he'd forgotten about.

Irritated, Mitchell sighed, knowing his only choice was to bury the arousal he was experiencing. In the past he could've acted on this type of stirring, probably indulged in some meaningless flirtation with Jazelle—any other woman for that matter—however an intimate, physical relationship was a component of life he couldn't have. Not now. Never again.

He flung the newspaper onto the glass coffee table, and sprang up exasperated. The shower was calling him. He had to go sedate his trippin' hormones.

ЅꙨᏟᏒ

"I gotta quit smoking these stupid things," Amanda muttered wryly as she blew out the smoke from the menthol cigarette. "But those kids are preventing me from stopping. Got my nerves all screwed up. It's a shame I was forced into smoking for the first time in my damn thirties."

Jazelle frowned, surprised. "You only recently started smoking?" she asked. They were outside in the smoking area sitting on a bench under a lighted pavilion. The night was lukewarm and they preferred being in the fresh air during their break. Plus, Amanda had been craving nicotine.

"Mm-hmm," Amanda mumbled, nodding while she took a hard puff. "Crazy, huh? One day I was over at my sister's, and the kids had been driving me nuts, so she offered me a cigarette. It started slowly from then on. Some days I want 'em more than others."

"Well, hope you're able to stop soon, 'cause—"

"I try," she interrupted, "but when things make me lose it, then I start craving a quick puff."

Her kids probably needed an ass whooping, Jazelle considered. She faced Amanda, rested an arm on the back of the bench, the other in her lap. Until now, her day had been fairly normal. Now that something had cropped up she was somewhat relieved it had nothing to do with her. "I thought the talk y'all had the other night did some good?" She felt sorry for her friend. It wasn't encouraging that her own kids were torturing her that way. Jazelle wondered what she could do to help. She told herself that if she ever had kids she wouldn't allow them to mess up her head like that, because she knew they would certainly run over her if she let them.

"It did ..." Tears started forming on the rims of her eyes. She began slightly trembling. "But ..." She broke down into a sob.

Jazelle embraced Amanda, attempting to console her. It was a pitiful thing that a grown woman was unraveled this deeply by some grade school kids. She wondered if Amanda was one of those pushover parents who permitted her kids to run over her. She'd seen some weak women putting up with rude, misbehaving, ill-mannered kids. She even remembered as a little girl in a store or some other public place with her mother, or grandmother, witnessing little kids falling out on the floor, kicking, whining, and hollering like they'd lost their damn minds if they didn't get their way. They ran through the aisles like they had no home training. Their mothers would only perfunctorily plead for them to get up or stop, like they didn't have a lick of authority over their own kids. Jazelle hadn't believed what she was seeing, because where she came from, you'd get the black knocked off you if you acted a fool in public like that. She felt that those women needed to visit a good old fashioned black household to see how disciplining kids was done. After that schooling, they'd know that all it took was a menacing stare-down in public for the kids to quickly get their little asses in line.

Part of the problem nowadays was tolerant laws weakening a parent's ability to discipline their own children, she realized, but if Amanda was tolerating that type of behavior, she'd better do something to curb it while they were still young. Once they were older, it was likely to escalate into a hopeless struggle, and by then it would be too late. She'd lose her authority, and they'd disrespect her and treat her like she was nobody.

She wanted to tell her friend all these things, but it wasn't her place.

"Amanda, you okay?" she asked soothingly, offering a paper towel she'd yanked from the bathroom dispenser earlier.

Amanda took it and dabbed at her teary eyes, smearing her eyeliner. Jazelle helped clean up the smudges.

"Thank you," Amanda mumbled dismally, and slowly rose from the bench. She moved to one of the posts supporting the pavilion, encircling her arms around it. "Sorry for breaking down like a big cry baby."

"It's okay," Jazelle chided softly.

"I know, but ... there's something else, Jazelle." Feeling ashamed, she kept her back to Jazelle.

Jazelle bounced up, moved to Amanda, and lightly planted a hand on her shoulder. "What is it, Amanda?"

She turned and peered at Jazelle. Anger and pain highlighted her expression. "It's actually not the kids." She went silent for a moment. "I think Steven's having an affair."

Jazelle absorbed the statement without flinching. Men's extra-marital dalliances were like a normal way of life. To her, married or not, they were all at one time or another up to no damn good! Men could always be counted on to dabble in infidelity. The earth was full of no-good, starved-dick assholes forever dogging women. She'd never met Steven, but like most men, she wouldn't be surprised if he was out marinating in some other woman's pussy. "You sure?"

"No. But the way he's been acting lately—secretive like."

"He's been absent with the loving too, I'll bet?" Jazelle knew one sign of a man having a side ho' occurred in the bedroom. The sex just didn't click like normal.

"Not exactly—it's his hours. He comes home later than usual. Seems to be a little too tired to please me like he ordinarily does, though." She looked like a sad little girl.

"What are you gonna do?" Jazelle asked.

She shrugged. "Heck—I don't know."

Jazelle glimpsed at her watch. She almost forgot they were at work. They were two minutes over their break time. "Amanda, we'd better get back up to work." She pointed at her watch. "We're late."

Heading for the elevator, Jazelle hoped that Amanda was wrong about her husband. She didn't want her going through that round of hell. Heartbreak was a bitch. *If Steven is cheating on her, Amanda ought to pull a Lorena Bobbitt on his two-timing ass! Cut his pride and joy off, pitch it in the wind. His ass wouldn't two-time anybody else.*

Her resentment toward men was climbing another notch.

6

Prior to class starting, Mackenzee handed Jazelle a picture. Jazelle perched herself on the edge of her desk to check it out. Before she could get a good look, several of her students strolled into the room. The little voices spoke as they passed her heading to their desks.

"Morning, you all," she happily greeted with her normal good-spirited temperament. She believed a cheerful teacher boosted kids' esteem and morale, making school more enticing.

Examining their appearances as they straggled by, she noticed one of the boys, Willie Randolph, hadn't tucked in his shirt, his tennies were untied, and his pants sagged a little. He looked like a tramp, and she couldn't stand a child looking tacky. "Willie," she sighed, tilting her head with a wry stare, "why do I always need to remind you to fix your clothes?"

He gave her one of those dumbfounded, I-forgot looks, but quickly fixed his clothes.

Jazelle shook her head and forced a smile. "Thank you. But, Willie?" He glanced at her sheepishly. "I don't want to keep reminding you, okay?"

"Okay, Miss Johnson." He dragged on to his desk.

While the last of the students drifted in, she stole a look at the picture of Gwen, Carla, Quincy, Mitchell, herself, and some others from the club. Gwen had promised her the picture. She grinned with amusement at the pathetic images staring back at her. The picture humorously exposed the pitiful, torn-down condition of everybody, except Mitchell. He'd probably been the only sober soul in the entire club, because he'd only drunk orange juice, or 7-Up. The bartenders had stared at him disbelievingly, and so had she, knowing how teenagers usually took full advantage of an opportunity to get their drink on. In there, no one would've stopped him from drinking as much as he wanted.

It had been a fun night, she reminisced, taking a long look at the photo. To her displeasure, she had some unwanted thoughts upon eyeing Mitchell in the picture. Instantly, a surge of guilt rushed over her, condemning the thoughts toward that *jail bait*. Quickly, she slipped the picture away in her desk, trying to rid herself of any thoughts of that boy.

She focused on the kids and proceeded to do roll call. She then instructed them to get ready to say the alphabet out loud, one by one. The drill enabled her to determine who had or hadn't been practicing their letters. With a meter stick in hand, she called on Tommy Clausen, one of her brighter students, a red-headed, freckled boy, to begin the exercise. He was seated in the last desk in the column farthest from her right. Right to left, row by row, the students would all get their turn.

"Do I have to start it, Miss Johnson," he asked bashfully. He was very shy.

"Yes you do. Last time we started on that end." She pointed the stick toward the last seat in the row farthest from him.

"Aw, alright," he mumbled, realizing his bad fortune.

She aimed the stick at the first of the letters over the chalkboard, and the exercise began. Though they were familiar with the drill, not all knew the alphabet like they should, and she noted who needed some individual time with her. Most whizzed through the drill, citing the letters like singing a song; that was how they'd been taught by their parents for the most part. The more they practiced, the more the letters stuck in their minds. Soon they'd recite without having to harmonize.

Amongst those who needed to put in more time with the letters, Nikki, who hadn't caused any problems so far during the week, was considerably lacking, which concerned Jazelle. She'd done better the second week of school. Jazelle was looking forward to having a chat with her parents.

℘℘℘

Travis was reclining in a deep, leather swiveling chair behind his desk, engaged in a lazy phone conversation and twiddling a pen. He motioned Mitchell into his office once he noticed him leaning on the door frame looking amused. The past couple of days, Omnity had been receiving plenty of attention due to Main Man's new contract; they'd had calls from prospective clients, colleagues, competitors, and acquaintances. Even the media had been contacting the office more than usual.

Mitchell grinned at Travis lounging behind his messy, grand, mahogany desk, resembling a powerful business tycoon ruling his empire. The spacious office fit him well. For a white dude he had some style, and had certainly hooked up the entire office building when they'd remodeled a couple of months ago

"What's up, Mitch?" Travis asked, hanging up the phone. He stood and stretched. Tall and slim, he sort of resembled Tom Cruise a little, thought he was much taller. "We may be getting our first female client," he continued. "She's a WNBA player, unhappy with her representation at the moment, but trying to be loyal. I told my source to tell her to be patient. Wait and see what happens."

Mitchell nodded, pondering the prospect of a woman on their roster. "Is the source reliable?"

"I believe so."

"Hmm, well you know how the saying goes, if it happens, it happens" The addition would be cool. Welcomed. But he was anxious to talk about something else. "I know of two future stars in the making," he said, with a touch of enthusiasm.

"Serious?" Travis's curiosity was piqued as he sat back down. "Who are they?"

Mitchell dropped into one of two smaller, identical versions of the chair Travis occupied and propped the heels of his tasseled loafers on the shining mahogany. A faint breeze from the churning ceiling fan settled over him. He gazed blankly at a photo on the wall behind Travis of the two of them with Main Man after he signed his first contract. He had the exact same picture in his office.

"Who?" Travis's impatience was beginning to kick in.

"Just—" Mitchell purposely cut off what he was about to say, knowing Travis would get aggravated. He was toying with his partner and loving it. At times they carried on like two big kids.

" 'Just', who? Damn you, Mitchell Thomas!" He wanted to sock Mitchell.

Mitchell nonchalantly leaned forward, brushed a speck of lint off his shoes. "My little brother and my cousin." He'd been itching to tell all along, but was enjoying tormenting Travis. "You should've seen 'em, T-Dub."

Travis's eyes became animated. "Wha' did they do?" His annoyance from a second ago had vanished, and he spoke quickly, running the words together.

"My brother—he plays tight end and linebacker—and Li'l Q, my cousin, he plays running back. They're both freshmen on the same team. Anyway, I made it to their game a second after kickoff, and Li'l Q was halfway into a hundred and two yard kickoff return." Mitchell was animated like he was the one running for a touchdown. "Aw, man, he has moves almost like Barry Sanders, and his speed is ... *whoosh.*"

Travis was excited. "When're they playing again?"

"… and Montell caught a seventy-five yarder, breaking about three, four tackles before scoring!" Mitchell went on, ignoring Travis's question. "I didn't know my li'l bro' could move like that! On defense, he hits like a man possessed. He was hitting so hard, he caused three fumbles, picked one up and took it to the house—eighty-three yards. Had those dudes on the other team too intimidated to run the ball."

Travis was as much in awe from the recount as Mitchell must've been when he'd been watching the action in person. "Next time you're hopping your butt across the state to see your family in action, you can at least tell somebody. You know I love to watch young talent."

"Man, they're only freshmen. Wish they were already in college performing like that."

"When are you going to another game?" Travis asked impatiently, hoping his playful partner would finally answer him. "When?" He slapped Mitchell's shoes without thinking, prodding him to take them off the desk.

Mitchell yanked his feet down and sprang from the chair. "They're playing an away game farther north of Tulsa next week, so I'll probably go watch 'em the week after."

"I'll be right at your side then," Travis said, matter-of-factly.

"Cool. You're gonna be in for a treat, dude."

He and Travis often checked out local high school and other sporting events together, sometimes simply for entertainment, sometimes for business. Now and then, they discovered an unknown with potential; a prospect to watch for the future. Travis liked to have the upper hand with youngsters for Omnity, if a sighting emerged.

Reminded about going somewhere, Travis tentatively yanked a sheet of paper from his desk and hesitantly handed it to Mitchell.

"What's this?" Mitchell asked skeptically, seeing the hesitation in Travis's eyes.

"Read it."

Mitchell scanned the paper then studied Travis suspiciously. "Why're you showing me this?" he asked, shaking the paper at Travis.

Travis knew Mitchell wasn't going to take too kindly to what he was about to confess, but went on anyway. "I, um, entered you in that," he mumbled, averting his eyes.

"You *what*?" Mitchell exploded.

Travis hesitated a second, struggling to suppress the grin trying to break through. "I entered you in the auction. Paid the donation fee and everything." He refrained from looking at Mitchell, knowing his eyes were burning a hole in his face. "Katie and I will be attending too." Katie was his wife.

"Man, are you *crazy*?" Mitchell looked wounded. "I'm not gonna have my black ass up on a damn stage with a bunch of sex deprived women gawking at me!"

" 'Sex deprived?' "

"If they were getting laid they wouldn't be out paying for a date."

Travis wasn't sure how to counter that, so he said, "It's charity. It's for a good purpose."

"That's like ... prostitution."

"Prostitution? How's that? You're not auctioning yourself for sex."

Mitchell glared at him.

"Come on, Mitch," Travis cajoled. "All you'll be doing is getting up on stage, they'll bid on you, and some nice, single, successful woman will get to take you to dinner or something."

" 'Or something?' "

"Yeah. Dinner, maybe a movie. A Play. Opera. Something entertaining." Travis was amused by how frazzled Mitchell was. "What're you afraid of?"

Mitchell's cell went off. Annoyed, he checked the number, glaring at Travis. "It's my mama." He pointed at the flyer. "We'll discuss this garbage later." He balled up the paper and threw it at Travis as he left.

Travis leaned back in his chair, laughing. He picked up the phone and punched the numbers for his wife's office, anxious to

fill her in on how their scheme to reignite Mitchell's social life was developing.

7

"Oh yeah! Miss Johnson, I forgot to tell you that Mitchee said hello." Mackenzee was headed to the monkey bars, but stopped to pass on the information. The class was on recess and Jazelle, along with a few other teachers, was out monitoring the playground.

"Hold on, Mackenzee," Jazelle said, heedless of her sudden interest in what Mackenzee had said. "When did he tell you that?"

"Yesterday," she answered, antsy. "He came up here to see my brother, Monty's football game."

Jazelle wondered what had put her in his thoughts. "And he told you to say 'hello' to me?" Jazelle wasn't sure why but it sort of delighted her that he'd thought about her.

"Yes, Ma'am." Mackenzee was itching to go play. Her expression begged if she could.

Jazelle read it. "Go on and play, Mac." She hadn't thought about Mitchell since the day her car broke down. Now he was back in her head, and for someone who wasn't grown yet, he'd surely touched a nerve in her somehow.

She aimlessly looked around the playground, appreciating the nice weather that allowed the kids to play outside. The storm earlier in the week, had kept them inside. The sun was happy today, keeping it clear and warm on this side of the state. The storm must not have effected Mitchell down in Norman, she considered, since he'd come up to Tulsa to watch his brother's game. The news had mentioned the havoc wreaked in the western portion of Oklahoma.

Irked that she was thinking about Mitchell again, she attempted to squash the thoughts by returning to the task at hand.

She sought out her students and slowly began pacing each play area. She saw everyone but Nikki and Tiffany. Slightly exasperated, she slowly circled in place, her wide eyes covering the entire playground. After not seeing them, she started asking around for their whereabouts. To her dismay, another student, Curtis, pointed them out by the fence line in a section where her view was obscured by a part of the school building; a place which was off limits to the kids. "That damn girl is always doing something," she muttered under her breath. She was sure Nikki had bullied Tiffany into going over there, since Tiffany was too scared to break any rules on her own. She was just right— submissive—for a bully like Nikki to take advantage of.

Feeling like she wanted to shake some good into Little Miss Bad Ass, Jazelle hurried over to the two, her emotions on full display in her expression. With her arms akimbo, she glared at them and immediately discerned the fear in their eyes.

She didn't speak a word before Tiffany started spilling the beans.

"Nikki made me come ovah here," the scared little girl mumbled, her eyes wide and cowering with raindrop tears forming. "She said sh-she was g-gonna beat me up if I din't come ovah here wit' her."

"She lyin'!" Nikki defended ominously.

Internally, Jazelle was applauding her scare tactics because they were working perfectly. She knew Tiffany wasn't lying; she was just the stool pigeon of a baby delinquent. "I don't ever want to see you over here, Tiffany." She kept her voice soft, yet firm. There was no need to scare the hell out of the little girl.

"Y-yes Ma'am," Tiffany mumbled remorsefully.

"Wipe your face and get back over there with your classmates," Jazelle ordered Tiffany, knowing she wouldn't get tangled in anything else, forced or otherwise.

On the other hand, Nikki was an enigma. She hadn't started the school year causing problems; it was like she'd suddenly caught Miss Jekyll and Hyde syndrome.

"I din't tell—"

"Quit lying, Nikki!" Jazelle cut off the fib before the little girl could start it. She didn't want to be harsh, but sterner methods were needed with this child. She squatted eye to eye, shaking a finger. "I don't know what your problem is, Nikki, but you're not going to keep misbehaving in my class. I've already had enough of your disruptive behavior."

Eyes studying her shoes, a finger in her mouth, Nikki nodded sheepishly. There was shame wafting from her, yet no tears formed in her eyes.

"I'm contacting your parents today. Something has to be done about your behavior, or you'll end up getting put out of school for a while. You want to be put out of school, Nikki?"

Nikki shook her head, her beaded braids rattling.

"Come on, let's get back to the rest of the class," Jazelle ordered. She'd had enough of this scene, being that she was forever uncomfortable about confrontations with students. "Also, I want you to tell Tiffany you're sorry for getting her in trouble."

Nikki nodded remorsefully.

Jazelle wondered how this child with such angelic features could turn into such a she-devil. "You hear me, Nikki?"

She nodded again.

Jazelle briskly pulled the finger from the girl's mouth and forced the downcast face to look at her. "Do you hear me?"

The first sign of tears appeared, slowly inching down Nikki's pretty butterscotch cheeks. She swiped her face with a backhand. "Yes, Miss Johnson."

Jazelle was grateful she only had one bad seed to contend with so far. Two or three more troublemakers ...

She sighed, and not for the first time, found herself questioning her choice of occupation.

∞∮

Attempting to parallel park in the only space he'd been able to find within reasonable distance to the campus recreation facilities, Mitchell adeptly squeezed between a narrowly spaced car and truck. After grabbing his towel and bottled water, he hopped out of the car and chirped on the alarm before taking off in a trot. He'd changed into shorts and a tank top before leaving the office.

Jogging the short distance to the facilities, he inhaled then exhaled what was likely some of the last of the summery air. The weatherman had said temperatures should be dropping in the coming days. Evening students were hurrying to classes, and he was glad not to be walking in their shoes. He loved school, but was thankful he'd been there, done that.

Before realizing it he was already opening the door and entering the oft busy recreation center. He produced his ID for the attendant to verify, then made his way to the weight room.

The infinite mustiness and lingering smell of hard earned sweat filled the room as he joined the other patrons. Intense men and women were grunting, huffing, puffing, and grimacing from their workout routines. The clinking sounds of steel weights and machines reverberated through the building, as did the blare of ear-aching rock music coming from speakers posted up high in the corners of the walls. The bench press was fortuitously unoccupied, and he quickly made a move for it.

Bret Tucker, a muscle-bound law school buddy of Travis's who could pass for a competing bodybuilder, slid up to him. "What's up? Mitchell, isn't it?"

"Yeah, that's it," Mitchell answered. "Just came to get in a few sets." He wanted to ask the massive white dude what type of steroids he was on to get so damn big. *I wouldn't ever want to be even close to that huge. Wonder if he knows he looks like a damn freak? Men who bulk up like that must have some masculinity issues, because that's too much size.*

"That's how you get to be big like me." It was a cocky, arrogant statement. Hulk thought he was *all that.* "Where's my buddy, Travis? He still in happy land after the contract he negotiated?"

Up until now, Mitchell had put his meddling partner out of his mind. He'd come to work out to blow off some steam. Now, T-Dub and that auction business rambled back to the front of his mind. "Yeah, I guess you could say that," he said with some stiffness in his tone. "He's probably at home with his wife right about now."

"Isn't she pregnant?"

Mitchell wanted to tell him to go on back to his damn workout. "Yeah."

"I'm gonna get back to what I was doing then." He boastfully flexed and made his pecs jump and dance. "Tell my buddy I said good job when you see him again."

"Yeah," Mitchell replied uninterested, with no intention of mentioning him to T-Dub.

Hulk gestured his hand, forming an imaginary outline of a pregnant stomach as he backed away. "And tell 'im congratulations."

Glad the Hulk was back to adding more unneeded mass to his already oversized frame, Mitchell frowned, annoyed that his mood was soured again. *I could just kick your ass, T-Dub!* With his back flat on the bench he energetically tossed two hundred and twenty-five pounds up and down, barely letting the bar touch his chest. He hadn't warmed up, but his face was intense as he pumped twelve solid reps.

As he tried his best to concentrate on the workout, the thought of T-Tub signing him up for a damn bachelor's auction without his permission distracted his concentration. He wasn't as angry as he was uneasy about the thought of having to socialize with women. The farther he stayed away from that particular activity the better.

And even though it was for a charitable purpose, he would have to compromise that stance, and ...

Hell! I'm not open to meeting any females—romantically for certain. Business purposes are cool, but if I intended to become acquainted with women, I'd join one of those online dating sites.

However, he didn't consider himself an eligible bachelor. Eligible meant ready to be chosen. Qualified.

Well ... I'm not ready for that!

He replaced the bar on the rack, sat up, grabbed his towel and wiped the perspiration from his forehead. Normally he would've shot some hoops and followed with a weight workout. Tonight though, he'd aimed straight for the weight room, since he was not in the mood to deal with physical contact. He couldn't have tolerated the trash talking that happened on the basketball court. He'd probably end up getting rubbed the wrong way, wanting to throw some blows.

While he added more weight to the bar, some fat youngster—probably a freshman, he assumed—who needed to spend a whole lot of time jogging around the track, less time in the cafeteria, approached and asked if he could join in. Mitchell nodded. He didn't ask the kid's name or classification, he'd just spot the hefty youngster, and vice versa.

Once Fat Boy positioned himself on the bench, Mitchell unracked the bar and released it. Because of his size, Mitchell assumed Fat Boy could handle the weight. His mind began wandering to the auction business, stealing his attention from spotting.

"Say ... man ... help!" Fat Boy breathed out brusquely, unable to budge the bar from his chest. He struggled and squirmed to push, but it was hopeless. His jaws formed a big Dizzy Gillespie bubble as he strained for strength that would never come.

"Oh shit! I'm sorry," Mitchell said apologetically, looking minimally alarmed after being yanked from his untimely thoughts. He easily lifted and returned the bar to the rack. He'd just violated one of the most important rules in the weight room: always pay attention to your workout partner when he was performing an exercise. *The damn weight was too heavy for him anyway*, Mitchell thought, slightly irritated by dude's cluelessness regarding his own strength. "Some of that weight needs to come off."

"Duhh," Fat Boy said. "You're s'posed to be spotting me."

"You're right." He didn't want to upset the yellow skinned youngster. He could see his pride was injured. He'd turned red, and beads of sweat had already formed on his forehead. Mitchell felt bad for his negligence. *You need to be doing aerobics or something requiring some serious motion anyway*, he thought, trying to justify his carelessness. Still he was upset with himself for being distracted when he should've been paying attention.

Unwilling to jeopardize this boy's safety again, Mitchell snatched up his towel and water and abruptly left the weight room without saying a word. Fat Boy quizzically looked his way as he disappeared through the door.

"Wonder what chickenhead got his mind all fucked up," Fat Boy said to himself. Intimidated by the free weights, he jiggled on over to a weight machine.

ഏറ

Mitchell trotted to his car and headed home. Once inside the townhouse, he fingered through his mail, finding nothing of relevance. In his room, he hung his suit in the closet, stripped off his gym clothes and dropped them in the hamper before getting in the shower.

The steady pulse of the water against his tense body eased the throbbing emotions he was battling. At the moment, it was the closest thing to emotional healing.

After exiting the shower, he dried off then went and fell on his bed, succumbing to the soothing frame of mind the shower had caused. He was oblivious to the fact that he hadn't eaten a bite since lunch. It didn't matter; he only wanted to lose himself in the comfort of his bed, let the conflicts of the day take a hiatus for the night.

Like a swift breeze blowing over him, he was soon overcome by a deep sleep. In the course of the night, he dreamed about an auction.

8

The next morning, Mitchell knew he'd woken up too early after squinting to get a look at the clock on the nightstand. He felt well rested as he sat up and realized he'd fallen asleep butt naked, because the towel he'd been wrapped in was on the floor.

He vaguely remembered dreaming during an anguish driven sleep, but for the life of him couldn't remember what about. His stomach growled notifying him that he needed to eat something. He grabbed the remote off the nightstand, clicked on the TV and surfed the channels to see if anything significant had happened while he slept the night away. After finding nothing interesting, he sauntered to his bathroom and slapped some cold water on his face, wishing he was at a hotel where he could order a hungry man's breakfast and have it promptly delivered to his room.

At least it's good to be able to wish, he thought, as he headed downstairs.

In the kitchen, he grabbed a bowl and spoon from the dish rack and poured himself a big bowl of Frosted Flakes. He took a seat on a bar stool and got busy. When he finished that, he devoured two micro-waved chopped ham sandwiches.

Hunger satiated for the time being, he clicked on the stereo before going back up to his room. The late Esther Phillips sounded from speakers positioned throughout the house. It was her 1972 album, *From a Whisper to a Scream*, a rhythm and blues gem by a diva that people from his generation and beyond really knew nothing about; because of his maternal grandma, his love and familiarity with many obscure 'oldies but goodies' went way back before his time. He mostly listened to old school anyway, whether it was R&B or rap, because he felt the current music greatly lacked the substance of songs from back in the day.

Upon re-entering his room a news report on TV caught his attention. He upped the volume loud enough to hear over the music. A woman had reportedly shot and killed her husband in self-defense after he'd allegedly beat her with an extension cord. She pulled a .38 from under a couch pillow and shot him twice. It was reported that he'd been abusing her off and on over the past five years, and she had taken the abuse for so long because he'd threatened to kill her if she ever tried to leave. Like in so many other cases of domestic abuse, he always claimed to be sorry for kicking the ass of the woman he supposedly loved. Police records showed they'd visited the residence before after 911 calls reported domestic disturbances at the address.

"If that's love I wouldn't wanna experience hate," Mitchell mumbled ruefully. *That woman was probably better off killing that son of a bitch because he would've kept beating her. No man has the right to put his hands on a woman that way. Married or not. Coward! A dead one now. That chump got what he deserved. If some fool ever put hands on Mac, there is no telling what I'd do to the bastard.*

While getting dressed, he realized the report had got under his skin. Legislation on domestic violence had improved over the years, but the abuse of women had gone on for so long without effective law enforcement that it was obvious why so many women remained in those relationships. They were brainwashed to believe there was no help or hope in support of their plight. Helpless and afraid, they became used to the beatings until it was a way of life. Being emotionally and physically traumatized, they inevitably submitted out of fear, and a lack of self-esteem. A beat down a day kept them from running away.

The thought of it sickened the hell out of Mitchell.

He jerked his tie, tugging it too tightly, almost choking himself. Struggling to catch his breath, gasping for air, he stretched both arms toward the ceiling allowing some air to flow through his lungs. As his breathing stabilized, he thought of how easily he'd been getting riled up lately; small, frivolous things had been annoying him, and that was so not his character. It normally took something major to tap his angst. Even T-Dub and that auction mess should never have gotten to him like it had. Something that insignificant wasn't cause for him to be losing his cool. Not that he would normally roll over like a friendly puppy; when someone signed him up for parading before a pack of fawning women who undressed him with their eyes, he was going to speak his mind. When T-Dub first told him what he'd done, he'd almost taken on his mama's persona and begun cussing like crazy.

Good thing she had interrupted when she had, because Mitchell did not want Trav receiving a taste of his ghetto side.

He brushed his fade, yanked the bed clothes from the bed and pillows, swapping out with fresh ones. Then he sprayed on some cologne, and headed downstairs, where he straightened and cleaned what needed it. He wasn't exactly a neat freak, just orderly, and liked to keep his crib spotless. The thought of nasty ass roaches, like those they'd dealt with when he was growing up, invading his pad wasn't an appealing thought at all. Just thinking about the six-legged creatures hording up in his house gave him the chills.

Satisfied, he clutched his briefcase, and clicked off the stereo. When he opened the door to leave, beams of friendly sunlight greeted and blanketed him. He thought of Ice Cube's

"It Was a Good Day." Then the newscast about the battered woman killing her husband flashed in his mind, and he amended the thought. "At least for some of us," he muttered, shading his eyes with his free hand."

ଚ୍ଚର

Quitting time was nearing, and throughout the day Mitchell had avoided Travis. He was now studying a spreadsheet on his monitor about quarterly income taxes. He was pretending he was still pissed at Travis because he was confident Travis would come to apologize before the day ended. Was it a silly game between two adults? Definitely. Childish as it was, he wanted T-Dub to squirm with guilt for what he'd done, and Mitchell didn't want to see him til he was ready to own up that he'd been wrong.

He'd never tell but he wasn't tripping about the auction anymore. He needed to do more charitable activities since he was doing so well, plus he loved seeing people's faces light up when they received an unexpected gift. The thought of that was the reason he wasn't going to have it out with Travis. It was a way of giving back, and a reminder to never forget where he came from.

His issue with the auction was being in the spotlight. Standing out in a crowd wasn't his thing. He couldn't care less about that type of attention. It was too much like arrogance or narcissism, so he diverted that type of attention away from himself whenever it came his way. He let T-Dub deal with the more public aspects of their business, because T-Dub loved being a public figure. Mitchell preferred being in the background as the somewhat anonymous component helping propel Omnity's success. More importantly, for now, he wanted to keep his family from learning about his position as a co-owner of a flourishing company until he was ready. That was why his face was absent at press conferences, and why he was never quoted or mentioned in newspapers.

He was thinking about all of that when he was interrupted by his assistant.

"I posted those expenses, Boss. Everything balanced," she said.

"Hunh? Oh. Yeah," he muttered.

She planted her hands on her hips. "What're you in such deep thought about? Bet it's that auction, ain't it?"

Desiree was a little, half-pint Latino woman in her thirties. To Mitchell, she stood tall as an Amazon because she was his right hand woman. Dependable, efficient, prompt and energetic, she provided the office with spunk and some down home humor.

"You know about that?" Mitchell asked, surprised and slightly irritated that the auction business seemed to have spread through the office before he even knew about it.

Desiree had heard about Mitchell's reaction from Travis. Uh, yes. I'm the one who gave Trav the bulletin. So I think you might just be mad at the wrong person, Boss."

"I'm not mad."

Stepping to his desk, resting her stubby hands on the edge, she detected the defensiveness in his voice. "Yeah, right, Boss." She gave him the look to go with that response.

Mitchell's eyes focused on her hand. Her manicured fingernails matched the fuchsia of her cotton outfit. He knew her eyes were focused on him. "I'm not."

Desiree had been around him long enough to know something was bothering him. She knew Travis's actions had gotten to him. "Why've you been avoiding Trav like the plague, then?"

His eyes remained on her hands. He didn't answer.

She sat in one of the two chairs facing him. "I didn't know he was gonna enter you without asking first, or at least mentioning it to you. But I did run it by him, so he could maybe try to talk you into entering."

Mitchell raised his eyes from where her hands had been, and looked at her flatly. *This is the culprit behind the auction mess.* Unlike T-Dub though, he knew Desiree's intentions were plausible. She meant well. In a way she was like an older sister to him. "I wasn't angry—I mean I'm not angry." He manufactured a disappointed expression. "Just a little pissed he did it without my permission."

Ain't that the same as being mad? Desiree thought, but instead said, "I see. But," she raised her hands, palms up, and shrugged "you know how impulsive Trav can be."

He nodded. "Even though I would've declined initially if he had asked me, if it was your idea to begin with ... you should've said something to me about it. You would've eventually convinced me to participate, though I would've still been reluctant."

She smiled regretfully, knowing now that she should've gone to him first. "You remember how I told you about the shelter helping me ..." It wasn't a question, she was reflecting. "If I had the money to play around with, I'd go bid on one of those bachelors myself. I wouldn't mind hooking up with some hardworking *hombre guapo*."

Mitchell could only laugh.

"I'd show that *ventoso* the time of his life," she continued, frolicking in the seat. "Desiree'd have 'im beggin' fo' mama!"

Mitchell was cracking up. ""Desiree, you're something else. But no thanks to you"—he gave her an artificial frown—"and that damn T-Dub, I'm gonna do it anyway."

"I already knew you would," she said, smiling gleefully. "Might as well, 'cause, as handsome as you are *jefe*, and with that body, *dios*, you're gonna have older and younger women just droolin' over you." She released a cackling laugh.

Mitchell couldn't help but laugh along with her.

"Fo' real, Boss. You're gonna have those women all wet between the thighs, and it's gonna help that auction raise some serious moo-lah." She made a gesture of rubbing her thumbs with the middle and index fingers of each hand. I wouldn't be surprised if one of 'em threw her panties on stage at you."

Mitchell just shook his head.

She stood and looked at Mitchell seriously, but affectionately. "I gave a small donation myself. I'll forever be thankful for what that shelter done for me."

A minute after Desiree left, Mitchell was still smiling, thinking about her. He now realized she'd gone to Travis first because she didn't want to conjure up her past in order to persuade him to participate in the auction. *How magnanimous of her.*

He'd met Desiree when they accidently ran into each other at the unemployment office in OKC, a week following his graduation. She was leaving the office in a dejected hurry after unsuccessfully obtaining a job and, with her head down, bumped into him head to chest as he was entering. He was there to post a job opening for Omnity.

"Oh, I'm so sorry," she'd said, looking tired and frustrated.

"That's okay, just an accident." Mitchell saw her anxiety, and it compelled him to ask her what was wrong.

At first she'd been dismayed, wondering what gave the young, cute *niño* the audacity to ask a complete stranger about her problems. But at the same time, his concern was touching, considering he was just a teenager; and she felt a tinge of gratification that someone had taken the time to regard her, and seemed genuine about it. So, she reluctantly told him.

"I'm trying to find a job, but ain't having no damn luck. I got two kids to feed and clothe, and at this point I don't really care what type of job it is, as long as I can put some money in my pockets."

For Mitchell no more had to be said, because the fact that she had kids grabbed him. It was a familiar echo to him: struggling, single mom trying to support her kids. She'd already sold herself to him.

"I have clerical training and experience," she explained, "but no positions are out here for me."

"Know anything about bookkeeping?" Mitchell asked, though it was irrelevant to him. He was only being professional; he couldn't believe he had the role of being an employer.

"Not really. But ..." Her eyes got wide and hopeful. "You know of somebody hiring or something? I'll learn bookkeeping, or any da—'scuse me. Or anything else I need to. I'm a quick learner."

He showed her the job opening he was about to advertise, then offered it to her on the spot. She'd cried with joy, then become suspicious, because he was just a boy who definitely couldn't be responsible for hiring anybody. He'd had to provide her with his business card, prove his age with his driver's license, and let her have a brief chat with Trav on his cellular to verify the authenticity of the company and position. After that, she was happy to accept.

True to her word, she learned quickly, her typing skills were past adequate, and he'd helped her with speed and accuracy on the ten-key machine. He taught her what she needed to know about their accounting system, and sent her to computer courses. Later, as they'd become closer, she confided in him how her husband used to jump on her, verbally abuse her, and how, after being unable to take the abuse any longer, she had found the strength and courage to take her little boy and girl and get the hell away from Arkansas. The shelter in OKC had accommodated her, and helped with the process of getting an apartment.

She'd turned out to be the perfect assistant, was very resourceful, and had become a good friend. So, out of deference for Desiree and all the other helpless, fearful women from the past, present, and future of domestic abuse, Mitchell had decided to participate in the auction. If it allowed him to help only one woman escape the wrath of an abusive partner, that would be worth his trouble; and in spite of his feeling about the auctions itself, there was no doubt of his moral obligation to participate in it.

His mind was still there when Travis breezed into his office carrying a bag of glazed donuts with one partially protruding from his mouth. "Peace offering," he said, dropping the bag on Mitchell's desk.

Mitchell didn't acknowledge him. He just grabbed the bag, plucked out a donut and bit into it. "Mmmm, now that's a fresh donut. Melt-in-ya-mouth good."

Travis grinned then sank into the chair Desiree had recently vacated. There was a moment of flagrant silence.

"Before you say anything," Mitchell finally began while licking glaze from his fingers, "I want you to know I'm not mad at you; never was."

"Coulda fooled me."

"Ticked off is what I was. You went behind my back. That wasn't cool, T-Dub."

Travis feigned remorse. "Yeah, you're right." He wasn't the least bit sorry, but in order to get Mitch to the auction, he'd do a little sucking up; at least appear to be apologetic.

Mitchell dipped into the bag, pulled out the last donut and frowned. "Why'd you only bring three damn donuts?"

Travis chuckled. "There were five, but once I ate one, almost couldn't stop."

"Greedy ass! Should've gotten a dozen to begin with."

Travis was still laughing. "Sorry guy, but those were the only fresh ones they had."

Mitchell looked at him flatly, halfway grinning.

Travis's laughter abated, turned into a tentative smile. "I'm also sorry about, you know ... entering you without your permission." He shrugged. "What can I say? Sometimes I tend to go a little too far."

Mitchell contemplated before saying anything. T-Dub was a sap. He'd fallen for the bait. *Sucker.* "Okay. But next time you pull some shit like that,"—he pointed at Travis—"Your ass is mine, homie."

They laughed.

Eventually, as he gathered his things to leave, Mitchell explained to Travis that he'd decided to participate in the auction after seeing the newscast about the woman who killed her abusive husband. "I'm still gonna find something devious to pay you back with though, buddy boy!" Mitchell exclaimed as they headed for the door. He flicked off the lights in his office, and locked the door behind them.

9

"**I** really don't feel like going out tonight," Jazelle told Dawn as they leaned on the fender of Dawn's car in the parking lot by Jazelle's apartment. She'd just made it in from work, and before she'd even got out of her car, Dawn had swooped up next to her, attempting to persuade her to go to the club. "I'd rather stay home and relax."

Dawn frowned. "Except for last weekend, you've been doing too much fuckin' relaxing."

Jazelle knew Dawn was referring to her recent depressed state over being played by that no good Kevin, and grimaced. "So what, I was in recovery."

"I know, but, hell! You went all the way into hibernation like a fuckin' bear." Dawn couldn't relate to Jazelle wasting so much time mourning over that dead-beat. He wasn't worth the emotions she'd wasted on that busta. Dawn's motto was: lose one, find another. Men came and went, just like time. "Girl, you can't keep letting that ol' sorry dog hold you down. You need to get his scrub ass out of your head. You know nigga's already think they control us as it is."

Jazelle didn't reply. She'd already had something of a draining day, and right now just wanted to go into her apartment and put her mind and body on lay-away. A crowded room, noise and come-ons by a bunch of wanna-be, good-for-nothing, so-called players, didn't appeal to her. Not tonight.

She tilted her head upward. The infinite, twinkling stars seemed to wink at her. The night was peaceful, which, with the appropriate companionship, could be intimately idyllic. She wasn't in the mood for going out.

And that was what she explained to Dawn, but very carefully, since the last time she'd refused an outing, Dawn had avoided her for two damn weeks.

"Sell out!" Dawn barked, obviously disappointed.

Seconds later, as Dawn backed out of the parking space, Jazelle considered flagging her down and going with her. But she quickly erased the thought, realizing she'd only be going to appease her friend. *No*, she decided adamantly, *I'm always doing things to please other people. Not this time. I've got to quit being so easily persuaded into satisfying everyone else's wants.*

They had been friends since sixth grade. They'd been through some shit together, good and bad. So, if Dawn wanted to act petty and not talk to her for a while, well, that was her prerogative.

Jazelle entered her apartment, plopped on the couch like she was even more exhausted than she felt, and dropped her purse next to her. She now welcomed the mellowness of the apartment. Today she'd had a rueful meeting with Nikki's mother, and she only wanted to lay back and loosen the annoying kinks their talk had twisted in her head.

Nikki's mischief had started after her daddy moved out, so the classroom wasn't the only place Nikki had been misbehaving lately. At home, stores, the doctor's office, even at her grandmother's house, the little girl had been venting her pain and confusion the only way a child of her age knew how: by rebelling.

Needing someone to talk to about it, Mrs. Smith told Jazelle why he'd left. He'd taken up with an older woman, who was more sophisticated.

"And," Mrs. Smith had divulged, tears inching down her cheeks, "he said she's nowhere close to being as argumentative as I am." Jazelle had listened, feeling very sorry for the woman. Lately it seemed like many people—women—she knew were facing marital problems. Crazily, the thought of it all gave her a bit of relief that she wasn't alone in getting done in by those good-for-nothing …

Instantly ashamed for having such selfish thoughts, as if being made a fool of initiated her into some type of honorable female society, she scolded herself. There was nothing good about being hurt.

Nothing.

Unfortunately, this particular set of circumstances affected one of her students, consequently flowing over into her classroom. It wasn't a simple problem to manage, because Nikki was only a baby. How would one even find an adequate solution? Did Mr. Smith even care what he was doing to his little girl? From her own experiences, Jazelle didn't think he did.

Bastard!

Anger began sweeping over her as she thought of him not having the decency to consider his daughter's feelings. She kicked the flats off her feet and massaged her temples, trying to force resentment and depressing thoughts from her mind.

After finally settling back, her cell rang. She retrieved it from her purse. "Hello?"

It was Dawn, calling to see if she'd changed her mind.

If I'd changed my mind, I would've called. "No, girl. Still don't wanna go." She expected to get a snide, saucy reply but Dawn merely gave her a surprising "Okay."

"You're not gonna give me the distant treatment again, are you?" Jazelle asked.

Dawn acted dumbfounded.

"You know," Jazelle said, "like you did when I wouldn't go on that blind date with you, Marco, and … I can't remember ol' boy's name. It was last year."

After Dawn's assurance that she wouldn't go AWOL on her, they hung up. Jazelle dragged herself to the bedroom and peeled off her clothes. After a shower, she draped herself in an oversized shirt which hung to her knees and sat on the carpeted floor at the foot of her bed, ensconcing herself in a Blackboard bestseller. Sections of the book seemed to parallel her present status: single professional woman, lonely, a terrible track record with men.

The quietness of the apartment started to smother her, engulfing her like a sinking ship being swallowed by the ocean. In a short span she went from wanting to spend a quiet, solo night at home, to wishing she'd accompanied Dawn to the club.

Hell!

Self-pity started kicking in, causing her to wonder what was wrong with her. *Am I that dense when it comes to choosing a decent, honest man? Why can't I connect with a good brotha? One, who's intelligent, gainfully employed, has his own place … and car. Considerate … and the almost unheard of: m-o-n-o-g-a-m-o-u-s; someone not trying to plug any and all female crevices that will open for his dick. Am I some type of female billboard where these dogs see me and start barking, "There's a ripe victim for the taking?"*

What the fuck is it?

Out of nowhere she started hearing a female panting and moaning. She slightly tilted her head and listened. The noises were coming from the apartment above her; a slight squeak of the bed, rocking and the soft clack of a headboard tapping against the wall. The tenant above her was a girl of about twenty-three, who'd moved in a month earlier. Katrina was her name. Jazelle had only chatted with her briefly on a few occasions. She'd never seen any men going up there. Then again, there wasn't much opportunity to see much of anything around the complex, since she virtually worked all day and evening during the week. *Katrina must've caught herself somebody recently, because some one's up there sexing her down.*

Annoyed, Jazelle felt like pulling her hair out. *Must be nice,* she thought sarcastically.

The girl moaned pleasurably from her climax, and that disgusted Jazelle more, and made her jealous. She hastily jumped up, snatched a pillow and comforter from her bed, and went and crashed on the sofa. "Everybody isn't able," she said, scowling at the ceiling.

Close to an hour later she still couldn't sleep. The erotic noises wafting through her bedroom had somehow coaxed her hormones awake. Pleading to be pleased. Surprisingly, she found herself sliding a hand toward her panties. Dawn had told her women didn't need a dick to reach orgasmic bliss.

Her fingers slid inside, feeling the moistness. She worked herself a little, stirring it, trying for that pleasurable stimulation, but she wasn't feeling it.

Self-flagellation was just not the ticket for her. *A man is what I need for this damn job.*

Irked, she snatched the hand from inside her underwear. She just lay there, horny and miserable till sleep finally came.

10

The weekend passed by with nothing much to speak of. Saturday had come and gone like it never occurred. Sunday saw the sun retaining its diligent presence over the city, partnered with clear blue skies. For Jazelle however, gloom lingered like an immovable force. It seemed like a dispiriting presence had come and force fed her a plate full of desolation, pitifully leaving her in a state of purgatory. She didn't know why, but that's how her weekend had been. She had slumped around the apartment doing nothing but watching TV, and the minute house cleaning needed in her sparsely furnished apartment. Times like these—lonely and boredom—she wished for a large family so she'd have a choice of sisters and brothers to visit, along with a gang of nieces and nephews to enjoy or get on her nerves.

To her disappointment though, a big family was merely a figment of her imagination. The closest she had to family was Dawn and her folks. She did have a brother, Sonny Jr, who was four years older, but she hadn't seen him in over six years. After graduating high school, he'd joined the marines vowing to return home only for visits. He'd stuck to that promise, only visiting twice over the past nine years: for Jazelle's high school graduation and their maternal grandmother's funeral. He only came for that because Jazelle pleaded and begged him. He called once or twice a year from different locations, but other than that contact, Jazelle rarely heard much from him. He'd written only twice throughout that time. He'd gotten married the year Jazelle graduated from college, and now had two sons. Jazelle had never met his wife or the boys.

She missed her brother like crazy.

Her mother had died from an overdose when Jazelle was five. She'd been turned out by different types of drugs, and no one knew exactly which had killed her. The autopsy suggested it had been a combination, since there was so much indistinguishable junk in her system.

Her father had deserted Jr and her a year following their mother's death, leaving them to be raised by their grandmother. He hadn't lived with them at the time their mother died, but up until that point he'd come to take them places and still spent time with them. Jazelle's only contact with him since he abandoned them was the measly child support checks he sent monthly until they'd each turned eighteen. The heartless bastard hadn't shown up for either of their high school graduations. She'd personally delivered her announcements to his house, giving the envelope—her senior picture included—to his new wife. Supposedly he wasn't home at the time. Jazelle had tried to act as though his no-show didn't bother her, but on the inside she cried a torrential rain storm.

She'd never tried to contact his sorry ass ever since.

Her grandmother, who everyone called Mean Mamie, had been a strict, unaffectionate, bitter and mean old bitch. Once she was old enough to analyze and rationalize things, Jazelle understood how her mother had been so fragile. The older Mamie had gotten, the grouchier the old hag had become. She'd given Jazelle and Jr the blues from the day they moved in with her until the day they'd each moved out of her house. She was obsessed with cleanliness to the point of being petty. If they even wasted a drop of water anywhere inside that house other than the kitchen she'd sniff it out and they'd end up getting a verbal beating. Sometimes, regardless of who'd done it, she'd whoop both their asses. So whenever they ate or drank anything they sat at the kitchen table. Because of that, Jazelle, to this day, regarded housecleaning with disdain.

Before becoming teenagers, they weren't allowed to sit on her living room furniture. They sat on the floor. As a result, most of their time at home was spent in their rooms. And their rooms had better be neat and uncluttered or she'd come down on them. Friends could never come inside the house; even when they became teenagers. They had a nine o'clock phone curfew until the day they left because she wasn't about to allow her line to be tied up by what she called a bunch of mannish, too-grown-for-their-britches kids. Jr got more lee-way on weekends when it came to staying out late. His curfew was twelve am, maybe twelve-thirty, but being a girl, Jazelle couldn't stay out past eleven pm. Mamie didn't want a *fast-ass* girl living under her roof. "Live unda my roof, you're gonna abide by my rules," she would grumble sourly whenever one of them protested. Jazelle's school counselor had to beg her to extend Jazelle's curfew for the prom.

They couldn't get out of that woman's house fast enough.

Jazelle didn't get her first boyfriend until she went to college. The boys had been afraid to contend with a grandmother who was wound up so tight.

Mamie was killed when an old gas stove heater with an undetected leak caught fire and burned her and the house to a crisp. At her funeral neither Sonny Jr nor Jazelle shed a tear. It had been that mean witch and their absentee, deadbeat father who'd run Jr away, and she had little love for either.

She stood listlessly, looking out the front window, remembering those awful days. *What's my brother doing right now? He's probably so into his son's that he'd have to be pried away from them each day just to go to work.* The words he used to say sounded in her head. "Whenever I have kids, I'm gonna spoil 'em rotten. I ain't nevah leavin' 'em to suffer like we have." He'd always hug and pacify her when she cried for their mama, or when she just cried because she was a sad little girl. Mamie never embraced her, nor comforted her with compassionate, loving hugs as a grandmother should.

Right now she yearned for Jr's brotherly love and comfort, wishing he could be there to help assuage the barren state she was in. But as she absently gazed out the window watching early rising kids play, church-goers hurrying off to morning services, and an outdoors generally more animated and spirited than she was at the moment, she was aware of her life's inadequacies: a much missed brother who left to escape the agony of an almost tormented childhood; a father who'd deserted them, washing his hands of his own offspring; herself, a lonely young woman with no accessible blood family to share her existence. No familial camaraderie whatsoever in her world.

As the realization blanketed her, unconsciously, in a whisper, Jazelle cried a futile plea for her long deceased mother to come wrap her tightly in her arms, and smother her sadness.

෨෬

Following a late breakfast, Jazelle sat cozily in the corner of the couch, legs folded under her, intractably immersed in the football game on the TV. Football was her favorite. With her brother always watching football, slowly she'd been reeled in as a fan, and learned all about it as he explained the game to her. The more familiar she became with how the game was played, the more she fell in love with it. Once upon a time in her youth she'd even wanted to play. That had been the clueless tomboy in her. Now she was almost as knowledgeable about football as a dude.

"Go! Run! Ruuuun!" she yelled animatedly from the edge of the sofa. "Touchdowwwn! She cheered excitedly, jumping out of her seat after Main Man scored on a long run. "Knew he'd make a difference. Knew it."

She happily watched as the camera showed Main Man reach up and hand the ball to a fan in the stands. As the camera zeroed in on the elated fan—an athletically built teenage boy—a boy next to him around the same age, patting him on the shoulder, caught her attention. "That looks like ..."

The camera zoomed out, then back on the boy with the ball, and the boy next to him.

Jazelle quickly rushed up to the TV—eye to screen—staring into it. She squinted discerningly before the camera moved. Was it him? "Mitchell?" She looked harder. "That is Mitchell," she said to herself, surprised. *How in the hell did he get tickets to a Cowboy's game*? "This is too unreal," she mumbled enviously as she dragged herself back to the couch and dropped back into her previous position. She often dreamed of going to a Cowboy's game, hoping the opportunity came before she was too old and decrepit.

To her annoyance, she realized seeing Mitchell on the TV screen had somehow highlighted her day. Just as she'd been stirred up by the picture Mackenzee had brought to school for her, the visual of him generated an unwelcome sensation inside her.

Why were her insides trying to betray her? Her emotions should remember that he was jail bait; a one way ticket to the *big house*. So she ought to be ashamed of herself for what she was feeling.

Annoyed with herself, she willed Mitchell from her mind like she'd been doing frequently. For good this time. He was becoming a nuisance. Without reason, he'd begun creeping into her head too damned often.

No more of that.

For the remainder of the evening she lay on the couch watching TV. She wished she had cable, but had to let it go a couple of months back. An expense she couldn't afford for now. She did get up and cook a decent meal though cooking was one of her weakness. Mamie's limitations prevented her from really learning how to cook, except for frying and boiling certain foods.

After eating the baked chicken, baked potato and corn, it struck her that she'd been hungrier than she realized.

A while later, Dawn called and told her the club had been kind of whack. "But girrrrl, guess what?" Dawn said with mischief in her tone. "'Member ol' boy, Calvin, I told you I'd met about a month ago?"

"Mm-hunh," Jazelle mumbled.

"Well, he treated me to Denny's after we left the club. I met him up there. After eating, we were in his car in the parking lot, and that fool damn near molested a bitch. I had on that cute skirt I bought last weekend, and he was all over me—especially since it was easy access."

"Girl, that is a come-fuck-me skirt," Jazelle assured.

"I know," Dawn said scandalously. "Anyway, he wanted some of the coochie so bad I pushed his head down south and fed his ass some dessert alright." She laughed.

"Nasty slut."

Dawn kept laughing. "Naw, girl, just got it like that. After I let 'im slurp up my sweet cream—"

"Uhhhn, you nasty ..."

"... his ass thought he was gon' fuck me right there in the parking lot. I got outta that crazy boy's car so damn fast. 'Awww, that's how you gon' play a nigga?' he cried. I told 'im it's better to give than receive."

Jazelle laughed. "Girl, you're a trip."

"He sixty-ate-it and I owe 'im one he'll never collect."

Jazelle cracked up, thinking about how she admired her friend's boldness. Dawn was crazy, but she had the game down.

"Sometimes we gotta dog them out like they're always doggin' us out," Dawn said. "Strike first and get our stroll on."

"If only I could be like that."

"You can—just do it. Ain't that what those Nike commercials used to say?"

After hanging up, Jazelle realized that the dismal mood she'd been in most of the weekend had evaporated since the football game, mostly because her team had won. Still, she was glad the weekend was ending.

11

The laser red Tahoe pulled into the driveway. If not for the three or four houses bearing dimly illuminated porch lights, the neighborhood would look like a black hole. The lone street light on the corner of the block had a black eye.

The four inside the SUV were almost lights out as well, struggling to keep their eyes open, because they'd been up and at it since five in the morning.

Being in the Cowboys' stadium to watch them play in person was one thing, but meeting the team, shaking their hands, and getting autographs and pictures was more than Quincy, Montell, and Li'l Q could've ever imagined.

But it all happened.

Before the Tahoe was completely parked, the door to the house slowly opened. Carla had been waiting for their return and headed for the door as soon as she saw the headlights shine through the living room window. She stepped onto the porch wearing a housecoat and house-shoes.

Quickly, Terrence and Rodney appeared from behind her, racing to the vehicle before she could stop their anxious acceleration.

"Terrence! Rodney!" she screamed. But it was too late. They were already yanking on the SUV doors.

"Hey, you li'l runts," Mitchell happily said when the passenger side front door opened. "Aren't y'all supposed to be in bed asleep?"

"We was in bed," they replied together, breathing heavily. Both were wide-eyed and in pajamas.

Mitchell was crazy about these particular cousins, mainly because Aunt Carla and his mama were around each other the most. Like he did for Montell and Mackenzee, he usually included these three on his gift list. Anytime he came home, chances were that he had something for them too.

"When we heard Mama open the door we-we rant outta there," Terrence said, his breathing calming down a bit. Though older by two years, he could pass for Rodney's twin; they looked so much alike.

Mitchell chuckled and ruffled the two heads that sported Mohawk haircuts.

Li'l Q and Montell straggled down from the backseat wearing Cowboys baseball caps and jerseys. Montell was gripping a football he'd gotten from Main Man, and Li'l Q was holding a plastic bag with souvenirs in it.

"What's that, Li'l Q?" Terrence asked his big brother.

Li'l Q initially thought about teasing his little brothers, but lacked the energy to be clowning around, so he handed over the bag. "It's for y'all."

Excited, Terrence snatched the bag, dug in and pulled out caps and jerseys identical to Li'l Q's and Montell's. The jerseys had the boys' first names on the back. When he spotted the names, Terrence's eyes expanded with delight. "Hey, these got our names on 'em!" His grin stretched across his face. He handed Rodney the cap and jersey with his name on it. "Who's football, Li'l Q?"

Li'l Q had forgotten that his souvenir from Main Man was still in the bag. "Oh, yeah, leave that in the sack. It's mines."

The two little ones already had footballs, so that one didn't interest them. They enthusiastically tossed on their new gear and rushed to show their mama, who was still waiting on the porch.

Before strolling toward the house, Li'l Q gave a very appreciative thanks to Mitchell, who nodded, and he told Montell he'd see him at school.

Carla waved and shouted "bye" to her nephews, and thanked Mitchell before following her three sons into the house. Quincy, who'd spelled Mitchell behind the wheel on the return trip from Texas, remained behind the steering wheel, praising the Tahoe. He'd had the adoration of a child when Mitchell pulled up to their house the other day in the SUV.

"When you comin' back up?" he asked his Mitchell. His left foot was absently tapping a beat on the running board as it hung out the open driver's side door. He was wearing a Cowboys baseball cap, but sported a team T-shirt instead of a jersey.

"For the boys next game here in town most likely," Mitchell answered. Quincy was one of Mitchell's favorite people. Mitchell gravitated toward his happy-go-lucky personality, because he could bring life to a roomful of deadbeats like a comedian. Mitchell loved being around him. He felt like he'd known Quincy forever, because he'd been around since Mitchell was in the third grade, which was about the time he'd started sniffing around Aunt Carla. Mitchell had gotten plenty of basketball skills from him. Up until he was in high school, Quincy had been one of the best he'd seen on the court. He used to watch with awe when Quincy put it down on the court.

"Alright, nephew, guess I ain't gonna hold y'all no longer," Quincy said. "Thanks again for the game and stuff. All that was something else. And,"—he swept his right hand, alluding to the Tahoe—"this here got it goin' on, Mitch."

Appreciatively, Mitchell nodded, too fatigued to carry on much chit-chat. He hadn't told it to anyone in the family, but Main Man had given him the Tahoe to show his appreciation for the things Mitchell had done for him. Besides, Main Man had gotten it as a gift when he'd signed an endorsement deal with the automobile manufacturer, and since he'd already specially ordered himself something customized, he thought Mitchell should have this one.

"Man, I wish I could afford one o' these," Quincy went on. They gave each other some dap before he slid from the seat.

Mitchell thought about what Quincy had just said. If he was more financially responsible he'd be able to afford almost anything he wanted. He and Aunt Carla both worked decent jobs, and between the two, they made decent money. But poor money management crippled their finances. Mitchell had given Quincy some sound financial advice—planning, saving, investing—many times, but it always went in one ear and out the other. Until he started following some of that advice, they'd continue living from paycheck to paycheck. *My people and their irresponsible money habits.* He shook his head.

Mitchell climbed into the driver's seat, and shut the door. Montell climbed in next to him, pulled the door closed, and let his head fall back on the head rest. When the door to the house closed behind Quincy, Mitchell thought: *oh well, Quincy's only human.* In his mind he posted a contingent entry for this year's Christmas list.

Slowly, he backed out the driveway and glanced at his exhausted brother. As he drove from the neighborhood, he wanted to lay his head back just like Montell. Before he let it slip his mind, he asked, "Where're you gonna keep that ball, M-Morg? You know it'll probably be worth a li'l something-something one day."

Montell was yearning for his bed, at the same time, the memory of Main Man trotting to the stands, then tossing him the football he'd scored his first touchdown of the season with, then doing the same for Li'l Q, played repeatedly in his sluggish, teenage mind. He could barely believe his own brother was so tight with a pro football player. He knew they'd gone to college together, but the way they'd carried on in the locker room, they were like ... like tight homies. He was so envious of his big brother.

"In my room, I guess," he murmured almost lifelessly. The value of an autographed football, though of much more sentimental significance, was the last thing on his mind. All he cared about was getting to his bed and crashing.

Mitchell halfheartedly grinned. His little brother had no idea that the pigskin he was gripping could one day be a collector's item.

"Tell you what, li'l bro," Mitchell said, wanting to make sure the ball was kept safely in good hands, "I'll keep it til we can get a glassed-in trophy case to store it along with some of the other awards we've accumulated." Montell's trophies, plaques and ribbons from the sports he'd played were on a wooden shelf in the living room at home along with some of the awards Mitchell had won. A few others were grouped in Montell's room on the dresser and a little table.

Montell didn't respond. He was at sleeps threshold.

"Is that cool with you?" Mitchell implored lightly.

"Yehhh—guess so."

With Montell virtually sleeping, Mitchell straining to keep his eyes open, they traveled the remaining distance home mutely. Mitchell didn't even turn on any beats.

⁎⁎⁎

Shortly after twelve, they drifted into the house. It was quiet and almost dark except for the light over the kitchen stove, and a thin ray of light seeping from the barely cracked bathroom door. That light was kept on for Mackenzee's sake so she wouldn't have to encounter pitch blackness if she woke up late at night.

Dull, flickering light was also coming from the TV in Gwen's room. A night person, she was wide awake watching the tube. When she heard the front door shut she called out, "Mitch! Monty! That y'all?"

Montell aimed straight for his room and fell on his bed, clothes and all.

"Yeah, Mama," Mitchell answered, stepping into her room. Gwen was reclining on her pillows, focused on the TV screen. Mackenzee was sleeping soundly without a care in the world. He smiled wistfully.

Gwen caught sight of him. "Where's Monty?"

Mitchell easily dropped at the foot of the bed and laid back, resting his folded arms on his forehead. "In his room. He's dead tired. That ride wore him out."

"Is he gonna wash his rump? Or did he just go in there and get in bed?"

"Mm-hmm." Mitchell wanted to fall out himself. Especially to avoid the inquisition he knew his mama was bound to attack him with.

" 'Mm-hmm', what?"

"Mamma ..." Mitchell slightly whined, but knew not to show too much irritation. Gwen didn't like getting rebuked, and would let it be known without hesitation. Then her retort would wake up Mac ...

Maybe not Mac, he reconsidered. That girl could sleep through a tornado.

"He went to sleep, G-Lady. The boy's tore down. He can hit the shower in the morning—I mean when he gets up since it's already morning."

Most of her attention was still on the TV, watching some bootleg DVD.

"G-Lady, why isn't Mac sleeping in her own bed yet?" Mitchell asked. She didn't respond but he knew she heard him. "Mama?"

"Hunh?" Her eyes stayed on the screen. "Hell, I dunno. Guess she rather sleep in here wit' me."

"Mama's baby."

"You did it, too. You was the same damn way."

Mitchell considered denying it, but right now couldn't remember way back then. His mind wasn't functioning on all cylinders. Mac's bed was on it too heavily. He rose up to go answer the bed's calling when Gwen stopped him.

He almost flinched.

She lowered the volume on the TV with the remote. "How was the game?" She had to subtly ease into what had been weighing on her mind lately. This was the perfect opportunity since her crafty son was sleepy. When he was alert, he could be as evasive as a mouse running around in a house.

Can a brother just go to bed? "It was on hit. M-Morg and Li'l Q got autographs from several of the players on the balls they got from Main Man. Quincy, he was probably more excited about being at the game and meeting the players than them."

She laughed. "I know he was. So they finally got to see that—what's his name, Main Man? Yeah—Main Man they always talkin' bout."

"Yep. He gave'em footballs he scored touchdowns with."

Gwen didn't know a lot about football, but she'd been to enough of her sons' games to know what a touchdown was.

"Is that so? They gon' brag 'bout that for a while to they damn friends." She paused the movie and scrutinized Mitchell, seeing he was as tired as a marathoner within a few miles from the finish line. He'd done plenty of driving the past few days, and had been up yesterday before the break of dawn. She knew he was fiending for sleep.

Nevertheless, she had to talk to him while he was available. He'd be going back to Norman in maybe—she peered at the clock on the stand next to her bed—four or five hours, and there was no telling when he'd be back to Tulsa. She rose from her reclining position, patted the bed right next to her, directing him to come sit.

"I need to talk to you 'bout something, baby."

Mitchell's first thought was to make a plea for sleep, but sensing a serious tone, he took the spot next to her.

"What up, Mom's?" *Please don't let this take all night.*

She stared into his drooping eyes. The gaze slightly spooked Mitchell. It was pleading, but disarming. His drowsed state perked up some.

"Mitchell," she said, removing her glasses and rubbing her eyes, "where've you been gettin' all the money to buy and do the stuff you been doin'?"

He'd known the question would come sooner or later. It was surprising she hadn't asked months earlier.

"Aww, mama ... you had me kinda worried for a sec'. I thought something bad had happened."

Twin creases appeared between her eyebrows as she laid her glasses on the nightstand. "This *is* bad, boy. You always havin' all that money, getting brand new cars, those damn designer clothes you be sendin' that ain't knock offs—expensive shit. Expensive jewelry ... and everything else you been gettin'."

Mitchell almost laughed, but she was looking at him like he was crazy. She was overreacting. But he understood she was only being a concerned mother. With some of the unlikely merchandise he'd given them, what loving mama wouldn't? He was aware of what she was getting at though. She thought he was hustling. He'd bet money on it. Where he was from it was the thing to do. But the way youngsters were getting killed and locked up over that fast money, he knew it scared the hell out of her. Also, he knew there was always the thought of how his daddy had been killed at the back of her mind.

He studied her before saying anything. He didn't want to disappoint his mama. Not when he could avoid it. Love and Happiness like Al Green had sung about is all he wanted for her. "Look Mama, I know what you're thinking." He yawned. "I assure you, my money is completely legit."

She frowned. "How the hell you know what I'm thinkin', boy?"

Mackenzee stirred, interrupting her diatribe. Both gazed in her direction. She only snuggled deeper into the pillow.

Seeing his sister wasn't waking, Mitchell said, "It's obvious. I can see it in your eyes." Almost whispering, he declared, "You think I'm slangin' that mess, don't you?"

The conclusive look on her face was enough proof.

Curiously, she muttered, "Well?"

Mitchell grinned weakly. "Mama, I'm not crazy. A little sneaky, maybe slick, but not crazy. The compensation couldn't afford me. I'm David's son, but his attraction to easy money is where our similarities end. You can believe that, G-Lady."

The mention of David made her think of her first boyfriend. The man who'd taken her virginity and given her child number one. Whenever she looked at her son she saw a lot of David in him. Mitchell had his smile, hands, easy-going manner, and walk. He hadn't taken after his daddy's self-destructive ways, and she hoped that was still the case. "That still don't say where the money's comin' from."

"Mama, I am a professional." He enunciated each word with a touch of good-natured sarcasm. He stood up, stretched both arms outward, yawning. "You think professionals make chump change or something?"

"Professional my ass. That car out there you bought me, whatever that truck is,"—she pointed, referring to the Tahoe outside—"with those shiny, twenty-six inch rims that yo brother told me they were. Yo' *professional* ass don't make enough money for all that, and I ain't stupid enough to believe you do."

Fatigue relentlessly harassed him, and was right for doing so. For the second morning in a row he would be rising before the sun frowned down on T-Town. This conversation couldn't last any longer.

"Look, G-Lady, believe me, I'm not doing anything wrong, illegal, against the law, or anything else in that category." He had his reasons for not revealing his true source of income, but it wasn't time to fill her in. Not yet. "You don't have to worry about me getting in trouble. Promise."

He produced a tired grin, leaned in and pecked her on the forehead, and got ghost before she made another plea. He knew she was still curious and concerned, but she didn't have to worry about her eldest. Once he finally rid her of her worries, getting the new Cadillac would seem as insignificant as a pro athlete signing a measly million dollar contract.

Gwen gazed, shaking her head as he disappeared from her room. She mostly believed he wasn't doing anything illegal, because he said so. He'd always been honest. She couldn't remember him lying to her about anything serious. A white lie maybe, but something important, she was sure Mitchell would be straight with her. For now she'd have to take his word.

She sighed. One way or another she knew the truth would come out.

Out of habit, which mothers often resort to when feeling helpless, she prayed.

12

When Katie's Range Rover stopped and honked in front of his townhouse, Mitchell was already walking out the door, duffle bag strapped over one shoulder and pulling a carry-on with suitor. He chuckled boyishly upon seeing Katie behind the steering wheel.

"You mean to tell me that lazy bum husband of yours has you driving?" he teased. Travis was waiting outside the vehicle with the back hatch opened to help Mitchell load his luggage.

"Yep," Katie answered with generic disappointment.

Mitchell leaned in the driver's side window and pecked her on the cheek. "How ya' doing, K-Dub?" He lightly brushed a hand over her stomach. "And my Godson?"

"Good, all things considered," she said, giggling at the nickname she hadn't completely adapted to yet, while also rubbing a hand over her barely protruding stomach. "The both of us are. How 'bout yourself?"

"A brotha can't complain." Mitchell shot Travis a menacing glare. "Just anxious to get this crazy mess your husband got me into over with."

"I can imagine." She smiled wryly, feeling a touch of guilt.

Mitchell loved Katie. Like Desiree, she was like an older sister. She was very down to earth, artificial free, loved to talk, and with her, what you saw was what you got. She was perfect for her husband, because she could be just as bizarre as he was, and wasn't ashamed to show her crazy side. Mitchell had met her at one of those modern-wave clubs—he called them psychedelic hangouts—one night. Her hair had been dirty-brown and in dreadlocks. She'd had on bell-bottomed jeans, a polka dot vest, and some of those platform sneakers. At first sight he'd thought she was loony as hell. Katie had noticed him staring at her with amusement, and shamelessly walked over to him.

"Wanna dance, homeboy?" she asked with an infectious aura, using her best black person's dialect. Mitchell had cracked up, tickled by the boldness which instantly won him over. They danced together through four straight up-tempo songs. She had rhythm for a white person; some soul in her funk. He'd told her he had a crazy white friend he'd love for her to meet.

"Crazy as me?" she asked, feigning disbelief. "When can I meet your homeboy?"

Almost four and a half years later now, she and Travis, very happily married, were expecting kid number one. He'd put together a match made in heaven.

"Are you nervous?" Katie asked Mitchell over her shoulder a minute after taking off.

Seated behind Travis, Mitchell, who was always amazed when comparing this mature, wifely Katie to the one he'd first met, was trying not to get nervous about what was soon to be taking place. He was still sort of laughing inside at how Katie had worn her hair in those dreadlocks. She was a natural brunette with shoulder length silky hair that was now gorgeously tussled.

"Slightly, at the moment, but the butterflies will probably be swarming once we get to T-Town."

"Mitchell, Mr. Spice on the basketball court, nervous?" Travis teased. "You've gotta be kidding." Mitchell lightly slapped him on the neck. Travis chuckled.

Mitchell then thought of something. He'd been the best man at their wedding, and Travis had been so nervous he'd forgotten part of the vows Mitchell had helped him write. So, Mitchell, sensing he was struggling with his memory, stepped up to Travis and whispered the forgotten parts to him. Travis had never gotten over the embarrassment of his faux pas. Now was a perfect time to rag on him with that recollection.

"Not nearly as nervous as some absent minded person who forgot his wedding vows," Mitchell said.

Travis went stiff, remembering the embarrassment. Their wedding had been videotaped, but he'd hid the only copy of the tape, and it hasn't been seen since.

Katie cracked up. "He gotcha there, T-Dub," she mocked.

Travis's face reddened.

Mitchell knew he'd gotten the desired result, so he changed subjects. "Tell me something you two ... do y'all think there will be any sistas participating in this auction?"

"Sisters?" Travis and Katie said in unison, both unsure of what he meant.

"You know—black women. African American honeys. Women of color."

"Ohhhh," Travis breathed.

"I knew that," Katie lied. She and Travis glanced at each other and shrugged. "I'm sure there will be." She thought he was talking about siblings or twins or something.

"What's wrong, Mitch? Scared to get your jungle fever on?"

Mitchell shook his head. "No I'm not scared, nutty man. I'm just curious about the racial demographic options I might have. 'Cause I know the snows—I mean white women—will be there. Just hope some sistas will be representing." He didn't discriminate, just knew he'd be a bit more comfortable with some black women in attendance.

"The options aren't yours, my brother," Travis put in.

"True dat, but you know how I hate being at the center of attention and stuff, so I don't wanna be standing out like a virgin in an orgy of prostitutes."

Husband and wife cracked up; Travis more so than Katie, who was still stuck on Mitchell's dubbing of white women.

"Snows?" she murmured with good natured indignation, amused by the label somewhat. "Where on earth did you come up with that label, Mitchell Thomas?"

Mitchell shrugged as Katie peered at him through the rearview mirror. "You haven't heard that before? Sno' or sno'-ball? Picked it up in the hood somewhere. Either way ... just an innocent euphemism for white woman."

"Some euphemism," Travis said, laughing.

Mitchell turned sideways, resting his back against the door, and stretched his legs the length of the seat. "A nice fit I think."

" 'Sno' or sno'-balls,' " Katie huffed incredulously, laughing. "Do we need to make any stops before I get onto the highway?

Both men mumbled a "no," but they ended up making a pit stop at a convenience store anyway, bought some junk food and gum.

Katie was thrilled that Mitchell had given in to the auction, because *women* had been a very delicate subject for him for well over two years. She felt it was time he moved on. She was a psychologist, and had reluctantly refrained from unleashing some of her professional expertise on him. Not even as simply his friend had she broached the subject of trying to help him with his emotional conflicts. It was difficult for her to bite her tongue though, forcing herself to resist approaching him with some of her methods. She'd desperately wanted to drill in his head that as humans we're often faced with adversities that evoke our mortality, but we must be strong, endure as survivors, and move on with our lives. For the most part he had moved on, but romantically and socially, where women were concerned, it was a *no go*. With Travis constantly refraining her from expressing what he called *psycho mumbo-jumbo* to Mitchell because he felt he would eventually come around on his own when he was ready, she'd kept her mouth shut, leaving Mitchell to his own vices to cope as he saw fit. She hoped Mitchell, who she loved like a brother, would recover from the emotional abyss he was unfairly thrown into.

But God was she happy her husband had finally decided to interfere and try to nudge him along.

₭ℛ

In the lobby of the Double Tree Hotel, the site of the auction and where they'd be staying for the weekend, Mitchell took notice of the countless attractive women streaming by him in small cliques of four, three, or two, while some were solo. The diversity and attractiveness of the women even had the *square* he'd turned into half wide-eyed and attentive. Short skirts, pants that must've been painted on they were so tight, plunging necklines, and plenty of my-woman-is-going-to-slap-the-hell-out-of-me-for-staring-at-that-cleavage dresses. Mitchell felt like he'd been dropped smack dab in the middle of an estrogen fest. Some were too thin, too big, or just too damn odd-bodied for the outfits they were wearing. But Mitchell knew they couldn't be told that they weren't cute.

A fine, paper-sack brown sista, with a whipped short-crop hairstyle, walked by wearing some fitting leggings; her rump was plump as hell. P-H-A-T. Mitchell couldn't help but take a second, third, and fourth look. *Woo-wee that sista got ass for days! Hell, I wonder if she's kin to Serena with all that back she pack's.*

While Mitchell's eyes were occupied with that sight, Travis came up behind him, his gaze following Mitchell's, and tapped him on the shoulder. "Don't blame you, bro, she does have a *nice* one."

Mitchell slightly jumped before playfully elbowing Travis in the gut. "Eff you, T-Dub. And quit drooling before I tell your wife."

Their eyes found Katie. "I'm merely looking at what you're looking at. Looking doesn't hurt anyone." Katie was over chatting with some woman. With a fake challenge, he peered at Mitchell. "You won't tell. Homies don't rat on homies."

Mitchell shook his head, laughing.

Travis handed him the keys to his room. "Registration already started, so let's all try to be ready in forty-five minutes, and meet at the registration desk."

"Fine by me."

"The fun's about to begin. You ready?"

Mitchell just gave him the eye.

Travis stole one last sly glance at the women, being cautious of his wife's quick eyes. "There's enough vagina around here to make an immoral man think he'd died and gone to pussy heaven."

Mitchell couldn't argue with that.

After the valet sat Mitchell's luggage down in his fourth floor room, Mitchell tipped him with a new big face Ulysses S. Grant, closed the door after dude left and walked through the suite, inhaling the fresh, sweet scent of wild flavored air freshener, and soon found that the bathroom was equipped with a whirlpool tub. *That's what I'm talking 'bout.*

He unpacked, contemplated calling his mama, but decided against it; she'd get to probing him with an onslaught of questions about him being in Tulsa, and he wasn't in the mood to answer ten thousand questions. He'd spoken to her earlier in the week to let her know he'd be in town for the Fair next weekend.

With that resolved, he peeled off his clothes, letting them fall to the floor. He had about thirty-five minutes before he had to meet Travis and Katie for registration.

Fifteen of those minutes were spent in the whirlpool, unsuccessfully trying to stifle his slowly encroaching nervousness.

ஐௐ

"Honey, do you think this will be too overwhelming for Mitch?" Katie asked Travis. "This is something completely against what he cares for."

Travis slipped up behind Katie, wrapping his arms around her, and slowly guided his big hands under her shirt, gently rubbing her stomach while softly kissing the nape of her neck. "He'll be just fine, sweetheart," he whispered in her ear. He started nibbling on her ear.

The soft kisses, feathery brush of breath, and the nibbling, tingled her entire body, but Katie willed herself to disregard the sensations her husband was unraveling inside her. "But ... ooohhh ... but what if he's on that stage feeling out of place?"

"He's an adult, baby. He can handle it."

"I still feel guilty. The way we got him involved in this—"

"Don't worry," Travis murmured, nuzzling her silky hair, taking in its coconut aroma, "told ya' he made up his own mind about participating—no persuasion from me at all. We only initiated the idea."

"We did more than initiate."

"Honey, we've already been through this."

"I know, but—"

Her complaints tapered off as his fingers craftily trailed up to her breast, under her bra, and glided over taut nipples. She inhaled then released a low moan. "Tra-Travis ... wh-what're you doing?"

He turned her to face him. With a mix of pleasure and dismay, she saw that her horny husband was only in boxers. That long, slender body of his was a constant weakness of hers; she couldn't get enough it, or the parts which were known to take her on fantastic voyages of orgasmic proportions. She knew exactly where his mind was, and by the way his boxers poked out in the front, where that particular joint wanted to be.

He lifted her blouse, directed his tongue to the fully erect nipples.

"Travis we don't have time fo—"

The meager protest fell to the wayside after he gingerly walked her to the bed, gently turned her around, had her place her hands on the bed and entered her from behind.

13

Mitchell arrived at the registration table outside the banquet room on time. Mr. Punctual and his wife were nowhere in sight. He approached the table, and giving the names Mr. and Mrs. Wingham, asked one of the two women manning the table if they'd already gone in.

After skimming the list of names, she replied, "No, not yet."

Mitchell stepped away from the table and restlessly stood by the wall, glancing up and down the corridor, hoping to spot Travis and Katie coming PDQ—Pretty Damn Quick. Several fine-as-hell young ladies passed by, sizing him up. He nodded politely at some, averted his eyes when he sensed one looking his way flirtatiously.

"Girrrl, look at that," he overheard a chocolate sista say to her multi-cultured friend. "Hope he's up for bid." They lightly giggled like two teenagers, taking another glance at him before entering the banquet room.

That only unnerved him, and made his impatience intensify. Something was telling him to make a break for it. He peeked at his watch and cursed under his breath. The auction hadn't even started, yet here he was standing in the hallway already feeling like a black man stranded in a rural white part of Mississippi. All because his meddling, late-ass partner made it his business to sign him up for this ...

He let the thought pass as he considered cussing T-Dub out soon as he showed his melanin deficient face. Where the hell where those two anyway? He was getting pissed. It was already—he checked his watch again—five till seven.

The moment he took his eyes off his watch, Travis, wearing the smug grin Mitchell knew well, appeared hand in hand with Katie. At that very moment, Mitchell had the inclination to politely walk up and slap the shit out of him. "Forty-five minutes, hunh?" he said snidely, once they were face to face.

Travis and Katie looked at each other giddily, looking like teenage boyfriend and girlfriend who'd snuck around the back of the house and done something they shouldn't have been doing. "We ... um ... we lost track of time," Travis said.

Mitchell stared at them scornfully. Suspiciously. Travis wasn't a person who lost track of time. Then the reason for their tardiness registered. The foolish, guilty smirks on their faces were dead giveaways. He shook his head with disgust, trying to suppress a smile.

"Come on, let's go in you two and get this show on the road," Katie said, tugging a hand of both men.

They stepped into the banquet room and were impressed. Tables had centerpieces of red, white, and blue flowers representing a theme of Independence, with a burning candle in the middle, laid out on an elegant tablecloth. While they waited to be seated, they tuned into a band performing Kool and the Gang's "Ladies Night." The dance floor was already filled. Women were everywhere, and there were a few more couples than anticipated. Several single men were present as well.

Travis leaned over and said, "Oh yeah, Mitch, I forgot to tell you earlier ... Desiree is the one who paid your entry fee—or 'donation', as these people call it."

Mitchell was surprised. "Is that right?"

"I tried to persuade her to let me take care of it, but she insisted." Travis shrugged.

Mitchell halfway smiled. *So that was what Desiree meant when she said she gave her donation.* "I'll thank that sneaky woman when I see her Monday," he said mischievously.

A pretty, twenty-something brunette hostess escorted them to their table, which was positioned in a perfect spot by the platform where the bachelors would be strutting their stuff. A banner reading: 1st ANNUAL BATTERED WOMENS HOME CHARITY AUCTION hung in the background.

After being seated a waitress came and poured them water, asking if they would like coffee, tea, or some other beverage. Travis wanted coffee, the other two requested water. She picked up their name cards, informed them about their meals which had been pre-selected on the registration forms, then retreated toward the kitchen.

"By the way, you two oversexed lovebirds," Mitchell teased, "y'all look exquisite." He said the last word in a very proper English accent.

"Thanks. Kudos to you, my brother," Katie replied in the same accent, taking an approving survey of her husband and Mitchell.

Travis just grinned.

Both men were decked in sumptuous Armani suits, and Katie had on a fabulous Stella McCartney evening dress. The fit of the dress shielded her pregnancy, and she was glowing. The attire had been rewards to themselves during their last trip to the Big Apple after closing a deal for one of their major league clients. Mitchell had spotted the dress and told Travis Katie would look *queenilicious* in it. Travis always valued Mitchell's taste, so he bought it.

"Oh yeah, Mitch, I took the liberty of choosing ribs for your main course," Travis informed tentatively, not wanting to conjure up the recollections of his machinations which had Mitch in his present predicament.

"Amongst other things," Mitchell uttered sarcastically. Just to start something for the hell of it, he thought about asking, "How you know I didn't want the chops, homeboy?" but he left it alone.

Travis responded with a contorted expression.

Mitchell leisurely looked around, wondering if he knew anyone else in the room. The band played an old Janet Jackson cut, "Nasty Boy," and Katie pulled her husband onto the dance floor. T-Dub had no rhythm. As Mitchell watched his partner and wife try to shake a leg, he was conscious of his dwindling apprehension, and was feeling pretty much at ease. Across the room, he detected a table of women staring at him. Unlike usual, he didn't avert his eyes. In fact, he was uncharacteristically intrigued, though minutely.

The waitress returned with their drinks, and after placing them on the table, asked Mitchell if he was one of the bachelors. Mitchell smiled and answered, "Yes." For some reason her resulting blush relaxed him even more. She was dark-skinned and fair-looking. He guessed she was a college student earning some dollars to help with school expenses, because she looked like she was in school. He considered asking if she was a student, and if so, what school, but the covert glances she kept passing were a red flag. Keen on recognizing women's interest in him since it happened quite often, he decided not to ask. No need to send her mixed signals. He wasn't trying to flirt with any of these women.

Instead he asked for a Pepsi whenever she'd completed her rounds again. He was in no hurry.

As she walked away, he was resigned to the fact that he couldn't be inconspicuous in this cluster of females. *Might as well get with the program Mitchell and try to have a good time.*

After she dropped off his Pepsi and scurried to other tables, one of four females he'd spied gazing at him from across the room approached his table. Her unexpected visit startled him as he looked up into a gorgeous, olive face, which looked of Latin descent.

"Hello," she said smiling. "My name is Theresa." She pronounced it 'Tuh-ray-suh' as she extended her hand.

Her accent validated Mitchell's assumption, but her English was fluent. Always a gentleman, Mitchell immediately stood and took her hand. "*Hola, Theresa. Es un placer conocerte.* I'm Mitchell. Mitchell Thomas."

She smiled. Impressed. "*Habla Espanol. Muy bien.*"

Mitchell chuckled. He was proud of how composed he was being. "Only a few things." He'd taken Spanish in high school and still knew bits and pieces of what he'd learned.

He released her hand.

"The waitress told us"—she half turned, gestured toward her table of friends—"you are one of the bachelors."

He blushed. *That's what that waitress was up to.*

"After learning that, my girlfriends dared me to come ask you to dance," she said apprehensively.

Mitchell noted her slight apprehension. She had some of the biggest, prettiest almond eyes he'd ever seen.

"Would you? Like to dance?" She asked.

"No doubt," Mitchell replied without hesitation, hoping to ease the nervousness he sensed from her.

She smiled again and breathed a sigh of relief. "*Bueno.*"

"Wouldn't be right to turn down a pretty woman like yourself," Mitchell added, wondering where in the hell had he gotten the nerve to say that.

She blushed. "Thank you."

From the front this senorita has it going on. Images of J-Lo floated in his head, and he wanted to check out Theresa's backside to see what she was working with. Even through his self imposed distancing from the fairer sex, he hadn't buried a man's natural inclination to check out the physical assets of women.

When she led him to the dance floor he saw she didn't have J-Lo's *trunk-of-junk*—not even close—but he knew all Latinas couldn't be so fortunate.

To the pleasure of all Theresa's friends, he danced with each of them, downplaying their questions about his romantic status, and good naturedly rolling with the flow through all their flirting.

Katie and Travis surreptitiously watched Mitchell and the fun he seemed to be having with the women. They were hopeful. Maybe their plan had been a good idea after all.

☨

Most had completed their meals and dessert when the first bachelor was announced and strolled to the stage, turning the atmosphere into one comparable to a strip club. Whistles, wooing, cheering, and sexual epithets erupted all over the room. The ladies had been waiting for this moment, and they were expressing their enthusiasm.

Programs provided to everyone listed the name and background of the bachelors. Twenty-five were listed, and Mitchell was twentieth. The auctioneer was a mid-fortyish woman who had the look and air of a modern-day aristocrat. She had on a conservative dress and a stiffly erect posture which conveyed propriety. She'd provide a profile for each bachelor: name, age, height, education if any, occupation, interest and hobbies. Mitchell's profile excluded his age. Travis was well aware of his feelings about revealing his age, and requested the exclusion.

Bachelor number one was a fairly good looking, tall, sandy haired white guy, who looked sort of nerdish. He was dressed simply in khakis, tie and white shirt. He received animated applause the moment he walked across the stage, and when the auctioneer announced he had a foot fetish, and loved giving massages, the women erupted with loud approval.

At their table, Travis and Katie had been teasing and questioning Mitchell about the four women he'd been dancing and mingling with, but now they were focused on the stage, amused by the excited, rowdy women. Mitchell wasn't sure what he'd expected, but he sure hadn't expected this raucousness from the women. He now felt like he'd been ambushed. For a second he thought about acting like he had to go to the men's room then making a mad dash out of the place. Run like a chicken.

"Mitchell, do you give foot massages?" Katie asked playfully, but really was curious.

Mitchell thought for a second and shrugged. "I might." The question had drudged up a brief recollection, but he'd quickly blinked the memory away before it affected his mood.

"He does every now and then," Katie said, pointing at Travis. "But the further I get into this pregnancy, he's gonna start doing it more often ... or he won't be getting any."

Travis gave Mitchell a sideways glance, vibrating his head with quick shakes that said: No *I'm not*. But Mitchell blew that off, knowing Travis would walk across the North Pole bare-foot in swimming trunks for Katie if he had to. He sent Travis a dry smile, thinking, *Yeah, whatever, T-Dub.*

Mitchell's attention was jolted back to the stage once the bidding began. All bids would start at one hundred dollars. Each bidder had a small glow-in-the-dark tube which they raised up high when bidding. The modest lighting was perfect for the atmosphere. Mitchell was somewhat galvanized by all the tubes going up and down around the room. He speculated many of the women to be early to mid thirties, and could hardly believe there were so many single women in that age bracket. The dawn of the *Independent Woman* was certainly showing its presence.

The gavel came down at a final bid of three hundred seventy-five for bachelor number one, resulting in another round of loud applause. Clapping, Travis said over the cheers, "Mitchell, you're gonna beat that bid by at least five hundred or more—mark my words."

"You think so?" Mitchell was more enthusiastic than he cared to admit. His competitive spirit had been aroused.

"Hell yes," Katie jumped in, wanting to boost his confidence. She wanted him to enjoy this because that would absolve her of the guilt she felt for conspiring with Travis.

As his turn approached, Mitchell remembered the times other than his graduation ceremonies when he'd been the focus of an assembly of people. From elementary to high school he'd been the recipient of many honors—most outstanding student, certificates of achievement, spelling bee champion, Male Athlete of the Year, and others—and each time his name was called he'd taken the stage with pride. He'd never been nervous then. But this was a different type of crowd, gathered for a different reason. Back then he'd expected and welcomed the spotlight because he'd worked hard to be in that position. Plus, unlike tonight, back then there was no crowd of avaricious women honing in on him like a pack of hungry wolves.

"Next up we have Mr. Mitchell Thomas," the auctioneer announced.

Hearing his name, Mitchell's insides turned to mush. He glanced at Katie and Travis. They were clapping and coaxing him on. "That's my man," Travis chanted. "Go get 'em, Mitchell," he absently heard Katie cheering.

I can handle this. He took a deep breath, stood erect, and walked to the stage, blocking out the cheers, focusing on being cool, calm, and collected.

Before going on the stage a strange thought swept through his mind. It was the memory of the dream he'd had the very night Travis told him he'd entered him in this auction. The subject of that dream was who he'd been subconsciously hoping to spot when he'd been scanning the room of people earlier.

Miss Jazelle Johnson.

The moment he crossed to the center of the stage, some woman near the back of the room shouted "Seven hundred-fifty dollars!"

A staggered hush ensued as everyone glared toward where the voice had come from. Mitchell was appreciative of the momentary diversion. So many eyes were on him. But an instant later the babble started up again as the auctioneer announced "The bidding hasn't opened for this gentleman just yet."

"Damn! He's hot!" Several women could be heard uttering. "I just want thirty minutes with that hottie," some woman hollered.

"And I'd like to join you," came another voice. "You can use and abuse me anyway you like, you gorgeous thang, you," the same woman continued. People busted out laughing.

"Do you take cream with your coffee?" Some white woman shouted.

These women are a trip, Mitchell thought.

He was looking handsome and desirable to the women. His double breasted terra-cotta suit, along with some gleaming double monk-strap shoes, dazzled the eyes of the infatuated, loose women. "Take it off!" Several women screamed.

While his profile was being read, Mitchell sought out a spot to plant his eyes. Wearing a stylish pair of designer eyeglasses, he found the glow of an exit sign at the rear of the room and concentrated on it. He wasn't about to look at the crowd; they'd possibly cause him to tense up. At the moment he was maintaining his cool.

The bidding started at seven hundred fifty dollars to everyone's disbelief. As it increased, so did Mitchell's intrigue. Realizing what he was doing was somewhat similar to his everyday occupation—being an agent was about marketing his clients—he decided to sell himself to the women with a little flare. Hell, it was for charity, after all. He smoothly began stalking the stage like a model, doing it with swag, emphasizing his normally modest gangsta-limp.

The women ate it up, and the glow-in-the-dark tubes were going up and down like gasoline prices, increasing the bids. Katie and Travis were at their table stunned, disbelieving what they were witnessing. For as long as they'd known Mitchell they'd never come close to seeing him be so bold and theatrical. They gazed back and forth at one another with gaping mouths.

Mitchell felt the energy he was arousing, sensing the same type of electricity he'd generated during high school talent shows he'd been in. So with attitude, he glided across the stage, exposing an infectious smile, but never looking at the crowd. Then, to the enthusiastic delight of the women, he provocatively removed his jacket and slung it over his shoulder. The women went crazy. He thought about adding some gyrations, but decided that would be doing too much. If he started that the women would want him to start stripping.

The bidding quickly bypassed the previous high bid. Once everyone realized the amount, *oohs* and *ahhs* sounded off like a song.

It was all tripping Mitchell out.

Travis and Katie, still shocked over Mitchell's actions, continued looking at each other with astonishment.

"What I tell you?" Travis said to his wife, referring to his prediction. Katie shook her head incredulously, smiling.

Wherever the bidding ended she wouldn't need to feel guilty anymore.

At $1,250 the bidding slacked off, but a bidding contest generated between two women in the center of the room. The dimness prevented Mitchell from making out the two women, though he briefly tried to get a look at them. The two were going at it like sparring partners, shooting the bids to seventeen hundred. The room was intense with anticipation as everyone focused on the two ladies.

Then, like a boxing knockout, one of the two women yelled, "Twenty-five hundred dollars!"

The only sounds to be heard came from the kitchen, everyone else was virtually frozen, on the edge, quiet as a recently potty-trained child pissing on himself. Close to thirty seconds elapsed while everyone stared in suspense, waiting for a response.

But there was no counter bid from the other woman.

"We have twenty-five hundred for the final bid," announced the auctioneer, directing her words to the lady who hadn't countered yet.

After a few more seconds she didn't respond.

"Twenty-five hundred dollars going once," said the auctioneer, then pausing a second. "Going twice." Pause. "Sold! We have a winner," she announced.

The gavel came down with a thud to a room of cheers.

⁎⁎⁎

"Mr. Thomas, let me introduce you to the two ladies who were in that friendly bidding competition for you," the auctioneer said after walking up to Mitchell, both women—one black the other white—flanking her. The remainder of the auction had been anti-climactic after Mitchell's little performance. No one received bids over five hundred dollars.

Mitchell looked at the shelter's director and the two women with her. He smiled, uncomfortable with all the attention, but was riding it out since it was the right thing to do.

"This is Doctor Willette Reed," the director said, introducing the honey colored woman who extended a soft hand with manicured fingernails colored in blood red. She had on a figure hugging red dress and looked to be about 34. "She's a pediatrician—the runner-up in that battle of the bids."

Wow ... Doctor. And pretty. "Nice to meet you, Dr. Reed," Mitchell said, firmly shaking her hand. "It was cool how you helped benefit the shelter."

"Call me Willette," she replied flirtatiously, a slight look of disappointment in her eyes. "Wish I would've won you, though."

Mitchell blushed.

"And this is Doctor Susan Ladonis, the winning bidder of the night," the director said. "She's an Ob-Gyn."

Damn! Another Doctor! Mitchell wondered why this sno'-ball bid so much just to go on a date with him. She didn't look like the type who kicked it with brotha's. And she surely wasn't the type brotha's usually chased. Black men liked women with some meat on their bones. Squeezable flesh when it was time to mesh. She was about five foot-seven, maybe 37. Nicole Richie thin; not enough flesh for his liking. There was a sexy cleft in her chin though, and some men wouldn't mind introducing their tongue to it, he imagined. Her auburn hair was chopped off and styled soft and wispy, and she had enchanting green eyes which matched her pant suit.

"Nice to meet you as well, Dr. Ladonis."

She grasped his hand firmly, gazed into his brown eyes. "The feeling's mutual, Mr. Thomas."

Mitchell wasn't sure if that was simply a cordial greeting, or if it carried a double entendre. For some reason, something about her made him a little curious. She was an alright looking woman, but there was a tomboyish aura about her. Something indeterminable.

Katie came up to him, and, with mocking sarcasm, whispered in his ear, "I see you've been hooked up with a sno'-ball." She chuckled.

Mitchell glared at her.

Minutes later, several pictures were snapped, and when the band resumed playing, Mitchell danced with plenty of the women. They flirted with him all night long.

Susan had unselfishly told him to dance and enjoy the women's attentions. "Tomorrow I'll have you all to myself," she uttered sultrily.

Travis and Katie had been on the perimeter of the women surrounding Mitchell, and were amused but enjoying what was going on. They'd been close by when Susan made the statement to him and teased him about his newest acquaintance, chuckling like some hyenas.

Mitchell flashed them the middle finger.

14

Jazelle and Amanda were in a restaurant, sipping on strawberry daiquiris and scanning menus. They were doing some female bonding, plus giving Amanda some much needed time away from her kids.

Earlier, they had browsed more than shopped at the mall, and roamed around like two giggly, overgrown teenagers. With her tight budget, Jazelle only bought a pair of jeans and a sweatshirt. Amanda, out of guilt, bought her kids matching jackets and herself a pair of boots. The jury was out on her husband, so he got nothing. They had then taken in an emotional love story at the theater, and both had shed some tears. It had been Amanda's first visit to a movie since her kids' births without their distractions, and she'd enjoyed it to the max because they hadn't been there diverting her attention.

Jazelle had wanted Dawn to tag along, but she had to work.

"Jazelle, I can't thank you enough for coming up with this girl's day out." Amanda looked happy, the pleasure on her face an assuaging contrast to the stressed mien of late. "One of us should've thought of this week's ago."

"Alllready," Jazelle added. "A much better way to spend a free day than my boring, tired apartment."

"My house isn't boring, but—though I hate to admit it—this day has been like a breath of fresh air compared to being home."

"Come on now, Amanda, it's not that bad at your house, girl."

Amanda sighed, absently stirring the straw in her almost empty glass, her eyes still focused on the menu.

Jazelle caught the undertone. "What's happening now?" Her friend shouldn't be so unhappy with her home life. Unlike Jazelle's, Amanda's place had plenty of life, activity, and interaction. Family. Simple things people too often and easily took for granted. Besides, Amanda had recently told her the kids had toned down their irritating behavior, which had been the thing distressing her the most. The speculation about her husband cheating was just that—speculation. She hadn't found any evidence, other than a couple of late nights out, to prove he was fooling around.

"Nothing new really. Actually, your 're right, it's not that bad." Amanda was fishing in her purse for cigarettes. "But there's been so much tension between Steven and I lately, mostly from me and ..." She let the statement die, pulled out a cigarette.

"What're you doing? There's no smoking in here." Something Jazelle was glad for.

"Oh, yeah, I almost forgot," she whispered putting the cigarette away.

"So tell me Amanda, why haven't you confronted him yet?" Jazelle asked. She'd gone through suspecting an ex or two of cheating, but silently tried to dismiss that it could be happening. Now she knew that not knowing the truth was too agonizing. "You scared he might prove your suspicions right?"

Amanda was quiet for second. "I dunno, maybe?" She looked around for the waitress, wanting another Daiquiri. "Maybe I'm scared he'll leave me."

The waitress came over and Amanda asked for a refill. Neither woman was ready to order but promised they would be in a minute or so.

Jazelle observed Amanda. She didn't want to misjudge her friend's husband, but if he was doing Amanda wrong by having *split duty* with some other female, then he ... he ... hell, she didn't know. Life could be so screwed up. Even the good people got kicked around like a damn soccer ball. And Amanda was good people. She shouldn't be going through that stress. "Do you want to know?" she asked tentatively.

Without hesitating, Amanda went off. "Yes I do. And I'll kick the tramp's ass if I ever see her! She's probably one of those white trash bitches, giving him blow jobs whenever he wants one."

Holding in a laugh, Jazelle surveyed the room, hoping nobody was paying attention to their table. She knew the antique white couple at the adjacent table had heard Amanda, but it looked as if they were ignoring her, or they were too embarrassed to look.

"But, Amanda, you don't know if a woman's to blame for whatever's happening with your husband."

Embarrassed, Amanda was relieved when the waitress, a red headed cougar, returned with her drink and asked if they were now ready to order. Not wanting to put the woman off again they ordered, but not without changing their minds a couple of times. Amanda hastily got up and headed to the ladies room to release some liquid, but mostly for a moment to recompose herself in private.

When she returned she didn't mention her outburst, but did revisit their previous topic of discussion. "You know, Jazelle, when I build up enough courage, I'm gonna confront Steve. He's been kinda lost as to why I've been so testy with him lately—least he acts like he has no idea. But I've been with Steve since high school, he busted my cherry—"

Jazelle busted out laughing at the adolescent description of losing your virginity. She couldn't help it, though she knew Amanda wasn't being facetious.

"—and he's the only man I know that way—if you understand what I'm saying—and if I accuse him of cheating ... and I'm wrong, then what? He'll be so hurt."

Jazelle couldn't imagine being with one man for that long. *Wow.* Four or five months had been her longest stint in a relationship, and neither time had been real love; definitely not on any of the men's behalves. And with her pitiful history with men, she doubted ever being fortunate enough to experience that type of love and longevity. She couldn't empathize with Amanda on that level, but she understood the fear of losing someone you loved dearly. Losing a loved one, regardless of the form, was emotionally devastating.

"I understand where you're coming from, Amanda, but I wish you wouldn't let this"—she grasped Amanda's hands, comforting her, searching for the right words—"these possibly untrue assumptions affect you so stressfully."

Amanda eyed Jazelle wanly, wishing it could be that easy to dismiss the conflict of her non-abating suspicions. But until she knew the truth, her emotions would continue fluctuating between sadness, frustration, and anger. Yes, the best way to solve her suspicions was to confront her husband, yet she hadn't built up the courage. Until she was brave enough to do that, she couldn't continue saturating her friend with her fears and weaknesses. So, she smiled weakly, and sighed. "You know, Jazelle, we were having a good damn day until I started spoiling things like a big cry baby"

Still holding her friends hands, Jazelle smiled sympathetically. "Girl, you're not a cry baby. And you're not spoiling our day. What you think friends are for? You're supposed to be able to cry on my shoulder. A friend in need is a friend in deed. Support, in whichever form, is the basis of friendship."

Amanda squeezed Jazelle's hands. Smiled.

A little while later the waitress returned toting their fish and shrimp platters. Right when Jazelle was about to say something, she was completely thrown off by a vision crossing to a table on the other side of the restaurant.

 හ⊙Ɑ

Being a gentleman, Mitchell pulled out Susan's chair, nudged it forward once she was seated, then seated himself, and idly scanned the room in an effort to distract his uneasiness.

Across from them, a twenty-something white couple was trying to get their toddler, a boy who was sitting in a highchair, to stop hollering and pitching his food on the floor.

Mitchell remembered that type of scene with Mackenzee back in the day.

From the time he'd entered Susan's Lexus at the hotel earlier, he'd been struggling to relax in her company. Dating was almost Greek to him. It had been so long, and he wasn't the most comfortable person at the moment. It wasn't helping his cause any that his date was basically a stranger, and every so often, assessing him like a fox locked in a barn full of hens.

Their first stop had been to the Museum where they'd viewed some fabulous Native American art, which Mitchell had loved, wishing he could purchase and take some of the works with him. Though the museum had been a good impersonal way to break the ice between the new acquaintances, Mitchell still felt a touch out of bounds. He still wondered why Susan had paid more than two *stacks* to spend an evening with him. *Maybe she was lonely and hadn't been able to settle down with anyone worthwhile?* If that was the case he knew the lonely sometimes went through extremes to alleviate their loneliness.

Mitchell Thomas, those are some of the things you should be talking to her about, you wuss.

Susan wasn't nervous. She had the confident demeanor of a person in complete control. It was a date she'd eagerly anticipated, waiting impatiently for the previous night to end so it could begin. At the auction, she'd asked him if they could get the date over and done with since he lived out of town, because she didn't feel it necessary for him to go out of his way traveling back to Tulsa sometime in the future for a measly date.

After seeing Mitchell on stage at the auction she'd instantly become intrigued and curious about him because he looked so young. Even after he'd told her he was 21 earlier, she doubted he was experienced with a mature woman, but the deciding factor was her curiosity about black men, which she wanted to prove or disprove for herself. She had wondered about the stereotype for years, ever since she heard some of the looser girls at her Catholic high school gossiping about their sexual rendezvous. She had other friends with the exact same curiosity but who wouldn't dare make the move to find out because they either didn't know how to approach a black man, or were afraid of what people in their *circle* would think or say. She couldn't care less about what others thought anymore.

He had displayed choppiness throughout their short time together so far, and she wondered how to loosen him up. Maybe it was her? She hadn't asked his views on interracial dating. The subject seemed inappropriate once she'd sensed his trepidation. She figured it would spook him even more.

"Mitchell, are you a naturally shy person?" she asked. She imagined him being so young played a big factor with his lack of dialogue, but asking him could be a good start.

Mitchell thought if this date had happened a few years ago she would've never had to ask him that. He never had diarrhea of the mouth—he'd been able to hold his own, conversing with women.

He wondered what some of his old homies would say if they saw him with a woman acting scared. They'd certainly clown him; call him weak, scared of the draws, soft ...

He was tiring of the introverted nature he'd taken to. Though it wasn't something he was purposefully doing, he couldn't shake the condition. It was an emotional-psychological thing, he knew, but it held him captive like a bad dream he couldn't wake from. People said he would get past it in time, so when was the time for that?

Trying to downplay his uneasiness, he smiled and said, "People ask me that a lot lately. Actually I'm not shy. I think I just have to get used to you. Sometimes I'm a little reserved with new people." Under the table his right leg bounced non-stop. "Just gimme time, I'll loosen up some."

Susan smiled. "I can relate to that. I was like that as a kid. Actually until some—" She wanted to say, "Until some point after my divorce," but she'd bring the subject of her failed marriage up later. "—some point in my late twenties. Some of us need to adjust to new people. I think it's a comfort and trust thing. Some people meet no strangers."

Mitchell absently looked around, speculating. The latter part of what Susan had said described T-Dub and Katie. Those two talked to anybody. "I can agree wit' ya on that," he said, drawing the words out.

Susan lightly laughed.

She sensed he was loosening up some.

"Mitchell, are you gonna actually contact those artists from the museum?" The waitress came and placed their drinks on the table. Both thanked her and told her she could return in a few minutes for their meal orders.

"Yes. My partner's wife loves Indian—I mean Native American—art, and I'd like to try to get her some for Christmas."

"Hmm. Your partner's wife Native American?"

"Naw, Katie's white. Like you, she's a doctor. A psychologist though. But she's kinda"—he wavered a hand like an airplane tilting its wings back and forth—"out there, so to speak."

"Strange, you mean?"

"Nah. Not strange, or weird—just different in a humanitarian sort of way. She thinks of herself as a universal being desirous of connecting with all cultures and ethnicities."

Susan chuckled. "Guess I kinda understand. Those head doctors are on a different level. I think they analyze minds so much it eventually makes them a little quirky."

Mitchell laughed.

"So, what about you?" he asked. Her eyebrows drew together. "I mean, what made you want to be an Ob-Gyn?"

"Ohhh. That." For a second she thought he was calling her crazy. "I guess because I feel that men shouldn't be examining women's private parts. Men can't feel what we feel like. We can't feel what men feel. Physically that is. I once had a male doctor when I was a teenager, and to this day I still believe he fondled me inappropriately."

Sipping his Pepsi through a straw, Mitchell frowned, wondering if his mama's doctor was a woman. "Did you report him?"

"Nope. At the time I wasn't sure, so I kept it to myself."

"Hmm."

"I'm sure you've seen some of those news programs," she went on bitterly, "with those doctor's who got caught on tape doing unethical, disgusting, degrading things to their patients." It wasn't a question.

"Yes, I have, and I can understand why you feel the way you do." He paused in contemplation. "But I've never seriously thought about if I'd prefer a man or woman examining me. I—"

"It's different with a woman examining a man." She was emphatic.

"In a way." He didn't want to raise the double standard argument. He figured she had reasons for her point of view. "But but with me, it's a question of being comfortable. Even with a male doctor I've sometimes wondered if he was getting some thrills from feeling around my genital area. On the other hand, I'm not too comfortable being exposed that way to a female if, you know, it's not for intimate reasons."

The word 'intimate' struck a carnal nerve within Susan, and she wondered how uncomfortable Mitchell would be undressed in front of her. With that on her mind, she felt bolder than normal and changed the direction of their conversation.

"So, Mitchell, I know this question's coming from nowhere, but is it ... true what they say about black men? Or is it just talk?"

Mitchell's eyebrows furrowed. He almost choked on his drink once he realized what she was asking. He gave an embarrassed chuckle. Shrugging, he said, "I don't know. I can't speak for other men. With you being a doctor, you probably know more about that than I do."

"But I don't examine men. When you were in school and playing sports didn't you catch glimpses of the other guys in the shower?"

Mitchell smiled. In a communal shower with no stalls of course he'd caught glimpses of the other naked dudes. "Really wasn't checking out anybody else's family jewels."

"I'm almost embarrassed for asking you that, but for years I've heard you guys are supposed to have"—she made an aimless hand gesture—"you know, big, um, swipes."

Mitchell laughed, shaking his head. *Swipes*.

"The best way to really find out," she continued, "was to literally go to one of the sources. You're the lucky person." She smiled. "Hope you don't think I'm disgusting."

"Naw, you're alright. They say 'a closed mouth never gets fed.' A person's gotta ask about what they don't know. But like I said earlier, I can't speak for others; though I'm sure in some cases it's true. Sure all races have their fare share of men who're ... well endowed." He had to take the diplomatic route, hoping she'd end the subject.

"I wonder?"

Mitchell half expected her to ask if *he* was packing; thankfully the waitress came along and took their orders.

ഇരു

For a moment Jazelle was frozen stiff by the sight of him. It was Mitchell. She was surprised to see him. But was it jealousy gnawing at her because he was with a woman?

A white woman.

The feelings were alien to her, especially the possibility of being rubbed the wrong way about him being with a white lady. She'd never had any qualms with black men with white women. Not that she had ever been aware of. This was the first time she had experienced any negative reactions about it if that was the reason for her feeling pissed. But wouldn't it be hypocritical of her, being that *she* was there with a white friend?

Amanda noticed Jazelle's expression, immediately craned her neck to see what she was frowning at. "What is it, Jazelle?"

"Hunh?" Jazelle absently muttered, then blinked out of her stupor. She was instantly ashamed that she may be having prejudiced issues. "Oh, remember when I told you about my student—Mackenzee's brother?"

Amanda thought for a second. "Yeah, the one you thought was in high school?"

"Unh-hunh. That's him," Jazelle said, nodding in Mitchell's direction. "Mitchell is his name."

Amanda stole a look. "With the white lady?"

"Yes."

"I can't see his face well." Amanda got up.

"Amanda? Where are you going?"

"Be right back." She walked toward Mitchell and his companion.

Jazelle panicked. "Amanda, girl, what ...?" She hoped Amanda wasn't going over there. But she was. *Please don't let her say anything to him.*

Amanda came back to the table smiling mischievously. "You were right on the nail Jazelle, he is a cutie! Looks like somebody's little brother for sure, but very hot." She sat down. "How old did you say he is?"

Jazelle was shaking her head, slightly amused by what Amanda had just done. "I don't know for sure. Maybe nineteen?"

"You thought I was gonna say something to him, didn't you?" Amanda said. She saw Jazelle's expression when she came back to the table. "I just looked. But I don't believe he's nineteen ... more like sixteen, maybe seventeen? And that woman he's with, who's she?"

Jazelle wondered about that as well, though she hated to admit it. Suddenly a crazy notion started swimming around in her head. *Maybe Mitchell is a gigolo or something? It's obvious that woman he's with is older and looks financially able to afford those types of services. That's probably how he makes the money to buy those expensive gifts he gets his folks.*

"Jazelle, you should go over and speak to him," Amanda said.

Jazelle frowned. "For what?" Her heart was speeding for some reason.

"I dunno," Amanda shrugged, "to say hello. To be nosy and see what he's up to with that older woman. Aren't you curious?"

"No." She lied. "It's not like I know the boy that well or anything."

"Something about seeing him struck a nerve," Amanda reasoned matter of fact. She noticed how he grabbed Jazelle's attention; like she'd seen someone who had returned from the dead.

"It's just that his being with that woman incites questions I've been wondering about him." Jazelle explained the suspicions she had about Mitchell and how Mackenzee could be affected, though that wasn't what was actually bothering her at the moment. But she wasn't about to admit the jealousy she was feeling over seeing Mitchell with that woman.

She forced herself to eat, maintaining a calm demeanor. The whole time, Mitchell being with that woman nagged her.

15

"Come on in," Susan told Mitchell as she walked across the sparkling wood floor to hang her keys on hooks attached to a board which read: NO MISPLACED KEYS HERE. "Look around," she said taking his jacket and hanging it on a coat rack. "I need to get out of these heels."

Susan's home was a spacious downtown condominium. Mitchell walked in, appraising. He could see himself having a crib like it in Tulsa for when he came to town. Although nicely and tastefully furnished, he thought her dark furniture had too much of a masculine appeal for a woman's place. He eased his way from the living room into a room made into a den. A big screen TV and the bookshelves lining the wall all the way around caught his eye. He liked the set up of the room. The bookshelves contained many medical text books, a nominal selection of fiction, and at least half a shelf of gay/lesbian literature. He scanned that shelf closely, seeing titles covering rearing and raising children in a gay/lesbian household. He didn't think much of it, figuring Susan was likely staying informed about the subject for her patients' benefits.

"Mitchell, would you like a drink?" he heard Susan ask as he was digging an appealing crystal collection which made him think of the play, "The Glass Menagerie." Only these weren't just small figurines, but artfully detailed, seven-inch statuettes. His mama would love these, he knew, because he liked them, and they had similar taste in certain things.

"Mitchell?" Susan called out again. "How 'bout a drink?"

Mitchell knew she was offering alcohol. Even when it was recreational drinking, he had never understood why people easily drank something that didn't taste worth a damn and burned your throat all at once. He had no love for that *sauce*, as he called it. "Oh, I'm sorry Susan, I was captivated by your crystal," he answered, raising his voice for her to hear him. "I'll take a glass of OJ if you have it. I'm not much into alcoholic beverages if that's what you're hinting at."

"No OJ. What about tea?"

"That's fine."

When he made his way back to the living room Susan was at the stereo putting on some music. "Like jazz, Mitchell?"

"Sure." Jazz was good to chill and relax to, but he'd never purchased any. He was mostly into Hip-Hop and R&B.

He thanked Susan when she handed him the tea, fully aware that whatever she was drinking was laced.

He heard the base guitar and instantly recognized it was the homeboy Wayman Tisdale sounding through the speakers. Since Wayman was a T-Town legend, Mitchell had been meaning to buy all his CD's, but hadn't gotten around to it. He made a note on his cell to stop at Starship Records before he left town to pick up whatever they had available of the late WT.

Susan sipped her drink, closed her eyes, taking on a rapturous expression, and began swaying her narrow body to the music.

"So, what you think?" she asked, making a sweeping spread of her hands.

Looking at her now, it was the first time Mitchell had wondered why Susan was single. They had talked about numerous things, even his non-romantic life, but nothing had been discussed about her romantic life. Since he wasn't interested anyway, he hadn't asked. She was successful, decent looking, independent, smart as hell, and from what he could tell, would be a great catch for some worthy man. Plus she was minus any little rug-rats.

"Think about what?" he asked.

She tilted her head, making a wry expression. "My place, silly."

"Ohhh," Mitchell chuckled. "Nice. Comfortable. Cozy ... but not as feminine as I'd expect a woman's home to be. Classy though."

"Hmmm." Susan looked at him, pretending to be hurt. "I don't know whether to be offended or accept some of that as a compliment."

Grinning, Mitchell traced the sign of the cross over his chest with his free hand. "Promise it was a compliment."

It was only a quarter to nine, and since clubs usually started jumping after eleven or so, they had time to burn before getting ready. Subtly gyrating and sipping on her drink, Susan was debating when to make her move. She had him where she wanted him, but felt slightly reluctant. This was the first time in her life she'd done something so cunning. Being the product of a Catholic upbringing, she'd mostly walked a straight line, done what was expected of her; the perfect child afraid to do anything that would cause God or her strict parents to look down on her. Up until her college days she'd attended church regularly, and remained a virgin until marriage. That marriage ended because the wonderful man she married turned out to be controlling, possessive, and overbearing. Not so wonderful after all. In the beginning she believed that was how husbands were supposed to be, and wives were supposed to be submissive. Oprah, magazines, other talk shows, books, and living with that male chauvinist pig changed that rationale. Then she found out he'd had a mistress throughout the marriage, and the resulting divorce was the first time she had gone against the grain. She felt bad about defying the Catholic Church, but to hell with that, she decided. She got out. Once she gained her independence, she realized she had been living in a cocoon, dumbfounded as to the ways of the real world, especially men's imprudence. She had been brainwashed in regards to them. She went on to do some stuff neither her parents nor God approved of, but none of that included deceiving anyone.

She wasn't sure if her conscience could stand up to what she had planned for Mitchell.

Attempting to build up her nerves, she shot-gunned the remainder of the brandy, smoothly backhanded the residual wetness from her lips and hoped that display wasn't too un-lady-like.

The smooth warmth of the liquor sliding down her throat seemed to jolt her adrenaline. *What the hell*, she thought, feeling that she deserved to be a little naughty and live on the edge for once in her life. "Conscience, forgive me this one time," she whispered under her breath.

"Mitchell would you like to shower before you change clothes?" she asked aloud. "We have to share restrooms because the one in my room is being remodeled so it's out of order right now."

"Nah, you can go ahead, it'll take you longer to dress and prepare. It doesn't take me long to wash up and dress." He rubbed a hand over his jaw. "And my face is hairless, so I don't have to shave."

She narrowed her eyes, then teasingly, said, "Mitchell, is that a sexist statement?"

"Of course not," he defended, slightly grinning. "Women take longer in the bathroom. It's nothing new." He shrugged. "And since we aren't in a hurry, that'll give you plenty of time to do all that female junk you all do."

"I'd almost beg to differ, but I can tell you're being a gentleman." Her swaying was becoming more defined. She was into the smooth sounds of Tisdale. "And since courtesy is something we women don't get much of from you men these days, I'll let you off the hook."

After executing a ballerina-like flourish, she sashayed off. Mitchell used the opportunity to leaf through her CD's. The jazz had a melodic flow to it, and was too much on the romantic level. Though he doubted it, he wanted to see if she had any R&B with some up-tempo songs. He figured rap was unlikely; Susan wasn't the type.

He didn't find anything worthwhile and wished she had any of the classics by the King of Pop, but she didn't.

He decided to let the Jazz continue emitting its almost serene grooves when about fifteen minutes later Susan yelled, "It's all yours, Mitchell. The water's still nice and warm."

She had laid him out a wash cloth and towel, and though she assured him he could dress in the guest room, he debated taking his clothes and dressing in the bathroom after showering. He still felt a little awkward in a female's home.

From nowhere, a voice inside him said, *Man, what's your problem? What kind of man are you? Afraid of a little woman seeing you naked?* Then Charles calling him a sissy ran through his mind. Pride and ego forced him to undress down to his briefs, yank up the towel and wrap it around himself.

₧₧

Susan had gotten out of the shower and was peeking through her barely cracked bedroom door, waiting for Mitchell to go into the bathroom. After he went in she gently pushed the door closed, then easily pressed her back against it and sighed, her hand pressed to her pounding heart. It was thumping; nerves, adrenaline, and reluctance all balled up together. She had gotten a quick glimpse of his upper body unclothed. What she saw stirred the woman in her.

She threw on the most seductive garment she had: a skimpy red silk-satin negligee and matching gown that only snapped at the chest. Panties were excluded. She squirted Chanel on all her erogenous zones, and raked a finger through her hair, attempting to gain that feminine look of eroticism. After assessing herself in a full length mirror, she felt self-conscious about her thinness. It was a genetic trait; her mother was a small also. She couldn't really help it.

Minutes later, peeking through the slit in the door again, she watched Mitchell come out of the bathroom wrapped at the waist with the towel. The rivulets of water she glimpsed on his back were so sexy. Titillating. She felt her body temperature rising. Already felt *herself* getting wet.

Slowly, she counted to ten, inhaled deeply and exhaled before proceeding to do what would probably shock her guest stupid.

‪‬

Mitchell was slathering on some moisturizer when he spun around after sensing a presence coming up behind him. He encountered the most unexpected vision he could recall in a long, long time. Susan was coming toward him in a very provocative manner—movements and expression. She was thinner without clothes.

But Susan was still a woman.

A butt-the-fuck-naked woman under the negligee, he realized. He did a double-take after catching sight of the triangle of auburn hair down south as well as her small training-bra sized breasts with dark, perky nipples.

Has Susan lost her damn mind? What's she doing coming in here with ... without ...? He was almost unable to breathe, and got quieter than a dog walking through a Korean town. All he could do was swallow the fat lump forming in his throat.

Susan was convinced that no virile, heterosexual man in his right mind would be able to turn down what was basically free pussy on a platter. Married or otherwise. By nature it was impossible. Men were predators when it came to women and sex; to conquer was their thing.

Studying Mitchell, she saw shock in his eyes, but otherwise couldn't read him. She wondered what he was thinking. She mentally tried to map out the steps for seduction, but now realized, at this point, everything would have to be spontaneous. Improvised. She hadn't been with a man in over five years, and was lost with how to proceed. Her ex-husband had been the only man she had been with sexually; seduction had never been part of their routine.

She pleaded for her female instincts to guide her to the *promise land*.

Standing directly in front of Mitchell, she stared into his eyes. Her heart was pumping quickly. She wondered how he would react. Slowly, she moved her hand toward him, unsure if he'd reject her. Touching him soft as a feather, she glided her hand over his smooth, muscular pecs.

His eyes widened with … what? Surprise? Pleasure? Disapproval? She couldn't tell.

Mitchell flinched, but said nothing.

She felt his rapid heartbeat. His body was tense, yet motionless. Easily, she touched one of his nipples with the tip of a finger. He tensed up more, still said nothing.

With her other hand, she slowly began loosening the towel at his waist. He finally made his first motion to stop her, but before he could follow through with the meager, wordless protest, the towel fell to the carpet exposing his family jewels, and she swiftly grabbed his penis in a sensual, soft grip. It quickly got stiff, standing at complete attention. And … huge! Damn! Her curiosity about that black male stereotype was satisfied. For this particular black man, at least, it was definitely no myth.

Mitchell inhaled and gasped heavily, his head fell back as in defeat, his eyes shuttering.

Still, he was quiet.

Susan released her gaze on his face for the first time, allowing her eyes to roam lustfully over his body. He was an Adonis in the flesh. Every masculine inch of him.

Hell yes, he was a God.

She began planting gentle kisses, teases of the tongue from neck to shoulder. Shoulder to chest. Chest to navel. She felt the currents of electricity jilting through him as his mouth hung open, his eyes tightly closed.

It was intensely arousing.

His bland response, and absent protest still had her unsure.

Mitchell wanted to ask her what the hell she was doing. Push her away. But his tongue was tied, limbs immobile and powerless against the forces of feminine persuasion. She had no idea this was his first taste of any type of intimacy in months on top of months. That she was doing things inside him he didn't want to feel, and wasn't supposed to be feeling.

Yet, he was unable to stop her.

Susan slowly dropped to her knees, softly gripping the back of his toned thighs, lightly kissed his tip, licked around it. Measuring him, she slowly took him halfway in her mouth. His body tensed even more. She took him in as far as she could.

Mitchell gasped, drew in a deep, deep breath, squeezing his eyes shut in unbearable pleasure. *What ... is ... this woman doing ... to ... me?*

After years of celibacy he was too damn weak to fight the onslaught. With pleasures and sensations he had forgotten ever existed flowing through his vulnerable body, hell, he had no chance. He was gone.

Before being thrust into a trance-like state, he shuddered, and his knees buckled as he muttered, hissed, and cursed, then erupted like a volcano.

16

Jazelle entered her apartment and her emotions were tripping. She'd had a good time hanging out with Amanda, and they promised to do it again. She hoped Amanda and her husband were only going through one of those passing phases couples went through, and not headed to the marriage graveyard.

She prayed that her friend wouldn't have to ride that painfully rocky road.

She was still unable to shake the image of Mitchell with that woman. Though it was none of her business, though she had no idea what they had been doing together, or the nature of that relationship, she had jealous feelings. And that was crazy. Why would she even care what he was doing? Who he was spending time with?

Annoyed, she peeled off her jacket, flung it over the arm of the couch, flopped down on the couch and huffed. *Mitchell Thomas, why have you been fucking with my head, boy?*

Why?

She dug into the sack that held the paintings she'd bought earlier that day: an African king in his royal garb, another of his queen in her royal garb. She studied her mostly empty walls, trying to picture the perfect place to hang them. The walls were certainly in need of some art. It depressed her that she wasn't able to embellish her apartment like she wanted. When she and Dawn lived together their apartment was *boss* thanks to Dawn's parents. They had bought them new furniture, decorations, the works, but when Dawn moved out, the two friends decided she should take it all for when she got her own place. It was all in storage for now. Back then Jazelle was able to buy furniture and accessories, but it hadn't been necessary. Now she was broke as a joke because of debt, and couldn't afford to buy most of what she desired, so she worked with what she had. If not for the Rent-to-Own store, she'd probably be sitting and sleeping on the floor.

She hardly remembered a time when she wasn't struggling with some type of issue. Since her mother's death it had always been something. Back then it was emotional. She wanted her mama back. Then she went through adolescent growing pains; mainly coping with boys. Since Mamie wasn't having any of the boyfriend-girlfriend nonsense, she couldn't talk to her about it. Much of dating and relationships often encompassed what was learned from a role model, but since she really hadn't had a concerned adult for direction and guidance in that arena, she'd gone into the dating game clueless as a domesticated animal thrust into the wilderness. Her trials were always errors.

Now an adult, she was stacked with all the baggage she'd brought from childhood and then some. The only part of her life she wasn't struggling with was teaching. If not for that to clamp to, she'd probably go crazy or, she contemplated sadly, get twisted up like her mother and become submerged in a life of drugs and addiction.

Thankfully, she had so far bypassed the road her mother chose, refusing to be just another weak minded sista fitting the stereotypical description—high school drop-out, three or four baby daddies, on welfare living in public housing—that resulted from a dysfunctional childhood.

She was measuring by feel the right space for the paintings when she heard a knock at the door. Her watch said 9:45. She figured it was Dawn wanting to go clubbing again. *Maybe I will go out*, she pondered *if only to be around people*. She wasn't in one of those depressing moods tonight, but it could be a chance to end an okay day—even with that Mitchell image in her head—on a good note.

But when she cracked the door to the limit allowed by the chain and saw the face on the other side, she damn near slammed it.

Kevin!

The pit of her stomach started break dancing with hatred.

"*What the hell* do you want?" she asked sourly. "You got some damn nerve coming to my house again!" All the frustration and pain she was trying to put behind her because of him started rushing back to the front. She wished she could call up her brother and have him come open a can of whoop ass on Kevin's punk ass.

With the minimal glow from the porch light, she could see his hair was still cut close and full of waves, indicating his vanity was still intact. His shoulders were hunched forward, and he was blowing in his hands. The temperature had dropped and it was a little chilly. She wondered where his jacket or coat was, and why he wasn't wearing a hat. Unfortunately, his chocolate face was still fine. But he was still the same *dog* who had charmed her with his slickery, hurt her in more ways than just emotionally.

"Look, Jaz," he pleaded, shivering, looking jittery and nervous. "Can I come in? I need to talk to you. It'll only take a few minutes."

He must be outta his rabid mind! *What made him think I'd let him set foot in my damn house again*? "What do you want, Kevin?" she said, annoyed, not believing he had the audacity to show his face at her door.

"Jaz—"

"Don't call me Jaz. We are *not* cool like that!" She used to like when he called her that, but now, hearing him say it repulsed her. He wasn't worthy of resurrecting even a pinch of their past.

"A'ight, a'ight. Can I come in?" He kept peering over his shoulder mysteriously.

"Does dog shit smell like roses?"

"I know you're pissed—"

" 'Pissed?' " she echoed contemptuously, cutting him off. "That's not the half of it. And I'm not about to give you the satisfaction of rehashing it with you, so you might as well forget about coming in here! In fact, I don't know why I'm standing here talking to your worthless ass this long."

"Come on, Jazze—"

"'Bye Kevin! And don't come back. Matter of fact, make like a paper towel and wipe me completely out of your fucking mind." She easily closed the door in his face and waited for him to knock again. He didn't.

She had met Kevin at a fruit and vegetable stand of all places. He came up to her and said, "Yo' man is wrong for lettin' you out and about all alone." It was his smooth way of flirting, scheming to find out if she had a man. She'd thought the line corny but cute, and him funny. Attracted to his mixture of tall, dark, and fine to go along with his charm, she gave him the digits after he asked.

Many a woman had fallen for a fine, charming man, not realizing he was using those very devices to eventually get in the panties, and anything else a woman had or could access that would benefit him. Love and commitment weren't on their agendas. Kevin had been charming alright. Smooth. Smoothed his black ass into her life, home, and finances.

But never again, Mr. Ballard, she thought angrily. *I may have been a fool once, but your ass will never get to swindle this sista again, playa. Believe that.*

"Fuck you, Jazelle!" she heard him yell.

She went to her window and watched him walk until he was out of her view. She wished she could see the exit of the complex to see if he was leaving, but she didn't have that luxury. *Where is his car? Why is he on my side of town walking when he lived farther out north with his baby's mama? His damn problem*, she decided sensibly. *Do wrong to others best believe wrong will come back for compensation and kick you in the ass.*

She imagined something had to be up with him to have the gall to come to her apartment after the shit he'd done. She was relieved that she hadn't had to dial 911, but she had the phone ready just in case.

She ended up falling asleep on the couch with Kevin on her mind, but dreamed what was a strange nightmare for her, because in the dream, Mitchell married that white woman.

₞⌒

Mitchell woke up in a haze, yawning, and wearily rubbed his eyes. He felt so drained. Turning to glimpse at the digital clock on the nightstand next to his bed, it wasn't there. *What the ...? This isn't my bed! It's too soft.* Then he realized he was lying on and covered by ... silk? Satin? Something unfamiliar. The room was dark, and smelled of a woman. And ... sex.

He began adjusting to the darkness somewhat, mainly because shallow light from the hallway was seeping into the room. A toilet flushed, and it blanched him into reality. *I'm at Susan's place.* Everything that occurred after she alighted from her room in a skimpy negligee and stalked toward him with feline sultriness flooded his memory.

Shiiiit! What have I done? The moments of untamed sex struck him with two hundred volts of guilt. After Susan had orally uncorked him, she led him to her room like a puppy on a leash. From there it was like he'd been hypnotized, acquiescing to her desires like a robot instructed to do exactly as programmed. It had been mind boggling and feral. Susan may be a thin woman, but *damn*, she had more energy than a utility company, triathlon stamina, and was freaky-deaky adventurous. She used her tongue and fingers in ways he never imagined.

He moved to sit up and winced. It was aches and pains from what Susan had unleashed on him. She virtually wore his black ass out. Devoured him like a hostage who got fed after being starved for weeks.

Damn. He almost felt like he'd been abused.

Susan stepped in the room and saw he was sitting up. She illumined the touch-lamp on the nightstand with a soft touch of her hand.

"Morning," she said gleefully. She was wrapped in a chenille robe, sipping coffee from a mug.

Mitchell felt ashamed. Embarrassed. Stricken with guilt.

"What time is it?" he asked, sounding raspy.

"About four-fifty."

" 'Four-fifty?' " he gasped incredulously. How had it gotten so late? They had been getting ready to go to the club when ...

He looked away, remembering.

Even after the physical night she'd had, Susan was up and energized. Great sex was invigorating. She had to be at the hospital by 6 A.M. for fill-in rounds for a colleague. She and Mitchell had dallied in horizontal recreation for almost two hours, but she'd managed nearly four good hours of sleep. For a doctor used to being on call at all hours of the day, that was plenty.

Surely was earned.

She explained to Mitchell why she was up so early, asked if he wanted breakfast or coffee. Mitchell, in his reserved state again, turned down the offer, only wanting to shower, but was reluctant to get out of bed in the nude, fearing she'd try to seduce him for another round of sexscapades.

Susan sensed Mitchell's reluctance. "Something wrong, Mitchell? I know it's early, but I get the sense you're bothered."

Mitchell ran a weary hand over his face, feeling awkward and self-conscious about sitting up in this woman's bed, naked. "I didn't expect what happened tonight to happen," he admitted, scanning the room for his clothes. Then he remembered they were in the living room. So was the towel he had been wrapped in.

Susan had no idea what to expect either, but she'd hoped for what happened.

"Well, you do recall that I made sure we were protected, right?" She put that in figuring that might be what was bothering him.

"Yeah, right," he murmured. However, the two condoms they'd used were the furthest things from his mind.

"Mitchell, I was married once, right after completing my undergraduate degree." His expression conveyed a speck of surprise. "During those years, I'd never had a night quite like this. Not even close."

He recognized she was giving him his props. Complimenting him. But learning he had upstaged her ex sexually wasn't stroking his ego. He wished he could wipe out what had happened. Travel back in time to before the auction and eliminate his name from the entire program. But the marriage revelation was surprising.

"You were married?"

Susan gave him excerpts of her history up to the divorce that was so heartbreaking. Then she made an admission which tripped Mitchell out.

"Something else you're not aware of Mitchell, is that ... that I found comfort in another woman some years following my divorce."

Mitchell's eyes widened, his mouth parted momentarily. He thought about the gay/lesbian books on her bookshelves. Was she trying to tell him she was lesbian?

She recognized the inquisitive expression.

"Yep, I've been in a lesbian relationship the past three years." She motioned toward a Polaroid shot wedged in the dresser mirror. "That's her: Rachel."

Mitchell squinted, but without his glasses couldn't see the picture clearly. Though she'd already seen him naked, he still wasn't about to get out of the bed for a closer look. But her disclosure had gained his interest, momentarily steering his mind off his guilt.

"Y'all still seeing each other?"

"Well ... it's a tangled situation." She had strife in her eyes as she pulled on some pants. "I'm not gay, first of all. Sounds crazy that I've been sleeping with another woman for a while, but claiming not to be gay, huh?"

Mitchell had heard about straight women finding emotional solace with another woman after getting dusted by men, which eventually lead to physical comfort as well. Women understood women and could relate, unlike a man. But he wondered if Susan had always felt an attraction to women, or if she'd been pushed forward because of the pain her ex had caused her.

Not his business, though, so he didn't ask.

"Rachel has been aware and comfortable with her sexuality since adolescence," Susan went on. "She claims she'd known she liked women since her Barbie doll playing days. Said she never dated a man, never had sex with one. She felt she'd be being false with herself if she did."

Intrigued, Mitchell listened.

Susan said, "She came along when I was vulnerable and lonely." She began putting on a front snapping bra. "Our offices were housed in the same building—she manages a temporary employment service—and we eventually began doing lunch together, then dinner and other leisure and recreational activities women do. I'd learned about her sexual orientation after our third or fourth lunch together, but it didn't scare me off because I had lesbian patients."

She walked to the mirror, pulled the picture and handed it to Mitchell. Both women were on it. Rachel was a brunette, and appeared to be near Susan's height, but *butch* looking.

Susan said, "Besides, she was a good listener, sympathetic, and I felt comfortable with the friendship we'd developed. One day I asked her over for dinner. She'd never suggested or intimated anything other than friendship, so I had no reason to think otherwise. Plus, she was seeing someone at the time. But that night, while we were sipping on cocktails, talking, listening to jazz ... out of nowhere it happened." She was quiet for a moment. Reflecting. "She kissed me, and ... somehow, it felt so good. Compared to what I'd remembered with my husband, it made me tingle inside."

Her husband must've sucked, Mitchell thought.

"And it had been eons since I'd felt any intimacy. Felt wanted."

I know the feeling. Then, regretfully he thought, *until ...*

He drowned the thoughts, not wanting to think about what he'd allowed to happen with Susan.

"She made me feel reborn," Susan continued. "Pleasured me that night in ways I could only fantasize about. I may as well have been a virgin. Afterwards, I was ashamed and embarrassed that I'd felt so good from those acts with a woman. But Rachel convinced me there was nothing to be ashamed of.

"Still, there was a not-so-good aspect: I had to be secretive and hide the relationship. My parents would've never accepted it."

"Yeah, lotta parents wouldn't," Mitchell finally said. "Wouldn't *even* believe it." He figured there was something about Susan when he first met her, but wasn't able to put his finger on it. Now he knew.

Susan said, "So finally, about a month and a half ago, after months of internal conflict, I told her I wanted to break it off. I felt there was no future in it for me. Though she was good for me in some ways, I was—am still—too attracted to men. Plus I was tired of vibrators and dildos. I had been yearning for the real thing after learning how good it could be." She looked at Mitchell with a wistful smile. "And thanks to you, I have a ray of hope that Mr. Right is still out there somewhere."

Mitchell smiled sheepishly.

Susan kept on going like an energizer battery. "She'd influenced me to a point where I was thinking more man-like— hairstyles, dress code, even decorating this place—but she taught me to be uninhibited, explorative, and in essence, showed me a different side of femininity. That's where I got the confidence to go after you, and for what happened with you and me. Before her, I was a dud. Prude as could be. Timid and dull sexually because my ex never took the time to show me anything."

She waited for a comment from Mitchell. Nothing came.

"Mitchell, in case you're wondering why I'm telling you my history, I sense that you're conflicted with some ... confusing feelings," she explained, looking sympathetic. "Last night when, you know ..."

Mitchell caught on to what she was implying and gaped at her with a frown. "You think I'm gay?"

"Well, you—"

"Wrong answer, Susan!" he said, consternation all over his face. "Nope, I'm not a fairy—excuse the choice of words, nothing personal. Yeah, something is bothering me, but it's difficult for me to talk about. I know it's obvious that I'm a little flaky, but I have my reasons."

Susan realized she had offended him and expressed her sorrow for the insinuation, but wondered what was tearing at him.

Mitchell jumped up, clutching the sheet raggedly around him. "And hell naw, it hasn't a damn thing to do with another man." He looked her straight in the eyes. "Susan, best believe I'm one hundred percent Mandingo."

Susan could fully believe he wasn't gay, or bi. He had sexually contradicted it; defied the sexual conduct of a gay man as far as she was concerned. She didn't think a gay man would give a second thought to sleeping with a woman. A bi, yes, but not a gay. She felt bad for even considering that of him.

Mitchell tromped to the living room, snatched up the underwear and clothes he had intended to put on before Susan re-routed their evening. Susan followed him, trying to apologize, but he kept moving.

In the shower he let the water pelt against him. Soothe his embattled conscience and emotions. But unwillingly his thoughts played dirty, replayed how he had succumbed to the sensations Susan sent streaking through his body as she baptized him with her mouth. How, like a building gone up in flames, he collapsed, fell into the sexual foray, losing all restraint to the pleasures that had been unknown to him for so long. Then, Susan murmuring, "Ooooh, yes, that's *it*, Mitchell," in the way some horny, good-feeling women were known to do when they were on fire with passion, hummed its echo, causing him to squeeze his eyes closed.

It hadn't been right for him to enjoy what he had done. The guilt ate at him; had him feeling shitty like a teenage girl after losing her virginity.

He tried to scrub the smell and residue of sex, and of Susan, from his body.

17

The sounds of the Tulsa State Fair flooded the atmosphere, and Jazelle and Dawn walked, soaking up the excitement. Swarms huddled around the game booths, watching and cheering. Queues of eager young kids and overgrown kids flanked the rides. Anticipating the temperature dropping once night crept in, Jazelle was dressed in a leather coat, the jeans and sweatshirt she'd purchased the previous weekend with Amanda, and some comfortable ankle boots. Dawn was dressed similarly.

Jazelle was hyped. She always looked forward to the fair, because she didn't get to attend for years after her mother died. Mamie wouldn't waste her money on what she called an overpriced rip-off. Jazelle was seventeen when she was finally able to attend the fair again. She never wanted to miss it again. "Come on Dawn, let's get some tickets," she said anxiously when they were near a ticket booth. "Then we can grab something to eat, 'cause those corn dogs are calling a sista."

They purchased a few tickets to share since neither was brave enough to ride anything that left the ground. Minutes later they were buying foot long corn dogs, and lemonades.

"Dawn, I could just hug your mama to death every time I think about her bringing me back to the fair," Jazelle said. The time Dawn's mother had brought her was her fondest memory of the fair next to the last time she came with her own mama.

"Mama still talks about that too," Dawn said.

Jazelle bit into the corndog as they left the vendor and closed her eyes with delight as she swallowed. "Mmm. That's the best taste in the world, girl. I know now, since I was never big on the rides, this"—she instinctively shook the corndog—"is what I missed the most when Mamie wouldn't let us come. Fair corndogs have always been the bomb."

"You ain't never lied, girl," Dawn co-signed, swiping mustard from the rim of her lips with her tongue before dabbing it with a napkin. "Think they use Jiffy to make 'em with?"

Jazelle shrugged. The cup of coke was upturned to her mouth.

"I don't know, but this batter is what makes 'em so good ... kinda sweet, and feels like it just dissolves in your mouth."

They walked a little ways, finishing their eats, then decided the bumper cars would be their first ride since they were safe and earthbound. They waited in line about ten minutes with a bunch of surprisingly patient kids, and once their turn came, they hurried into a car each and, once started, repeatedly rammed into each other, laughing and giggling like all the kids around them.

Afterwards, while they walked and contemplated their next move, Jazelle saw a teenage interracial couple holding hands, looking so much in love and carefree. It stirred up thoughts of Mitchell and his *Miss Pale and Frail* at the restaurant, but she quickly shook it off. *Young, dumb, and in love*, she thought when they passed the couple. She wondered if she would ever walk the fairgrounds hand in hand with a boyfriend, fiancé, or husband. So far, since she had matured to a dating age, she had never walked hand in hand with any male other than her students.

Dawn nudged her, gesturing at a dart throwing booth. Neither woman was great at any of the games, but they usually won a little something popping the balloons, so they stopped and tried their luck.

Both won a little stuffed lizard no bigger than the size nine boots they were wearing, and quickly moved on because the attendant tried to persuade them to keep trying for a bigger prize. But they weren't about to waste twenty dollars or more for a damn stuffed animal.

"These fair workers sho' got game, Jaz," Dawn said, rolling her eyes at a booth attendant motioning for them to come try a game neither had a chance at winning. "They'll try their damnedest to talk somebody into blowing their hard earned money for one of those cheap ass stuffed toys that probably cost less than two dollars to make."

Jazelle recollected Mamie calling the fair a rip-off.

"Yeah, they'll definitely get you if you let them. But people need to know when to quit. Can't be a damn fool and just give all your money away." *Mamie was frugal anyway. Plus she would've concocted any excuse not to bring us to the fair.* "But Dawn, I wanna win one of those big ones," she said in a girls voice. "We've never won anything big."

Jazelle still had a desire to put a few of the large stuffed animals in her bedroom, along with each of the small one's she had won over the years which were similar to what she had just won.

"I do too," Dawn admitted. "But we ain't spending all our dead prez's just to come up with"—she thumped the little lizard she just won—"one of these puny ass things. Wonder if we flirted with one of these men working these booths, would they let us buy one for a li'l or nothin'?"

Jazelle laughed. "Girl ... hell-to-the-no. You remember we tried to buy one before."

"I know, but that's when we were teenagers. Titties were still miniature peaks,"—she struck a pose, swept her hands over her body symbolic of a model modeling an outfit, moving the leather jacket to the side to show off her butt and luscious body—"and didn't have all this heeuh."

Dawn was about a neck shorter than Jazelle, pecan complexion, with straight chin length, gold colored hair, curled inward at the ends. She had a wicked body that men lusted for. As she posed, two teenage boys walked by gawking, and almost bumped into somebody. Jazelle cracked up at them. *That's what they get for lusting.*

The basketball shoot then attracted Jazelle's attention because of the large prizes. She stared wistfully. Neither she nor Dawn could shoot a lick of basketball. "Dang, Dawn, why didn't we ever learn how to play basketball?" she said rhetorically. "One shot in and you win. One, girl."

Dawn absently nodded, watching some husky Latino dude trying his luck. He couldn't even hit the damn rim. Though the rims were purposely warped, making it difficult to make a basket, it could be done.

They were standing there, watching people constantly missing, when they heard a little voice yelling, "Miss Johnson!"

Jazelle whirled her head toward the yells. She instantly smiled. Her favorite student was quickly coming toward her.

"Miss Johnson, I knew that was you," Mackenzee said, slightly out of breath, breathing hard from running to her teacher.

"Hi, Mackenzee," Jazelle said. She was about to ask Mackenzee where her mother was when Gwen appeared, followed by a small entourage. Looking beyond them, she specifically took notice of one individual.

Mitchell.

She frowned non-perceptively, quickly focused on the others—Carla, Quincy, three boys she presumed were their sons because they resembled Quincy, and Montell, whose face she remembered from the game on TV that Sunday. They were all wearing starter jackets. She figured she would possibly run into some of her students, but running into Mackenzee and her family with Mitchell in tow hadn't crossed her mind. Seeing him sort of riled her, because the image of him and his *Miss Pale and Frail* was still fresh in her mind.

She spoke to the group. Introduced Dawn.

Dawn leaned over to Jazelle and whispered, "That's the little girl you like, ain't it?" Jazelle nodded. "When you said her name it rang a bell. Is one of those boys the brother you told me about?"

"Un-hunh. The one in back with his cap turned sideways." Jazelle noticed that, unlike last weekend, Mitchell was back into his hip-hop dress code.

"Hmmm-unhh ... his young ass could cause *Michelle* to wanna step out on President Obama, girl," Dawn said, drooling. "I can see why your mind be trying to rob the cradle. If I was about seven years younger, I'd hook his young ass. Have 'im sprung on Miss Dawn."

Jazelle softly bumped Dawn with her hip, shaking her head, halfway grinning. "You're a hot ass mess, girl."

"Miss Johnson," Gwen said as they caught up to Mackenzee, "I don't know how Mac knew that was you in this crowd of folks, but she was right."

Jazelle smiled, holding Mackenzee's hand. "How long have you all been here, Mac?"

"We just got here," Mac answered.

Terrence and Rodney were itching to go attack the rides, and were tugging at their parents to get the fun jumping off. Jazelle felt the same eagerness in Mackenzee.

"So, what're you riding first, Mackenzee?"

₧₨

Glad he wasn't right near Jazelle, Mitchell covertly looked at her. After last weekend, females were on his *avoid* list. He hadn't forgotten the affect she had on him at Mac's school, or G-Lady's party. He had been in the dumps all week with guilt eating away at him like maggots on a decomposed body. The tryst with Susan had caused him the type of contrition felt after doing something so wrong that being removed from the face of the planet seemed like the only reasonable punishment. Time after time he'd heard the general consensus of women that men had no feelings, and were incapable of expressing emotions; men were not sensitive, and couldn't care less about hurting others; when it came to sex, had no problems boning one female then going on to another; even if they had a steady woman, had no shame or guilt about sexual conquest after conquest.

Well, he must be an anomaly or something, or have inherited too many effeminate traits, because he was so messed up by the sexscapades with Susan, that he was unable to forgive himself. He had become more withdrawn than normal, and everyone at the office wondered why he was being so incommunicado. Travis had broadcast the news of the auction, but Mitchell had been rather dismissive about his theatrics on stage, getting the high bid, and certainly the outcome of the date. Travis and Katie had questioned him the entire ride back to Norman to no avail. He only downplayed the date, telling them he had an okay time.

It was tearing at him. Not only had he let things go too far with Susan but, whether he wanted to admit it or not, he realized he had enjoyed it.

He wondered what kind of person he was. What about his promise? How could he let what had happened happen?

Tired of the questions and unwanted attention at work, he took off Wednesday, and decided to break for the remainder of the week. Since it was Fair season it was a good time to hang out with family for a distraction from his guilt.

His enthusiasm for the fair hadn't dissipated from when he was a little crumb snatcher. For him, the amusement was contagious. But he had not considered running into Miss John— Jazelle. Just his damn luck. Like when he had last seen her, she was looking good. Her friend had it going on as well, he noted. He remembered her from G-Lady's party, though he never met her that night; Jazelle had only pointed her out on the dance floor.

He sighed, looked at his sister's irresistible face as she stood by Jazelle. No matter how miserable he was on the inside, seeing her enthusiasm, along with his little cousins', was more than enough ammunition to dismiss the misery for the time being. Their excitement rubbed off on him, so he cheered up.

Feeling the kids' anxiety, he said, "Come on y'all," pointing at the basketball shoot. "Quincy, Li'l Q, Monty, let's see who can make the first shot this year. Q, you go last since you won last year."

"Can I shoot too, daddy?" Terrence begged.

"Me too?" Rodney followed.

"That's all y'all men know—always trying to have a damn contest," Carla complained.

"Like y'all women don't," Quincy challenged.

"Miss Johnson, you comin' with us?" Mackenzee asked.

Mitchell feared his sister would ask her that. He hoped Jazelle said *no*.

"Yeah," Gwen joined her daughter. "You and your friend might as well hang out with us."

Jazelle looked at Dawn, who shrugged and said, "Fine by me."

"Alright." Jazelle gently squeezed Mackenzee's hand. "Guess we're hanging with the crew, Mac."

Mackenzee's dimples flexed. "Yesss."

Damn! Mitchell thought.

Before anybody shot, Mitchell pulled out a wad of money. He had intended to separate two hundred dollars from the stash ahead of time, but forgot. He felt the eyes beam in on all the *cheddar*.

"Yesterday was pay day," he said defensively, lying, but slightly smirking. He could imagine what his mama was thinking, but it was the fair, and he had to make sure there was plenty of money for them to have hella fun. "Who wanna shoot first?"

Jazelle frowned, hissing under her breath. That roll of money convinced her he was nothing more than another neighborhood thug.

The fellows each took a shot and missed. The women and three little kids were cheering them on. Second time around, Monty and Quincy badly missed. Li'l Q's circled the rim before falling off the side, and everyone *awww'd* disappointedly.

Mitchell stepped up for his second shot. "That first one was practice, this's for you, Miss Mac." He winked at his sister and released a high arcing shot. The ball rattled the rim, danced for a second, and went through the nets. "Wet," he boasted.

The kids yelped and cheered, jumping up and down, and when Mitchell asked the attendant to give Mackenzee the big red tiger, her dimples deepened happily. He made two more and gave Terrence and Rodney the stuffed animal they chose because they were complaining about Mackenzee getting something but not them. Quincy made a shot, but Monty and Li'l Q kept bricking.

During his shots, Mitchell had felt Jazelle's eyes glowering at him. When he subtly glanced her way, she wore a serious expression. He wondered if that was her way of willing him to make the shot.

Since everyone wanted to ride different things, everyone branched off into different directions. Dawn saw a guy she knew with a couple of his friends and broke away to kick it with them for a while. Jazelle stayed with Mitchell, Gwen and Mackenzee and they headed to a rollercoaster, because Mac had been talking about it since they loaded up to come to the fair.

For someone scared to sleep in her own room alone, Mitchell couldn't comprehend Mac's lack of fear for the rollercoaster. She had ridden it for the first time the year before and loved it. Mitchell looked at his sister as they walked in the direction of the ride, wondering how kids could be such contradictions.

Jazelle wanted no parts of a rollercoaster, and was adamant about not riding. However, she was getting some strong cajoling from Mac. With a puppy dog expression, she pleaded, "Come on, Miss Johnson, I'm riding, and I'm a little girl. It's fun. And you can ride with Mitchee. He won't let nothin' happen to you."

Mitchell and Jazelle exchanged dubious glances.

Unlike normal, Jazelle paid no mind to Mac's faulty grammar, feeling apprehensive and cornered by this little girl she was crazy about. Riding anything that lifted her too high from mother earth had been a no-can-do ever since she rode the Ferris wheel as a little girl. She had screamed at the top of her lungs, and cried like a baby in search of a nipple swelling with milk when it had ascended her closer to God's crib than she wanted to be. She rode basic, on-the-ground rides now.

How could she explain to Mac that her teacher was nothing but a big chicken?

Mitchell considered protesting. He had no desire to be paired with Jazelle in any form or fashion. But that sounded sissified and punkish, so he'd let it ride. Besides, when it came to his little sister, he generally incarcerated his feelings. Locked them up like a repeat offender. Unless it was something outlandish, what little sis wanted, little sis usually got.

Damn!

Mitchell said, "Miss Johnson, I assume you're probably scared." He gestured at Gwen. "She used to be scared too."

"Sho' the hell was," Gwen co-signed. "Use'ta couldn't pay me to get on that damn thang. Last year I only got on 'cause this girl"—she gestured at Mackenzee while frowning good-naturedly—"cried for me to ride wit' her. It still scares the hell outta me, but it is fun."

Jazelle smiled a bit, but was quiet. Contemplating. She wanted to bite her fingernails like she did as a child when she was nervous or scared. She watched the present group of jubilant riders screaming, yelling, and stretching their arms up high, waving with excitement.

She glanced at Mackenzee, then back at the rollercoaster. *How did I get in this shit?*

"Ohh ... alright." She was scared as hell.

Being concerned about the rollercoaster, she unconsciously abandoned her anger toward Mitchell. Fear had invaded her space, usurped all previous resolve. Mitchell would have to help her through this rollercoaster ride.

When they were about to climb into the cart behind Mackenzee and Gwen, she whispered, "I don't think I can do this, Mitchell."

Mitchell was amused by her frightened expression. He almost smiled but held off. "It won't be that bad, Miss Jo—JJ." He unconsciously used her initials after remembering she had told him not to be so formal with her. "It'll be over before you know it."

She paid no attention to him calling her JJ. When the ride began moving, she looked like a cat about to be thrown into water, and was ready to shriek and leap out of the cart, but the bar had her secured in the seat.

On the first curve she clung to Mitchell like they were in love. It wouldn't be until a future moment when she would remember the delicious scent of his 212 cologne. When they plunged into the first downward dive, her screaming and yelling was reminiscent of her childhood ride on the Ferris wheel, and she gripped Mitchell so tightly she was on the verge of ripping his jacket.

She inhabited that safe harbor for the remainder of the ride.

Mitchell yelled and threw his arms in the air, feeling the thrills along with the other enthusiastic fools. Even with her almost in his lap with her face burrowed into his neck, he allowed the rush in the pit of his belly to beam him to the high that rollercoaster's took their thrill-hitchhikers. Amazingly, the way Jazelle was congesting his space wasn't the least bit cumbersome.

When the ride finally halted, he gently tapped her to let her know her reality nightmare was over. Warily and slowly, Jazelle raised her head. *We really have stopped. I'm safe now*, she thought, realizing she was still living and in one piece.

She peered at Mitchell expecting a teasing expression to be staring at her.

It wasn't.

What she saw in those below-the-surface-sad-browns wasn't mockery; wasn't one of those smug adolescent contortions she expected from a male, and she was shocked.

Aware of her grip on his jacket, she quickly released it, and looked away self-consciously. Embarrassed. She knew she had been looking like a pure monkey's ass on the rollercoaster. She felt like the most pathetic woman in the world. Thank goodness Mac had ridden the cart in front of her, and hadn't seen how big of a coward her teacher was.

Startling her, Mitchell extended his hand to help her out of the cart. The unexpected chivalry would pop up in her mind at a future date.

"See there," Mitchell said when she was on her feet, "it wasn't that bad."

Relieved to be on firm ground, Jazelle blushed, exhaled, thinking: *I can't tell. I was stuck to you like you were my daddy protecting me.*

"Miss Johnson, wasn't that fun?" Mackenzee sang. "I wanna ride again, Mama!"

"Naw, girl," Gwen interjected. "We goin' somewhere else. Know I'm goin' to get me somethin' to eat."

"Aww, mama, one more time?"

"No, girl. We'll come back a li'l later."

Mackenzee wore a dejected frown, but moved on with her mama. Mitchell retrieved Mackenzee's stuffed animal, which he'd left with the attendant, and he and Jazelle followed.

Jazelle said, "Mitchell, if you all come back, I won't be joining. I still can't believe I let that girl talk me into riding in the first place. I'm not ashamed to admit I'm a big chicken. Tell me to chirp and flap my damn arms like one, and I sure in the hell will."

Mitchell laughed. "I feel ya. It's actually the most intense ride I'll get on. I'm not brave enough to ride any of the other adventure rides. Leavin' 'em for the nutty people. Plus I'll be calling earl if I ride the ones that go round and round and get you dizzy. I'd throw up right on the spot."

"Even the Himalaya?"

"Yep. It got me when I was little. Soon as I got off, corn dogs, funnel cake—whatever else I'd eaten came right outta me. Haven't been on it since."

Jazelle made a face.

As they headed to a feeding spot, they looked up at some frightened little girl on the sky ride, screaming to get off. She was *stuck like chuck* till her transport reached its destination, though. The scene brought back memories of the Ferris wheel ride when she was little, which Jazelle told Mitchell about. While Gwen and Mac remained ahead of them, they pointed out rides they wouldn't dare get on, how people where crazy for riding them. Other than those skits of dialogue, Mitchell said little else, and Jazelle thought about how aloof he was, but also how mature he seemed to be for his age—whatever it actually was—and how delicious he looked. She wished she was younger, because she would be getting her flirt on, trying to come on to Mr. Too Young For Her Now, since back then she didn't have it in for the gender that she and other women equated with the four legged animals known to dig up bones.

Wondering about Dawn, Jazelle periodically scanned the crowds looking for her, wondering if Dawn had enticed ole boy into winning a large stuffed animal. If Dawn showed up toting one, she'd be jealous. She looked at Mackenzee's big tiger.

"Mitchell, I've wanted to win something that size since I was little, but never have."

"A stuffed animal?" Mitchell said, gesturing at the tiger.

"Unh-hunh. My game playing skills are garbage."

Mitchell chuckled. "I got you covered Miss—Jazelle," he said impulsively. Then quickly scolded himself for speaking without thinking.

Jazelle looked at him quizzically "You're going to win another one? For me?"

"Fo' sho," he said confidently.

"How do you know you can?"

Mitchell looked at her dubiously, grinning crookedly. "Cause my name is Mi-tchell. That's what I do."

Jazelle thought he was so cute the way he said that.

18

Heading home, Jazelle figured the world must be ending. A man had actually kept his word. From the passenger seat in Dawn's car, Jazelle turned and looked at the two stuffed animals that Mitchell had won, sitting in the back seat like passengers. He said he'd win one for her and had stayed true to his word.

She smiled. He was still puzzling, though; different than other youngsters his age in the most subtle of ways. The parts about him she didn't know were what categorized him with other guy's she'd known. Seeing him with that woman ... the wad of money he pulled out at the fair assured her of that. He was renting time from an illusionary lifestyle. *Tick tock, tick tock before the cell block locked.*

She still couldn't understand why it mattered. Why he was such an issue for her.

"Dawn, since you're supposed to be a—what would be the opposite of womanizer?" Dawn could supposedly read men like a book, but Jazelle couldn't think of the appropriate label for Dawn. Dawn had played her share of brothers; broke many a heart. She was infamous for kicking it with many a dude, leading them to a place called *nowhere*, and then handing out walking papers like they were leaflets for an upcoming party. Only the leaflets said: *Go wherever you like, but get the hell on out of my life.*

" 'Womanizer?' " Dawn asked, not comprehending as she steered with one hand, lightly patting her thigh to the beat of the music playing with the other.

"Women who play men," Jazelle made clear.

"Oh. *Me*. Miss Dawn Rashawn Lovelace." She chuckled. "A-K-A Lady Mac."

Jazelle laughed. "Okay, Miss Mac Mama. What did you think about Mitchell?" She tried to sound indifferent.

"Other than how cute the boy is?"

Over the last month Jazelle had mentioned Mitchell more than the number of commercials that showed during an episode of "*The Young & the Restless's*" not-so-hour long broadcast each day, Dawn ruminated, but she hadn't been paying it much mind. That was likely because she had never met him before tonight. Now there was a face to go with the name, and she wondered about her friend's interest in the youngster. She knew Jazelle wasn't interested in him as a boyfriend—he was too young. But this particular question hadn't been tinged with contempt, like when she had mentioned him other times. "I don't know, but wish I was whoever the heifah is he's running game on daily. My bad, lemme make that plural. *Hei-fahs*. Why? You still think he's a wolf in sheep's clothing? If I hadn't seen how good he was with those kids—even with you and I— and based on that wad he pulled out, I'd be thinking the same way you do about 'im. But I don't know what to think about Mr. Too Young But Fine."

"I sense another but. But what?"

" '*But*' there's more to him than meets the eye. If I could spend an hour or so alone just talking to him, and get him to say some—"

"Isn't he quiet, girl?"

"He sure didn't say any more than necessary. He still better be glad I'm not younger, 'cause he's a fine young thang like you said, and I'd put the *mack* down, have 'im sprung like I do all the rest of them stupid, try-to-be-hard niggas. He'd sure be talking to beg for some o' D-Mac. All that money he had tonight, he'd be spending it on yours truly."

Jazelle laughed, shaking her head. How had she been around Dawn for so many years but not latched on to her scandalous, take-no-prisoners ways? She wished she was more like Dawn when it came to men.

"He must have some type of mouthpiece, because he and that *Miss Pale and Frail* surely hadn't hooked up from nods and hand signals. And it sure wasn't a damned business dinner."

"Coulda been," Dawn said.

"Yeah, you're right. If he's some kind of escort or gigolo, it was business and pleasure."

Jazelle's insides winced. She hated thinking of him stroking *ol' girl*. Hell, she hated her reaction to the mentioning of Mitchell's name. No man, even during her teenage crush days, had the perplexing, lingering effects on her that Mitchell had. And that shit was confusing. He had struck something deep inside her without doing a thing. She couldn't understand it. And with her history with men, wasn't too anxious to understand.

Dawn said, "I know God was wrong for bringing his fii-ine ass along after we got outta high school and shit. Mitchell oughta be outlawed for being that young, and looking so damn good. Teasin' and temptin' us older bitches. Shit, I'm almost jealous of the heifahs who get to go to the split shop with him."

"Split shop?" Jazelle questioned.

"Legs are spread, and the coochie's split when there's an incoming dick."

"Unh," Jazelle huffed indignantly, imagining him with some *bitch.*

19

After clocking out from job two, Jazelle hurried to her car, started it and turned up the heater. Before long, she was pulling into a parking space outside her apartment, and briskly made it inside to a ringing phone.

She snatched it up. "Hello?"

"'Bout time you got home, girl." It was Dawn as she'd expected.

"Just walked through the door."

"I figured that much. Your cell is going right to voice mail. I let the house phone ring till you picked up."

Jazelle frowned, remembering she had forgotten to turn her phone back on after leaving work. "Why? What's up?"

"I was anxious to talk to you," Dawn said anxiously. "Girrrrl, guess what?"

₧₧

Thirty minutes later, Jazelle was out of the shower, in her sleep shirt, thinking about ole boy Dawn had talked to her about. Not that she was actually interested, but Dawn's run down of the brotha was worthy of a second thought. His name was Philip, he lived in Dallas, and worked for the airlines in some IT function. He was originally from Broken Arrow, a suburb of Tulsa, and was the friend of the guy Dawn had hung out with at the fair, and he wanted to hook up with Jazelle when he came to town again.

"And, one of the best things," Dawn had emphasized, "he doesn't have any illegitimates or otherwise running around."

Dawn's always doing something, Jazelle thought, slightly annoyed, but glad Dawn had the sense not to give dude her phone number, though she had promised him she'd persuade Jazelle to go on a double date when he was in town.

"It ain't gonna hurt just to go on a friendly get-together with the brotha," Dawn had prodded. It wouldn't hurt, true, but first impressions were the initial point of deception. Men knew how to sugar coat, making themselves appear to be more upstanding than they were. They were good at portraying a person with good qualities which a woman would be foolish to pass on since there was a shortage of the so-called *good men*. But once the stage of getting-to-know— compliments, endearments, romantic gestures, sweet nothings, wining and dining—wore off, the real *him* kicked in. Time to get the panties—if he hadn't already—and that was when the dog in him started barking. The true playa came to light.

Jazelle was sure Philip was no different.

Lying back on her bed blankly staring at the ceiling, she wondered why women had to go through the tedious, often complicated, always unpredictable dating process. There should be an easier method for men and women to fuse. Something more reliable so a woman could know beforehand the real person she was getting involved with.

Like clockwork, what had developed into an almost nightly routine started happening again, disturbing her thoughts. Her upstairs neighbor was at it again—shaking the ceiling, moaning, groaning, bumping and grinding. Fucking.

Having learned it never lasted longer than eight to twelve minutes after timing it a few times, Jazelle put her pillow over her head until the soon-to-come ending.

Sometimes it had her feeling envious, though, and hornier than an inmate on twenty-three hours a day lockdown. It would be better if she swapped apartments with ole girl, then the heifah and her beau could pound each other 24/7 without aggravating neighbors; especially her. They certainly wouldn't need to worry about her rattling the ceiling and making noises. There definitely wasn't any action between the sheets in her apartment.

No boot knocking.

No hittin' that.

Nothing.

Her *split shop* was shut down indefinitely. A mere kiss wasn't even happening.

ഇരുള

"Mitchellll! Mi-tch-elll! Help! Help me ... please ... Help!"

The voice was filled with desperation, fear, and pain. It was dark, and raining heavily, but the ground flares, flashing lights of police cars, ambulances, and a sea of bobbing and weaving flashlights circled the indiscernible area of the voice's source. Mitchell heard the voice clearly, desperately wanting to rush through the hazy, foggy area from where it came. But for some reason he was paralyzed, and couldn't move a muscle, though he was trying to with stubborn determination.

Distraught and scared, he tried to yell, "I'm coming, I'm coming," but no sound would come out.

What's happening to me? he wondered, panicking.

After a moment he realized the voice wasn't calling out anymore. It had gone silent. He tried to listen intently for any sound. Who was it anyway? Who was it?

Not another sound came.

I got to get to her, he told himself. Then all of a sudden "Mitchellllllll!" sounded off in a shrilling scream ...

His heart pounding like an Indian war drum, Mitchell woke up with a start; suddenly sat up. It was pitch black, and he realized he was in bed and had been having a nightmare.

He put both hands to his face, rubbed his eyes. Tears had formed.

Exasperated, he muttered, "Damn!" The dream felt real as hell. His t-shirt was damp, and after rubbing it, realized he'd been sweating up a storm, though it wasn't a bit hot in his room.

Slightly dazed, he clicked on the lamp next to his bed and ran his hands over his face, and sighed. He jumped up and yanked off the t-shirt and shorts he was wearing then did the same to the damp sheets and pillow slips, dumping it all in the hamper.

His heart was beating faster than Usain Bolt hauling ass in the hundred.

Certain dreams meant something. What they were trying to tell you may or may not ever come to pass. He didn't want to read too much into the dream, but didn't want to discount it either.

Ideas floated in his mind, but ...

He looked at the time, thought about his mama, sister, and brother like he always did after having a nightmare relating to death. He didn't want to call home at three in the morning, but he was concerned, so he yanked up the phone, pressed *67 to block out his number on the caller ID, and dialed his mama's number.

After several rings, Gwen answered in a groggy, dry, sleep-filled voice. She'd been in a deep, deep sleep he knew, which was a good sign.

Sorry Mama. He hung up.

Knowing they were safe, he could relax now.

20

On an overcast, muggy day, the school was bustling because of parent-teacher conferences, with many parents in a hurry to get back to work, some on a time leash to report in for the first time of the day. Reorganizing areas of the room that had been disarrayed by some of the kids who'd accompanied their parents, Jazelle glanced at the clock; her final conference of the day was due shortly. Half her class had been scheduled for today, the other half tomorrow.

She was stepping to the table where she'd set up refreshments to pour herself a cup of punch when she looked up and spotted Gwendolyn Miller in the door-way.

"Hello, Ms. Miller," she greeted. "Come on in." She sometimes forgot Gwen's last name was different from Mackenzee's, incidentally calling her Ms. Morgan, but this time she got it right.

"Hi, Miss Johnson," Gwen replied, coming in smiling. "How you doin'?"

"Good, since my conferences have been proceeding without any problems." She scanned Gwen enviously, wearing an olive leather swing jacket, underneath, a turtleneck sweater and tailored pants. She liked Gwen's style. The woman knew how to dress. The majority of times she'd seen her, she was open casket sharp. If she hadn't known her background, she would've assumed Gwen was middle-class, the way she dressed. And from what had become a normal train of thought lately, she suspected Mitchell had plenty to do with Mackenzee and his mother's wardrobes. "Ohhh, Ms. Miller, I love that jacket. It's gorgeous." She wished she had one like it.

"Thank you. I love it too. It's the first real leather I've ever had," Gwen said proudly. "My baby¬—Mitchell got it for me."

Mitchell! Jazelle thought a bit disdainfully, staring jealously as Gwen dropped her keys into an expensive Prada shoulder bag. *We all aren't able.* She was sure the bag was from Mitchell also. She offered Gwen some punch and snacks, but Gwen only accepted punch.

"And where is Mackenzee this afternoon?" she asked, handing Gwen the Styrofoam cup. Like some other parents, she assumed Mackenzee would be with her mother.

Gwen pivoted toward the door. "She should be comin' through any second."

Jazelle briefly glanced that way. "Oh, she is with you." She remembered it was a little warm in the building and pointed, indicating a coat rack in a corner. "Ms. Miller, you can hang your jacket over there if you like. I know it's kinda stuffy in here. They try to keep the building warm when it's cold. I wish they could keep it cold when it's hot as … you know what."

As Gwen slipped out the jacket and hung it on the rack, Mackenzee's little smiling face poked through the door frame. "Hi, Miss Johnson," she sing-songed.

Jazelle smiled, but before she spoke she realized Mackenzee had company. Linked hand in hand with her was Mitchell. She momentarily flinched, then relaxed.

"Hi, Mackenzee," she said. Then very tentatively, "Hello, Mitchell. Surprised to see you here." She was trying to hide a slight blush by continuing to smile. The rollercoaster moments still had her a bit embarrassed.

"Miss Johnson," Mitchell spoke, nodding as he and Mackenzee came on in.

Jazelle passed a subtle gaze beyond Mackenzee, taking in Mitchell unfastening a handsome trench, and saw he was dressed professionally underneath, minus the suit jacket. Wearing his eyeglasses, he looked intellectual and professional, but the baby face wouldn't allow him to look adult. She had to admit he looked scrumptious. She wondered why he was dressed up, and why wasn't he at school? Either his class schedule was very light, or he skipped class a lot. He sure was in Tulsa more than he should be.

Happily, Mackenzee said, "Miss Johnson, I wanted Mitchell to come so he could see how good I'm doing in school. He told me if I did good in school I could grow up to be"—she looked at Mitchell with a question on her face—"What's that word, Mitchee?"

"Successful," he enunciated for it to stick in her mind.

"Yeah! Successful," she exclaimed.

Jazelle looked at Mackenzee with adoration, scanning over the cute little parka, mittens, and boots she was wearing. *Mitchell's behind that get-up too*, she imagined, but quietly appreciated her student being able to dress nicely.

"Your brother is right." She avoided looking at Mitchell, directed them to the coat rack with a finger.

₧₧

Mitchell tried to prepare for seeing Jazelle again by telling himself it was simply a meeting with his sister's teacher. It was halfway working. He was relaxed. Flashes of the fair kept popping in his mind however, and the thought of her clinging to him like she was scared for her life, had his insides a little antsy.

He shook off the thoughts, helped Mackenzee out of her coat and stocking cap, and fiddled with her fluffy pony-tails. He had met his mama and sister out front by the curb after just arriving in Tulsa. When Gwen had come in the building, Mac and he had stayed behind for a quick listen to some new music he'd bought.

He stole a glance at Jazelle dressed in a pull-over knit tunic, same color pull-on pants. She wore no make up again on her smooth face, and the glimmer of the gloss on her sensuous lips was tantalizing like before. In days long gone, he would've wondered about the flavor of her gloss. Better yet, he would've wanted to personally kiss and nibble on those lips, learning firsthand about the flavor and texture.

As it was though, those days were a thing of the past. He concentrated on hearing about what an outstanding student his sister was.

He proudly listened while Jazelle praised Mac, who was standing beside him. Simultaneously, he viewed her painting of a soon-to-be turkey on her easel. The picture was in its early stages, and took him traveling down memory lane, where he vaguely remembered making a similar picture when he was in pre-school. Mac had jaggedly outlined her fingers with paint, and he quietly explained to her that she should start it over and trace her hand with a crayon first, then trace it with a paint brush.

"How you know, Mitchee?" she asked, wondering how he knew so much about this kind of turkey.

Grinning, he said, "'Cause I made one like it when I was in pre-school."

Her eyes lit up. "You did, Mitcheee?"

"Sure did. Bet G-Lady has it boxed up somewhere at home."

"I wanna see it."

"You'll have to ask your mama if she knows where it is." He gestured at their mother."

The incident with the little girl, Nikki, was the only non-laudatory remark against Mac, but something like that was bound to happen sooner or later, Jazelle explained, because Nikki was going through some things at home, therefore acting up at school.

Mitchell briefly wondered what problems Nikki was having at home, but the thoughts abruptly vanished when Jazelle said, "Well, Ms. Miller, unless you have any more questions, I think we've covered everything about Mackenzee. It's such a pleasure teaching her." Mackenzee came over and stood by her, and Jazelle leisurely flanked an arm over her pupils shoulder.

"Naw, Miss Johnson, I don't have no more questions. I just don't want this girl at this school fighting again." Gwen gave Mac the eye.

"I don't think she'll be doing any more of that." Jazelle looked down at Mac, who was looking over her shoulder at her teacher. "Isn't that right, Mackenzee?"

"Yes ma'am," Mackenzee answered shamefacedly.

"She bet' not," Gwen chimed in. "She knows how crazy she is 'bout school." She nodded at Mitchell. "She smart like her big brother, so I know she's doing good, but she'll be looking foolish if she couldn't come."

Gwen and Mackenzee decided to use the restroom before leaving, leaving Mitchell and Jazelle alone. Jazelle spoke first.

"So Mitchell, what are you majoring in?" To avoid eye contact, she was straightening things in the room that didn't really need it.

"Hunh?" Mitchell was thrown by the question. He assumed his mama, with how she always ran her mouth about her kids, had already told Jazelle he'd graduated from college.

"Your major—what are you studying for?"

"Accounting," he answered as if he was still in school, realizing she really didn't know.

She was amused. She'd taken an accounting course in college. Hated it. Couldn't understand it one bit. "You like dealing with numbers, huh?" She was trying to get him to talk more than he usually had the few times she'd been around him. Even during the conference he only looked and listened while she and Gwen discussed Mackenzee.

"Yep, that's me: numbers." They called him *Numbers* at the office sometimes.

That was just like him to answer without elaborating.

"Is there a specific area of accounting you're planning on getting into?" She remembered there was public, private, and governmental accounting, and somewhere within the three, taxes fit in.

She's definitely a teacher, 'cause that's the same question teachers and counselors asked me in high school.

"I'm very drawn to taxes." It was easier to answer her that way. "While taxes are so complicated for most people, I've been blessed with the ability to delve through the complexities of the tax code as if it's second nature to me. I actually love researching different tax situations." If he'd gone to work for a firm, corporate taxes would've been his specialty.

His articulation threw her a bit. She wasn't used to youngsters speaking that intelligently. His being knowledgeable about taxes was even more impressive because, like many people she knew, trying to figure out taxes for her was like being lost in a damn jungle somewhere. When tax filing season came around each year she hopped her tail right on over to H&R Block and let them do what they do, otherwise she'd be clueless. "So, what year—"

"Sorry for interrupting, Miss Johnson," Nikki's mother cut in, right after knocking at the doorway. She gave Mitchell and apologetic smile, "but I came to see if you can fit me in today. A family emergency came up ... and I can't be here tomorrow."

Jazelle absently wondered what the emergency was. She glanced at Mitchell, then the clock, back to Mrs. Smith. "Yes. Yes, I can fit you in."

"It won't be a problem?" Mrs. Smith asked tentatively.

"Well, Ms. Miller and I just finished up, and they're about to leave when—"

"Hi, Nikki," Mackenzee greeted her classmate as she and Gwen re-entered the room.

"There y'all are," Jazelle said.

"Hi ... Mackenzee," Nikki responded sheepishly.

Nikki? Mitchell looked at the little girl closer. Her hair was French braided when he'd seen her in the office that day, now it was in ponytails, and he hadn't recognized her. She didn't look like a troublemaker ... favored her mother, who was fine, with a hazelnut complexion. After noticing the ring on her finger, he wondered where her husband was. He noted mother and daughter had sad dispositions, and wondered what was going on with them.

Anyway, he was glad to see Mac and Nikki seemed to be getting along. "Guess we better get ready and head out, you two." He grabbed the three coats off the rack.

Jazelle was slightly disappointed by Mrs. Smith and Nikki's impromptu appearance, but concealed it, and felt bad for feeling that way. But the interruption had come when it seemed she was on the verge of getting Mitchell to open up some.

The three put on their gear, exchanged good-byes. Jazelle hated to see them leaving for some reason; especially Mitchell.

₧⁖

Blankly sitting behind her desk in an otherwise empty classroom a little while after Nikki and her mother had left, Jazelle was feeling glum. It turned out that Mrs. Smith's grandfather in Arkansas had had a mild stroke and she and

Nikki were headed there to give her grandmother some support. She also told Jazelle that her husband had filed for divorce.

"I'd hoped he wouldn't do that to us," she'd said almost in tears. "I actually believed he'd find his senses and come back home." She and her soon-to-be-ex-husband had explained the situation to Nikki.

It had Jazelle experiencing patches of memory of when her father walked out on them. It was the turning point for the Johnson family. The turning point in her life ...

Her mother hadn't taken it well at all. Who could? Being left for another woman was the ultimate slap in the face. It was like being stabbed in the back, never having the knife removed. The pain was piercing and infinite. Her self-esteem, self-respect, and self-worth had been snatched away, leaving her believing she was less than a woman. Jazelle remembered hearing her mother crying late at night when she thought Jazelle and Jr. were asleep, questioning what was wrong with her, what had she done wrong, what hadn't she done right.

Her parents had married right out of high school, him too anxious to claim his manhood, her desperate to get out from under the mean, strict clamps of her mother soon as possible. He had enlisted in the Army and gone off to basic training a month following their secret marriage by the Justice of the Peace. Jr. was born eight months later. During basic training he tore his Achilles—Jazelle never learned how—and received a medical discharge. After the discharge he became certified as a carpenter, and it was on one of his jobs that he'd met his present wife two years after Jazelle was born. He'd been having an affair with her for a while before deciding to leave his family and move in with her.

Jazelle knew exactly what Mrs. Smith was dealing with, the confusion Nikki's small mind was struggling to understand. Jazelle hadn't understood at the time herself, but saw the pain in her mother's eyes and disposition daily until she could no longer cope.

Courageously, Mrs. Smith seemed to be taking it in stride, grieving in a way not to fray and ruin her already confused daughter. Those two had trying times ahead, and Jazelle hoped Mrs. Smith had the strength to keep keeping on, because the agony and pain could break a woman down to hopelessness. Create a woman who has lost the will to go on. She needed toughness of mind, and then some. For herself. For her daughter.

With all that picking at her, Jazelle was thankful she hadn't had to meet with Nikki's father. The thought of him left her feeling bitter, re-opening childhood wounds that, in a matter of speaking, had molded portions of her adult life. He would've been too much of a reminder of her father and what he had done. She would've gotten pissed just being in the same room with the bastard.

She sprang from the seat, irritated by the thoughts. The room was getting stuffy, making her feel claustrophobic. She needed to go to a different part of the building. Leave the memories behind. The dismantling of another family was too close to home and disheartening.

Life's a bitch, then you die. That's what echoed in her head.

⁊

Gwen had to get back to work, so Mitchell took Mackenzee after she persuaded him to stay in town till morning. Now they were heading to their maternal grandmother's house since she'd recently complained that Mitchell didn't visit her often enough. Because it was the truth, he made a vow to himself to visit her whenever he was home. His father's mother had moved back to Tennessee when he was four or five, and he vaguely remembered her. One day he planned on finding exactly where she lived and paying her a surprise visit.

As soon as they entered the house, they spotted their grandmother, Erma, sitting in her favorite recliner watching something on Oprah's network, peeling potatoes. Joy covered her face when she saw Mitchell. They had a special bond that started the day he was born. At 37 seven, Mitchell made her a grandmother for the third time—her two eldest kids had made her a grandmother twice already—when he anxiously forced his way into the world before they could get Gwen into the car to rush her to the hospital. On that cold, morning, Erma helped deliver him right in the snowy driveway. From then on he'd been her special grandchild.

"Come here and give old Erma a hug, boy," she told him, grinning, with her arms spread.

Mitchell went to her, bent over and flung his arms around her, and pecked her on the cheek.

"How's the first lady of the family?"

"You know yo' granny's hangin' in there with the best of 'em."

Mitchell stepped back, grinning, studying her. She'd played a major role in raising him since Gwen had been so young, and he remembered the healthy, energetic woman Erma was when he was a kid. Some years back, she fell and broke her hip on some slick stairs, and the resulting surgery went awry somehow, so now she wasn't too mobile. She walked as little as possible because walking was painful. He hated the discomfort she dealt with daily, and hoped to one day persuade her into seeing a specialist to right the problem. So far he'd been unable. She was too afraid of letting another doctor fool with her.

"Hey Gramma's 'Kenzee, girl." She spread her arms for her granddaughter.

"Hey Gramma," Mackenzee said going to hug her.

"It's about time you brought yo' butt to see me, boy," she scolded Mitchell when Mac stepped back.

"I know," Mitchell responded, feigning contrition. Erma was freehearted and mild-tempered, and Mitchell believed he'd inherited her easy ways. He shrugged his shoulders, then playfully said, "I should be 'shamed of myself. I don't know what's gotten into your Anxious Boy." She'd given him that name right after he was born because it seemed like he was so anxious to come into the world from his mama's wound.

She chuckled.

They rambled on about Mac, who had went to Erma's room to watch cartoons, and the parent-teacher conference; Erma's husband of ten years, Ted, who wasn't father to any of her kids, and how his detail shop was doing steady business; Sissy, her eldest sister, who was having high blood pressure troubles; cousin Johnny, who was trying to run an escort service in Vegas.

"I 'on't know why they try to use that *escort* name," Erma said. "They know damn well that's a damn whoring operation ... and he a broke ass pimp."

Mitchell cracked up. The expressions, metaphors, and adjectives she told her stories with tickled him to death. He looked around the living room walls, covered with pictures of her five children, grand-children and great grandchildren, that tended to take him down memory lane, evoking reflections of good and bad times he'd shared with most of them. Until looking at the pictures, he'd never realized he had so many cousins. And there were new additions he hadn't met. He'd have to remember to give his mama some money to go buy presents for the new babies.

"So, you ain't got you no new girlfriend yet, Anxious?" Gwen hadn't mentioned anything about women lately but she wanted to hear it from the horse's mouth.

Mitchell expected the question. She asked it whenever he talked to her on the phone. "Nah, Gram's, I'm not looking for one. I have way more important things on my slate."

Erma knew the subject was touchy for him, and knowing when to back off, she dropped it. "I wish your cousin's was patient, and had some sense like you. They just be screwin' outta each pants leg. Keep makin' dem babies left and right, and ain't got a pot to piss in."

Introspectively, Mitchell scanned the pictures, thinking about what she just said. Two or three more babies would probably be added next year. He was surprised Erma wasn't babysitting any of her grandkids today. Often, two or three were running around the house getting on her nerves. He couldn't understand how they struggled, living check to check, public assistance in most cases, yet continued bringing those poor kids into impoverished conditions after they had grown up under similar misery. Their laziness and lack of ambition to create better lives for themselves and their kids vexed him sometimes; especially when they blamed white folks for '*holding them down*'. People like that always wanted something given to them, or felt they were owed something for nothing, when they could get off their butts, go out into the world and put in the effort to get it on their own.

He wondered if they would ever quit being so lazy, and abort that defeatist mentality. Based on history, he doubted it. It was that way before he was born, hadn't changed yet. It was his family, though. He still loved them.

Seeing the expression on his face Erma asked, "What're you frowning about, Anxious?"

Broken from his thoughts, he said, "Oh. Just ... how big our family tree is."

On the way home an hour later, light drizzle softly sprinkled the car, and Mitchell's mind aimlessly wandered while Mac sang along with Beyonce.

Blankly listening to her go word for word with one of the superstars in music today, something compelled him to ask if Miss Johnson ever mentioned a boyfriend. Mac made a twisted face and said, "Boyfriend? Uhhhhnnn, yukk! Boys are yuck-kky!"

Why he'd asked her that was a mystery to him, but the answer she'd given was his exact sentiments in regards to women, only in different terms. 'Off limits' was his choice of words. Still, Jazelle remained on his mind, and a few times lately, he'd wondered about her relationship status. If she had a man, whomever he was sure was invisible.

When they made it home, an unfamiliar Chrysler 300 was behind Gwen's car in the driveway. Whoever it was, Mitchell hoped he or she wasn't distracting his mama from cooking. He was so hungry his stomach was trying to snack on his back.

"You know whose car that is, Miss Mac?"

Still into the music, Mac perfunctorily lifted her head.

"Yeah, that's Aunt Joyce's."

Joyce was neither a blood aunt nor related by marriage, but a long time friend of Gwen's and her sisters, whom they'd known most of their lives, so she was like another sister. To Mitchell, she'd been more than a fake aunt. He didn't know she used to jive around with Gwen about fucking him once he turned eighteen. Even Gwen thought she was playing.

Joyce was for real, though.

Two days after he graduated high school, she'd taken him shopping for a graduation present, which turned out to be some clothes for college. Then they stopped by her house and she told Mitchell to come in. While in there, she uninhibitedly introduced him to sex with an older woman. To this day he still didn't know what she'd put on him. But it was so good, it scared him, and he felt he'd be sprung as hell if he'd gone back for more. So since then, he had avoided her like the plague every time she came over, until he'd gone off to college.

Knowing he was about to see her again made him uneasy. He considered leaving and coming back after she was gone, but the hunger pang wasn't trying to hear all that.

Fuck it. He parked, and he and Mackenzee got out.

When they went inside, Aunt Joyce was sitting on the love sofa. Seeing her after all these years, Mitchell could only blush. He wondered if his mama knew about *that* evening. He wouldn't want to know if she did, because it would feel uncomfortable knowing she knew about her teenage son getting *busy* with one of her best friends.

Mitchell could tell Joyce had put on a few pounds; her face was fuller, breasts looked larger. She looked a little older than her forty years. Gwen had told him she was an undercover alcoholic, if so it was working on her a bit. With a honey complexion, she was still as attractive as when she'd seduced him. More sophisticated, he hated to admit. Idly, he compared her and Susan in the sack. *Susan was good, but Joyce would probably run circles around her. Whoever Joyce's present man is, if she had one, he was sprung as hell. Straight whipped.*

"How're you doing, Aunt Joyce?" He spoke with more resolve than he felt, resisting the urge to turn and go back out the door. She was already goo-goo-eyeing him, and for distraction, he helped Mackenzee out of her hat and coat for the third time that day.

"Hi, Aunt Joyce," Mackenzee sang.

Joyce stood up, eyes still on Mitchell.

"Come here, Mackenzee, and give Auntie a hug." Mackenzee went to her. "You too, Mitchell Thomas. Look at you, the big college graduate. You know I haven't seen yo' tail in ages, boy."

Coyly, Mitchell stepped to her. The sweetest scent he'd ever smelled wafted from her. He wondered what it was as he came conscious of its disparate contrast to the aroma of the chicken he was pleased to smell his mama was cooking.

"Mmmm. Look at you, boy. I could almost eat you alive," she said, wrapping her arms snuggly around Mitchell, thrusting her pelvic region into him, slightly grinding, purposely mashing her firm, hard nipples into him. "Damn! You're so damn handsome."

It was obvious to Mitchell that the lust and infatuation she had for him as a teenager were still burning like an oven pilot light.

He wanted to yank out of her embrace and cop a quick stroll.

21

Right now Jazelle hated her upstairs neighbor for waking her up with those annoying noises pounding the ceiling. *What in the hell are they doing at this time anyway*? They'd already run her from her room again last night with their ostentatious fucking, now they were interrupting her sleep on a day she wanted to pull a *Rip Van Winkle*. Sleep the whole damn day away. She flung the comforter off and sat up. One thing she knew for sure was she'd better have a talk with homegirl up there soon before they drove her crazy.

She dragged over to the window, poked her fingers through the venetian blinds, and upon seeing the fluffy clouds, wished she was floating on one just for the peacefulness. An oil-hued dude was emptying ashes from a barbecue grill into one of the complexes dumpsters, and she wondered if he'd smoked a turkey.

Turkey. The word swirled in her head, and she knew it would echo all damn day long. Why couldn't those dang people above her have just let her sleep?

Knowing more sleep was out of the question, she found herself going to the bathroom for the just-getting-up routine. She figured Dawn and her family would soon be around a table grubbing it up, and a tinge of disappointment accosted her, causing her to frown. *Dummy*! *You should've gone with them if you're going to be whining about it*, a voice in her head said.

The thought of eating had her wondering where she'd go to get a plate. Her first choice was Mrs. Green. She figured she could throw down in the kitchen because older women usually could. *Hell, I might just sit at home and bypass Thanksgiving this year.* Maybe it would be good not to follow the tradition just because everyone else followed it. As long as she was alive, the same freaking day would come year after year after year.

Food was on her mind, though. She grabbed the box of Rice Chex off the top of the refrigerator, got the milk from inside the refrigerator, retrieved a bowl and spoon from the drawer, and flopped in a chair at the dining table. When she tilted the box to pour the cereal, memory stopped her. "Damn!" she muttered exasperated, slamming the box on the table. "I'm out of fucking sugar."

Rubbing a frustrated hand over her face, she hopped up and went to her room to throw something on to run to the store.

₧ʠʡ₨

Mitchell woke up to the blended scent of turkey, ham, sweet potato pie and other foods wafting through his nose. He knew the smells well. Sitting up in his sister's bed, he lazily slid his feet into some sports sandals, stood up, stretched and emitted a deep, waking-up yawn. He then massaged the overtaxed fingers on each hand, loosening the kinks from the three or four hours spent till 2:30 A.M. standing over the kitchen sink cleaning chitlins. He'd felt like a gangbanger after an initiation beat down once he'd he finished with those things: relieved as hell. It was more manual labor than he'd done all year.

He wore a lethargic happy face as he moved like a senior citizen to the window and pulled back the curtain. Since he wasn't averse to a sky full of cottony clouds, which was the case as he peered out the window through squinted eyes, it was a gorgeous day to him. A diminutive breeze had blown hordes of dead leaves huddling along the chain link fence line separating their house from the one next door. Neighbors' yards and curbs were already piled and lined with cars of family and friends. The representation roused thoughts of Travis and Katie dividing time at both of their parents' home, and Desiree and the kids spending the holiday with her mother and family in Arkansas.

Except for the sounds he was making, the house was lifeless. His mama was dead to the world after being up most of the night cooking, and according to the digital clock on Mac's nightstand it was 9:57 A.M. and he knew his brother and sister were still in a deep sleep.

Like he normally did Thanksgiving and Christmas morning, he went to the kitchen to inspect and check on the food left cooking on low. He got a fork and dipped into the chitlins to see how close they were to being done. Everything else was coming along just right.

He opened the front door to gauge the temperature, and found it to be somewhere in the mid-fifties. He wondered if the neighborhood kids would play football—touch in the street, tackle in the grass—like they played when he was growing up. He knew most kids nowadays seemed not to do that sort of thing anymore. Facebook, video games and texting usually consumed all their play time now.

He passed a brief glance down to one of the only neighbors he knew, Toya, and saw her car wasn't home, so he figured she was gone to kick it with her folks today. He dragged himself back to Mac's room to lie down another hour or so, when everyone else should be getting up.

To his disbelief Mackenzee of all people stalked in the room forty minutes later, shaking him to go check on the food. Normally she slept so hard she didn't turn over until past noon, maybe later if no one woke her.

"Li'l girl, what miracle transpired to get you up this early?" Again he'd glanced at the digital clock. He'd only had his eyes closed, daydreaming about much of nothing.

"*I did*," she answered, still hovering over him. "Mama said for you to go check on that food!"

The likeness to their mama with that command was noted by Mitchell. The similarity was almost frightening. He wanted to say, "I already did," but since that was close to an hour ago he said, "Okay-okay, little fat head."

"I ain't no fat head!"

He bounced up, slid his feet back into his sandals, swiftly scooped Mac up and swung her over his shoulder like a sack of potatoes, inducing pleading, squirming, and giggling. The racket earned them a dry, throaty yell from their mama to "cut out that damn noise!"

Within minutes, Montell came dragging from his room in baggy gym shorts, no shirt. Half hour later, Gwen got up.

A short while later, Mitchell and Montell were sitting in the living room in front of the TV watching the football game. Gwen was in the kitchen finishing the food with minimal assistance from Mac.

"I'll be damn!"

Mitchell heard his mama's disgust even though he was into the game.

"What happened, G-Lady? Miss Mac mess something up?"

"No!" came his sister's defensive reply.

Gwen came in the living room looking tentative, wearing a self-deprecating smile, and stood in front of Mitchell.

Mitchell sardonically stared at his mama's manipulative expression.

"What I tell you?" he muttered, shaking his head, re-focusing on the game. "What you forget?"

Gwen didn't want to admit her son had been right.

"I need you to go to the store and get me at least three cans of cranberry sauce. It's the only thing I for—I didn't put on my list. But I coulda swore I saw two cans in the cabinet the other day."

Shaking his head as he went to throw on some jeans and tennies—there was no need to complain—he hollered, "Miss Mac, I hope you don't end up being absentminded like your Mama."

"You *go to hell*, Mitchell," Gwen countered.

Mitchell laughed on into his sister's room.

ꙮ

The grocery store nearest them was closed. The closest QuikTrip was out of cranberry sauce, so Mitchell headed to the next closest convenience store.

He slid in a CD of old school slow cuts as he drove and a surreal feeling pervaded, jarring a memory from exactly four years ago, when he ran a similar errand for his mama. He went to get some pie shells because the ones she was about to use had crumbled apart. It almost felt as if that occasion was now. Only he rode alone today. That day he had a passenger …

"You think they'll have some shells at the store we're going to, Mitch-Mitch?" asked the voice from that day.

Mitchell looked skeptical. "I hope so. I sure don't feel like running all over Tulsa looking for some dang pie shells. That mama of mine! With her, something always ..." He let the statement die, shaking his head.

"It wasn't her fault those shells weren't any good."

"She should've checked 'em ahead of time."

"Don't blame her; you're just mad you're missing that stupid football game."

Mitchell cut his eyes at his passenger, partially smirking. Calling the game *stupid* was typical female haterism. Yes, he hated being disturbed when one of his games was on. A lot …

As if the Tahoe was driving itself, Mitchell found himself turning into the parking lot of a QuikTrip without realizing it. The memory had completely absorbed him. Shook him up like some Bingo chips.

Grimacing at the recollection, he parked in front of the store, killed the motor, jumped out and blew off arming the alarm since he should be in and out of the store like a minute man's sexual brevity.

But some crazy, dingy, smoked out looking dude wearing a blazer he must've found in a dumpster was leaning on the trash can near the store's doorway, eyeing the Tahoe. Mitchell checked the door, making sure it was locked. Though he couldn't imagine some fool jacking him for his ride in broad daylight, he knew there were some nuts out there who'd try it. He would've hated coming out the store to someone smashing off in his roll-out.

He chirped on the alarm. *Always better to be safe than sorry.*

"Hay, Young Bruh, can a po' man borra a dolla' off ya?" asked the bum when Mitchell approached the store entrance.

Borrow? I'll never see you again in my life. Mitchell could smell ole boy's funky odor from a mile away. He smelled like pure shit! Against his better judgment, knowing Mr. Bum would probably go find the nearest dealer, he dipped in his pocket and pulled out a five.

"Happy Thanksgiving, Mr." he said holding out the cash, not wanting their flesh to touch.

Mr. Bum exposed a yuck-mouthed grin.

" 'Preciate ya, li'l bruh." With an inebriated, wobbly stroll, he hastily got him some yonder like a farm boy hearing the dinner bell chiming.

"Hope you don't go somewhere and OD," Mitchell mumbled to the air at ole boy's back.

Inside the store, he respectfully asked the big headed Middle Eastern flavored clerk, who was jocularly consumed with someone on the phone, directions to the canned goods. Big Head momentarily lowered the phone from his ear and directed Mitchell with a pointed finger.

Mitchell had slid that way after giving Mr. Big Head an unacknowledged "thank you" when a lady in a leather jacket, baggy blue sweats, and gray and blue baseball cap emblazoned with the Cowboy's logo abruptly stopped in front of him as she was leaving the aisle. She looked at him, then did a double-take.

"Mi-tchell?" she murmured, startled.

The voice was familiar, but the cap was pulled down low, concealing her face. Mitchell squinted. Then it hit him.

"Miss Jo—I mean—Jazelle?" he sputtered, very surprised to be seeing her of all people.

Suddenly mindful of her appearance, knowing she looked like a new millennium Aunt Jemima or somebody, Jazelle ran a self-conscious hand over her upper half. Her jacket was unzipped, revealing a jolly Mickey and Minnie on a T-shirt. She barely resisted the urge to zip up.

"Hi. It's a shock running into you here—especially today."

"I know, right? G-Lady—I mean my mama—forgot the cranberry, so I had to go on a hunting expedition. I've already struck out at two other stores. And the Thanksgiving meal isn't right without the C sauce."

Damn, he actually offered some info without being asked.

"I agree with you on that," Jazelle co-signed. "Thanksgiving meal without cranberry sauce is like ... it's just not right."

He motioned at the box of sugar she was clutching. "You forgot something too, hunh?"

"Uh ... no. I just needed some sugar."

"You cooking Thanksgiving dinner?" Mitchell recalled when he was in college, the girls—unless it was something basic, like boiling ramen noodles—were lost in the kitchen. His generation of women couldn't really cook worth shit. They burnt toast cooked in a toaster.

She made a face, softly grunted. "Me, cook for Thanksgiving? Ohhh no."

He easily laughed. "Guess that means your culinary skills aren't up to par?"

"You don't *even* wanna know," she said, shaking her head and smiling.

"So, who's doing the cooking for your family? Your mother, right?"

She winced internally. "My mother's deceased."

Mitchell instantly turned contrite, and felt stupid. "Oh ... I'm so sorry, Miss Jo—Jazelle."

It was kind of cute to Jazelle how he always seemed to fumble with her name.

"That's quite alright. You couldn't have known. She's been gone since I was a little nappy head."

Mitchell forced a smile, still feeling shitty for blurting that out, even though he couldn't have known. "I'm still sorry, though. It was thoughtless of me to be so presumptuous."

She waved a hand dismissively. "Don't worry about it."

An awkward silence ensued.

Mitchell then said, "So, if you're not cooking, where are you eating Thanksgiving dinner?" Instantly he felt like a doofus. Of course she had other family or friends besides her mother.

After a millisecond, she shrugged. "I don't really know."

Mitchell scrunched up his face a bit.

The expression compelled her to explain where she normally spent Thanksgiving, why this year was different, and that she hadn't joined her surrogate family in St. Louis because she didn't want to take her welcome for granted.

Mitchell thought about asking about other family besides her mother, but he'd already put his foot in his mouth once. Then sympathy or something must've caused an invisible rock to knock him over the head, because he impetuously said, "Why don't you come to our house? G-Lady would love to have you over. And I don't have to tell you how Miss Mac would feel about that." He blanched, marveling at himself for what he'd just done.

Jazelle blinked with surprise. Was this really the same Mitchell?

"Nooo, I couldn't just show up at you all's place like that." She was thinking of how delighted Mac would be if she showed up at their house, though. "I have other invitations, just haven't decided yet. I may just stop by each one."

" 'Show up?' " Mitchell said wryly. "You wouldn't just be showing up. I'm inviting you. Shoot, you can take your car home," he suggested, figuring the Corsica parked in front of the store was hers since the only other car on the lot had to be Big Head's, because it was parked away from the store, "and I'll follow you, then you can ride with me." Inviting her was shocking, but this suggestion was off the chart. It didn't show on his face, but he'd stunned himself again. Had someone slipped him a drug he didn't know about?

Jazelle blew some air, astounded. *This couldn't be the same Mitchell.* Unconsciously she was pondering the invitation when Big Head, finally off the phone, asked if they'd found what they were looking for. Mitchell and Jazelle blinked, realized they were idly standing in this man's store blabbering. Mitchell pulled out a twenty and paid for both, putting up a hand to wave off her attempt to reimburse him. She thanked him.

"You sure your mother won't mind?" The question slipped out on its own. *I'm not really considering accepting his invite, am I?*

"Heck naw," Mitchell answered. "It's Thanksgiving. The more people come to eat, the less leftover's wasted. Besides, she'd talk crazy to me if I told her what you just told me and didn't persuade you to come over. And I guarantee you'll love G-Lady's cooking."

After another moment of conflicted contemplation, more and more she dreaded the thought of going back to her dull apartment. She sighed.

"Ooo-kay." She looked down at her attire. "But I need to change."

When Mitchell pulled into the parking space next to her in her complex, she wore a man-killing expression that emerged after they had walked out of the store and he approached his vehicle and deactivated the alarm. Disappointment, contempt, and disapproval fueled by the resurfacing of her feelings about him doing illegal shit spread through her. She felt like cursing him out. *A damn Tahoe*! That was too much. The thought of this day turning out well wasn't looking good.

No older than nineteen at the most, poor family, in college—which she was rapidly starting to doubt—with all its expenses, yet, he had bought his mother a brand new Cadillac. Now, now he was driving a Tahoe.

She exited her car, impetuously slammed the door, swimming in disgust.

Mitchell hopped down from the Tahoe, rounded it and came toward her. She had avoided looking directly in his eyes in the store, but now she fixed her gaze right there. "Is that yours?" she curtly spit out, motioning at his ride.

Mitchell nonchalantly cut his eyes toward his vehicle. "The Tah?" he said, reflexively lifting the plaid bucket hat sitting haphazardly on his head and scratching.

His casualness amused Jazelle instead of irking her more. And it was good the bulky sweatshirt smothered his upper body.

She remembered how it was capable of making her hormones twitch. She was already struggling to hang on to the bit of incredulity she had.

"Nah, the boat!" she said rigidly, then almost wanted to apologize for the sarcasm and sounding so stony. "Yeah, the T ... Tah—whatever it is."

"Yep."

If he recognized the contempt in her expression or the curtness in her voice, he didn't let on. She noticed there was neither cockiness, nor boastfulness in his reply or his body language. Add that he was standing there with his hands tugged deep in his pockets, looking too scrumptious, and she started questioning her motives. What would she gain from probing him? Even if he revealed something to her, then what? It wasn't like he'd tell her a damn thing anyhow.

She sighed, trying to stifle her exasperation. A door opened and the sounds of music blared from that apartment. Kids were running around playing the games kids played nowadays. Absently, she looked at a car pulling into a parking space across the way, stole a surreptitious glance at Mitchell. He looked innocent, and it was lulling. Her irritation started hiding under something, her resolve wavering. *Thanksgiving must be having an effect.*

"Something wrong?" Mitchell asked.

Yeah. You! "No," she answered softly, concealing the left over aggravation. "Coming in so I can find something to wear?" If someone had told her a teenager was capable of fucking with her head like he had, she would've wagered everything she owned that it couldn't happen in a million years.

She would've lost it all.

Uneasily, she scanned the living room after walking in, hoping it wasn't a mess. She didn't want this boy thinking she was trifling. She swiftly rushed over and snatched up the comforter strewn across the sofa that she'd slept under, folded it neatly. The box of cereal and bowl were still on the dining table. Otherwise the place was cool.

With a forced smile, she motioned Mitchell, who was standing near the door, to come on in. He looked so innocent and unlikely to be involved in anything illegal.

Looks deceived to make you believe. She knew that all too well.

She wondered if she should go with him to his mother's. Because of that ... 'Tah', as he'd called it, outside in her parking lot stirring up the issues she had with him, she was reconsidering. Simply hanging out with him would be like being an accessory after the fact to his hustler's lifestyle. And that would make her a hypocrite.

Mitchell motioned at the TV. "Mind if I turn the game on while you do the clothes tango?"

She'd forgotten about the game. It wasn't her team anyway.

"Yeah, go ahead." She pointed to the coffee table. "The remote is right there." She paused. " 'Clothes tango?' "

Mitchell lightly chuckled. "Finding something to wear. You know it's a work in motion with women."

"That's cute. I have to bite off you one day for that one. Would you like something to drink? I have water, Pepsi, or orange juice."

"Umm, no thanks. Keeping the ol' belly good and vacant for all the eats I'll be gorging on later," he responded, patting his stomach.

Jazelle had still been contemplating the invitation until that comment. A bowl of cereal versus some turkey and dressing was a no brainer. She was going to get her grub on.

When Mitchell clicked on the game, taking a seat on the sofa, she hesitantly excused herself, telling him she was going to do that "tango." In her room she looked at her cell and saw she had missed a call and there was a voice message. She accessed the message, assuming it was Dawn calling from St. Louis.

It wasn't. It was Philip. Dude who she'd gone on a blind date with along with Dawn and her present fling to the bowling alley. He was calling to ask if she was interested in getting together later. *Can't he read the damn signs that I'm not interested in him like that? Doesn't common sense inform him when a female Is avoiding him, like kinfolks calling on payday?* He had called the day after the date, asking to get together and she turned him down. He'd called two more times when she was at her second job. She listened to both messages he'd left, didn't return either call. He texted her, she didn't respond. He was becoming a pest. The next time he called she'd better be straight with *Li'l Phil*—he was shorter than her, which was a turnoff—and foreclose on his Jazelle pursuit.

∾

Looking around the apartment, Mitchell was amused at how basic it was, and that there were only two paintings on her walls. A graduation picture of a bland-faced Marine dude sat on the TV. No other pictures of family or anybody else. It tripped him out that this was a woman's place. He wondered if the black GI Joe was her boyfriend. Homeboy off serving the USA would explain why she was never with a man when she was out and about. The dude sort of resembled her, though.

It then struck him that there was no green life inhabiting her crib that he could see. *No plants in a woman's house?* G-Lady would have a fit if she came in and saw such horticulture famine.

On the TV, a receiver dropped a wide-open pass, and Mitchell grunted audibly.

Jazelle heard the grunt, blew Philip off and commenced hastening her search for something to wear. Unable to make up her mind, Jazelle marched into the living room to consult with Mitchell, calling out his name before reaching him. Leaning forward, more engrossed in the game, he jerked his head around just as she appeared.

Jazelle's insides reacted with a sudden tingle. He was looking sexy as hell with an earnest expression. She almost meowed like a cat. "Do you think jeans will be ok?" She spit it out before she lost all propriety and impulsively jumped his jail-bait bones. *Someone so young shouldn't be so damn sexy.*

"Hmm hunh," he mumbled, partially looking at her and the game. "What I have on is what I'll be wearing all day."

Wish I were the clothes you have on. I'd be on you like stink on shit. "You sure?"

"No doubt." He briefly but fully looked her way. "Jeans are perfect. This day's about eating, not styling."

"Mitchell, I don't want to be looking like an odd ball."

"You won't." A Home Depot commercial came on. Something about it jarred his attention. "Oh, Mi—Jazelle? I noticed you don't have"—he circled the room with his eyes—"any plants in here."

Though a bit embarrassed by that fact, Jazelle found it amusing that he noticed. *So not like the average young boy.*

"I did have a few, but fooled around and let them die. Days of neglect."

"That'll do it. Gotta give plants a little water, sun, and some love—just like humans."

Too damn wise beyond his years. "I know that now."

The game came back on, his attention went with it.

"Well, let me hurry." She shuffled from his presence, ambivalent as hell over the youngster in her living room.

She ended up in jeans, a long-sleeve ottoman ribbed top, but wasn't sure about sporting the baseball cap. After an indecisive analysis in the mirror, she elected to leave it off, exchanged it for a French twist and strap-style headband. *Mirror, mirror* didn't tell her she was the *finest*, but it was good enough for her.

"Mitchell, don't you think we should call your mother to let her know I'm coming over with you?" she called out to him, talking into the mirror.

"No, Ma'am. We'll just surprise her and Mac."

Showing manners and being respectful was a good thing, but the "ma'am" shit, she didn't care for it coming from him one bit. It tacitly reiterated that she was a woman and he was a baby. On opposites sides of grown.

Mitchell barely looked her way when she re-entered the living room. The game held him in bondage. Jazelle was fine with it, unsure if she could withstand him examining her appearance without feeling insanely self-conscious and insecure.

But right before she let the door close behind her as they were leaving, he craned his head a little and said, "You look just fine, JJ."

Jazelle paused, looking at him, oblivious to him calling her by her initials. *He's been checking me out all along.* He's sneaky as well. She didn't know whether to thank him or run back in the apartment and lock the door to put up a barrier between her and too-young-but-fine Mitchell Thomas.

22

Charles Morgan wasn't fully wasted yet, but if he got his way he'd be pissy, can't-remember-what-happened drunk by nightfall. Alcoholic bliss. It was a holiday and they were made for drinking until you thought *blackout* was the location of your residence. To hell with what anybody said, if he wanted to get drunk, then that was damn well what he was gonna do. The whole wide world could kiss his natural black ass!

Like an old man, he trudged through the one bedroom shotgun house he and Ralph Lucky shared, tripping over, stepping on, and bumping into filth. It looked and smelled like the city dump had relocated from its isolated location, and moved in with them. Apparently Mr. Clean, Miss Mop, Mr. Broom, and Mrs. Potpourri had pulled a double elopement, and Brother Pine-Sol had gone along to be their witness. In the kitchen, dirty dishes, pots and pans were piled sky high in the grotesque sink, as well as strewn over an old, tattered dining table. Hundreds of roaches moved around fearlessly and boldly like Mandingo warriors, like they had as much right to be there as anybody else. They huddled around a noxious plate of indeterminable-day old eggs like anxious throngs of bargain hunters at a swap meet. Right off the kitchen, since the water was cut off, the bathroom smelled like shit and old piss. It might as well have been an outhouse. In the little-bigger-than-a-closet bedroom, a piss-stained, queen sized mattress lay on the floor, and filthy clothes were strewn over it as well as the rest of the nasty room. The front room was furnished with somebody's antiquated castoffs: a divan from the seventies, a torn leather recliner with holes and cigarette burns all over it, a shade-less lamp, a broken-down coffee table, and a used-to-be beige rug that was the color of mud. Ashtrays that hadn't been emptied since the slaves were freed pungently flowed over with butts and ashes.

Charles looked around the hell hole, blew some air. Since Ralph was at his folks' stuffing his face, he was alone, feeling left out and sorry for himself. Moping. Sometimes he admitted he'd made an ass of his life. Looking around the place where he laid his head every night, no one would argue. But was it his fault his daddy occasionally let him drink home brew when he was a young buck? Or, when he started doing it more no one stopped him? Hell, the brew got good to him. Grew hairs on his chest and made him a man. He started wanting it all the time. By the time he was a full-fledged teenager, instead of chasing flocks of young pussy, he was chasing the flavor of Corn Whiskey, MD 20/20, Gilbey's, Black Velvet, or *his main squeeze*: Windsor Canadian. Whatever he could get a hold of. It got to a point where a bottle of anything warm and potent was all he needed and wanted.

His folks had known what he was doing, but their country asses couldn't care less, so why would he? He went through a long span where he got it under control and only sipped on weekends, but he missed it too much, and the pull was too strong.

Now he was alienated from his family, kids, even some of his old partners. He didn't give a rat's ass, though. Fuck 'em. Fuck it. No one gave a shit about him. Just because he chose to do with his life what he wanted, every bitch-made-body wanted to wash their hands of him. Dismiss him like a company that was downsizing.

To hell with all o' them!

Well, not his baby girl, he retracted. She wasn't like the rest. Not his sweet little Mac. She hadn't disowned and judged him like all the other better-than-thou self-righteous ass folks had done. It was her punk ass mama feeding her a bunch of bullshit about him. Keeping him from seeing her. Punk bitch! Who was she anyway? What did she know?

Hell, he was able to ease up on the booze or stop anytime he wanted. He'd been sober enough when he was with her. But when he did drink a little something, try to have a bit of fun, she'd always nag, bitch and pester him about drinking around her damn kids; especially that spoiled, sissified Mitchell. Her *baby. I shoulda kicked his little bitch ass. Obedient, sweet natured fucka. Wimp ass punk! Probably got my son soft as cotton. I wouldn't doubt if he was still suckin' his mama's titties.*

Charles drifted outside and stood on the porch. He cussed which ever dog shit the pile of turds on the yard near the porch. He stepped back inside the tattered screen door to pull the front door closed behind him, then stumbled down the three steps, almost falling, but keeping his balance, went to Ralph's car that was parked in the gravel driveway, and got in.

Not giving a good-fuck about his suspended license from a few DUI arrests, or warrants for his arrest for failure to appear, or the fact that he was intoxicated, he got the key to the Oldsmobile from its normal hiding place under the floor mat and started it up. He then reached under the passenger seat and got a fifth of Night Train in a brown paper sack, pulled down the opening of the sack, untwisted the cap, turned up the bottle and took a long-throated swig. He twisted up his face, made an *ahhh* sound, his head shuddering a bit when he brought the bottle down.

After putting the car in reverse, he backed out the gravel driveway and slightly careened down the road doing a turtle's twenty mph. So-the-hell-what if he got stopped. Wouldn't be the first time, and probably wouldn't be the last. He didn't give a rat's ass.

It was Thanksgiving.

He wanted to see his baby girl.

23

Pushing her feelings toward the vehicle she now rode in to the back of her mind, Jazelle continued having reservations but kept them to herself, aware that she strongly desired spending this day in a familial atmosphere. The ride found them conversing about football, giving her great pleasure in seeing Mitchell's expression after revealing how football competent she was for a female. They even liked the same team.

The fact that he was talking was a welcome change from his usual dialogue deficiency. She thought about bringing up what she really wanted to discuss with him but figured going down that avenue would likely spoil a good mood. She didn't want to drop rain on the holiday, so she kept that topic on the shelf.

When they pulled up to the house jitters emerged inside Jazelle, like she was about to meet a boyfriend's parents for the first time. "Mitchell ... you're sure Ms. Miller won't mind?" she asked, seized by a tinge of trepidation. Before answering he was quickly out and around the vehicle, opening her door.

Jazelle wondered if she was dreaming. *A man opening the door for me*? That hadn't even happened in one of her fairytale laced dreams.

"Um, thank you," she uttered.

Mitchell extended a hand to help her down. Jazelle took it, recalling the sensation the first time his flesh clasped with hers. *These soft hands again.* She doubted if he'd ever done a day's hard labor in his young life. "Why are your hands so soft, Mitchell?" she asked, walking beside him toward the house.

With one hand holding the sack of cranberry sauce, Mitchell impulsively turned the other over, looked at the white side. "Because my name is Mitchell," he said, being funny.

She looked at him quizzically. "You said the same thing at the fair. What does that mean?"

"That's just what that is."

She frowned. He smiled.

At the door, he unconsciously grasped her hand again, holding her back so he could enter first. "Relax," he whispered, feeling what he assumed was apprehension from her. "No need to be a 'fraidy cat."

She was relaxed. It was him holding her hands. This closeness to him.

The door was unlocked when he turned the knob. He opened it enough to poke his head inside. The delicious aroma of his mama's cooking gushed out. Both of their nostrils reacted like ants at somebody's picnic. The game sounded from the TV and Mitchell expected his brother to be in the same spot watching it from when he'd left to go to the store, but Montell wasn't.

Somehow, though, Gwen's *animal* senses kicked in, and from the kitchen, she yelled, "Mitchell, that you, boy?"

How did she hear the door open? "Yeah, Mama, it's me," he yelled back, amazed at her hearing.

"'Bout damn time," Gwen exclaimed. "Where the hell did you go just to get some damn cranberry sauce, China?"

Mitchell looked back at Jazelle, shaking his head, not a bit embarrassed by his mama's dialogue. "You gotta excuse her, she think she's a comedian."

Jazelle smiled. "Your mama is funny," she replied, dismissing the apology.

Jazelle wasn't sure what she'd expected, but the sight before her surely wasn't it. The crib was laid. She took in the comfortable-looking furniture, pictures, flourishing plants, and the whole décor had her saturated with envy.

Mitchell said, "I have the same reaction when I come in here. I gotta give G-Lady some serious props when it comes to decorating."

Right then Gwen bounced from the kitchen, wearing an inquisitive expression. Before she could say anything, Mitchell said, "Look who I ran into." He stepped from in front of Jazelle.

"Miss Johnson?" Gwen said, surprised.

After the mention of the name Mackenzee zapped into the living room like *"I Dream of Genie."* "Miss Johnson?" she echoed her mama, then rushed to her teacher and threw her arms around her. "What you doing here?"

The embrace put Jazelle a little more at ease. "Hello Mackenzee, Miss Miller."

"Girl, call me Gwen. We ain't at that school house. What're you doin' here? You stayin' for dinner?"

Jazelle shot Mitchell an uncertain glance.

"Um, well..."—Mitchell was nodding almost imperceptibly—"Yes. I ... guess I am." *Shouldn't you be explaining to her?* her eyes pleaded to Mitchell.

Montell came from the kitchen stuffing something in his mouth. Jazelle still found it hard to believe his big self was the younger brother, and only fifteen.

Gwen saw his jaws working. "You been eatin' in that pie?" It really wasn't a question. She slightly smacked him across the forehead.

He chuckled. "Sho have. It's bomb!" He had on a hat like Mitchell's, but it was all white with a crimson band around it. "What up, Miss Johnson?" He was casually scanning her. "You kickin' it wit' us today?"

Gwen bopped him on the head again. "Boy! What I tell you 'bout talkin' that damn slang to grown folks?"

Montell flinched, chuckling. "Chill, G. It ain't like she's an old woman."

"Yehh, she's kickin' it with us today," Mitchell finally spoke up. Gwen dirty-framed him for mimicking his brother. He only grinned, explained that Miss Johnson and he ran into each other at the store, and that he had invited her over. To squash his mama's ensuing questions before they started, he manufactured, "She doesn't really get along with that out of town part of the family, so she stayed in T-Town." He winked at Jazelle.

Jazelle sent him an incredulous look for the lie.

"You're eating with us, Miss Johnson?" Mackenzee asked.

"Yes I am." She bent and touched Mac on the cheek.

"Yesss."

"Good," Gwen said. "Mackenzee take Miss Johnson's jacket—no Mitchell, you can, and hang it in the closet. I wonder where Carla them are. They shoulda been here by now."

On those words, the front door opened, and Terrence and Rodney stumbled in, then Li'l Q, packing a covered dish. Carla and Quincy walked in seconds later asking was it time to eat yet. The quintet fell in and spoke, reacting to Jazelle's presence like it was normal for her to be there.

With a teasing twinkle in his eye, Mitchell relieved Jazelle of her jacket. "Welcome to our crazy home," he said in a low voice.

"Mackenzee!" Gwen yelled from the kitchen seconds later. "Quit hounding around Miss Johnson like you ain't neva seen her before. Mitchell, where's the cranberry, boy?"

Mitchell shook his head. "Whatever happens today, Jazelle, don't hold it against us. My peeps don't mean any harm."

Jazelle softly laughed.

❧⬥☙

Jazelle was soaking up the holiday camaraderie when Mackenzee came from the kitchen and whisked her off to see her room. Stuffed animals covered her queen-size bed and a corner of the room making it obvious what Mitchell had been doing with his fair winnings. Posters of Venus and Serena Williams were on the walls, and the entertainment center and accessories she remembered Mac telling her about occupied its space in the room. Jazelle thought of how a five year old had more stuff than she did.

"Mac, your room is pretty," she told her.

Mackenzee was looking proud. "Thank you. You wanna talk on my karaoke machine?"

Jazelle touched her on the cheek. "Maybe later." At that moment she had a yearning to one day have a daughter and be able to decorate the child's room pretty and neat.

From up front eating time was announced. When Jazelle and Mac headed that way, Jazelle peeped into Montell's room. He and Li'l Q were entrenched in a video game grudge match, taunting each other like males tended to do. Typical for a male teenager, posters of rappers and pro athletes hung on the walls. She felt wistful. She thought of Jr and wished she could see her big brother.

"I see my baby sister took you to show off her domain," Mitchell said when they re-entered the living room. Quincy and he were disinterestedly watching the end of the first Thanksgiving pro football game.

"Yes, and it was pretty for a pretty girl."

"This game needs to hurry and end," Quincy complained to no one in particular.

Mitchell nodded his agreement with Quincy, but commented on Jazelle's statement. "Yeah, and she's a little brat." He playfully grabbed Mackenzee onto his lap and folded his arms around her.

"I ain't no brat," she retorted.

"I'm not a brat," Jazelle corrected.

"Ok, you're a spoiled brat, then," Mitchell amended.

"Unh-unhhh."

Watching brother and sister play, Jazelle had a brief flash of her and Jr. way back when.

"Mackenzee," Gwen called, "you and Miss Johnson come in here and get a plate."

"Those're the words I been waitin' to here," Quincy said. "Hurry up, Carla girl, and fix my plate. I'm hungrier than a used-to-be-rich white man in a soup line during the Great Depression."

Terrence and Rodney were already seated at the table while Gwen and Carla were fixing plates. Being this close to the food, Jazelle realized she was hungrier than she'd realized. Other than everyone gathering around the table for grace, everything was informal and unconventional; even the blessing, where Quincy said, "Good God, good meat, thank you, Lord, let's eat," and everyone couldn't help but laugh. The women and little kids ate in the kitchen, the men and two older boys in the living room, watching the game. It reminded Jazelle of the holidays with her family before the breakup, but instead of feeling sad or sorry for herself like she normally would, she was cool. They were making her feel part of their family.

Gwen held court and had everyone at the table cracking up, while in the front the men were debating over talents of this or that player and expressing opinions on different teams' chances of making the playoffs. With Gwen's humor, Jazelle had a hard time trying to finish up the food on her plate. Mitchell was right: she loved Gwen's cooking. Sista could burn. She admitted to herself that it was better than Mama Mamie's was; Dawn's mother's as well. She learned that Gwen had never been married in the legal sense; her first boyfriend—Mitchell's father—was killed before Mitchell was old enough for pre-school, her other real relationship ended because Mac and Montell's daddy was a drunk.

"What about you?" Carla said to Jazelle. Jazelle responded with a quizzical expression. "You ever been in deep with a man, on the verge of getting married?"

"Ohh. No. Not yet," Jazelle answered, uneasy about the subject; especially around the kids.

"All the women in our family since our great grandmother got hooked and pregnant when we were teenagers, girl."

"Sho did," Gwen co-signed.

"For real?" Jazelle found herself tripping that neither sister had any shame about their teenage pregnancies, making it seem like it was the thing to do. She had issues with teens simply having sex, let alone knowingly getting pregnant. She believed one of the major problems on the map was mere babies having babies, resulting in the millions dependent upon Uncle Sam's monthly allotments for the poor. But she kept those thoughts to herself.

"Whatever you do when you do find that man, girl," Gwen said, grinning impishly. "Make sure he knows how to lay pipe."

Jazelle didn't catch on until Terrence started giggling and said, "Oooo, lay pipe. That's how my daddy said he made us: he laid some pipe with mama." Her eyes dilated, and her mouth shaped into a capital O with shocked embarrassment. She couldn't believe this talk was happening in front of the kids! Gwen was a trip. Reminded her of Dawn. She still found herself laughing, though she knew she shouldn't be, because kids shouldn't know about grown folks' business like that.

"Damn Gwen, girl, you put yo' foot in that sweet potato pie," Quincy said, coming into the kitchen. "Hook a brotha up with anotha fat slice, Carla. It's so damn good, I wanna go slap my mama, with her no cookin' ass."

Everybody in the house cracked up.

Jazelle was glad for the diversion, because her social life was the last topic she wanted to be discussing. Even though she was stuffed, Quincy's compliments persuaded her to get up and cut herself a tiny slice of the sweet potato pie. When she bit into it her eyes closed with delight, her thoughts paralleled Quincy's words. "Ooo, Gwen, you need to go public with this pie, girl." She cut herself a bigger slice.

"That's what I'm talkin' 'bout," Quincy yapped from the living room. "My team's time to get busy."

"Men and that damn football," Carla complained, conveying the sentiments of thousands of women on that particular day. "Why do men wanna watch other men running around in tight ass pants trying to hurt each other? I'll never understand it."

"You sho won't," Gwen said.

Halfway grinning, Jazelle looked at the other two. "I hate to tell you all but I'm football crazy too." Gwen and Carla just looked at one another with no expression. "So, if you all don't mind, I guess I'll go join the fella's, cause my team's 'bout to play."

"Girl, go knock ya' self out." Gwen waved her on.

Jazelle wasn't the least bit tentative when she got up and made that move.

24

Watching the game turned out to be hopeless because other family and friends started flooding the house, turning it into party central. Gwen's oldest brother James brought out a big bottle of Jack Daniels, and from then it was on. Gwen unveiled a bottle, Quincy had a bottle, and others produced their choice of *crazy liquid* to the revelry. Paper cups began circulating like the collection plate at a church. The sound on the game was turned down in preference for some old and new school music, and kids started dancing until Gwen momentarily halted that activity to move her fragile furnishings and decorations into the garage. The space was needed just as much as preventing her stuff from getting broken, because it had gotten deep up in the not-big-enough living room.

Jazelle accepted a cup of Ciroc and juice, squeezed in glimpses of the soundless game while sipping and bobbing to the music. The kids were back in the center of the floor showing off their moves, and through the window behind the TV she could see Mitchell outside with his cousins gathered around, admiring his Tahoe. She forced herself to blow off the disdain she felt about that subject and concentrated on the kids' dancing.

Montell came from his room and plopped next to her on the sofa. "They still losing?" He was referring to Dallas.

"Just about to take the lead, hopefully," Jazelle answered. "I think it's first and goal from the three."

"Man, I still can't believe a female knows about football like you do." Before it got crowded, she'd enlightened them on her football knowledge while they watched the game.

She smiled, noting how Montell seemed extroverted compared to his brother. "My brother got me hooked when I was little."

"Speaking of brothers, did you know Mitch and Main Man are homies?" He pointed at the TV to emphasize his point.

She blinked. "Whaaat? They are?"

"Yep. They're pretty tight." He supplied her with details about the trip to the game in Dallas. "He don't like tellin' people though, because they either think he's lying or ask him to get 'em an autograph to test if he's telling the truth. To me, my big bro's just too modest."

Modest was an understatement. She realized it wasn't by coincidence that Main Man had thrown him the football that day. "I saw you all on TV that day. I hear you're a pretty good player yourself."

"Yeah, me and Li'l Q do our thang on the field, b-ball court, and in track. But Mitch ... he mostly taught me how to play everythang. He's the one with the game. You oughtta see him play some hoops." In high school, Mitchell had promising potential as a point guard, but tore up his knee before the start of his senior year during a summer AAU game on a simple drive to the basket. Schools that were recruiting him dropped him off their radar, plus the knee didn't heal correctly until his junior year in college. By then he'd given up on playing collegiately, only sticking to intramurals and pick-up games. Montell believed Mitchell was the best. He cried when Mitchell blew out his knee. He told Jazelle all of this.

"I figured he was pretty good when we were at the fair."

Montell blew some air. "Aww, you ain't seen nothin'."

Jazelle almost instinctively corrected his grammar but caught herself, let it slide. Good teacher's always wanted to teach when necessary, but this wasn't the time.

Li'l Q hollered for Montell to come finish their grudge match, and as he jumped up, asked Jazelle to keep him informed on the game.

She said, "Okay," as she watched Mitchell and the others pile into his ride, then ease from the curb.

"This crazy family of mines ain't driving you crazy, are they?" Gwen asked, coming out of the kitchen.

Smiling, Jazelle shook her head. "Not at all. I'm having fun." This atmosphere was certainly livelier than what she was used to with Dawn and her family. "Do you all get together like this every Thanksgiving?"

"Pretty much. But we usually stack up over to my mama's. I don't know why everybody decided to bunch up over here today." A little girl was getting her dance on; doing moves she most likely got from watching music videos. "That's my nephew's daughter."

"She's so cute. I've never really been to a family get-together as animated as this," Jazelle said. "Not even a family reunion." The twin creases between Gwen's eyebrows cajoled her into giving a shortened version of her history.

Confused, Gwen said, "I thought your folks went to St. Louis?"

Ashamed about allowing Mitchell to misinform his mother, Jazelle smiled deprecatingly. "Actually that's my best friend and her family. They're the closest I have to family, with my only brother being wherever he's been over the years. I didn't go to St. Louis with them because I really don't want to wear out my welcome, 'cause I'm always spending holidays with them."

"Oh well, hell, girl, you're welcome over here for any holiday—"

SLA-CLACK!

"Twenty-five dat way said da nigga slaya'! Now gimme two mo' playas. Get y'alls no playin' asses up!" It was one of the men in the kitchen playing dominoes and talking shit.

Gwen hopped up, went toward the kitchen, raising hell. "You fucka's betta quit slammin' them damn dominoes on my table!"

"Aww, Gwen, girl, jus' go back in there and play hostess. We got dis in here." It was her brother, James.

"I know y'all can get y'alls good-getting drunk ass's outta my damn house if y'all keep slammin' them thangs. Host that!" She walked out. "Act like they ain't got no damn home training," she mumbled.

She took her seat next to Jazelle. "Black folks always gotta act a' ass when they get together—especially when they drunk."

Jazelle chuckled, knowing Gwen was telling the truth.

Minutes later, Mackenzee and some of the other kids who weren't dancing came from outside, hollering. "Grandma is coming!"

The matriarch of the family hobbled in assisted by Mitchell, with other cousins following. Everyone fussed and doted on her. Though she had bits of gray hair, it was hard to believe she was a great grandmother. Facial wise, she looked as if she was just Gwen's mother. For Jazelle it was obvious where the source of the family's youthfulness came from.

Jazelle learned it was rare for her to get out the house because of her hip, but Mitchell and his cousins had persuaded her to join everybody at Gwen's, since her husband had gone to his son's for a little while. The love and affection they showered on her, and how she reciprocated, was a far cry from what she'd experienced with Mama Mamie. It brought about a pang of sorrow and bitterness for what she'd never felt from her grandmother. How she'd been robbed of that type of love.

The rue was short lived, though, as something odd she'd been minimally mindful of since Mitchell returned with his grandmother caught her full attention. Aunt Joyce, who'd arrived minutes before Mitchell came back, was staring at him in an unusual manner for an aunt. She was actually ogling him. Jazelle was tripping as she watched her go over to him with her arms spread for a hug. Swore she saw hesitance from him. When they finally embraced, he appeared uncomfortable. Then Jazelle gasped silently.

Aunt Joyce covertly copped an affectionate squeeze on his ass!

Jazelle was embarrassed. *With her own nephew? What type of incestuous ...?*

The uneasy blush on Mitchell's face as he retreated to the back somewhere proved she wasn't imagining something crazy. He had looked like a preacher trying to discreetly exit a strip club after seeing one of his church members.

She felt her temperature rising. Her pissed-off thermometer was approaching frying temperature. She gulped her drink in a swallow and quickly hopped up for a refill.

But once she came back to cop a squat, her anger was instantly replaced by alarm, when a chorus of kids darted in the house frightened, breathing hard and crying, "That man got Mackenzee!"

℥Ω

Hoping for a peaceful, fun day without drama was too much to hope for, Mitchell concluded, as he fishtailed down the block. The kids told him Mackenzee had only been a block and half from the house when the man put her and her bicycle in his car. Of all the people to use to start some shit, that idiot Charles had to enlist Mac. Mitchell knew he was the one behind it, because Mac wouldn't have gotten into anyone's car willingly unless they were family. That had been drilled in her head often. Only someone she was real close to could get her into a car without force. Since Charles was her daddy …

After whipping a right turn off their street, he spotted the car the kids described heading south bound a distance ahead. *Lucky's car.* The Oldsmobile wasn't moving in a big hurry, which decreased Mitchell's anxiety a bit. Possibly drunk, a speeding Charles could mean a whole world of trouble, and he hated considering the possible ramifications.

He contemplated calling the police then thought better of it, picturing a high-speed chase, resulting in a crash. He definitely did not want to panic Charles. Not with his sister in the car with that fool.

Intense and worried, beads of perspiration formed on his head, and he could feel his pulse trying to set a new speed record. His hands were damp as he tightly gripped the steering wheel. Not even concerned about *Johnny-the-god-damn-law*, he pressed the accelerator, cautiously trying to shorten the distance between him and the nut-case picking up speed. The Olds was swerving, and almost swiped a car in the other lane. Mitchell saw the driver making a pissed-off gesture at Charles with a fist.

Mitchell closed within forty yards or less. Either Charles detected him, or Mackenzee noticed him and told her daddy, because the car sped up again, abruptly made a sharp right, and almost veered into a honking Ford F-150. Mitchell winced at the near crash, felt the rate of his heart beat go into overdrive. Some enjoyment without distress in his family was hopeless, he thought. Adversity was always riding shotgun, ready to start some shit.

Calling Charles every pejorative he could think of, he impatiently turned the corner. His eyes widened with alarm and fear. He never heard the screeching of skidding tires, or the cacophony of a crash, yet the Olds was rammed into a fire hydrant. Angry water spouted like a 4th of July fireworks display. They were in a residential area, and alarmed, curious and concerned people had already started assembling.

The most painful period of his lifetime flashed before Mitchell. He tried to force it from his mind. The dream he had a while back, when a voice kept calling out to him, was conjured up. His heart was trying to burst from his chest as he propelled the Tahoe to a curb as close to the wreck as possible. He scanned the unpleasant scene that involved one of the three people he loved most in this world, mumbling a litany of prayers.

When he jumped out, he saw Quincy and some of the others had tailed him because they were rushing up also. Someone must've called 911 because a sirens crescendo was getting stronger, though the shrilling peal of the wailing horn from the Olds was trying to drown it out.

Mitchell pulled an umbrella from under the seat and flicked it open as he scrambled to the wrecked car, excusing himself as he nudged on-lookers out the way and approached the passenger side. Through the water blurred windows, he made out Mac hovered over an inanimate body slumped over the steering wheel.

He snatched the door open, calling Mac's name, asking if she was alright. There was no blood flowing from anywhere that he could see, no glass shattered and splattered all over the place. Though minimal, he felt some relief, but the screaming horn was irritating as hell.

Mac turned to him. A trail of tears crawled down her despondent face. "Mi-Mitcheee ... m-my daddy w-won't get up."

Mitchell could feel his heart breaking into a thousand tiny pieces. His earlier thoughts of yanking Charles out the car and beating his ass like a stepchild disappeared like the money from a crack head's welfare check. No matter how pissed he was, he didn't want his siblings' daddy to be dead.

Cooing and soothing his sister with soft words, he released the seatbelt at her waist, scooped her up and out of the car, handing her and his umbrella to Quincy, who was now behind him, and told him to take her to his car.

He'd learned CPR way back in high school, and figured this would be his first chance to put that training to use as he leaned over to check for a pulse from Charles. He noticed a bottle in a sack was wedged between the seats, and he shook his head. Then a stench abducted his nose: a concoction of ass, tart, liquor breath, feet, mustiness, and piss. Charles was funky as an outhouse. Flat out careworn, with frayed clothes and boots, and a disheveled kinky bush of a beard that was probably home to all kinds of mites. He was worse than the bum Mitchell had seen at the store earlier. For how Charles felt about him, Mitchell thought he'd find some cynical satisfaction at seeing his ex-step daddy's dilapidated state. But because it wasn't in his nature to wish bad on someone, the only thing he felt was disgust.

Slightly holding his breath, he grabbed Charles's wrist. His pulse seemed to be normal. He called his name over the horn, which was giving him a deaf headache.

Charles murmured something.

Mitchell called his name again.

Like a scene from a horror flick, Charles languidly lifted his head. The howling horn went quiet. He mechanically craned his neck, and stared at Mitchell with menacing, bloodshot eyes.

The stare was so eerie Mitchell thought of the "Exorcist" and almost recoiled. Charles was ugggggly!

"Why couldn't ya'll assholes just leave me and my baby be?" Charles sounded like he had murder on his mind. "And yo' punk ass!"

Mitchell almost fled from the liquor vapors Charles released until he said what he just said. Seeing nothing seemed to be wrong with Charles externally, Mitchell's earlier sorrow was replaced with animosity. The alcoholic son-of-a-bitch had put his sister's life in jeopardy, and now he wanted to talk shit! Mitchell glimpsed at the sack of whatever it was and his anger transformed into rage like he'd never known, as *punk* echoed in his head.

Just as he raised his fist to knock the stink off Charles, someone latched hold to his arm and jerked him from the car. Mitchell turned, looked into the eyes of a black po-po in a yellow slicker.

Charles's savior.

"Yeah, you better get me away from that drunken fool!" he shouted as the officer and his partner ushered him away from the car. "And that idiot's not hurt at all. Too damn drunk to be injured."

The officers commanded Mitchell to calm down, released him when they were a distance from the car. Mitchell chilled out. His thoughts went to Mac. He glanced to where he'd parked; saw that G-Lady and Montell had arrived, so had Jazelle, as well as EMSA, because a paramedic was talking to them while Mac was in Montell's arms, clinging to his neck.

He heard Charles cursing at the officers as they pulled him from the car. He sent a grimacing glance in that direction then turned and started toward his family. With all the people clustered around, Thanksgiving had turned into a fucked up spectacle, diverting these folks' holiday bliss. For that, they needed to kick Charles's ass, take him to jail, and lose the key for a long while. Maybe he'd sober up some. Those were Mitchell's thoughts.

Hearing that her daughter was painless and injury free after the medics checked Mackenzee over, Gwen, boiling with anger, stalked to the police car where they were about to stuff Charles. All the pain, resentment and fury he'd caused her and her kids over the years finally peaked with this stunt. She hadn't been cruel or unfair to him. She had been too fair in fact, providing him reasonable conditions and opportunities to see Mac. Montell was old enough to decide on his own whether he wanted to see his daddy or not. She knew Charles loved his kids, only he chose not to put his daughter and son before the bottle. All her prayers for him to change hadn't worked.

Lips pursed, she pierced her virtually unrecognizable ex with a menacing stare as she approached him. His skeletal, dingy, dusty, sickly looking ass was no resemblance to the person who'd given her children two and three. She almost puked.

But she was too pissed. After the crap he'd pulled, she couldn't waste a damn thing on his tore-up-from-the-floor-up ass.

"I told you not to come around my baby drunk!" She got all in his space, hauled off and slapped the Oklahoma-shit out of Charles. The slap bore the pain, frustrations, and anger of thousands of women, alive and dead. Gwen's quickness surprised him and the officers. Charles's head jerked back, he staggered a bit. "Didn't I, you drunk ass fool!"

Mitchell could've sworn he saw mists of dust, perspiration and funk jump off Charles. Sort of wished he was the one who'd socked him.

One of the officers pushed Gwen away. Charles looked like he could've committed homicide on his ex if he wasn't shackled.

Gwen didn't flinch at his evil glare. "Let 'im loose! Wish he *would* ...! I'll kick his *mutha*—"

The officer calmed her down, asked if she knew who Charles was. She explained what the officer needed to know.

Minutes later, when they were gathered near Mitchell's Tahoe, one of the officers came and read off some of Charles's charges: DUI, driving under suspension, no insurance, reckless driving, endangering a minor, destruction of city property, and others, and there was already a warrant out for his arrest. Everybody was speechless, knowing without doubt he'd be locked down for a hot minute.

"Guess he'll meet the hollow walls of the penzo," Mitchell said, "and wish like hell Johnny Cochran was alive to come help his helpless ass out."

The melancholy expressions of his mama and brother tugged at Mitchell's heart. He wished he could erase this entire incident. He was so sick and tired of the trials his family had to endure. Fortunately Mac had cried herself to sleep, and was lying on Jazelle's lap in the Tahoe, oblivious to the needless scene she'd been a major part of. But he knew when she woke up the memory would manifest in her mind.

Watching the image of the back of Charles's head fade in the squad car, Mitchell's determination to influence the bad his family often experienced with good was at the forefront of his life's purpose stronger than ever. Some things he *could* control.

Night was descending with the briskness of elapsed time, and he stared up at the sky. The North Star was already visible, though barely. He thought back to his childhood. The simple times. How he used to wish he could reach up, pluck that twinkling ball of fire from the sky and put it in his pocket. Back then someone had told him it would always lead you home.

Time to head that way, since my baby sister's safe and sound.

25

Those who'd remained at the house converged on the returning group. Even Erma got out of her seat to see about her granddaughter. With darkness pervading, the earlier energy of the neighborhood had faded and cars were departing, probably heading off for stops with other family and friends. Mackenzee woke up asking about her daddy, but Gwen and Mitchell assured her he was fine without mentioning his appointment with a cell. She told them that she'd been more scared about ramming into the hydrant and the spouting water than anything else. She'd tried to get her daddy to rise from the steering wheel so they could get from under the gushing water, and was crying because he wouldn't.

Other than from movies, she'd never been exposed to a human's death, and no one mentioned the word or asked if the possible thought of her daddy being dead had crossed her mind.

Later, after making sure Mitchell would still be home when she returned, Mac left to spend the next two days with Gwen's older sister Renee and her girls. With the evening winding down, the rest of the family was leaving as well. Once he, Montell, Quincy, and Li'l Q put the furniture back in place, Mitchell was ready to take Jazelle home. Emotionally drained, he was glad the evening was about to end. When everybody was gone he could find some solitude to gather the dreadful thoughts stirring around in his head.

As Jazelle and he were about to leave, she said her goodbye's, embraced the hostess. "Thank you for the most wonderful and fun Thanksgiving, Gwen," she said euphorically.

"You and everybody else made me feel just like family. It was the best time I've had in ..." She raised her hands, unable to verbalize her feelings.

Gwen, who had volunteered to take Erma home, made Jazelle a to-go plate, and also a whole sweet potato pie since she'd loved it so much.

"Like I told you earlier, anytime you wanna spend a holiday with us, you got my number." Apologizing for her ex's stunt, she added, "And I'm so sorry about that ... other situation."

ဆာ၏

Driving down the street minutes later, his thoughts wandering, and a full stomach after downing another fat plate, Mitchell sluggishly existed. So much so, he wasn't heedful of Jazelle's sideways gaze at him as she lazily leaned against the door.

They were barely up the block when they were held up by a truck struggling to parallel park in a tight space.

Eyes still surreptitiously fixed on Mitchell, Jazelle was amused that he appeared to be unfazed by the momentary hold up. Had she been driving, she would've been impatient and irritated. She figured he was probably too drained to be annoyed, especially after the emotional energy she was sure he expended on the incident with Mac and her father. She sure had. When those kids stormed in the house yelling, "Some man took off with Mackenzee!" she'd almost lost it. The thought of her favorite student being snatched up and abducted by some fool was scary as hell.

She felt a pang of sympathy for Mac's father. He had honorable intentions, but used the wrong method. At least he was desperate enough to do something stupid just to see his little girl. Some men didn't make an effort to see their kids at all.

Realizing she'd unconsciously alluded to her own father, she shifted her body to face Mitchell, placing her left knee on the seat, foot underneath her. She wanted to release the seatbelt from across her since it was getting on her nerves, but knew better. She didn't have the money to be paying for a bogus, no-seatbelt ticket.

Looking at Mitchell, she thought she saw a hint of a frown on his face. He looked a little weary. Added to Mr. Morgan's imposition, she was sure his present state also had something to do with family. They'd pretty much worn him down. His cousins had flocked around him constantly, like he was the *King.*

"Want me to get out and go show that driver how to park a truck?" she asked jokingly, surmising his mind was occupied by something other than the delay. But she was getting impatient enough for both of them.

He chuckled softly. "Don't think that driver would be too receptive to some stranger trying to show him or her how to maneuver."

"Bet it's a man?" She was impressed by his young self using *him* or *her.* "Some of you can't drive any better than women," she teased.

He looked at her and smiled wryly.

Thinking about patience, Jazelle recalled how he'd so easily put up with his family. Some were irksome as a mother-in-law, especially his drunk Uncle Sammy and cousin, Royce, who'd tried to flirt with her all evening. Anybody else would've been aggravated as hell, but Mitchell never displayed an iota of aggravation. And the way they all seemed to brag and boast about him, like he was a paragon, got to her a bit, knowing he wasn't as he appeared. *Do they know about his other side? The illegal activities?* If so, she was certain it wouldn't matter. With their ghetto mentalities, they'd simply qualify it as getting his *paper* by any means necessary, like so many of the other young brothers in the inner-city were doing. All money was good money to them.

"Mitchell, was it me or do your family treat you almost like a celebrity?"

"Hunh?" he asked quizzically.

"All of them look up to you—even your aunts, uncles, and older cousins—like you're some sort of star."

Mitchell was quiet for a long moment. He wasn't in the mood to talk about himself or anything, or anybody else. So what if they looked up to him? They were proud of their only family member who'd graduated from college.

"Aww, that's because they haven't seen me in a while," he said dismissively. "As far as my aunts and uncles are concerned, they're always proud I did something good with my life. I bet most black families show that kinda pride and love to the first in the family to go to college."

They haven't seen you in a while? How come? I seem to run into your young ass all the time.

"Well what about Aunt Joyce?" For some reason what she'd seen Joyce do to him was one of two or three things that perturbed her. Now that the holiday was mostly over, and there was nothing left of it to spoil—Mr. Morgan almost did that single handedly—and since she had him to herself, maybe she could finally get some answers. She noticed he tensed up some. "She seemed a lot more than proud from what I observed."

Mitchell thought about Aunt Joyce. Besides her groping his butt, in his ear she had asked when he was going to give her a visit. It was obvious what the invitation implied. He'd hoped no one had witnessed her brief indiscretion, now he knew Jazelle had. *Damn!*

"Actually she's not my auntie. She's a childhood friend of G-Lady and her sisters, so she's like an Aunt to us kids."

Jazelle noticed he suddenly wasn't as patient about their little hold up. That only heightened her curiosity, made her more irritated by what she'd witnessed than she should've been.

"Unh. So what I saw was a little ... innocent flirting, then?"

If only you knew. "Don't know what you saw, but she's teased me since I can remember." The truth. "It's innocent and meaningless." A lie.

The truck finally parked and Mitchell quickly accelerated. He was starting to get uncomfortable with her questions, and wanted to get her home and out of his hair. Not that she could know, but it wasn't a good time to be asking him shit. Personal shit definitely. Fragmented thoughts of what could've happened to his sister and Charles—like plunging head first through the windshield; a blood fest with their bodies all broken up and punctured with shards of glass or metal—was swirling in his head, and he was feeling a little touchy. He hadn't mentioned it to anyone but he'd been scared shitless when he hit the corner and saw them crashed. He'd just known they'd be rolling his sister to an ambulance on a gurney, or packing her away in a body bag. Nothing against Jazelle, but he wanted some time to himself to get the horrific images out of his mind.

"If you say so," she intoned with a touch of sarcasm. Instinct told her there was more to it than meaningless teasing. A woman knows a woman. That teasing was in search of some *dickful pleasing.*

Mitchell clicked on some music. Jazelle wondered if it was signaling no more questions. Dawn had told her several times to be more assertive and unwavering with men. That's one way to find out what they're hiding, their secrets. This was one of those moments, but she was concerned about crossing a line. Alienating him. Wouldn't that be a grateful way to show her appreciation for all of his Thanksgiving Day generosity? Thanks to his kindness, she'd unexpectedly had a Thanksgiving to remember. How would she look spoiling all that by pissing off the person most responsible? *But if you don't try to seek what you yearn to know, it will haunt you for a long time coming,* admonished a voice in her head.

At that moment she thought of Amanda's fear to confront her husband about his suspected cheating, and how it was tormenting her. How something about Mitchell had been jarring at her since the day she met him. Her father had destroyed their family with his thoughtlessness, and though of different circumstances, Mitchell could do similar damage to his family a lá a lengthy incarceration, or worse—death. It would hurt his folks something terrible.

Just like what happened with her mother.

In retrospect, maybe if someone would've appealed to her father before he dropped his bomb, chances were she'd be alive today.

Feeling foolish, Jazelle frowned at the lame reasoning. Who was she kidding? Her father's situation involved another woman. Whenever a narrow minded man—married or single—dibbled and dabbled with some new pussy and got hooked, it wasn't ending easily. Someone pleading to him maybe would've temporarily prolonged the inevitable, but he was going to do what he was going to do.

Still, what happened to her family boosted her need to protect Mitchell's family, and her intervening would be part of looking out for the benefit of her student, even if it indirectly had nothing to do with the classroom.

Nothing ventured, nothing gained she told herself as justification for her need to delve into his personal life.

"Mitchell?" He glanced at her sideways. She paused, still trying to build enough courage. They were getting closer to her complex, and she'd better quit stalling. This opportunity may never come again. "I don't mean to get in your business, but ... because of Mac, I feel the need to say something."

She waited for him to respond. He remained quiet.

"It's none of my business, I know," she went on, "and I might be out of line, but the illegal stuff you're doing"—a furrow developed between his eyes—"to make your money, don't you know you're bound to get busted? Outsmarting the law only lasts so long. They'll eventually catch on to your illegal ways."

G-Lady must've planted that mess in her head. That woman's always running her damn mouth.

" 'Illegal ways?' " he uttered incredulously. "Who said I'm doing something illegal?"

"What do you mean, 'who?' Don't you think it's obvious?" She said it like she was appalled he could even ask that question. "The cars—your mother's, this one we're in," she tapped the seat for emphasis. "Clothes, jewelry—I've seen some of the things you've bought your mother and sister—"

"That doesn't mean anything."

"It does for someone whose family is poor. Someone who is *supposedly*," she enunciated the last word, "in college, which I'm skeptical of, 'cause you seem to always pop up in town at times when a college student should be in class. And that wad of money you pulled out at the fair? Explain how a financially challenged person can accumulate a stack like that if you're not hustling."

Slightly up ahead, police lights flashed. Tulsa's finest had hemmed up some brotha in an old school candied out sedan sitting up high on some big ass oversized rims. Mitchell grimaced as they passed, knowing the image ignited the stereotype of that being a drug dealers car, right when Jazelle was harassing him about being a criminal. He could feel the censure come from her. Without looking at her, he knew she was now more focused on his so-called involvement in a lifestyle similar to what was presumably the lifestyle of that dude. He wanted to laugh, but didn't have the energy. He knew he should be *checkin'* her for her misplaced belief, but her accusations had no legs to stand on. None at all.

She was neither a threat nor an obstacle to the secret he'd been harboring for months, but since she was in his shit right now, it must've struck something, because he was starting to want someone, other than those friends connected to Omnity, in on his secret.

Before he could fully rationalize this bizarre occurrence, dignify her ridiculous accusations by responding to her last question, he made up his mind.

"Mitchell, you passed the turn to my place," Jazelle alerted him.

Mitchell's expression was impassive. He said nothing and kept driving.

"Mitchell, where ...?" Though mystified, Jazelle went quiet. He was ignoring her.

He passed by the turn to her place and kept going, so Jazelle assumed he was making a stop somewhere, since he was being mute. She sensed he was pissed at her, but she didn't feel bad about bringing up the subject that had been bugging her. But after riding a ways southbound, Mitchell flipped on a blinker, headed on to the expressway, and she became a bit wary. *What the hell?*

"Where're you going?" she asked mildly, not wanting to anger him more than she figured she already had. "Mitchell?"

Already today she'd caused him to do out-of-the-ordinary stuff, as if she'd cast a spell over him. When around her, part of him was wary, while part of him liked it. Shrugging off her periodic appearances in his thoughts during times when his mind should be on business or anything else besides a woman had been occurring off and on since the day they had met. He'd been blowing it off as simply coincidence. He tried to rationalize being nervous at the mere sight of her as just a reminder to stay away from women for the sake of not jeopardizing his promise. And when they randomly crossed paths, like today at the store, or were brought together for reasons such as the parent-teacher conference, he was often non-willfully more reserved.

He wasn't an expert on human behavior, but it didn't take one of the psychological professionals to tell him something was going on with him psychologically because of Jazelle Johnson. All he knew about this woman was that she was a pre-school teacher, a football fan, and by coincidental circumstances, where she lived. Hell, he didn't know her actual age, if she had a boyfriend or not, or, thanks to the escapade with Susan, if she was lesbian. His only connection to her was through Mac. He had no doubt she knew much more about him.

But what was it about her?

He subtly glanced her way. She looked a little apprehensive. "I'm taking you to Norman," he said matter-of-factly.

She looked at him like he was crazy. " '*Norman*?' "

"Yeah. You told me to explain how a"—he searched for her exact words—" 'financially challenged person can accumulate all that,' so that's what I'm gonna do. But I'm showing you instead of telling you. I think visual effect will be a lot more believable than me merely telling you."

" 'Norman?' " She repeated again, puzzled. "But ... but—"

"No ifs, ands, maybes, or buts. You wanna know what I do to get paid, and I'm about to show you."

"I don't really wanna know. I'm just concerned, because eventually you'll get caught and tear your family's hearts apart. Things done in the dark do come to light. It's cliché but true."

Mitchell just listened. She meant well but ...

"And Mitchell, I do know how it is for a family to be torn apart—"

"Oh, and I don't?"

The retort surprised her until she remembered what Gwen told her about his father.

"Yes, you do know firsthand, so why would you want to add fuel to that fire? Don't you think that's insensitive?" When he didn't respond she guessed she'd struck a nerve. "But Mitchell, it's not necessary to travel all the way to Norman. I just wanted to make a plea for Mac's sake. I wouldn't want to see her hurt. I see how much she loves you. I understand all the hardships you've had—money, family dysfunction, other stuff—and your desire to help them, but your way is the wrong way."

Amused by how presumptuous she was, he merely listened to her spiel. She made a good argument, only none of it applied to him. His lifestyle had absolutely nothing to do with what she was referring to. Nothing.

Actually, his mind had wandered off to an odd place. Though he wasn't looking at her, he imagined she was sitting over there looking good, all earnest, and imploring. He smiled at himself and said, "Has anybody ever told you you're pretty when you're riled?"

"I'm pretty when I'm riled?" she repeated, dumbfounded. "What's that all about? What does that have to do with what I've been saying?"

"Nothing. Nothing at all."

Tulsa was quickly passing by, Jazelle noticed. Lights from houses, stores, and other businesses and buildings twinkled at them as they zoomed past. Soon they were passing rows of right-off-the-expressway motels on either side. The motels rehashed one of her *almost* teenage sexual encounters. Spending the weekend with Dawn their junior year of high school, they had gone joyriding with two senior boys from another school when they were supposed to be at their school's football game. They ended up in a double-bed room at the very same Motel 6 Mitchell just passed. The boy's threatened to leave them stranded if they didn't give up the *draws*, until a sheriff patrolling the lot spooked them. The boys eventually dropped them off at the game, calling them DTs—Dick Teases—and cock blockers as they drove off.

Jazelle scrunched up her face at the crazy memory, and returned to the present.

"Mitchell, you're serious about going to Norman, hunh?"

"Serious as a heart attack."

Seeing a sign for the turnpike assured her he was. *Could what he was doing be considered kidnapping*? A man with a bundle strapped to his back walked along the shoulder, and Jazelle wondered if some trying-to-be-humane person would be brave enough to give him a lift. With all the distrust, fear of dangerous and unscrupulous people in the world and repeated warnings for drivers not to pick up hitchhikers, it was a wonder that people still hitchhiked. She wondered how far he would actually walk.

They rolled on, leaving Tulsa behind. Soon they were climbing an incline and her hometown got smaller and smaller, the lights dimmed, becoming a blur. Barely able to discern Tulsa's skyline, she definitely believed Mitchell's intentions now. She thought about acting a damn fool, but being the non-confrontational person she was, sensing it wouldn't change his mind anyhow, told herself to chill and roll with the flow. See what would happen.

Besides, though she was ashamed of herself for it, she was way more curious about what he'd be showing her than she would admit.

26

With the student population on Christmas break, Norman was tame when they arrived. Jazelle had dozed off at the halfway point of the journey after realizing Mitchell wasn't answering anymore of her questions, and now as they rode through *Sooner Nation*, he softly called her name to wake her.

Jazelle slowly opened her eyes and sat up, groggy and disoriented. Looking at Mitchell, she remembered he'd sort of abducted her.

"Wh-where are we?" She was trying to focus on the surroundings passing her by, but with the darkness hindering her vision, she squinted hopelessly, trying to make out what she could.

"Norman," Mitchell answered. Kendrick Lamar was rapping on low volume and Mitchell was bobbing his head.

She contemplated, continued looking around. Nothing was familiar.

"You were serious about bringing me to Norman. What time is it?" Though she had a watch on her wrist, like many people just waking up, her head hadn't completely cleared, and the question just came out.

Mitchell pointed at the time illuminated in the instrument panel. Now that he'd reached his destination after impulsively reacting he wasn't sure how to go about unfolding the real deal to her. He was used to having certain things planned and mapped out. What he was about to do felt too ambiguous. He had however thought to call and let his mama know where he was, and told her he had an emergency come up.

Finally shaking off the cobwebs, Jazelle surveyed her surroundings, finding Norman wasn't as she expected. She'd imagined more of a rural town, but it was pretty urbanized from what she could see.

Minutes later, Mitchell was pointing out the obviously vacant OU student dorms to their right, then to their left, where she got a vague view of some buildings which, he told her, made up the operation of the university: classes, faculty offices, student union, library, *et cetera*. A little ways down that same side was the football stadium.

Expecting to be going to the student dorms, if he actually was a student, because dorms were where freshman generally resided, she was bewildered when Mitchell continued by the entire campus. He hadn't answered her questions on the way there so she figured there was no use asking him anything now, and decided to ride contentedly until they got to wherever they were going.

It wasn't long before they pulled up to some apartments? Condos? She wasn't sure. "What are these?" she asked.

"Townhouses." Mitchell shifted into park, cut the engine.

"Who lives here?" She wasn't sure if her notion of him taking her somewhere to harm her was resurfacing.

"You coming in? I've got to get something. You probably need to stretch anyway, or maybe use the bathroom."

"I do, thank you. But you still didn't say where we are, or whose place this is." His evasiveness was starting to work her nerves. He was about to piss her off.

Without answering, as he'd done at his mother's, he was at her door opening and helping her down. This time though, she paid no mind to the gesture or his soft hands, because her growing frustration partnered with leeriness at being in unknown and unfamiliar surroundings.

He sensed her trepidation.

"Come on, Miss—Jazelle. You want to bring that food? I'm sure it needs to be refrigerated." He ducked inside and grabbed the plate Gwen had fixed her from the backseat.

It was chilly, and Jazelle already missed the warmth of the Tahoe. Wherever they where was quiet, well cared for, and looked pretty expensive. A light was on inside and she expected Mitchell to knock or ring the doorbell, but he used his key to unlock the door, opened it and used the remote to deactivate the singing alarm.

She warily stepped inside. The sight before her could've been snatched out of one of those home decorating magazines. She thought his mother's place was laid, but this crib was the *shit*. Lush earth tones suffused the spacious living room majestically. She knew the oversized furniture was cozy as hell. A lazy person's haven. She easily imagined getting lost in its comfort. The fluffy, thick beige carpet was so flawless she was reluctant to walk across it even after taking off her shoes.

She was about to ask whose place it was again, when a poster-size framed portrait over the fireplace mesmerized her. Mackenzee's dimpled smile reigned over the room with the aura of a Picasso or Rembrandt. Anyone who knew her would want to steal it and hang it on their wall. It was that gorgeous. On the mantel, a picture of a smiling Gwen stared at her, as did one of Montell posing with a basketball in a set-shot stance.

Smiling internally, Mitchell watched her reaction. He now had a game plan to let her know what his life was really all about. This stop at his crib was merely a prelude, though it was unplanned. He'd left his office keys here when he'd taken off for Tulsa, so he had to come get them.

"You live here, Mitchell?" she asked, sounding stunned. *What a dumb question*, she quickly checked herself, *why else would his families pictures be in here?* But people did or said stupid stuff when they were frazzled. And she was frazzled.

"Yes I do—for about six months now." He'd owned it longer but hadn't moved in until the renovations were completed. "I need to run upstairs a sec, but feel free to look around."

"How many bedrooms are there?" She was comparing her mediocre apartment, and the one's she'd shared with Dawn. Even together those had nothing on this.

"Three. All up stairs," he said, pointing upward. "The downstairs bathroom is that way."

The bathroom could wait, Jazelle told herself, stepping over to a glimmering hexagon-shaped glass cabinet displaying small shots of Carla and Quincy together, individuals of their boys, Mitchell's grandmother, and some of his other cousins. Small trees in urns, and other plants were arranged about the place. African statuettes, African American paintings, and some other whatnots showered the place, which showed his mama's influence. She wondered if Gwen had a hand in decorating the place.

Enticed, she continued her tour, impressed with everything, including the small office with a laptop opened up at a small workstation, a sparkling kitchen with a big stainless steel refrigerator, which she opened and unbelievably saw it was filled to the hilt. She scoped around for signs of a roommate—mainly a female—other than all that food, because this was too much for one person no matter how much illegal money he made; especially a man. No way could a man maintain a fresh-ass crib this neat and clean without a woman's help. No way. It was too much like perfection.

She frowned at the thought that Mama Mamie would've loved the spotlessness.

Like anyone else, she had to ride out being awestruck before coming back down t o earth. Being astounded was fading as she checked out the built-in bookshelves containing a varied selection of books, as well as trinkets and whatnots for embellishment. She considered what it took him to get all this. *Illegal business must be damn good! Thriving like pimping back in the seventies.* He was living high on the hog while she struggled to pay bills.

Coming down the stairs dangling keys, Mitchell paused at the bottom landing, looking at Jazelle riffling through some books. Something about her in his home was a touch idyllic; like she was meant to be there doing what she was doing. Other than Katie and the women who worked at Omnity, she was the only female to enter his home.

"Did you find the bathroom?" he asked, lacking anything better to say.

"Hmm hunh." Jazelle flipped through a Michael Baisden novel, then placed it back on the shelf and turned to him. "I haven't used it though. Mitchell, do you have a roommate?"

He detected a slight nuance in her tone. Something must've set her off again. Glancing at his watch, he started toward the kitchen. "Are you gonna use it? There's someplace we need to go." He wanted to get to Omnity before it got too late. Being at an office building on a holiday was suspicious enough, and being there this late made it worse, and after today's drama he didn't want to possibly have another encounter with *One Time*.

Jazelle impulsively caught him by the arm before realizing it. "You still didn't say if you had a roommate or not." She wasn't letting him off the hook this time. *Enough of that shit.* She wanted him to answer. Now!

He still didn't answer. In spite of knowing she was waiting for a reply, something about the word *roommate* drew his thoughts to the dorms early in his freshman year.

"My roommate withdrew from school after only one week," Mitchell responded to his guest's question, who was observing the pictures taped to the wall above one of the two twin-size beds in the room. "Something about the finances he thought he had being gone."

"That's messed up. Did he say what happened to the money?"

"Naw—just that it's not there."

His guest sat on the bed. "Do you think he would've been cool?"

"During the time he was here we had no problems. We hung pretty closely since we were *fresh meat* to this college scene." Mitchell put a CD in the stereo and Li'l Wayne filled the room. "We had different taste in music though. He was a white dude that liked that grunge type of stuff. Other than that, who knows?"

"So, have they said if you'll be getting another roommie yet?" Mitchell sort of shrugged his shoulders, while his guest continued, "At first I was concerned about how my roommate and I would get along but so far we're okay. It's kind of good having one."

"My RA told me they probably will, but if it doesn't happen within the next couple weeks, I'll probably be livin' solo till next semester."

Mitchell cringed at the memory, sensed Jazelle's impatient, chiding eyes on him. He glanced at her, quickly looked away. "You ready to go?" He idly dangled the keys.

"You still haven't—"

He interrupted her by holding up a placatory hand. "I'll make everything clear soon. So unless you need to use the bathroom, can we roll, please?" He said it so politely.

Jazelle rolled her eyes before strutting to the bathroom.

₧₧

She assumed he was taking her to some run-down projects or somewhere with a bunch of crack heads running around, because even though she'd toyed with the idea of him being a gigolo or escort after seeing him with that white woman, she actually believed he was a drug dealer. With all he'd accumulated, that was the most logical explanation. The money was fast and came in bunches. From what she'd seen of his, very hefty bunches.

They parked in the lot of a business building near Norman's tiny downtown area, and he whisked her inside, into the lobby. Jazelle didn't know what to think. On the way there she'd forced herself to shut up, not ask any more questions. But curiosity was jabbing at her left and right. She needed some answers PDQ—Pretty Damn Quick.

She was about to open her mouth when Mitchell said, "Welcome to Omnity Sports. Professional sports management for some of the famous pro athletes you're familiar with, mainly your favorite football player." He sounded professional, as if he was trying to make a pitch for a sale. "I'm part owner. In other words"—he made a spreading gesture with his hands—"all this is what I do."

Jazelle looked at him like he was a damn fool. *What did he mean my favorite football player? What cockamamie bull is this impassive-ass little boy trying to put over on me? And something about being part owner?*

She looked around, trying to understand.

"Mitchell what does this building have to do with what you do?" she asked tersely. "And how does it connect to all the money and stuff?"

He smiled, and no matter how annoyed she was, it was so disarming, she couldn't help but pause. Then he drew her by the hand, led her through a corridor of closed office doors, where she abruptly stopped at a section of wall adorned by two rows of framed, autographed portraits. Twin creases formed between her eyebrows, because one looked like ... Main Man? What

Montell had told her about Mitchell being good friends with Main Man popped into her mind.

That's ..." she trailed off, unsure. It looked like his upper half in a suit and tie, but out of his football uniform she couldn't tell.

"Main Man," Mitchell finished for her, thrilled by her bemused expression. He then led her to an office, unlocked and opened the door.

Jazelle's head was still turned in the direction of the portraits, when she turned and brought her attention to what was now in front of her. At the doorjamb she looked inside and around the office. It was roomy, befitting an executive: cozy swivel chairs, computer station, large desk, a couch, all fronted by a beautiful oriental rug. Easing on in up on Mitchell's request, she scanned the glossed bookshelves, sighting accounting, corporation, tax, and other books pertaining to business.

Mitchell remained silent, allowing what was taking place to happen at its own pace.

Not until she rounded the desk and saw pictures of his family sitting on it, did Jazelle gasp. Her mouth shaped into a capital O, and wide-eyed marvel emerged. Reflexively, she turned to the wall behind the desk blanketed with plaques and awards. *Surprised* wouldn't completely describe the effect of what she saw there. Shocked. Stupefied. So stunned, her heart was beating a big bass drum. This couldn't be. *My eyes must be playing tricks ...*

Mitchell intervened, knowing she was drowning in disbelief. "I know this is turning out to be a journey of shock, Jazelle, but what you're looking at is how Mitchell Thomas *really earns his money.*"

Jazelle's eyes were riveted by framed degrees with his name certifying he'd earned a BBA, an MBA, and there was even a framed CPA certification.

"Mitchell, how old are you?" she asked, almost whispering, turning to look at him, totally deranged in the head.

In a condensed version, Mitchell gave her an earful: his age, how easy school was for him—including him advancing and breezing through a couple years early—the story behind Omnity, the fact that his family knew nothing about it, why he was keeping it a secret from them. "And by the way, I live in the townhouse by myself. I own it."

Jazelle was dumb struck. Felt like the ass of a funny joke.

"You're *twenty-two*?" she said blankly, having difficulty absorbing him being a legally grown man, but looking like he should be gearing up for his junior prom. "And you really are good friends with Main Man?" She was staring at a photo on the wall of him, Main Man, and a white guy Mitchell told her was Travis, his partner.

"We're pretty tight," he said, crossing his fingers, indicating there closeness. "He's our client, but we're friends and real cool outside of business."

Reaching for the desk to steady herself, Jazelle slowly turned, looking at Mitchell apologetically. She was so outdone she could hardly speak. The cars, things he'd gotten his family, that tight townhouse ... all acquired by legal means. He'd earned his money honestly. It was so unbelievable. Something inside had told her there was something *good* about him. Honest. And vaguely she'd listened, but it was hard for any objectivity with her cynicism toward men, so she spent misdirected energy suspecting him of being up to no good like most men she'd known.

Now here he was, telling her he wasn't the teenager she thought, or the college freshman she'd assumed, but was twenty-two, with undergraduate and graduate degrees with honors, and part owner of a very successful company. She had misjudged people before, but this flat out took the case. It was damn near unforgivable how far off she had been about him. She felt dumber than a box of rocks and three times as stupid.

Seeing how she looked right now was kind of amusing to Mitchell. He started grinning.

Jazelle frowned. "What're you smiling about?" She didn't see a damn thing funny!

"You—the way you're looking. I can't tell if you're mad or about to cry."

She had nothing to say. Not one damn thing. The way she felt she could only imagine how her face looked.

"You thought I was dealing drugs," Mitchell said, more as a statement than a question. "That is what you were insinuating, right?"

Her blank, guilty expression provided the answer.

"Did G-Lady—I mean my mama—put that mess in your head?"

Jazelle looked bewildered. "No. Why would she do that?"

"Because she thought—thinks—the same thing. She's been harassing me about it too." He told her about the chat he'd had with his mama. "And she's supposed to know her own son better than anybody. So, I figured she said something to you. Me a drug dealer? That's so ludicrous."

"Well, I just assumed—"

"Like so many others ... people are always wanting to stereotype and think the worst about somebody—especially black folks."

"No—that wasn't it. It's ... hard to explain."

It amused Mitchell watching her squirm. What she'd suspected him of wasn't a big deal. Misconceptions were part of the territory when secrets were involved. It was human nature to assume, accuse, or misrepresent when there was a shortage of facts. For the hell of it though, he wanted to hear what she had to say.

"Oh really?" He leaned on the doorjamb, folded his arms.

Earnestly, Jazelle started toward him. "We've never discussed it but I thought you were only 17 or 18. Actually, the first time I saw you I could've sworn you were just 15 or 16, until that was subsequently rectified at your mother's party."

Mitchell thought back to the party when she'd somehow confused him with Montell. "You thought I was 15 or 16?" he said, feigning incredulity. "And ever since G-Lady's party you've thought I was only eighteen and perpetrating being a college student?"

She nodded blankly. "So with me thinking you were just a teenager, and with your families ... you know, *financial status* contradicting the things you were buying, there was no choice but for me to suspect what I did."

Mitchell shook his head, grinning. "Now I've heard it all."

Jazelle started explaining how stupid and sorry she was. "I don't normally go around passing judgment and stereotyping people, but with you ... I got emotionally caught up. I didn't want Mackenzee getting hurt like I did at that age. And then, with me coping with Nikki's problems, the little girl Mac had the skirmish with, I was sorta coerced into judging you."

By now she was directly in front of Mitchell, ruefully looking into his eyes. Mitchell couldn't stand anyone looking sad around him.

"Miss—I mean—Jazelle, thank you for looking out for my sis." He had to let her off the hook, glad he'd dispelled her ill-conceived notions about him. "Not all teachers are that concerned. And I'm sorry you had to think the worst of a brotha before I cleared it all up. But if my own family is clueless, there's no way you could've known what I have going on."

She looked into those browns of his and, before realizing it, raised a hand to his face, tracing it lightly, oblivious of her disdain toward men. Right now that was obsolete. Mitchell had shown her not all men were assholes, and the decency in him was pushing her to him. He had morals, character, wasn't insensitive, had a giving nature, and he was a gentleman. Qualities women only fantasized about a man having.

The moment she touched him, Mitchell stiffened, looking into her eyes. His heart rate began speeding up.

Jazelle gave no thought to what she was doing. The way he was looking at her had her thinking of only what was in front of her.

She kissed him.

Mitchell knew it was wrong, but the feel of her lips meshing with his felt right. He was unable to stop it. Against his will, he closed his eyes, allowing the sensation to subdue him, knowing a storm was brewing.

With pleasant sensations between her thighs, sensitivity in her breast and general untamed arousal throughout her body, Jazelle's arms went around his neck. She easily parted his lips with her tongue, initiating an awkward tongue slow dance that shortly turned adept.

Responding, Mitchell's hands glided over her spine on their own, creeping down to her butt, where he lightly squeezed, prodded on by the firmness. The kiss deepened and became passionate as their bodies began slowly grinding.

It had been a long, long time since he'd felt the passion of a kiss—the most intimate part of physical affection. Natural instincts took over as he worked kisses downward, placing them on her neck, a tongue tease to the ear, making her catch her breath.

"Ohhh ... Mitchell," she breathed as he tugged the sweatshirt off her shoulder a bit, planting kisses there.

At that point their intent to stay clear of the opposite sex was non-existent. They didn't have that type of fight in them right now. Man and woman were meant for this.

It had been a while and Jazelle was overdue for some maintenance.

Pulling back, they stared at each other. Neither said a word. Desire cried out from their eyes. Jazelle took his hand, lead him to his desk. The only sounds other than their labored breathing came from the low hum of the heater through the vents.

Jazelle perched herself on the desk, drew him into a hungry kiss, softly moaned when his hand covered one of her breasts. Looking into his eyes, she ran her hands over his chest, rubbing the pecs beneath his sweat shirt, then she started pulling it up, raised his arms, cleared it over his head and let it drop to the floor. She kissed his chest, teased and softly sucked on his tiny nipples, got more aroused by his soft gasps and subtle shudders. She was getting real anxious as he worked her sweat shirt up and over her head.

Unclasping her bra, Mitchell felt the warmth when flesh touched flesh. They exchanged kisses, tongued each other's ears and traced each other's spines. Slipping the straps from her shoulders, liberating her breasts, he kissed one nipple then the other.

Hissing and tilting her head back, Jazelle was becoming impatient with lust. She unfastened his jeans, then slipped off the desk and slid them down his legs, running her hands over his toned thighs as he stepped out of them. He was already bone rock. She shuddered internally when he tongued her navel as he pulled her pants from under her feet.

Underwear was hastily pulled off, and they hungrily eyed one another's nakedness. She had never seen a more gorgeous brotha and he saw a soul sista's image of beauty and femininity. He ran a hand through her hair, removed what bound it, loved how it fell to her shoulders as she shook it loose. Dallying his tongue over her taut nipples, he eased a hand between her thighs, rubbing over the patch of hair, traced the perimeter, then the slit of her vagina.

She was wet, warm, and wanting.

So wet.

She almost lost it as he stirred her creamy center, and thinking about Dawn telling her to *assert her will on men, be the driver*, Jazelle pushed Mitchell's head south, perched her bottom back on the desk. He entered the cooch with his tongue, licking, nipping, sucking, and savoring the sweet juice like it was sustenance for survival. She swung both legs over his shoulder, giving him full access, and almost had a fit of pleasure it felt so damn good.

"Ooooo ... da-uuum ... Mi-tchell," she moaned, urging him out of it for a breather because she couldn't take it.

Mitchell rose, reached around her and swept everything on the desk to the floor, and easily entered that orifice of delight. Jazelle closed her eyes, catching a very deep breath, arched her back, desperately pulled him deeper inside her, as if wanting to weld their bodies together.

Eyes closed, stroking passionately, it all seemed too good to be true. Feeling like he was about to die and go to heaven, Mitchell pulled out, squeezed his tip, repressing the gush on the verge of erupting. He re-entered when that sensation waned.

Panting. Grinding. Moaning. Groaning. Humping. Faster and faster.

Jazelle started climaxing, then Mitchell did as well, both uttering incoherent expletives, her fingers digging into his back, his hands franticly clutching her ass, and it so happened that she came twice in succession before the two sweaty, spent bodies disconnected, fully exhausted.

ഇ◌ଔ

Breathing like they'd been running from a grizzly bear, both were speechless, looking at each other, unsure of what to say, or if anything should be said. They'd gotten caught up in the emotions of the moment, responding to their hormones like two unstructured adolescents.

Jazelle warned herself not to let emotions intervene and get all sappy, wanting to cling to him like he was now her man. That action had simply been sex. Something that happened on a humbug. *So, heifer, don't try to read more into it than it was.*

Subtly becoming self-conscious, she instinctively covered her breast with one arm and her vagina with her free hand, wondering what had come over her to cause her to act like a ho. Through all her bad choices with men, she'd never given it up this spontaneously, and felt a little embarrassed, if not ashamed by her sluttiness.

Feeling what she was feeling, she kept quiet.

Normality began setting in for Mitchell as well, and though the constricting feelings of guilt hadn't struck yet, he knew what he'd just succumbed to wasn't right. Not at all. He hated the thought of facing another stint of the guilt he'd dealt with after the episode with Susan. Man, was he disappointed with himself for his lack of self-control. Yes, he was human, flawed, but he hadn't made promises which he maintained for such a long time just to break them twice within such a short span for quick dips in some enticing coochie.

He just knew the guilt was going to attack his black ass.

Both found their clothes, and started dressing. Without preamble, he asked if she was ready to go. Not willing to risk falling asleep at the wheel driving back to Tulsa, which Jazelle agreed with, they went back to his place to crash for the night.

When they got there, Mitchell told her where the linen was, extra toothbrushes, and that she could use the washer and dryer to wash her clothes if she needed.

After some assuaging relaxation, Jazelle emerged from the Jacuzzi tub and put on his terry-cloth robe. On the bed in the spare room, he'd lain out a black T-shirt for her that hung just below her knees when she slipped it on, and gray draw-string gym shorts that were baggy as hell on her.

Downstairs, she found him quietly sleeping on the couch. *Just like a man to fall asleep afterward.* He'd taken off his tennies. She smiled. Her earlier shame for giving up the draws so easily had dwindled. Reliving the entire office scene, a tremor shot through her body. *I wore him out. But he did fulfill one of my secret fantasies to the fullest. Fullest.*

Shamelessly, she imagined stripping off his clothes while he slept, surprising him by coaxing him into round two.

Exhaling, she quickly went and threw her clothes in the washer before she ended up having to take a cold shower to calm her greedy hormones.

Before climbing the stairs to retrieve one of the comforters to spread over Mitchell, she thought about waking him to shower, but changed her mind at the thought of him sleeping with the scent and remnants of her dried juices caked on him.

27

Finally waking up, Jazelle smelled something good, remembered she was at Mitchell's, and looked at the digital clock on the stand next to the comfortable bed, that illuminated 12:45 P.M. *Damn! I Slept that long*? She had slept like a baby for real. It had been a while since she'd rested so well. Peacefully. She thought about the reason she'd been so exhausted and grinned like an inmate after a conjugal visit.

Curious about the wafting aroma, hungry, she got up, stretched and went to the bathroom to do the hygiene routine. After pulling on the terry cloth robe and tying the sash, she finger combed her hair in the dresser mirror, a little self-conscious about how Mitchell would take her morning appearance.

Pfft, he's seen me naked, too late to worry about impressions now.

She damn near fainted once she got to the source of the aroma. A bunch of BS—lies, deceit, pain, anger—was the only thing a man had ever cooked for her, but to her disbelief, arranged on the dining table, was French toast, omelet, hash browns, pork sausage, turkey sausage, bacon, milk and orange juice. Her feelings for Mr. Mitchell Thomas swelled like a fat woman.

"I was just about to come wake you," Mitchell said when he came from the kitchen and saw her standing there. He gestured for her to sit.

Still shocked, half opened mouth, she did.

"Guess it's safe to say you slept well."

Jazelle blushed, thought about the reason why again.

"Mmm-hunh. Wish I didn't have to get up. At home I'm sleep deprived. My upstairs neighbors are the shits."

"I know the feeling. Had the same problem in my first apartment while I was still in college."

He being a college graduate and all the other stuff she'd found out last night still had her tripping. She quickly learned he had some of Gwen's talent in the kitchen, too, because the food was good. "I see you have some culinary skills."

"Thank you. So am I off your shit list now?" Mitchell playfully asked.

She frowned good-naturedly. "Do you deserve to be? I know how slick you men try to be. You're probably hiding something else major."

He threw up his hands, palms upward. "Who, me? Slick? Hiding something else?"

She laughed; so did he. Surprisingly neither was feeling awkward after last night. He told her he'd put her clothes in the dryer and ironed them. He even apologized for conking out on her. Jazelle considered pinching herself, unable to believe she'd actually met a man with Mitchell's too-good-to-be-real attributes. Thought of how she could get used to all that he brought to the table.

Will you marry me, Mitchell?

߷

"So Mitchell, have you traveled to lots of places?" Jazelle asked, assuming agents did plenty globetrotting. They were now on the way back to Tulsa.

"From one end of the US map to the other, up and down."

"Is New York like they say—fast city that never sleeps? I would love to go there one day, but know it'll likely never happen."

"Yeah, it's a different kinda place than what we're used to. There, the Windy City, City of Angels, places like that are like a culture shock for us smaller city folks. And a place like Oklahoma would surely be a culture shock for them. We're like the turtle to their rabbit."

"I bet."

"But you know what's messed up? For some idiotic reason, especially East Coast and up North, those people are under the stupid impression that we're still riding horses and buggies in Oklahoma."

"For real?"

"Fo' real. Tripped me out when I was in Chi-town sporting an Oklahoma T-shirt and told this curious thirty-something sista I was from Tulsa, Oklahoma. She asked me aren't we still doing the Cowboy-Indian and farm thing. And plenty others have come at me with the same perception."

Jazelle made a face. "That's effe'd up."

"And they try to call us *country*, when they need to move around, check out some other places on the map. It offends me. I have much Oklahoma pride. Now when we travel—T-Dub and I—we carry postcards of Tulsa and OKC to let 'em know they are cities, just not as large and congested with overpopulation. And I let 'em know I've never been on a farm in my life. Never."

"Neither have I."

"While they're playin', I've never been on a horse."

I have, Jazelle thought, pertaining to Mitchell.

Mitchell couldn't believe how he was going along as if last night's office tryst never happened. He was trying to leave it where it happened. At work the coming Monday at least he could face the office without Jazelle around. He hoped she wouldn't dwell on it today.

A freely talking Mitchell was unexpected. Jazelle liked him being conversational. "Mitchell how many women do you have?" she asked all out of the blue. She'd been thinking about it though. She never found any signs of a girlfriend at his place, though there could've been something in his room. She wasn't ratchet enough to look around in there. "I know there's someone somewhere."

Not this subject. "Can't a brotha just be solo if he chooses?" It was time to evade and be vague.

"Shoot no. Men always have a woman stashed somewhere. Sometimes several." In a perfect world she'd be his woman. The *one* and *only*.

"I've never seen you with a man or heard you mention anything about one. Where're you hiding him?" The old 'flip the script' on her. But abnormal for him, he was actually curious. But he didn't like that he was. "What up with that?"

"Can't a sista just be solo if she chooses?" She chuckled. "We have gotten to be pretty darn independent in these days and times, you know. Women *can* make it just fine without a man." Though true, it was her cynicism talking. Deep down she wanted someone to share life with.

He chuckled. "It's possible. And yeah, many women are without by choice, but like men, usually somebody's getting the draws."

"That's true in many cases, but my cat's been caged up." She turned both thumbs down. "Because the idiots I've been not-so-fortunate to come across have been ... Let's just say, they weren't worth the time and pain their mama's splayed their legs for."

Even though he was a man, he agreed with her for the most part. G-Lady, Desiree ... so many other women he knew had had worthless men.

"Women do travel a hazardous road trying to find a decent dude. Someone worthwhile." He elected not to give his opinion that many women often settled for less than they should; got what they paid for, so to speak. "So you don't have a man?"

"Nope. My grade with men is a freakin' F minus."

"Well what about the picture of the Marine at your crib?"

"That's my big brother."

"Ohhh, now that I think about it, he did favor you."

"You should see us together in person."

She doesn't have a man. Why did he feel like a little broke boy who just found some money?

Jazelle thought of what she'd meant to bring up last night before certain circumstances erased it. "Mitchell, I was wondering ... I was with a friend one Saturday, and we saw you with ... a white lady."

Mitchell tensed up, hoped his facial muscles didn't sell him out. He'd put the Susan episode way behind him. "You were at the restaurant that evening?"

"Sure was."

"It's embarrassing, but she won a date with me at a bachelor's auction benefitting the Home for Battered Women. Guess it's better to say she paid for a date." He explained how he'd gotten involved in the auction but mentioned nothing else about the *date.*

"I vaguely remember hearing or reading something about that." She wanted to jump with joy that that *Miss Pale and Frail* wasn't someone meaningful, but thought it was very kind and generous of him to contribute to the cause.

They reached Tulsa city limits, oblivious of having made it so fast. Conversation had carried them through heedlessly. Still, Mitchell had tactfully avoided answering questions about his romantic life, but now knew she was single. He didn't know why, but felt good about her being unattached. And after gaining her promise not to mention it to anyone along with everything else she'd recently discovered about him, he showed her his best kept, most important secret. After seeing it, Jazelle was *d-o-n-e*!

In her parking lot, he remembered to give her the plate of food and pie she never touched.

"By the way, Jazelle," he said, standing outside the Tahoe, reaching inside to get a business card from the visor, and handing it to her. "If you ever have any financial matters you need assistance with, holla at a brotha. Finance is *my* thing."

She wanted to frame the smile on his face, box him up and take him in her apartment and hold him hostage. He was a one-of-a-kind man-child. She scanned the card. "Not that I'd ever have any reasons for your *professional expertise*," she wished he could help with her finances as broke as she was, "but thank you all the same. Oh, and I know I told you earlier, but thanks again for the lunchtime breakfast. For a bo ... I mean ... man, I gotta give you your props."

He chuckled, almost said *"anytime."* "You're welcome. And thanks again for the compliment. Like mama, like son in the kitchen."

Both hated that their time together was ending. Jazelle hated it the most, because he'd left without so much as a hug or peck on the cheek.

28

"You shittin' me, girl!" Dawn yelled in disbelief, trippin' on Jazelle's account of her eventful Thanksgiving. Only minutes after returning from St. Louis, after getting situated at home, she'd called Jazelle.

"No, every bit is true." Jazelle had covered some of everything but the sex part. She'd ease into that. "If I hadn't seen with my own eyes, I would've never believed any of it. I'd still have him convicted without trial for being a juvenile delinquent headed for a nice, cozy cell in the penzo. He had this chick fooled for real."

"You? I still can't believe his young ass is twenty-two."

"Twenty-two, girl, intelligent as hell, and sittin' on something *phat*. I'm talking phaaaat." It was Sunday, and Jazelle was still floating on cloud nine, happy to pass this *tea* to her BFF.

"So why's he keeping all this from his family? He trying to keep all those spendables on the down low to prevent them from begging all the damn time? If so, I wouldn't blame 'im one bit. Know how black folks are when somebody they know has a little money."

Jazelle scoffed. "Heck no." If Dawn only knew how generous Mitchell was, she'd never let her mouth speak something that absurd. Mitchell had told her it wasn't planned that way; initially he'd kept his occupation from his family in case it failed, but once it started flourishing, he'd come up with the idea to reveal everything after his *main surprise* was completed. She wasn't mentioning that to Dawn, though. She'd already said too much. "He's waiting till Christmas. He's spilling the beans to them then."

"Shoot, I'd love to be a fly on the wall at that house come Christmas."

Jazelle laughed.

"So, Jaz, what did you and Mr. Not-As-Young-As-We-Thought do in that fresh-ass townhouse all by y'alls lonesome at that time of the night?" Dawn was teasing, knowing all too well Jazelle had shut the door and padlocked it on men. That *coochie* was off limits.

Jazelle paused for a second, thinking. "Nothing but sleep and eat." The truth. *But at the office he did me on the desk, which was my fantasy come true.* She was hesitant about telling her about the office, knowing Dawn would make a big deal of it. Jazelle already couldn't get Mitchell out of her head as it was.

"Eat and sleep?" she said with disgust. "That's all?"

"Uhh ..." Jazelle faltered.

"Oh hellll-to-the-naw! I'll be there within twenty minutes, heifer." She hung up.

Better than her word, she was there before twenty minutes, knocking on Jazelle's door.

Trying to make light of it, Jazelle simply told her they'd got caught up in an emotional discharge and done the *do* without realizing what was happening.

"I can't believe ... Jaz, you hoochie, you finally gave—"

"Aww, girl, it ... we just got a little carried away." Jazelle was being vague from fear of showing more feelings for Mitchell than she cared to convey.

"Okay, but was he 'bout any damn thang? Did he hit *that* like it needs to be hit? Did Miss Coochie go snap crackle and pop? Can his fine ass pay the cost to be the boss?"

Ohhh, he did all that and then some. "Don't keep asking a bunch of crazy questions Dawn, girl, there's not much to tell." Truth was, she'd never felt like this before. In the past, she'd thought she had strong feelings for someone, but this was on an entirely different level. "What happened just happened, and that's all there is to it." She was trying to convince herself as much as she was Dawn, but really wanting to describe how he'd *rocketed* her to the moon.

Studying her suspiciously, Dawn yielded for now. She knew Jazelle almost as well as she knew herself, and her best friend could never open up her *gold mine* and let some hard head start *digging for the treasure* without some feelings being involved. Call it woman's intuition, but she knew her homegirl liked that boy.

ഓരു

The next day at school, seeing Mackenzee only amplified Jazelle's thoughts of Mitchell. She had to keep telling herself what she'd told Dawn: *what happened just happened, and that's all there is to it.* She had to force herself not to make something out of nothing.

Still, she couldn't help but think about knowing he wasn't on a one way path to the big house, and what he had in store for his folks was too wonderful not to think about.

That night at job number two her continuous thoughts of Mitchell were temporarily abated when Amanda announced Steven hadn't been cheating. "He'd been taking some fucking cooking classes at night up until the Friday before Thanksgiving week to surprise me and the kids with a Thanksgiving dinner," Amanda said incredulously. She and Jazelle were in the break room. "Can you believe that? And he wants to relieve me in the kitchen often."

"Must be nice."

"But I cried when he didn't show up at my parents' house Thanksgiving eve. He'd been at home all night cooking. Every Thanksgiving we stay at my parents' the night before so I can help my mother cook and stuff. When he did show up Thanksgiving morning it took all my will power not to attack his ass like a wild animal on the prowl. If the kids hadn't been around I would've."

Jazelle laughed. "See. Now don't you feel foolish?"

"I looked pathetic when I learned the truth. He told me he figured I suspected him of infidelity. But mom and dad knew the whole time what he was doing. He'd discussed it with them before taking the friggin' class."

"Like the saying goes, 'the spouse is usually the last to know.' " To herself, she thanked God her friend's marriage was safe.

"But Jaz, I sure did make up for it with some great loving that night, and told him how sorry, sorry, sorry, I was for not trusting him."

"You go, girl."

Both laughed as they high-fived.

"You weren't alone apologizing on Thanksgiving for some misguided notions," Jazelle said, then went on to supply details of her holiday for the second time in two evenings, omitting the *horizontal recreation.*

"I know you were shocked silly."

Jazelle harrumphed. "That's the understatement of the year."

"Did you ask him about that woman we saw him with at the restaurant?"

Jazelle told her about the auction, still feeling a tinge of joy that it was simply a friendly outing for Mitchell.

ഔന്ദ

Jazelle made it in from moonlighting to a pressing message on her answering machine from Dawn to watch the news.

She watched it.

Kevin Ballard had been found dead in the kitchen of the house he shared with his girlfriend, from a gunshot wound to the chest. Speculation stated a large sum of money he owed someone could be the motive.

Numb, Jazelle slumped back on the sofa, tears skimming down her cheeks. She'd been hurt by Kevin, and mad as hell at him, but she didn't want the brotha killed. *Damn!*

The night he had come by and she wouldn't let him in flashed in her mind. He'd been a little jumpy and acting peculiar, like he was trying to dodge somebody. Spooked. *Maybe that had something to do with what happened to him?*

Dawn called and they sadly chatted.

The funeral was held that Saturday, and because it seemed the right thing to do, she attended it with Dawn to pay her last respect.

29

For two weeks following the funeral, though she tried to fight and deny it, she knew without a doubt that she was really feeling Mitchell. She had feared these types of feelings would blossom, leading her into more disappointment and heartbreak. It was the story of her life. She wished she could erase it, but the desktop scene was a daily replay in her head. Foolishly, she wanted to create more scenes like it. She couldn't front, she wanted him stirring up her cocoa with his potent spoon.

Something else was clear also: what she'd felt at seeing him with ol' girl at the restaurant had nothing to do with race. Jungle fever was fine by her. True love should be cultivated when and wherever found. Happiness should be snatched up when it came. Simply put, she'd been jealous about him being with a woman, period. Nothing more nothing less. Aunt Joyce ogling him and squeezing his butt had plain and simply ignited her jealous gene as well. Her anger that day had nothing to do with thinking something incestuous was going on.

These revelations had hit her at once, bringing to light that she'd been falling for him even when she thought he was a teenager, meaning the feelings were budding during her discontent with men.

Because of Mitchell, she'd found the courage to get Philip off her trail. The day Mitchell brought her home from Norman, Phillip had called, and finally she'd told him she didn't feel that type of chemistry with him. She didn't beat around the bush or contemplate hurting his feelings, just told him straight up.

Mitchell. For the last few days, she'd been pulling his business card out, staring at it, wishing she had a legitimate reason to call him; ask him about mutual funds, or certificates of deposits, or IRA's. Something. She was holding the card at the moment, yearning to hear his voice, feel his soft yet masculine hands rubbing her down. Wishing she could be his work in progress.

Absently, she eyed the blinking Christmas lights she'd put up in the living room window earlier, feeling the urge to talk to Dawn. But her home girl was out with some brotha she'd met in St. Louis, who'd come to check out Tulsa since his company was considering relocating him to the area.

An image of Mitchell knocking at her door from out of nowhere pervaded. *I wish.*

She hoped he would've called sometime after he'd dropped her off that day. Just for the hell of it. But it hadn't happened, and likely wouldn't happen. Shoot, she hadn't given him her number. Though Gwen had it, she doubted Mitchell would even bring her name up to his mother.

She sighed. Couldn't believe she'd allowed herself to have a one night stand. She couldn't blame the man this time, because she'd been the aggressor, practically threw the draws at him.

Wanting to get out of the apartment, she pulled on a coat, hat, and gloves to go for a walk. It had been a while since she'd strolled around the hood.

Walking in the neighborhood, looking out for stray dogs, she almost couldn't believe she was walking in the cold, even though she was dressed for it. She wasn't a cold weather person. But shit on the mind made people veer from the norm. Would the type of problems that had her out in the cold be a lifelong occurrence for her? She hoped not. She'd seen a therapist on one of those talk shows discussing symptoms causing certain behavioral patterns, especially those causing women to be quick to emotionally latch on to men—mainly older men—and how that was often subconsciously attributed to an absentee father when they were growing up. The need to have a male figure, no matter how bad he was for her, blinded them from seeing his flaws or their own neediness. Emotional-psychological attachments also occurred with people who'd lost someone very dear to them. That group clung to other loved ones because of that loss.

Both scenarios easily applied to Jazelle. Her father deserted her as a child. She lost her mother to death. She'd been in denial before, but now had to admit the theory fit her. The older men she'd dated and their resulting mistreatment. Because she'd lost so much family wise, her students substituted for her family, and she got emotionally attached to them, wanting nothing bad happening to them.

Three youngsters cruised by in a four door sedan, slowed, whistled and yelled out some sexual epithets. Not acknowledging the crudeness, Jazelle made like she was going into someone's yard, and they rode on.

She went back to her thoughts, mainly her father. Since she couldn't actually hate anyone, whatever was close to hatred was how she felt toward that man. His ass was to blame for her psyche being all fucked up. Still, she knew her life was her own. What he had done couldn't be changed. She had enough experience to know circumstances in life resulted from the choices a person made; good or bad. True, others were to blame for certain things at times, but your life was your own, and her father hadn't made her make the stupid choices in men; she'd plunged into those farces very aware of the risks, but naïve and stupid enough not to respect the possibilities of tricked-off outcomes. And she'd paid for the idiocy.

A foolish female schooled every time.

Well it was time for change; time to quit placing blame. Sonny Johnson Sr. helped create the being, but had nothing to do with Jazelle Johnson the woman. She wasn't dwelling on what he'd caused her family anymore. It was time to pack that old news away in a chest for bad memories.

Some boys playing basketball on a portable goal in the driveway conjured up Mitchell and his attempts to show her how to shoot at the fair. She wondered what he was doing. At least he hadn't used her for his own benefit like the other rejects she'd fooled with. *Did he have a woman or what*? He never made that clear.

Near to her complex, she grinned wickedly. There was more than one way to milk a cow. She had a phone call to make.

Making a face, she realized Dawn's influence was slowly but surely rubbing off on her.

೫ఎఇ೪

Mitchell slowly drove through the gates of the cemetery. How he remembered the location of the grave-site was a mystery, because the only time he'd been there his mind was far off in a world of pain, mourning, and despondency. He'd been a passenger while Gwen drove his listless body, and was oblivious of his surroundings.

That was over three years ago, yet somehow he knew where he was going.

He hated rehashing that visit, more so, the events leading to it. Nerves had him quivering as he followed the gravel road. The sky was nebulous and dispiriting and, like all graveyards, this one was murky and depressing. A modest assemblage was gathered around a plot, proceeding with the burial of a loved one. What those people were feeling was palpable to Mitchell even though the person being buried was alien to him. The vacuous feeling of putting someone you cared for in their final resting place was indelible to anyone who'd experienced it.

He despised cemeteries. Along with the eeriness, the finality they represented was depressing blows to the heart. That was why he'd spurned visiting over the years, though guilt had dogged him many a day and night for being MIA. Even now he was sparring with second thoughts, unsure if he could go through with it.

Surprisingly, this visit was finally inspired by two women, of all things. Susan Ladonis, Ob Gyn seductress, had surprisingly called him at the office two days ago, seeking some investment suggestions and, to his embarrassment, to thank him for his part in repairing her incongruous life. "That sex we had," she'd said conversationally, "helped untangle the confusion over my sexual orientation. I'm no longer struggling over whether I'm lesbian or bi. Since that night I know all I want to be is straight. Excuse the French, but I'm strictly dickly."

Taking him off guard with her straightforwardness, Mitchell didn't know how to respond, but noted the guilt he'd experienced after that night didn't resurface.

"And guess what, Mitchell?" she continued happily. "I've met someone. I told him about you. He's mixed—Canadian & black—handsome, not endowed like you are but hey, everyone can't be so lucky, and he's a doll, though he does say I can use a little more weight on me."

He laughed at parts of what she said, and was embarrassed by bits of what she told him, but he told her he was glad to hear the good news.

"Mitchell," she said before hanging up, "if, or when you do find a special someone, embrace her and share life together like there's no tomorrow. Don't throw away something that may never come again."

Her last words had resonated in his head that day non-stop. Added to that conversation was the fact that he was suffering from some non-physical ailment which strangely wasn't guilt. At least with guilt he'd know what was plaguing him; this was something on a spiritual level. Making things worse, going home everyday to an empty house was starting to play out, especially with the memory of Jazelle having blessed it with her presence. She'd been on his mind non-stop as well. Her sweet smell. Her luscious curves and soft body. The feel of her wrapped around him flesh to flesh.

Not once had he felt guilty about the thoughts.

A year ago or so, he'd overheard Katie telling Travis, "Mitchell would recognize when the post-trauma stress he was experiencing, but refused to own up to, was showing signs of unshackling him." He still wasn't buying the PTSD diagnosis, but agreed his uncharacteristic actions incited by Jazelle corresponded to Katie's prediction. The signs were apparent. And weirdly, the distinct feelings she caused had happened only once before in his life.

The combination of all that catapulted him to suddenly journey to Northeastern Oklahoma, to the last place on earth he ever cared to be: a cemetery.

He located the vicinity, parked and got out, clutching a bouquet of flowers. The wind seemed stronger, the breeze making it colder. Pulling the parka hood over his head, he slid his hands into gloves lined with wool, languidly walked to the plot.

⅘⅚

Her name was Elaine. He'd met her his freshman year during physical therapy sessions to rehabilitate his knee. She was a sophomore, pre-med, intent on becoming a physical therapist, and one of her classes had her assisting patients with their rehab. Mitchell was her first assignee, and they bonded instantly. Though pretty and well-dressed, she was basically a *plain Jane* and a homebody, who was studious as could be, a complete bookworm, and a *virgin*. But she intrigued Mitchell like no other girl ever had. Paper-sack brown, a curvaceous 130 pounds, about 5 feet 7 inches, her father was a doctor, mother a teacher, so education and success were paramount with her. It had taken weeks of almost begging and cajoling to get her to loosen up some, but he eventually did. They started hanging out during their spare time. He even persuaded her to go to the court, where he tried to teach her some basketball basics. One evening she accompanied him to his dorm room for the first time, they ended up in bed together, and he consensually laid claim to her virginity. Feelings had been swelling prior, but after that evening they were inseparable.

She was like a miracle downpour of showers during a severe summer drought, and except for their socio-economic backgrounds, they were as homogenous as opposite sexes could be. That following year they got engaged.

The memories abruptly faded as he approached the grave. An urge to turn and flee to his car surged, but something compelled him to stay. Queasiness caused him to close his eyes momentarily. He studied the headstone. Seeing it for the first time rattled him more than he'd imagined.

IN LOVING MEMORY OF ELAINE DENIECE SAMUELS, he shakily read. Tears glistened in his eyes as he read her date of birth and date of death. He continued through the epitaph: LOVING DAUGHTER, SISTER—she had two older brothers—AUNT, FRIEND, AND PERSON. OUR LITTLE ANGEL FOREVER. THANK YOU FOR ALL THE WONDERFUL MEMORIES.

Mitchell didn't cry at the funeral; he'd been too numb to emit any emotions. But now tears flowed, splattering onto the dull grass. He knelt, placed the flowers against the headstone, removed his gloves, and rubbed a hand over the cold stone, then the stubby grass, wishing he could touch his Elaine once again. Just one more time for old time sake.

He sighed deeply. In his mind he could.

On TV he'd often seen people talking to the graves they visited, and he wondered if some people truly believed they could supernaturally communicate with the dead.

"E ... E-laine," he whispered awkwardly. The name felt ominous. He'd virtually been unable to say it since her burial. It hurt too damn much. "I hope you're doing fine up there."

He went silent for a spell, wiping tears with the back of his hands. Car doors slammed off in the distance. He turned, blankly seeing the service had concluded.

Facing the headstone, slightly off to the side, he sat on the ground and leaned back some. "Bet you're wondering why I've finally come to visit?" He was trying to talk conversationally. "I'm sure you know I've wanted to come before now, but ... you know how I feel about these places. They aren't my thing."

In spite of the tears, he forced a smile, recalling how she loved when he smiled. She once told him his smile could cure folks with terminally bad attitudes.

"Anyway, I know you forgive me for the lengthy MIA. You were always a forgiving person—sometimes too forgiving." He recalled when her roommate once loaned out Elaine's car to her boyfriend without permission for a supposed quick run to a store while Elaine was in class. The sucka' came back five hours later acting like he wasn't in violation. Mitchell wanted to beat hell out of him, and wanted Elaine to kick her roommate's ass. Instead, she blew it off and forgave her like Jesus would. She grew up having everything and anything she wanted, so material possessions weren't as big a deal to her as they were for Mitchell. But despite knowing how she felt, what those two did still pissed him off all these years later.

He reached and pulled one of the flowers from the bouquet, brought it to his nose. He knew she would've loved them. "They're fresh with a sweet aroma just like you were." He laid back. "So sweet you were."

He bundled deeper in his coat. The breeze seemed to be picking up, and it was getting colder. Realistically he knew there was no reason to be, but he was still unsettled in this setting. It was a little spooky. The few times he'd been to graveyards it was always overcast, a couple of times light drizzle accompanied. *Why is the final resting place of people who were supposedly going to heaven always so dismal?*

The guilt of neglecting to visit for so long kept him put. Out of respect for the woman he intensely loved, he owed her that.

"Well, E," it was what he usually called her, "my actual reason for finally coming ... I met someone. Someone very nice. Remember my li'l sis, Mackenzee? She's five years old now. Can you believe that? Anyway, that someone—a woman—is her teacher." He sighed deeply. Even though she was dead, it was difficult discussing another woman. It seemed disrespectful. Hurtful. "Yeah, I made you a promise, and E, baby, I tried desperately to uphold it to the point that I became withdrawn, abnormally introverted, and purposely avoided even the friendliest socializing with women. It didn't matter if they only had platonic intentions, I kept my distance."

While Elaine had been comatose in the hospital ICU he'd adamantly promised to forever honor their engagement, and never get involved, nor fall in love with another woman. "You're the only woman for me until I leave this earth," he'd declared, fully believing it himself. He now understood he'd been in shock, traumatized, delirious, and scared. For months on top of months he'd upheld his promise, until human nature finally prevailed.

"This woman—her name's Jazelle. Jazelle Johnson. I think you would like her. She has good morals, independent, intelligent, and like you, she's very caring. He omitted physical characteristics; they were irrelevant. "We haven't discussed becoming a couple—actually I've only recently decided myself. But if it's okay with you, I think I'd like to explore the possibility with her. You see, these feelings she's awakened inside me ..."

He stopped, uncomfortable mentioning his feelings for another woman to Elaine. It was like continuing to pounce on a badly beaten fighter who'd thrown in the towel. But the feelings weren't some simple infatuation, or hormonal cravings; they were way more serious than that. And he needed to be honest like he'd always been with her.

So he continued.

"Anyway E, not to make comparisons, but the feelings I was referring to are so ... so indescribable, what you used to do to my insides is the only thing I can equate it with. They're that powerful."

Now that he'd made that admission, he half expected a mystic retaliation of some sorts. When nothing happened moments later, for some reason, he foolishly considered the unlikely possibility of receiving a sign from Elaine that she understood his quandary due to his loyalty to her; that she approved of him settling down with another woman with her complete blessing.

Out of deference to Elaine, and knowing this would be the closest he'd ever get to her again physically, he stretched completely out, lying next to her headstone. An affection that he'd come to a type of closure with the first love of his life encompassed him.

He cried freely, releasing all the suppressed emotions held back for so long.

"I'll always love you, Elaine Deniece," he whispered through the tears.

He remained in that position til the edge of nightfall.

‽‽

Jazelle dropped her cell phone on the couch, dejected and hurt. She'd come in from her walk and called Gwen, carried on some small talk before gaining the nerve to ask if Mitchell had a woman, but she finally asked. Now she wished she'd never called.

She curled up in her favorite corner of the sofa, remote in hand, clicked on the TV, and started channel surfing. Though she hung up before Gwen could give details—actually before she said he had a girlfriend, because she played like she had an emergency—Gwen's long pause before answering was enough evidence.

The teenager-looking ... has a damn woman! Mr. Innocent isn't so innocent. He's just like all the rest of these no good d-o-g-s'! Oooo! I'm so through with men! From now on, if one of them bastards just looks my way I'm cussing him, his mama, daddy ... the rest of his family the hell out!

She meant what she was thinking.

30

Jazelle sat at her desk almost in a daze. Since the brief phone conversation with Gwen, she'd been having an affair with misery. Learning that Mitchell had a woman was a low blow, crumbling her far-fetched fantasy of the two of them having a picturesque wedding, and thereafter, sharing a life with the fruits of family, home, and happiness.

How ignorant I was to have conceived that bullshit.

As it stood now, she wouldn't dare accept Gwen's invitation to join them for Christmas. She couldn't bare being around him, acting as if she was *cool* in his presence. The torment of wanting to be with him would be like getting molested but too afraid and ashamed to tell anyone. Even worse, *she* might even be there. Jazelle certainly couldn't be in the same space with his girlfriend.

Disdainfully, she wondered who the lucky wench was. Why didn't he tell her he had a woman? It would've been a simple enough admission. But what else could be expected of a damn man? Mitchell had only been true to form: a conscience lacking SOB who couldn't give a rat's ass about a woman's feelings. He had let her make an ass of herself; spread her legs eagerly, and let him take the *nasty* plunge like she was some hot ass hoochie. And, she'd let his black ass go in without a life jacket. He could've given her the damn heebie-jeebies! That gotcha! Something bleach couldn't remove and penicillin couldn't cure. What the hell was she thinking?

She hurt like hell, wished he would've been considerate enough to tell her about whoever *she* was, but shamefully, she still wanted to be with him.

Adding to her anxiety was Nikki acting up again, and the rapidly approaching Christmas vacation. It was already the week before the break, and she'd have to play the solo role again, which she wasn't looking forward to. Thankfully, she had her surrogate family to ease some of her blues.

Putting personal issues to the side, she wistfully looked over her class after they were all seated to start the morning. "Everybody," she said, getting their attention, "I'll be leaving early today. There's something I must tend to."

"Is you comin' back, Miss Jackson?" one of the little voices asked.

"*Are* you coming back," she corrected. "No, I'm not, but I will be here tomorrow." She often wished she could take them all home with her and protect them from life's ugly surprises; the one's people wished they could tear off and throw away. In return they could help alleviate her at-home loneliness.

₭₡ℂℂ

Mitchell was able to break early for Christmas and was back in Tulsa. Thankfully they had renewed an endorsement deal they'd been working on earlier than expected, which freed some time. He had some shopping to do and other important loose ends to tie.

Then there was Jazelle. Yesterday he went to Travis and Katie's for dinner, provided them with some music to their ears. "You two bet' not make a big deal of it," he said, passing threatening glares at them, "I met a woman."

Travis and Katie exchanged stunned but curious glances. Travis spoke first. "You, uh—what's her name?"

"Miss Jo"—Mitchell stopped and waggled his head—"Jazelle. She's Mackenzee's teacher, and for some reason I'm always absentmindedly calling her Miss Johnson—which is her last name."

"You met her and ...?" Katie queried, being the consummate analytical therapist.

"And I think I'm going to pursue a relationship with her." He then poured out a shortened version of his history with Jazelle, excluding the sex part.

"I can't believe you," Travis said, feigning hurt feelings. "You've been keeping this from us all this time?"

Katie gazed at her husband with a shit eating grin. "What did I tell you, ho-mie?"

"Whoop-dee-do, Katie," Travis mockingly shot back at his wife. "Mitch, I thought we were brotha's, man, what ...?" He spread his hands.

Mitchell laughed at his partner, aware that Katie was referring to his supposed PTSD which she'd predicted would start waning, though they had no idea he overheard that particular conversation back when. But since he knew, he told them about his visit to the cemetery, and they turned sentimental, until he declared it had been an emotional healing of sorts. Closure.

"I'm slowly coming back to my old self, you two," he said before leaving their house.

Now at the school, he pulled into the parking lot. This visit was motivated by something Mac had told him over the phone the other day. With this deed hopefully he could enable a child to have a joyful Christmas.

Once inside, a middle-aged white woman behind the office counter, wearing what was almost a bouffant, told him Mrs. Green was filling in for Miss Johnson, who'd left early. *Good.*

Not running into either of them would make what he wanted to do a whole lot easier.

For a second he wondered what had taken Jazelle from work. She'd told him only an act of God could keep her from her students.

Since Mrs. Bouffant seemed occupied with paper work, he thanked her then discreetly slipped out of the office. The corridor was inactive, and instead of leaving the building, he put on a fake mustache, which remarkably looked real, and some funny-looking oval glasses. Taking a quick scan, the coast was clear, his target was as Mac had explained, and he stepped that way.

His task would be as easy as ripping off a passed-out drunk.

ꕥ

"Well, Miss Johnson, your test is positive," the doctor said.

Positive! She felt like she'd just been tackled by Ray Lewis. All the wind gushed from her body.

"Positive," she mouthed disbelievingly.

The word echoed in her head the rest of the day and into the night, disrupting her attention to everything else. She couldn't eat, sure couldn't sleep. The next day she woke up puffy-eyed and jaded. This time her neighbors weren't to blame. Her head was spinning, and damn was she in a daze! She'd made some stupid mistakes before, but this was like the *dumbass* jackpot winner. Since twelve years old, she'd been warned and threatened by her grandmother, not to mention the cautions about abstaining or practicing responsible sex, yet, in spite of all the warnings, she went and ...

"How could I be so fucking irresponsible?"

Slowly, she got out of bed and went through the motions of getting ready for work. Christmas was just around the corner and it was already turning into a piss-poor holiday season. It would be a chore facing her students today. She almost felt like a hypocrite. Daily she tried to stress right from wrong, and now she'd gone and done something *wrong*. So wrong.

At school, two unusual things occurred, vexing her, but shifting her thoughts away from the incessant anxiety of finding out she was pregnant. Nikki, minus the expected sad disposition, but exhibiting the spirit and happiness desired of a child, got up in front of the class on her own, as composed as an adult, and said, "Everybody, I'm sorry. I'm gonna be a good girl from now on." With an endearing smile, unseen for days, she slightly twisted Jazelle's way. "Promise, Miss Johnson."

Perched on her desk, Jazelle was speechless as she watched the little girl calmly walk just outside the door and sit in the outcast's desk. Did what she think happen actually happen? *What in the world caused that*? As a teacher, she'd learned to expect the unexpected from these small fries, and though this was one of those times, she was completely astounded.

For the lack of a better response, she asked two of the boys to get Nikki's desk and put it in its proper row, and had Nikki come join her classmates. She wasn't sure why, but she had a feeling the child would be totally fine from now on.

Later that day she stopped by the office and a lovely bouquet of red roses in a beautiful clear vase was sitting on the counter. She was envious of the lucky colleague they were for.

"Jazelle," Mrs. Green called, emerging from one of the offices. "I'm glad you came down." She saw how Jazelle was admiring the roses. "They're for you."

Did she hear that correctly? "For me?" Her fingers tapped her chest questionably. She was mystified.

"Yes—for you. There's a card. You must have a new admirer you haven't told me about." She knew Jazelle hadn't been dating anyone since the last *loser*.

Jazelle smiled shamefacedly. Blushed. "Not that I know of." Never in her life had she received flowers of any kind. Men weren't romantic or thoughtful like that nowadays. Her senior prom date had even forgotten to get her a corsage. Mrs. Green had to be mistaken.

She plucked the small envelope from the arrangement and removed the card.

To Miss Johnson. A woman of unrivaled affect on a brotha. It was unsigned.

"Who delivered these?" she asked.

"A woman from a flower shop. I forgot the name of the place, though, and she didn't leave a business card; something about forgetting to put some in her van this morning."

Jazelle knew Mrs. Green was itching to know what the card said, and who'd sent them. She indulged her. "But who they're from beats me." She held up the card for her to see. "The person didn't sign it." Suddenly she had a thought: *Philip. He must be in town for Christmas.* After telling him there was no haps with him and her, was he still going to try? God, she hoped he wasn't one of those psycho types.

She thought about giving the roses to Mrs. Green, but since this was a first for her, Philip or not, she decided to keep them. No need to not enjoy what could easily be a simple Christmas present, was there? She'd thank him when he called—she knew he would—but firmly reiterate her stance on dating him. Hopefully he'd accept that sensibly.

31

Early Christmas morning, Mitchell awoke and duplicated the routine he'd followed on Thanksgiving, but this time his movements were more animated. After inspecting and finding the food satisfactory, he pulled on some Dockers and a polo shirt, sprayed on his favorite cologne and, after an approving examination in the mirror, put on a coat and stocking cap and grabbed his keys. He contemplated waking Montell to tell him not to let G-Lady sleep too long, but decided he'd call later.

It was clear and blue outside, but chilly. Not at all the picture of what this day should be. *It should be snow everywhere*, Mitchell thought. A White Christmas was rare, seeming like merely an image from a fairy tale.

While letting the car warm up, he riffled through his CD's for the one that would get him amped. Old school BDP's "By Any Means Necessary" was the choice, and he turned up the volume. Like when he'd first heard KRS-1 dropping the lyrics to his favorite cut, "Poetry", he allowed the man he felt was one of the greatest hip hop lyricists of all time enter his conscience and get him started. He'd fallen in love with this classic 80's hip-hop when he was a broke pre-teen. Something about it always took him on some type of spiritual high.

He started thinking about the talk he had with his mama Christmas Eve in the kitchen while he helped her prepare some of the Christmas dishes. "Mitchell, boy, you know Miss Johnson like you, don't you?"

He stopped chopping celery. "Hunh?"

"Miss Johnson—Jazelle, she like you." Gwen told him all about the brief phone conversation she'd had with her daughter's teacher.

"So she thinks I have a girlfriend," he said ruefully.

"Yeah, baby, and I feel bad, but she didn't gimme a chance to explain. Mitch, now I've tried to quit counseling you about your life where Elaine's concerned, but since I'm yo' mama, your pain's my pain, and it hurts me that you're not happy like you should be. Being a mama is a lifetime job, and you already know I know how losing someone you love is hard as hell to live with, but I'm gonna be straight with you. Yeah, it's a fucked up thang that she died, but what you need to start doing is letting her spirit live on through the things you do with, and during, the rest of yo' life. The fact that you were able to know her, and the little time y'all had together was a blessing; you should start rejoicing instead of agonizin' and feeling sorry for yo 'self over it. You're too damn young, to be keeping other women at bay like you do. You might find someone that you'll like a whole damn lot. It's time you came up outta that mourning and stuff—"

"Mama, I went to visit Elaine's grave."

Her spiel interrupted, Gwen suddenly stopped peeling sweet potatoes, and stared at him.

"I've come to realize that ... I like Jazelle too, and before I could start anything with her I had to find some closure to that."

Gwen looked shocked. He knew she was thinking how hard the visit to the dead must've been for him. "I cried and cried, Mama, but, it was overdue. I finally realized that going to her gravesite and talking to her would help me move on."

He yanked a paper towel from the roll on the table and handed it to his mama as a tear glistened in her eye.

"As for the promise I made," he continued, "I think Elaine would happily look over it for me to be happy with someone like Jazelle."

Gwen smiled. "I didn't know Elaine all that well, but what I knew of her, she was a sweet person. She came from a good family."

"The person she was made me a better person. She tamed the little wildness that I did have in me."

"Boy, yo' ass ain't neva been wild."

He made a dubious face. "G-Lady, if only you knew..."

She chuckled. "I do believe she'd give you her blessing. She'd want you to be happy."

"That's what I think too, Mama."

Now his desire to see Jazelle and try to straighten out the misunderstanding she had with his mama was pestering him. He could almost see her disappointment after that conversation. He imagined she called him every dirty name in the book.

He rode into her complex nervously excited. Several kids were already putting their new toys to the test when he got out the car. A little girl, assisted by a pre-teen girl, was tentatively trying to get the hang of her roller blades. A little boy was being tutored on a training wheel by a woman who was likely his mama. Three boys looked to be playing villains and superheroes. Mitchell smiled reflectively. *There are no better times than your days as a kid.*

It wasn't 9:00 A.M. yet, and he imagined Jazelle was still sleeping. He knocked on her door, hoping he wouldn't encounter an embarrassing situation like her having another dude over. Although she'd told him she didn't have a man, things could've changed since then.

Jazelle was sleeping on the couch and vaguely heard what she imagined was a knock. She stayed in her spot, thinking she was only dreaming.

Mitchell knocked again, but harder, resigned to stand there til he knew for sure she wasn't home. Upstairs a door cracked and someone peered out for a second then quickly shut the door.

That was at my door, Jazelle finally realized as the knock sounded again. Groggily, she sat up. It could only be one damn person bothering her: Dawn. What time was it anyway? She tried to focus on the hands of the clock on the wall. At around 2:30 A.M. or so she'd finally fallen asleep, wishing she was able to push time past Christmas into the new year, thinking maybe next year would be better.

"It's too damn early for this heifer to be effin' with me!" she grumbled, seeing the time.

She threw the blanket off, yawned, and stood up. Only in a big sleep shirt and panties, she dragged to the door and without even peering through the peephole she slid off the chain, unlocked and opened the door.

"Girl, what the hell do you—"

Her words died abruptly. It wasn't Dawn. It was ...

"Mitchell?"

Seeing her, Mitchell was instantly sorry for disturbing her sleep. Her hair was in disarray; she was frowning, and looked like she wanted to cut his nuts off. His gaze caught the peaks of her nipples through the thigh-length shirt. Knowing she was bra-less aroused him. In fact, her being in sleeping attire straight up made his dick hard.

"Merry Christmas, Jazelle," he said tentatively, hoping she didn't slam the door in his face. "Sorry I'm not a 'girl.' "

Instantly self-conscious, she covered her chest and used the free arm to grab two fingers and a thumb full of shirt sleeve, wet it with her tongue and began wiping at the matter in her eyes.

The coldness coming through had her shivering.

"Oh hell!" If she wasn't awake before, she was now. "Wh-what are you doing here?"

"Would ya believe I'm a black Santa Claus, and since you don't have a chimney"—he spread his arms and shrugged—"I had to make a door delivery." *Maybe the humor will loosen her up?*

Searching for something gift wrapped, she saw nothing, and didn't find his jab at humor funny at all.

Mitchell saw her frown as she looked for whatever he was supposed to be delivering. "Uh, Jaz, could I please come in? I'd like to talk to you 'bout something if you don't mind?"

Rolling her eyes, she reluctantly motioned him in with her head. If it wasn't so cold she would've let his ass stand out there.

"Thank you." He closed the door behind him, reflexively locking it.

"Excuse me," she said tartly, flouncing toward the back. "I need to use the ladies room."

He didn't miss the attitude in her voice, figuring he probably added to it by interrupting her sleep. At least she let him in, which was a good thing, not least because it let him know no other dude was in there. The strewn blanket on the couch told him she'd slept there. The generic, miniature Christmas tree on a stand near the window was a contrast to the too-big tree at his mama's, where there were so many presents, G-Lady had to rearrange and remove some furniture to make room. Though the content under Jazelle's tree was small, he had something for her that would surpass any present under any tree.

He hoped.

Brushing her hair, Jazelle suddenly thought of how her recent anxiety had as much to do with Mitchell as it did herself. *What the hell is his problem popping up at my door all out the blue so damn early in the morning? He almost got cussed out and the damn door slammed in his ... that damn handsome face of his. What does he want anyway?* Since his *no-good ass* was there, she might as well tell him the *bad* news. See how he slicked his way out of that. Would he react with some consideration? Sensitivity? Or act a fool like many a man was known to do, and say something real ignorant? Since she hadn't told anyone yet, not even Dawn, she was ready to spill it. Mitchell should be numero uno hearing it.

When she returned, Mitchell saw she'd done something with her hair, smelled the mix of toothpaste and mouthwash. Her appearance hadn't mattered to him, she'd been cool the way she was at the door: in a natural element.

"Sorry for dropping by like this," he said, "but there's been a misunderstanding—"

"No, there's no misunderstanding!" she shot back spicily. "You're just another bullshit man who did what comes naturally for ya'll. Got a free piece of ass because you could." She wasn't about to let him patronize her with some lame bullshit. She was too tired of men running over her and dogging her out.

Mitchell stared at her, looking humbled.

"To think I considered you different from the other scrubs I've fooled with. And dropping by here to try to sell me one of you men's full-of-shit dreams ... you can save that drama for some other gullible hoochie!" She glared at him. "This sista isn't going for the okie doke anymore. You did me once, gotcha little shit off, so let it be. I don't mean to be such a bitch, but I guess you can just go now."

A long silence ensued as they stared each other down. Mitchell assumed she'd be pissed, but hadn't expected this blow-up. *A woman scorned,* he thought, ending the stare down and moving toward the window, where he bent over and picked up some fallen icicles off the floor and slung them back on the tree.

"Her name was Elaine," he began reflectively, blankly looking out the window, figuring he'd better spit it out while he had the wherewithal to do so. He did notice that he used the past tense before *Elaine*.

Jazelle looked at him like he was stinking. "Mitchell, I don't want to hear about your girlfriend. You didn't tell me when I asked, no need to tell me about her now!"

"I met her in college," he continued, then relayed his beginnings with Elaine.

"Why're you telling me this, Mitchell? I don't wanna hear it, I told you."

Mitchell went on. "We hit it off, eventually got closer and, like the story goes, fell in love. That next year I asked her to be my wife; she said yes."

The more he talked, the sadder he sounded. By now Jazelle was enthralled.

"We'd planned to get married sometime after my graduation, but ... but at the end of the spring semester my sophomore year, I was studying for a final late one night, and she went to get me something to eat from Whataburger." He paused for a long minute. "On her way, a ... a drunk driver in a high speed chase with the police lost control of his truck, jumped a median ..." His eyes turned glassy and dazed.

The cracking in his voice weakened Jazelle's remaining austerity. She sensed she was about to hear something real sad.

Mitchell turned, facing her but looking into space. "The truck pounced head on into her car," he said, barely audible.

The funereal gloom in his eyes made Jazelle's insides want to go on strike.

"Some hours later, she died in the emergency room. I was holding her hand as she took her last breath."

The tears in his eyes caused Jazelle to tear up also. She now understood the reason for the melancholy she'd noticed in him since the first time they met.

"I'm sorry, Mitchell. I ..." She trailed off, not knowing what to say.

He waved off the condolence, recomposed himself. It was the first time he'd been able to utter *died* in the same sentence with *Elaine*.

"What I've come here to tell you is that I've finally found some peace and closure with my loss." He went silent, recalling the grave-side visit. "She—Elaine—was who G-Lady was about to tell you about when you abruptly ended y'alls phone conversation that day."

Jazelle indiscernibly inhaled, immediately ashamed of her reaction that evening."

"Until recently, I'd been unable to say her name," Mitchell admitted. "The aloofness, introversion—uncharacteristic traits for me—which I'm sure you've wondered about, were because of her death's effect on me. I didn't want to be close to another female, didn't want to love that much again for fear of opening myself up to the possibility of that type of pain again. So, I kinda climbed into a shell, keeping my distance. I loved her like nobody's business. And in a way—since she was driving that night because of me—I felt like it was my fault, so I owed her. Felt like I didn't deserve to be happy."

Looking at him sympathetically, tears easing from her eyes, she related to his pain, and the changes the hurt and loss caused in a person.

"For the first time in over three years, though, someone—a notable lady, who somehow broke through the shell—gained my attention long enough to force me to recognize that I needed to let Elaine go, and possibly give myself a chance with someone who may be just as wonderful." He sheepishly gazed at Jazelle.

Jazelle's stomach started fluttering.

"After Thanksgiving I ... I ..." he stammered, "Hell—I have feelings for you, Jazelle. Strong feelings." That was the only way he could express it for now, though he knew the "L" word was lurking.

Butterflies began flying around inside Jazelle. *He likes me.*

"I'm hoping you'll give me the chance to get to know you better, with the possibility of exploring life with you." He partially grinned. "I want to get to know everything about you that I can—your likes, dislikes, favorite foods, color, what size clothes and shoes you wear—and on my own, learn the small things about you that even you might not be conscious of."

Could this actually be happening? Jazelle was almost in disbelief. *Does this beautiful, unlikely, one-in-a-trillion, baby-faced black man, really want to get to know me? It can't be, especially after the static I gave him. After misjudging him, not just once or twice? How many surprises does Mitchell Thomas have for my hopeless ass?*

They studied each other in silence, both smiling sheepishly. Two people cut from the same cloth, but previously stitched to different brands, now possibly coming together to form a unique design.

She was in his arms, kissing him before either realized it. His hands wasted no time getting inside the robe, getting reacquainted with her flesh, mainly her butt.

Jazelle pulled away, looked at him menacingly. "Boy, if you're selling me a dream ... planning on dogging me out, I'm telling you now, I'm gonna *kill* your ass!"

Mitchell clutched one of her hands. "Don't worry, I wanna live til I'm old, cripple, and senile." Bringing her fingers to his mouth, he began sucking one at a time. Erotically.

Jazelle's legs almost buckled.

Continuing with the finger play, he started slipping off the robe, then cupped one of her small but perky breasts through her shirt, his finger teasing the erect nipple.

"Mitch-ell ..." She was so aroused and filled with desire. "I'm not ... I—ohhh—I want you."

After months and months of denying himself this type of pleasure without feeling guilty, with no hesitation, he lifted her up. "Guide me to your room, homegirl."

In her room he laid her on the bed. A glimpse of the red thong she was wearing hastened his motions, and he started peeling his own clothes.

Seeing his urgency had her ridding her body of the shirt and thong.

Hovering over her as she leaned back on her elbows, he ran a hand along and between her thighs, found *that spot* wet. Anxious. Her head fell back, her eyes closed. He then halfway straddled her, slowly kissing down her body until his tongue replaced his fingers at the shaved slit.

Jazelle tensed up as his tongue approached its target. Suddenly tidal waves of ecstasy like she'd never known rushed through her, sending her into a lascivious frenzy. She felt like she would lose her mind, it felt so agonizingly good. *If hell is the retribution for this act, at least half the world's population had to be making reservations.*

"Ohhhh ... sh-iitt, Mi-i-tchell. Ohhh ..." She quivered then suddenly came with force, almost ripping the sheet she was desperately fisting.

While she quaked from the explosion, he easily slid inside her. She caught her breath. Then slowly they began gyrating and humping in unison. Two people previously constricted by traumatic past finally brandishing in a sea of bliss without any personal shackles.

With excruciating pleasure, Jazelle cried out, unable to hold it back; not with how he was making her feel.

Ridding himself of all inhibitions and gentleness, he started pounded it. "You like this dick?" he asked, surprising himself, but realizing he'd surely come out of his shell.

Jazelle hissed from the impact, but being stubborn, didn't respond otherwise.

Feeling challenged, Mitchell shifted gears, pounded harder. "I said, you like this *dick*?"

Jazelle was a bit shocked by Mitchell's actions, but it turned her on even more. Increased her desire. Resisting a response to his machismo, she only moaned a little louder and moved with his motions.

Upping the ante, Mitchell went into overdrive, and the headboard started knocking on the wall. "JJ, do you like this dick!"

Jazelle hissed heavily, and unable to resist any longer, yelled, "Fuuuck meee! Ohhh, yes, Mitchell ... I liike ... it! Oooooh, do I ever like this dick!"

Within seconds, she came again. Powerfully. Filled with pleasure, she released a loud groan she couldn't suppress if her mouth was duct taped.

Right as Mitchell uttered his ferocious release, a knock came from the ceiling. Jazelle smiled a mischievous grin. *Now you know how it feels, ho'*. She was glad to be giving her upstairs neighbor some of her own medicine. But now she could relate to homegirl's through-the-ceiling broadcasts of pleasure. It was definitely relatable.

The bad news she wanted to talk to Mitchell about completely slipped her mind. And again, making sure he used *condom sense* never crossed her mind.

32

Both lazily chilled in post-sex serendipity, spooning, with Mitchell's arms wrapped around Jazelle. Now that she'd developed a level of comfort with him, she found it easy to spill out her insecurities, past mistakes, heartbreaks, and animosities toward men, including her father. How lonely she often felt without any blood family around. How she often missed her mother. How she eagerly wished to hear from or see her brother. Things she would've never considered disclosing to a man.

"With my luck and history, I never expected to meet someone like you, Mitchell. Never. Now here I am consorting with the enemy."

Mitchell laughed.

"Men like you just don't exist." She playfully elbowed him. "Should I pinch myself, or maybe I should punch you to make sure I'm not imagining this?"

Mitchell stroked the silky, soft skin on her shoulders. He never imagined feeling for someone this strongly again. He was listening to what she'd been saying but was halfway in a daze. "You are definitely a woman of unrivaled effect on a young brotha, Miss J. Johnson," he said dreamily. I think you voo-doo'd me." He hardly believed the giant steps forward he'd taken in his personal life.

A woman of unrivaled effect echoed in Jazelle's head. Where had she heard those words recently? Where ...? Suddenly she rotated her body to face him, catching a glimpse of the roses on top of the dresser.

"You ...?" She narrowed her eyes. "You sent those roses!"

He grinned devilishly. "Can't deny it, I'm guilty as OJ, though he was found innocent the first time."

She smacked his shoulder. "I thought—" She caught herself from bringing up Philip. *Never mention another man to a man at the wrong time.* One of Dawn's caveats. "Did you go to some type of school for surprising people? You're always pulling one over on some damn body."

He laughed. "Naw. Just a talent. I'm young, gifted, and black."

She nudged him, chuckling.

"I love 'em. Surprised the hell outta me when Mrs. Green said they were for me." She kissed him on the cheek. "Thank you, Mr. 'Me.' That was the first time I'd ever received roses."

"Word? Damn I'm good."

They laughed, and started kissing.

She suddenly pulled away. "I was thinking ... somebody made an anonymous donation—a very hefty one at that—to the school for a complete overhaul of the playground, supplying labor and everything. Would you happen to know anything about that?"

He made an innocent face. "Nah, can't say that I do."

"You liar!" She jumped on him and started wrestling him.

Giggling, he broke away, holding her back. "By the way..." he paused for a moment, making her irritated as he watched her inquisitive expression.

"What?" She was getting riled.

"How's Nikki?" he finally said, when she started impatiently struggling to tear her arms loose from his grip.

She stopped, thought about the scene at school the other day. It was so odd how that troubled child had promised to end her disruptive behavior from out of nowhere. Very odd.

"Mitchell ...?"

Scrambling out the bed, he dug in his coat pocket and pulled out a picture of himself in a Santa's helper uniform. Travis was in it, dressed as Santa. To a child, it was a convincing photo. Explaining that to Jazelle, he handed her the photo.

"Anybody with sense knows the easiest way to reach a child that age," he bragged, "especially during Christmas. Just mention Santa Claus and they'll melt in your hands. Mac told me about how Nikki said that her daddy was divorcing them, and I also remembered you mentioning her having problems. I put two and two together, figured that's why she'd been acting up in class. The past two years, T-Dub and I have been putting on these costumes and giving out presents to disadvantaged kids at a recreation center, and I sorta used some of my thespian know-how to help out the li'l girl."

Jazelle studied the picture, smiling. "You sure look funny, homie. But both of you are believable—'specially Travis."

"I dropped by the school the other day, cautiously approached her from the side, staying clear of your open classroom door—you had left early that day, by the way—showed her the picture, and told her I worked for the *man* kids idolized most, and explained how Santa wanted her to be a good girl for her mama and quit acting up in school. The other things I told her, I'll just keep that secret." He grinned. "Don't want anybody using my schemes."

"Wha' did you say to her? You can tell me, I'm her teacher."

"Wrong answer. If I tell you my tricks-of-the-trade, I'd have to hit you over the head hard enough to give you amnesia."

She glared at him defiantly. "You'd hit a woman?"

"In a country second, girl, I don't discriminate. Didn't I just *hit it*?" She punched him. He cracked up.

She marveled at his mystique. He had an immeasurable quality about him that she was so drawn to.

"The first time I saw you, I knew there was something about you as unordinary as I'd ever seen. That's why my interest was ignited that day in September."

Absorbing her words, he suddenly uttered, "Oh, hell!" and checked his watch. "JJ, we gotta get dressed."

"JJ? Who's JJ?"

"Hunh?" He hadn't realized what he'd called her. "Oh—duhh. You are. Jazelle Johnson—JJ."

She thought for a millisecond, then with the palm of her hand, smacked her forehead. "Sure are my initials. Dang, nobody's ever called me that."

"I can tell. You gotta get up Sista-Who-Doesn't-Know-Her-Own-Initials."

"Shuddup." She nudged him. "Why? What's the hurry?"

He gingerly hauled her from the bed as she slightly protested, and ushered her to the bathroom. "You'll know soon enough."

In the shower, hormones were aroused again. Water pelting their bodies, Jazelle dropped to her knees, feeling friskier than ever, and teased, nibbled, then gave him an oral baptism. She licked, sucked and smothered the length of his penis, working her mouth and tongue with a prostitute's expertise, and had Mitchell wanting to jump his ass out of the shower from the too good agony. Before the goodness made him explode, he pulled her up, turned her around and entered her from behind, stroking in and out until she couldn't take it anymore.

"Mi-tchell ... Mi-tchell ... I-I'm cum ... I'm cuuuuuuming!"

They came in unison, yelling pleasure-laced expletives.

ℰℭ

Minutes later, they emerged body wash fresh, cleansed of their sexual indulgence. Mitchell gave her fifteen minutes to be suited and booted and ready to roll. At least that was what he told her as she headed to her room. Actually, he wasn't taking her anywhere, just wanted her dressed for a surprise.

From the living room window, he saw the car he was expecting pull up. *Good timing.* He grinned like a little boy.

"JJ are you almost ready?" This time he was aware of what he called her.

So was Jazelle. "You called me 'JJ' again," she said from her room, liking it. *He has his own pet name for me. Goodness. I'm quickly getting addicted to everything about this boy.*

"My way of distinguishing you differently than anyone else, I guess."

Jazelle heard a knock and hurried to the front, buttoning the berry pullover top she had put on.

"Am I dressed okay?" She slightly posed, her hands feeling to make sure all her hair was under the hat on her head.

Mitchell assessed her, grinning, wishing he was the leggings she was wearing. "I'd eat ya."

"You're so baaad." She couldn't get over this Mitchell compared to the reserved one before his revelation.

She unlocked and opened the door after another knock, and looked right into the face of a taller, male version of herself, decked out in Marine garb. Her eyes almost popped out of their sockets.

"Junior!" she exclaimed in disbelief, rushing into her brothers spread arms. "It's really you." Tears flowed quickly.

"It's really me, li'l sis. Merry Christmas. Yo' big bro's home."

After a lengthy embrace, he introduced his wife, Shala, and sons, Daquan and Dejuan. With utter disbelief, Jazelle hugged the three of them like she'd known them forever. She then ushered them inside, started introducing them to Mitchell.

He interrupted her. "We've already met," he told her.

Smiling at Jazelle's bewildered expression, Jr. and he explained how Mitchell had a client whose high ranking Marine uncle pulled some strings, located Junior, and then how Mitchell had arranged and financed their trip to Tulsa. He'd picked them up from the airport the night before and put them up at the Double Tree downtown.

"Merry Christmas, JJ." He wore a triumphant grin. "This was actually why I had to rush you; your Christmas present."

Jazelle couldn't say anything. Not one damn thing. Un-fucking-believable is what Mitchell was. She simply went and hugged him.

"Thank you, Mitchell. Thank you."

33

Jazelle went with Mitchell to witness what he'd labeled the *Surprise of Surprises*, but planned on getting back with her brother later. When they pulled up to his mama's, Mitchell's favorite eight kinfolk were admiring the SUV Mitchell had had secretly delivered to Quincy that morning.

Nobody paid mind to Jazelle and Mitchell being together when they got out and joined the others, though Mac rushed to her teacher and hugged her. After the *thank you's* and display's of gratification from Quincy, Mitchell begged everybody to keep that he'd bought the SUV for Quincy on the down low. Just between those that were present, to avoid a family blow-up. "All hell would probably break loose if the rest of the fam' knew," he said persuasively. The adults agreed.

Anxious to get to the going, Mitchell urged everyone into either his or Quincy's ride. He was going to make it seem like he was taking the kids to see the biggest Christmas tree in Oklahoma while it was still daylight.

Jazelle sent a dubious look his away, amazed at how deceptive he could be.

Thrust by the three young ones' excitement, Quincy said, "Let's roll." He was ready to splurge in his new wheels.

Not to be separated from her teacher, Mac climbed in with Mitchell and Jazelle, as did Gwen after she secured the house. The other five jumped in with Quincy, who followed Mitchell's lead.

Mitchell drove to a location in West Tulsa that not many people—even those who had lived in Tulsa their entire lives—

were familiar with. The only visible home sat a distance from the only accessible street, which was surrounded by what looked to be fields of farmland on both sides, resembling a rural area. He turned onto that street, following its long, inclining and winding route past the single nondescript house.

At the top of the road, after climbing a somewhat steep incline, mouths popped open, eyes expanded. It almost equated Dorothy, Toto and the crew landing in Oz. Tucked away in a virtually hidden area was a community of luxurious homes of contemporary design. The affluent homes jumped out at them like a 3D movie. The exclusive homes afforded by those with some deep pockets made up what could pass as its own little utopia. *Oohs* and *ahhs* echoed inside both vehicles as they slowly cruised by each house. With features like vaulted ceilings, floor-to-ceiling windows, swimming pools, three and four car garages, and other upper income amenities they weren't accustomed to seeing in the hood, these were like mansions to their ghetto reared eyes. Benzes, Beamers, Range Rovers, Lexus's, and other top-of-the line cars lined driveways and carports.

"Shoot, these is like those houses they used to show on MTV Cribs or something," Carla exclaimed.

Mitchell approached one of the houses, and the electrical gate parted like the Red Sea. Onto property with newly laid grass, containing a sprawling two level brick house, he parked just inside, allowing enough room for Quincy to pull in. The gate closed and everyone jumped out of their respective vehicles after Mitchell.

The house was brand new and huge. A white man wearing a baseball cap and workman's overall's stood near the house, waving and smiling at them.

Amidst the questions of whose place it was and the sheer awe, Mitchell kept quiet, letting their curiosity build. It was the time of day when the sun had reached its crest, but it was cold enough that its presence was still ineffectual. Everybody had forgotten about the big Christmas tree they were supposed to be seeing.

Mitchell dipped into his pocket and pulled out some keys, keeping them concealed.

"G-Lady, M-Morg, and Miss Mac ... welcome home." He said it so nonchalant, no one really caught on. He held up the keys. "Merry Christmas G-Lady, li'l bro,' and sis. This is y'alls new crib."

They paid attention this then.

A reserved sign of happiness began as it started registering that Mitchell was being serious. Unsure, Gwen looked at him side-long with one of those stares allied with her fear of his method of getting money.

"Really, G-Lady, it's y'alls." He and Jazelle stood back after he handed his mama the keys, and watched the eight animated bodies bolt toward the house, with two or three almost tripping and falling.

Along with minimal input from an architect friend, Mitchell had designed the house. His dreams for his family since they'd moved in and out of more projects and other government assisted houses than he could count. Five bedrooms—each with walk-in closets—including master bed and bath, formal living room, family room, dining room, game-weight room, huge kitchen with commercial stove, swimming pool, Jacuzzi, and also a three-quarter full basketball court. He had hooked it up, and was looking forward to G-Lady making the inside come to life with her *Midas* touch.

"This all started out as a dream during my pre-teen days," he told Jazelle, smiling. "I thought it had all gone down the drain, though, when my dream of reaching the NBA crashed with my blown knee. I never imagined getting all this without being one of those well-paid pro athletes. Not as a black man from the ghetto."

Jazelle put an arm around his waist, admiring the house. "This is absolutely breathtaking," she said.

"You know something, though, JJ?" he said, scanning the beautiful property. "Only thing is, we're completely surrounded by white families out here. But that's all good 'cause we're 'bout to unleash some ghetto soul into this here community."

Jazelle laughed.

"I just hope they don't do like what has historically happened when a minority moves into their neighborhood ..."

"What's that?"

"Pack up & flee to the 'burbs."

Jazelle shook her head as Mitchell wrapped her in his arms, her back to him.

"Just the thought of that show's how far we've come, but how much further there is to go."

"True dat. But that's their issue."

"Allllready."

Thinking about where he'd come from, to where he was now, Mitchell said, "Man, it's all hard to believe." He stared up to the sky and mouthed, *Thank you, E,* then winked at his deceased love.

Jazelle had never felt as vital as she thought about Mitchell's words. She pinched herself to make sure this was all real. Within a short period, she'd met, denounced, accused of criminal activity, and fallen for this unreal man; gone from lonely and depressed to being fruitful, fortunate, and happy-as-hell. Her brother was back on the scene, too, so now she also had the family she'd been longing for. *God, I must be the luckiest heifer on earth.*

"When they ask how you got all of this, are you telling the truth?" she asked because no one ever knew what he had planned.

Mitchell rested his chin on her left shoulder. "T-Dub got my back. That was him on the phone on our way up here. He and Katie'll be here shortly. You'll finally meet my *padna'* and his better half, who's large with my godchild in her belly."

Jazelle grinned. Introspectively, she reached out to her mother. *Mama, I don't think that you have to worry about your baby girl any more. I think I finally have a family again.*

"And Mama," she whispered, *all men* aren't the same. There are some who'll surprise you. Good ones. You probably already know it, but I found me one."

"You found what?" Mitchell asked after hearing a whiff of her words.

"Oh—a family." She smiled nostalgically. "Something I've wanted for ... almost forever."

Thinking of family, Mitchell's hands were linked at her stomach, and she affectionately pressed hers on top of them, thinking of what he'd just said about Katie having a baby in her belly. Turning in his arms, facing him, she looked up into his gorgeous brown eyes, which twinkled happily now. Amongst all the day's excitement, she'd forgotten about what she'd been stressing over. Only now she no longer considered it *bad*. Still, a small part of her wondered if it would scare Mitchell off. Would it mess his head up, and make him run to wherever men run to when they don't want to face something?

If so, his bad, she was spitting it out.

"Mitchell, I have something to tell you," she said, still slightly apprehensive. "It's ... it's a biggie. And I don't know how you're gonna take it."

He looked at her, his head cocked. "Take ... what?"

"The *surprise* I have for you, homeboy."

ACKNOWLEDGEMENTS

It's Mary Lee's 2nd grandchild dropping my first literary gem, and I aspire to come at y'all with many more stories for yall's reading entertainment. It's been a long journey, but now I can present this work to the masses.

First I'd like to thank the Almighty for blessing me with a taste of talent for creating words that provide reading pleasure for a few folk.

Special thanks to Dana Felder for going over my manuscript in its early stages. You rock. Salute Lakeshia Williams for the encouragement, but not so much for misplacing my very first Short Story (LOL). Krystal Moulds for editing this thang. Lashon Wade of Creativision Design for the cover design.

Much love to Mom's Linda(Faye), & pops Clifford(Fess). Wouldn't be here without y'all.

Shooting some breeze to my brothers & sisters Li'l Clifford(Toonz), Marlon(Big-Burna), Marshall(Baby-Sikk), Micheaux(Suge), Myesha. They're the ones who kept a brotha at his best. Keep going with Sis Shay, Li'l David at The What Not Shop & his fam, Shamika and Mia & their fams.

Gotta hit up Oline for my daughters Ebonee, Essence & Endia. What up Dez, Deuce & Unique. Those are Ms. Riley's progeny. For my boys Elza, Desean & Monshae, yall gotta start doing what's right & leave what's wrong in the wind.

Then I gotta throw some good at my nephews and nieces Ricardo, Keisha, Krystal, Quandre(Dre), Marlon(Boog), Marshawn(Bun), Shaquan, Lazhontae, Quartnee, Clarissa, and Kiara. Holla at my Aunts Ruth, Opal(Squeak) Cozetta, Gail. Plus Aunt Michelle, Li'l Di, Aunt Dorothy, Angie, Rochelle, Tina(out there somewhere), Cathy, and my uncles Marshall Quabner, Peaches(Suga Bear), Lawrence(Onney), Calvin, AC,

ACKNOWLEDGEMENTS

Mike Tyson(not the boxer).   Shout out to my cousins: Corey(Free Big Cheez), Missy & Bo Mullins and their offspring, Shanita & her offspring, Chiquita & her offspring, Ebony(My cousin the Dr.) & her fam, Tyla & her offspring, Dominique & his fam, Kenny & his fam, Mike Tyson, Jr & his fam, Jerome, Shannon & his fam, all those Scotts: Malcom(Free Dirty Mac), Tabitha, Linda, Nora, Francis, Lisa(chill out kinfolk), Hank, Laura, Kenneth & David. Gloria, Rhonda & their fams. Louis, Jeff, Queeny, La-La & their fam's, Marie's kids, Jessie's kids, & Celestine's kids, and DaShon & her fam.

My other girls Ebony, Micyra, Myrakahl, Kennedy, the Twins Jasmine & Jameese, Shantell, Kewana, Kimbree, & Maqui. Try to "grow" to make a brotha proud. Same goes for Christian & Tivon.

Gotta show some love to my boy's Jeff(Free Federo) Bagby, Demarchoe(Free Minis)Carpenter, Clinton(Free T-Wax)Carrol. Marcus Carrol, glad you got outta "there," & Calvin at KeKez Fashions in The Town. The other pops Big David, sis&law Queesha as well as Tanza and Stephanie. Hustle and win to my boys Slo-Mo & Pep. Reggie & Skip P, y'all fam too. What up.

Gotta thank some native T-town ladies for their different influences: MLK, Rodie, Quisha, Gwana, Misha(Tink), Tamika Lynn, Lotrise, Gayla, Nikki, MD Reed, Kimberly Elaine, Tonya Stewart (waiting on that next Play, girl), Chamesta(We both SCORPIOS), Gladys P, Reebee W(Where are you, girl), Laura Bell(sister from a different Mr.) & Mama Sharon. Bridgette Rogers, miss ya girl. Jacqueline Yvette, yo.

For all you good peeps from Marshall, TX it's nothing but love. Special's goes out to my 'gal' Marian(Mer-Mer), Kim & her boys Zack & Kivon, Cretia & her two Malik & Da' Kata, their mom and pops Angela & Joel, their aunties Big Mary, JoAnne, Patsy, Betty Jo, Wanda, Mary, Sharon Anne, Robbie, Linda, Alice, Uncle Charlie, and all those cousins. Also, Aunt Freda, & Mama Johnnie Faye & their offspring. Ooops …

ACKNOWLEDGEMENTS

almost forgot. Cici, yo mom & sis' & Auba, yo mom & siblings, I'm shouting y'all out too.

Much love to all my fam & friends in T-U-L-S-A & other locales that's not mentioned. Blame it on my mind & the space, not my heart. Oh yeah, what up to my kinfolk up in Portland, OR. I gotta get up that way soon. My other family at JEL: Tracy, Alice, Lisa, Venicia, Deborah, Sharon, Analisa, Philip (Mr. D) Dixon III, John Langdon & those who passed through for a sec—Rachel, Cindy (crazy girl), Carla, Zach, etc—nothing I wouldn't do for any of y'all.

Mike Rhone over in OKC, & Keith Newby of Portsmouth, VA, my old college roommates. Haven't seen y'all in forever. Miss y'all cats; real talk. Get at ya boy. Timothy Bell you too. Maurice (Flip) King, so proud of you dude. Hank Armstrong, you don't know it, but you inspire yo' boy to always do better. Kendera LeAnne, holla at ya boy. Natasha Iris, word.

By the way, let me not forget The Dock Book Shop in E. Fort Worth, TX. Y'all are still providing a service in the hood that's a rarity nowadays. (Support our local bookstores!)

To the writers who's influenced & provided me with a good story, 'preciate ya, respect due. Y'all are "Heroes" & "Sheroes."

Everyone mentioned has inspired me to make some type of positive mark on society. And I'm trying my best...

I wanna give a **Thank You** ahead of time to all those who eventually purchase and read this book. **Good Looking Out**.

Thanks again!

Wow. I'm out

Until next time, Thug Town's one and only ... Tu sabés

M. D. Williams